Faction Paradox

WARLORDS OF UTOPIA

by Lance *Parkin*

mad norwegian press | new orleans

Also available from Mad Norwegian Press...

FACTION PARADOX NOVELS
Stand-alone novel series based on characters and concepts created by Lawrence Miles

Faction Paradox: The Book of the War [#0] by Lawrence Miles, et. al.
Faction Paradox: This Town Will Never Let Us Go [#1] by Lawrence Miles
Faction Paradox: Of the City of the Saved... [#2] by Philip Purser-Hallard
Faction Paradox: Warlords of Utopia [#3] by Lance Parkin
Faction Paradox: Warring States [#4] by Mags L. Halliday (upcoming)

SCI-FI REFERENCE GUIDES
Dusted: The Unauthorized Guide to Buffy the Vampire Slayer
by Lawrence Miles, Lars Pearson and Christa Dickson

Redeemed: The Unauthorized Guide to Angel (upcoming)
by Lars Pearson and Christa Dickson (edited by Lawrence Miles)

A History of the Universe [revised]: The Unauthorized Timeline to the Doctor Who Universe (upcoming) by Lance Parkin

About Time: The Unauthorized Guide to Doctor Who
six-volume series by Lawrence Miles and Tat Wood

I, Who: The Unauthorized Guides to Doctor Who Novels and Audios
three-volume series by Lars Pearson (Volume Four upcoming)

Prime Targets: The Unauthorized Guide to Transformers, Beast Wars and Beast Machines by Lars Pearson

Now You Know: The Unauthorized Guide to G.I. Joe TV and Comics
by Lars Pearson

All rights reserved. No part of this book may be reproduced or transmitted in any form or by any means, electronic or mechanical, including photography, recording or any information storage and retrieval system, without express written permission from the publisher.

Faction Paradox created and owned by Lawrence Miles, licensed to Mad Norwegian Press.

Copyright © 2004 Mad Norwegian Press.
www.madnorwegian.com

Cover art by Steve Johnson.
Jacket & interior design by Metaphorce Designs.
www.metaphorcedesigns.com

ISBN: 0-9725959-6-1
Printed in Illinois. First Edition: November 2004.

THE STORY SO FAR

The War. A conflict so primal that for most of the population of history, it can only be thought of as a "War in Heaven". Now in its forty-sixth year (at least from the point of view of those directly involved), but intersecting the continuum throughout the span of causality and across battle-lines too large to be recognised by non-combatants, it's a War that isn't just *fought* but re-written, re-defined and re-imagined with every new confrontation. It can best be described as a dispute over the twin territories of "cause" and "effect", and some of the participants are as follows...

The Great Houses. The immovable, untouchable bloodlines which have - traditionally - been seen as responsible not only for the current structure of history but for the fact that history *has* a structure at all. Ancient, aristocratic and prone to infighting, it's enough to know that the Houses were there before anybody else, and that all other known cultures (humanity included) can be thought of as nth-generation copies. Great House technology goes some way beyond gross machinery, but the Houses are best-known for their timeships, although "ship" might be a misleading terms as these vessels are complex historical events in themselves and tend to look like people on the outside anyway. The War-time enemy of the Great Houses is the first recorded challenge to their authority, and even the fact that there *is* a War suggests that something has gone very, very wrong. (The exact nature of the enemy isn't relevant to this current story. The politics of the Houses themselves is hard enough to follow.)

Faction Paradox. The Fallen Angel among Great Houses, the bloodline which has consistently refused to follow the protocols of House society and which has found itself utterly rejected by the Houses' Homeworld as a result. Made up of renegades, ritualists, saboteurs and subterfugers, the Faction is now part criminal syndicate and part "family", the only bloodline to recruit the lesser species (humanity included) into its ranks… something the other Houses consider to be in remarkably bad taste. And since the other Houses insist on seeing themselves as immortal, basic death-cult imagery is common among the Faction's agents. Their masks are made from the skulls of things that shouldn't really have been born; their weapons are bonded to their shadows, *not* carried; and underneath it all is a philosophy that's as much about sacrifice as temporal theory. Since natural childbirth is as disgusting to the Houses as the thought of dying, Faction cells throughout history - like many of the voodoo-cults on Earth - tend to use family titles: the Cousins, who make up the biggest part of the Faction's membership, are theoretically under the control of the Mothers, Fathers, Godfathers and Godmothers who rule from the hidden parliament of the Eleven-Day Empire. Technically Faction Paradox is neutral in the War, meaning that it'll get in *anybody's* way if it wants to.

For more detailed information about any of these subjects, see *The Book of the War*.

For Brie Lewis.

Thanks to Mark Clapham, Mark Jones, Lawrence Miles, Lars Pearson, Phil Purser-Hallard, Justin Richards and Jim Smith.

Quidquid latine dictum sit, altum viditur.

•

"The optimist proclaims that we live in the best of all possible worlds; and the pessimist fears this is true."
- James Branch Cabell (1926).

PART ONE: THE FACE OF HISTORY

I.

My name is Marcus Americanius Scriptor, I number among the ranks of the historians, and the day of my birth was the most significant date in the annals of our world. This may seem unduly boastful at first, and that is not my intent. All I need to say is that I was born on the eighth day of the month of Januarius in the year two-thousand six-hundred and sixty-one, and I am sure that the educated among you will immediately concede the point. As for those without a sense of history, please humour an old man as he tells you his life story.

The moment at which a story truly starts is often open to interpretation. Historians can always find an earlier link in the chain. If the son is like the father, then surely we must consider the father before turning to the son. And if the father is like *his* father ... then we are in for a long story. There was a fashion, long ago, to imagine that every event somehow had its roots in the age of the Greek heroes. Every major city had been founded by a refugee from Troy. Every hero on the field of battle could trace his ancestry to Hercules. That was fanciful even back then, and later scholars gently broke it to us that tracing events back to legends was an attempt to add grandeur to the life stories of often rather ordinary men.

We know now, of course, that history operates on a scale quite unimaginable a century ago. If the history of the Earth were the length of my arm then the whole of human history would barely inhabit the smallest fraction of the smallest part of the tip of my nail. Now that we have begun to quantify the true length of eternity, the age of legend seems so recent we could almost touch it, and the wars on Olympus seem like a family squabble. For millennia, all the priests, shamans, clerics, ministers, rabbis, monks, bishops, brahmins, lamas, abunas, druids, hierophants, flamens and hierodules of this world, all the holy *men* told us of the vastness of the domain of the gods. Yet we now know that multiplied together, the spheres of divine influence would not be a fraction of the cosmos of which we are now aware.

Our eyes were opened to the true nature of creation, at least some of the way, the day I was born. Is that what being a god is? To understand the infinite, to know the true scale that time and space operate on? If so, I think I am glad to be human. The wisest of men now say that a history book is an anachronism, that you can't conceive, nor can I, the appalling strangeness of the forces that shape the universe. This is not a history of the universe, this is a history of one man.

Let me start with a description of the world that I was born into. There was, then, unquestioning belief that the gods had blessed Rome, granted the city and its Empire good fortune. The course of history made sense when seen in those terms. It's something that the younger generation and those foreign to our ways can't truly understand. When I was a child, I knew that Rome would always prevail, as it had for twenty centuries. This wasn't faith, the optimism of politicians or the hindsight of historians, it wasn't even certainty. This was fact.

The world was controlled from Rome, greatest of all cities. The rule of the Emperor was absolute, his dominion encompassed every city of the world including the subterranean cities in the ice of Ultima Thule and the marine cities of the Atlantic and Indian Oceans. By the time I was born, there had been five centuries of almost unbroken peace and prosperity. The whole world accepted the authority of the Roman Emperor. How could anyone do otherwise, when the course of history pointed so unwaveringly in that direction? Why would anyone resist when Rome ensured they had water to drink, grain to eat, security, protection under the law? Not everyone prospered, and there is no possible system that will give all men everything they desire or true equality, but no-one suffered. Not a single human being went hungry, lacked work or died of a preventable disease.

The fundamental unit of social order on which our utopia was built was not the Emperor, the Senate or even the Army. It was, and is, citizenship. To be a Roman citizen is to have rights, protections and privileges in the law. Those that can state "civis Romanus sum" are heirs and beneficiaries of the most enduring political system the races of man have seen. It has always been a limited right. By the reign of Augustus, in the eighth century after the foundation of Rome, the Empire's frontiers were drawn at the Atlantic, the Rhine and Danube, the Euphrates and the African and Arabian deserts. In all, there were around three-thousand cities in the Empire. There were possibly a hundred million people; the records from that time survive, but do not live up to modern standards. Half the population, as now, was made up of slaves. Two-thirds of the remainder were provincials. A third, then, were citizens.

As the ideal of Rome spread, everyone in the Empire was proud to belong, but it was the citizens who belonged *most*. Roman standards became those of the known world; all traders learned that to make the best profits, they needed Latin and to know the Roman measurements. Law came to mean Roman law, and few dared transgress it. If you killed a Roman citizen anywhere in the world, then you died as sure as if you had thrown yourself off a cliff. The golden age had begun, exemplified by the eleven Golden Emperors who ruled in the tenth and eleventh centuries: Nerva, Trajan, Hadrian, Antonius Pius, Marcus Aurelius, Avidius Cassius, Septimus Severus, Publius Septimius, Claudius Gothicus, Domitius Aurelianus and Diocletian. As individuals, these were very different men. They had very different aptitudes, priorities and preferences. Some were soldiers, some were politicians. Some were cruel, some were liberal. But all were wise, and listened to wise counsel. All won great military victories, and promoted great building projects. They protected the boundaries of Rome, fed the people, left the treasury with more than they found, secured the value of coin. That done, the Rhine and the Danube were crossed, the Germanic people were defeated and the Empire's armies and engineers tamed the forests across the Rhine.

With the Western Empire prospering, Constantine moved East; his armies swept into Arabia, then Parthia, which had been ravaged by plague. His grandson, Julius Alexander, did what his namesake could not and reached India, securing outposts and trading routes there. Six centuries after Augustus, when Justinian was crowned in Rome, he was declared Emperor of India, as well as the Romans. By the time of his death, Justinian was also Emperor of what we now call America. Roman navigators had circumnavigated Africa and made Atlantic crossings almost routine.

There were periods of expansion, there were periods of consolidation. But Rome's rise was inevitable. Only two nations presented any resistance. The first were the Norsemen, a coalition of the German, barbarian and Scandinavian peoples. The campaign in the North, started by Carolus Magnus, ended by Octavian VI, saw them defeated.

The final nation to hold out was Seres. They were not expansionists, but had a philosophy of technical and philosophical innovation. Their vast country, completely surrounded by the Great Walls and ruled by their own Emperors, those of the Yuan and Ming dynasties, stood firm against Roman incursion as the rest of the world fell to our might. We knew almost nothing of what went on beyond those Walls, indeed we had only vague reports of the extent and lay of the territory. Barring a few naval skirmishes over spice islands, only the border guards ever had any contact with the Serics.

By the twenty-first century, Roman roads led to all parts of the world. It was possible to walk from Rome to Hibernia, India or to Mauretana, where you could join the vast trans-African highways. America and Oceania, vast continents the existence of which other nations had not even suspected, were slowly being colonised. Unlike many of the savage races we encountered, the native Americans were peaceful. Their chieftains were happy to be togafied, and we were happy to teach them techniques that allowed them to better understand and cultivate the land they held so dear.

On the other side of the world, the Emperor of Seres, Yung Lo, had secretly constructed vast fleets of warships. These he placed under the command of the eunuch Zheng He. The Roman Empire was caught completely by surprise by these lightning attacks. In a period of relative peace and security, many of our trading ports were lightly manned, and relied almost entirely on their defensive walls. The Serics had new and terrible rocket weapons. These smashed holes in the walls of over a hundred cities, which were then overrun by infantry. The Roman navy was sent to recapture these ports... and was routed, its boats sunk before they had even sighted their enemy. For twenty-eight years, this rampage, this "world war", continued. The Romans rallied, they stemmed the tide of the Seric advance, then contained the threat. But Rome had lost control of the whole Indian Ocean and the territory on its coast.

Then, something extraordinary. Yung Lo requested a private audience with the new Roman Emperor, Cosimo. They met on the Great Wall. Yung Lo set out the problem; he was not just a mortal, he was part divine. Almost all the Roman Emperors had also been deified, and Cosimo could expect this on his death. So, this was not a battle between human beings, but between demigods. The Roman Emperor countered that whatever happened, millions of human beings would die. Millennia of culture, history and achievement would be lost. Beautiful architecture and priceless art would be smashed. Neither side could call that victory. He agreed that they were evenly matched, but saw no alternative to war. Yung Lo responded in perfect Latin: 'Pax melior est quam iustissimum bellum.'

Yung Lo took a Roman coin from his pocket. He told Cosimo there was another way.

They could flip a coin. The winner would become the one, undisputed Emperor of the World. The loser would serve loyally as his first minister. Seric technology and philosophy would be married to Roman power and organisation. Cosimo was no soldier, but he realised that this proposition required a new form of bravery, and a particular loyalty in the gods. He agreed to Yung Lo's plan; they gathered their generals and made the men swear the most powerful oaths to the gods and ancestor spirits that they would all abide by the result. Cosimo said that *his* face, the face of the Roman emperor, would look up when the coin landed. He declared "heads". The coin was tossed. And a moment later, Yung Lo, commander of the mightiest navy the world ever saw, knelt at the feet of his Emperor.

Now, there was no serious threat to Rome. Almost five centuries of peace followed. But this was not a period of stagnation. The whole sum of Seric philosophy, art and technology enshrined in the *Yunglotatien* was added to that of Rome, and great advances were made from the fusion. A better society, a perfect world, was built.

All this is well known, and feels *right*, somehow. The alternative was humanity divided, a war-torn Earth. Ignorance, division and poverty. But while this utopia was the destiny of the races of mankind, and (whatever your religion) clearly part of the divine plan, not everything that happened was what we planned or foresaw. Obviously, if Yung Lo's coin had come up tails, not heads, then the whole course of history would have run with Seres, not Rome. History often depends on chance as much as human design.

There are other points with consequences just as profound. Take the Germans. Around the year one-thousand, the Roman armies under Claudius Gothicus took advantage of an unusually cold winter to cross the Rhine and overrun German defences. But we did not, as is popularly thought, exterminate the German people or drag them all to Rome in chains. Instead, we drove the majority of them from their land and to the east, into the territory of other barbarians. For centuries, the Germans fought the Huns, the Vandals and the Ostrogoths. We moved to kill one bird, and instead killed many more. Fighting amongst themselves, the barbarian hordes could not fight Rome, and for several centuries the Roman Emperors could concentrate their resources and attention on other areas of the Empire.

Many events worked to Rome's advantage. But while almost every Emperor has been exactly as prudent, wise, brave and compassionate as his times demanded, there were occasions where the unforeseen occurred. Just because Rome has always prevailed does not mean that its history hasn't, at times, been turbulent. Indeed, the prize of the Imperial Crown is all the more tempting because of the great power and wealth it represents. And the crown does not grant its wearer the gift of infallibility or immortality. For Rome to prosper in the long term, it has been necessary, from time to time, for the Empire to pursue the wrong path. It is by learning from our mistakes that we all grow, and Roman Emperors have made mistakes.

All we could know is that Rome, somehow, would prevail. All that happened, happened for the best.

What of the role of individuals?

Clearly, the ruling elite wield great power and influence. But dissenting opinion exists. There will always be a winning side, but it won't always be the obvious one, or the one favoured by the majority. So, despite Rome's manifest destiny, choices an individual makes are still important. And I was to be an important individual. All the signs pointed to the eighth of Januarius MMDCLXI being a particularly auspicious day. Both my father and mother, otherwise sensible people, employed astrologers; three men, representing the three major branches of the natural law. They agreed it was the most momentous of all days, that it would go down in Roman history with Actium, the Fourth Great Fire and Yung Lo's Coin - adding their usual disclaimers to the effect that all the rituals had to be approached with the proper respect or it would throw off their calculations - and my birth was duly induced when it became clear that I would rather have been born three or four days later.

I was born in my mother's bedchamber, in the north wing of the family's villa, which is situated on an elongated island between the Malum and Magnus rivers, on the East Coast of the continent of America. This island was discovered during the reign of Romulus Augustus, greatest of Emperors, when three ships carrying salt from Africa were caught in a wind that carried them across the ocean. The site of their first landfall is marked with a rather plain obelisk in the grounds of the villa.

By the time of my birth - indeed for over a century beforehand - the villa and its grounds had spread over the whole area of this island, which is around fifteen miles long and four miles broad. There is a central park, three miles long and some thirteen hundred jugeri in area, containing a zoo and a number of stadia. There are many theatres on the island, there's a marina. One tower was, at the time it was opened, the tallest building in the world. Another contains the largest atrium, and there are a number of renowned statues, squares and galleries. An underground railway links the major buildings and places of interest. In all, something like one-hundred-and-thirty-thousand men work here, doing little more than maintaining the villa and tending its grounds. It takes eight-thousand slaves working in four shifts just to wind the clockwork. Still there is room for nature reserves and any number of gardens, small vineyards and pretty terraces. All in all, my family, even using the most all-encompassing definition of the term to include every cousin and great aunt, consisted of around one-hundred living souls when I was born.

It is important, then, for you to know at the outset that my father and his father before him felt this family home so meagre that it shamed them. All our family's energies were directed at improving our lot. In a world of fifteen billion people, we were perhaps the thirtieth or thirty-fifth most wealthy family. We governed, unchallenged, the whole continent now known as Northern America, and had for a hundred and forty years, since my illustrious great-great-grandfather - known as Americanus because of his renowned lack of mercy - had been sent to quell a bout of republican revolutionary fervour. But we lacked *status*, that most Roman of commodities. We were many thousands of miles from Rome, and few there ever thought of our province. The ever-revered ancients - no less an authority than Horace - had warned that the gods would be angry if anyone tried to cross the Atlantic. Two thousand years later, most Romans were still superstitious about the trip, although they were happy to eat the grain, buffalo and pigeon from American farms that came the other way. Those that spoke of us at all mocked us for the slight regional variation of our spoken and written Latin or our reputed frugality and restraint; stark contrast, it was thought, with the grandiose, aggressive, triumphalist attitude befitting true Romans.

So, when my mother discovered she was with child, her first thought was that I was to be the one to restore the family's fortunes. It was what my father demanded of his firstborn. And it was what his astrologers had told him would come to pass. When they told him of the hallowed status of my birthday, he apparently registered no surprise or satisfaction. This was simply how it should be and no less an authority than the stars proclaimed it.

This was what I was told from my earliest days, but even as a very small child, my impression was that the three astrologers would say anything my parents wanted to hear, desperate for scraps of their attention and favour. The Aegyptian was the oldest, and his art depended on nothing more than a deck of cards that he'd scrawled hieroglyphs on; these supposedly spoke of some prehistoric wisdom. The Seric preferred star-charts, ones covered with even more ancient and indecipherable runes. Neither would let anyone else do anything more than glimpse the artefacts that served as the source of their insight.

This tendency to the obscure impressed my parents. I am not like them. Most, it seems, watch a stage magician and coo and clap at the stunts he performs. But magicians aren't sorcerers, whatever most of them claim. It's a small set of techniques; sleight of hand, distraction, cleverly-constructed props and willing assistants. It's a matter of constructing a set of expectations, then confounding them.

I was around ten years old when a troupe of flying acrobats performed for us, one feast day. Everyone else in the family, I'm sure, was transfixed by them as they swooped over us and dived around each other. I was looking up at the ceiling, trying to find the wires and assistants who must have been there. I did not see them. You must understand this about me: the acrobats' ability to contrive a trick so flawlessly that I could not see how it was done was so much more impressive, to my mind, than if the gods had granted them the gift of flight. When I look south over the bay of my family home and see the Jupiter Libertatis, one arm held aloft bearing a lightning bolt, my mind is filled with awe not for the father of the gods, but for the Gaulish sculptors who designed and built that vast statue.

So, it was the third astrologer, an Atlantean, who fascinated me. He was a crafty, political creature, ever looking to discredit his fellows. As you may have guessed, I confess that as a young man I found the strategies he adopted far more interesting than the matter of the state of the weather. He alone saw astrology as something akin to a gambling game. He confessed as much to me. The Atlantean used charts, but mathematical ones. He explained his arts to me one evening, and it was a simple matter applying numerical values to each outcome, then referring to probability and statistical tables to assess the most beneficial. He was, in short, playing the odds.

It is only now as I write this, over eighty years after he told me his secrets, that I realise his explaining of the charts was simply another strategy on his part. He knew that I was sceptical, that I was intelligent, that I was a creature of reason. He calculated that I would keep his secret from the rest of my family. I spent decades feeling secretly superior to that superstitious lot. If I had denounced him over dinner, gone through those mathematical tables with my father, showing the astrologer to be a charlatan, then it would have been a victory, but one that wouldn't have lasted the hour. The Atlantean would have been put on the first ship home, certainly, but he'd have been replaced by someone new, some Britannic druid, perhaps, or an African who my father would insist was a *real* astrologer.

My birth was not an easy one, and my mother was weakened by it.

As the physicians performed the caesarean, I apparently screamed and bawled in a way that my father felt to be most un-Roman. It demonstrated that I was healthy, though, and I had been successfully ripped from my mother's womb on this most auspicious of days.

It was in Rome, however, that history was not only being made, but entirely recast that day.

II.

The Forum of Rome is, as one might expect, the largest in the world. Yet, if every man, woman, child and slave who now claimed to have witnessed the events of the eighth of Januarius had truly been there at the time, it would need to be ten times larger still, at the very least.

And, by the most reliable accounts, there was nothing to see in any event. In the gap between moments, an elderly man appeared on one of the lowest levels of the Forum. If you had been looking the other way, then turned back to face him, then you would have noticed only his unusual clothes, not the materialisation itself. But some had seen him appear, and quickly word of it spread through the crowd. The old man was surrounded and confronted, grabbed and did not help his case by addressing them in an entirely unknown language. A pair of centurions arrived and led him away, worried that his presence was a challenge to public order.

How little they knew!

I, of course, was oblivious to this, being but a few hours old. I can't relate what happened with any great authority. What the official record shows is that the old man, confused and still gabbling in an unknown tongue, was taken to the Forum manager's officina, where the manager and the centurions attempted to converse with him. The man couldn't make himself understood. Doctors examining him knew that there were cases of men with head injuries who had lost the power of comprehension and communication. However, there was no sign that this man had such a wound. He was sent to the local magistrate, whose report described his unusual clothes and a strange item of jewellery that had been grabbed from him by the mob, then later retrieved by a centurion. The man tested sober, he behaved in a calm and dignified manner. The magistrate declared that the old man arrived in the Forum "unseen, by means unknown". Faced with a mystery, the magistrate, clearly a pompous and unimaginative fellow, chose to ignore it.

The old man was shown maps, first of the city. Every schoolchild knows these images. I was fifteen before I travelled to Rome, but by then I had spent ten years studying the maps and guides. Almost every instructional book had pictures of Rome. I knew my way around, having never been there. The old man did not recognise Rome. He seemed confused by a map of Europa. Only when he saw a map of the whole Earth did he react. He ran his hands over it, pointed at it, squinted at it. Finally, he looked satisfied, but was unable to point to his own country on it. His manner wasn't aggressive, it was - so the report says - almost apologetic.

He had no money, he could not make himself understood. What do to with him? He had committed no crime, but could not pay for lodging. Such an old man could not do manual work. The magistrate says that he tried to find out if the man had a craft or aptitude, but does not say how diligent he was in this undertaking. In the end, the man was sent to a hospice in the Alps that was funded by some rich patron or other. The whole affair was soon forgotten.

This is not how the story is officially reported nowadays. We Romans have grown used to the notion that history is written at the request of rich and powerful men who want to become richer and more powerful still. We were already cynical about history and historians; don't be surprised to learn that I already know you read this imagining it to be some form of fantasy. Let me assure you that not only is every word of what I write a true recollection of what happened, but you will soon understand that by all the laws of nature as understood by the wisest men of learning, it *has* to be so.

Acta est non fabula

How could such a significant event happen right under the noses of the most rich and powerful men in the world, without them even noticing? The way the story is told now, at least three or four of the most powerful Senators witnessed the old man as he appeared, and that very same day, they recognised his value and took him under their wing.

Nonsense, of course.

The man spent nineteen years in the sanatorium. In that time, he didn't have a single visitor. No-one interviewed him. The staff tolerated him and humoured him, but all they really did was wait for him to die, as they did with all the inmates.

One part of the magistrate's report, unknown to all, contained all the secrets of eternity and infinity. Yet it stayed confined to the report for nineteen years.

I grew up.

I was a healthy child, but a difficult one. I questioned. I was read to all the time, and I learned to read for myself almost before I could hold a scroll or tablet. Tablets, in particular, fascinated me; the clicking and clacking, as the blocks flicked round and a new page was formed, was music to me. New stories, new facts, were constantly with me. By the time I was six, my mother had bought me a tablet with an especially efficient spring. With it, I could read almost all day without it winding down. I pity the wrist of the slave whose job it was to turn the key. He or she must have spent all night at their work.

I did not confine this quest to my library. I asked about the history of the villa. As soon as I was old enough, I went out into the great land of America and visited many of the housesteads of the American people. The mosaics and painted walls were properly Roman, but many - and not just the oldest - contained images and motifs from the culture that had been here before, and depicted historical scenes. There was no written record of these American people, barring a few myths that had become children's stories. In my eleventh year, I declared my intention to write the official history of the nation of America. My father was delighted, and threw open the family archive.

'But, father, the history of this country starts long before the time of Americanus,' I told him.

He glared at me. I could not understand his anger; this was, after all, a fact. A moment later, I understood. There is a difference between History and Truth.

'I will, of course, concentrate on what shaped modern America,' I told him. 'I will pay all honour to our illustrious forefather, Tiberius Americanus.'

My father seemed soothed by this. Remember that I was but ten years old at this point. I was, as you can guess, something of a prodigy. I was not, by now, an only child. I had a brother, Titus Americanius, and three sisters, triplets.

The history of the American people proved an immense task, but it was one that I relished. It took two years to complete. I have not read it for many years. I imagine it's still a readable work, albeit one clearly composed by a precocious youth.

My father told me that now my writing was done, I should prepare for a career in the military. Why, you may ask, would a world united under one ruler – one *politic* - need an army? It is a long time since the army fought the great land battles that are so celebrated in our history. Ours was perhaps the best of all possible worlds, but it was not perfect. Local disputes would flare up, especially if there was a plague, earthquake or flood to disrupt the normal flow of trade. There were organised networks of criminals, and a huge black market trade in both legal and illegal goods. Politicians took bribes and sought to gain power by any means. The army maintained secret networks of spies and analysts, it enforced the law and protected trade routes. It investigated and punished crimes.

Truth to tell, though, the main duty of the army in those days was to protect the infrastructure. The great road networks, the bridges across the Fretum Gallicum and the Straits of Hercules, the tunnels, canals, sewers and aqueducts all needed skilled men to maintain them. This kept the men fit, it kept them disciplined, but I could think of no worse life than to be in charge of the men who ensured the cobbles of the road were laid well enough to ensure the passage of the land trains and steam carts.

I never told my father as much. The army still found itself dealing with enemies of the state. There was glory to be had. A successful soldier could still be awarded a triumph, a statue and favour with the Emperor.

This was my father's plan to return our family to glory. At thirteen, I was sent to military academy. This was in Britannia. I had never visited the Province before, but it soon became my adopted home. Used to hot summers and cold winters at the family villa, I found the perpetual grey skies somewhat unnerving, but grew used to them. I rolled my resentment into a ball, swallowed it, and learned the craft of a soldier. I was a strong boy, and I was respected there. I gained a reputation for ruthlessness. I found this ludicrous, until I recognised that I had such disdain for the cadets who actually wanted to be there that I had no compunction about hurting them in our training exercises. The more I hurt them, the more they respected me. The reputation of the original "Merciless one", my ancestor Americanus, did nothing but fuel the myths about me.

At night, I continued to read. Britannia, of course, has a vast literature. I immersed myself in it, sponsoring new clockwork productions of Concuthasta's tragedies of *Julius Caesar* and of *Anthony and Cleopatra*. These granted me a little money of my own, and respect in academic circles. Those who saw the showings remembered them fondly. For many years afterwards I was stopped in the street by members of the public full of praise. Puffed with success, I commissioned a prose piece ostensibly the autobiography of the first Emperor Claudius from one of my fellow soldiers, Sepulcrius, but ended up having to amend a great deal of it myself. If you are minded that my writing style resembles his famous book, then that is the reason.

By now I was sixteen years old, and seen as a sponsor of the arts. In all honesty, it was a way to get away from the barracks, with all their boorish traditions and attitudes. You met a better class of women my way, I found.

While in Britannia, I visited the ancient sites of the druidic religion. How odd, I thought, that the druids had been persecuted and hunted down, when their beliefs in the natural world were really not that different from those of the native Americans.

Amongst all this, almost incidental to my life, my military career continued. By now my brother, Titus Americanius, had joined me. This had both good and bad consequences: he was good company, not an academic man, like myself, but most certainly a wise one, and with sound judgement. Moreover, he quickly proved himself to be a fine soldier; he had none of my reluctance, and twice my ruthlessness. This took a great deal of pressure off me. My father had been worried by my ventures into theatre, feeling it would do nothing to enhance the reputation of our family. I argued that it did precisely that; it may not have been glory on the battlefield, but the Imperial Court and the citizens of Rome have traditionally been almost as impressed by spectacular entertainment. There was more chance of me gaining renown in Rome my way than if I led a legion of civil engineers.

Unknown to my father, my brother or myself, my mother had finally got round to reading my history of America. She was entranced, and sent a copy to a friend, who sent it on to a friend in the Court. From there, it reached the attention of the Emperor himself. So it was that six years after I completed the work, the old Emperor Emmanuel Victorius wrote to me. It was an excellent book, he told me. He enjoyed histories, and couldn't remember ever reading such a detailed report of the American continent. He cautioned me, though, that – while entertaining – I wasn't quite good enough a writer to rank among the best academic historians, and that I was right to join the army. He wished me well, and ended with a pleasantry to the effect that he looked forward to well-written military reports from me.

The etiquette in this situation is clear: one can write a brief note thanking the Emperor, but – unless he has asked questions of you – you are not to seek to prolong correspondence with him. I felt, perhaps through wounded pride, that I should set him straight on a point of detail. I wrote a short letter, explaining that my history of America was a juvenile work, completed when I was twelve years old.

I sent the note, and immediately regretted it. Its tone, though short, was petulant. The eighteen-year-old man who wrote the note was far less reasonable than the twelve-year-old who wrote the book. Whatever slight sweet taste the three volumes of the history book had left the Emperor would be erased by the bitterness of a three line note. Whatever chance I had of gaining favour had been permanently erased.

I had never been so scared before, I realised. While I had risked my father's disfavour, and risked my life on military missions, I had never before threatened to annihilate my entire future in such a way.

Hopes that the Emperor would ignore the note – or, better, that some blessed slave or secretary would dispose of it before he even saw it – were dashed when I received a letter bearing the Imperial Seal two days later. I read it … and was amazed that it was effusive praise from the Emperor's private secretary. He asked me (I use the term loosely, as I imagine such requests are rarely turned down) if I would compose a short monograph celebrating the thousandth anniversary of the Hercules Bridge, linking Hispanus and Africa. I had only a couple of weeks to do so. I showed my commanders the letter, and they gave me special leave before I'd even requested it.

I had never been to the Hercules Bridge. When my men and I had been deployed to Africa, we had always gone by ship or submarine. Longer bridges have been built in the last thousand years. But the Bridge of Hercules is particularly impressive. It was, of course, listed by the authorities as one of the Hundred Wonders of the World, and it had been the subject of a particularly turgid poem by Verbipretium. Over the years it has been expanded and reinforced to cope with ever-larger volumes of traffic. The statue of Hercules that bestrode the bridge as originally constructed was moved aside when the bridge was widened (moving the statue was itself a mammoth feat of engineering). It still stands, facing Africa, a powerful symbol of Roman strength.

Remember how, in school, you were shown that the strength of Rome was like intertwined laurels? A solid piece of wood would snap, but individuals have the flexibility to bend, and would never break. The Hercules Bridge had learned that lesson to survive ocean storms from the Atlantic and blasts of Saharan sand. It was constructed to be flexible, and even the top levels, the ones exposed to the elements, were rarely closed to traffic. It was the gateway to the Mare Nostrum, and therefore to Rome.

When I first saw the bridge, I gawped at it like a peasant. I arrived as the early morning fog was clearing, and the lanterns along it were still lit. The first hippopotami were being herded across one of the pedestrian walkways, and appeared as mere specks. It was a monumental piece of architecture, that much was clear, but I didn't truly appreciate the scale until I saw a Balaena passing underneath it. I was very familiar with that class of ship; the one I saw now was almost certainly out of the Eastern American ports. I had never seen such a behemoth of the sea dwarfed before.

I had an appointment at the naval base on the Rock of Hercules. There I met a young legatus, Quintus Saxus, who helped me find a route through the subterranean archive. Everything I needed was stored within, including the original plans, and contemporary reports of the opening of the bridge, attended by the Emperor Emmanuel Victorius. There had been great anxiety that Aethiopian rebels might find some way to sabotage the opening, or even to demolish the bridge. As I reviewed this material over lunch, on a viewing terrace alongside the bridge itself, I wondered how anyone could have thought it possible. Every Roman soldier is taught that nothing is impossible, that even the seemingly impossible task can be completed with enough men and the right strategy. So, how to bring down the bridge? All the gunpowder in Seres, piled along the roadways themselves, might do the job.

With such impregnable construction, with the fort and naval base at the European end, and – who knows? – with Hercules himself watching over it, the history of the bridge was almost ridiculously non-eventful. Romans often mock America for being a quiet backwater, but I managed to get three volumes out of the events and progress there. Lucky for me that this new commission was just for a monograph. Talking to Quintus Saxus, who was full of anecdotes about the running and maintaining of the bridge, I uncovered a new line of attack. I decided, once I had paid due attention to the circumstances of the bridge's construction, to discuss the present. I spent my time interviewing the toll-keepers and the merchants who used the bridge every day. There were a hundred or so people who lived within the structure of the bridge; generally African caretakers and masons, many of them living in lodgings granted to their ancestors by the Emperor at the time the bridge was constructed. Thousands of fishermen lived under the arches and supports, making a little money on the side by taking tourists around the base pillars… and, no doubt, very much more money from smuggling. Everyone was preparing for the Emperor's visit, and the bridge was being swept, painted and hung with bunting and flags.

I had two weeks. I used them to soak up what I could of life around the bridge, and the evenings writing up what I had discovered. I finished my assignment, arranged for a local printer to publish a limited edition of the work, bound in leather, and sent the first copy to the Emperor. It arrived early, giving him time to read and re-read it before he was due to visit.

By all accounts, it is fair to say that he loved the book. I was not present at the millennial celebrations, but Quintus Saxus wrote to me to say that the Emperor virtually read out the entire work during a series of speeches.

I was back in Britannia, preparing for a new mission. I had specialised in intelligence-gathering work, in hand-to-hand combat and in strategy. I had conducted covert operations on every continent, but these had mostly been straightforward and short-lived campaigns, ones designed to test my mettle. By my twenty-first year, I was due to start a more sustained piece of undercover work infiltrating a criminal gang who dealt arms and narcotics to the highest bidder and stole crates of spirae from a central warehouse, then smuggled them all around the world. It would take many years to destroy this organisation from within, and the personal risk was extremely high. The day before I was about to leave for that mission, my life took a different turn. I was told to go to Rome. I had been commissioned to write the definitive history of the Forum, which was, at that time, being comprehensively refurbished.

When my father heard this, he was astonished. I had gained a good reputation with the Emperor, but I was on the verge of throwing away my chance of military glory 'to write about shops'. The same thought had crossed my mind. This was not the stuff of legend. Father sent Titus Americanius to talk sense to me. But my brother was most keen for me to write the book. The Forum was the financial centre of the world. He ran down a list of the merchants, senators, vestals and priests who were proposing to sponsor my book. I would meet all these people, and make an almost unrivalled collection of contacts. Titus also found it impossible to believe that I wouldn't meet the Emperor himself, and become the talk of the Court.

This was only the third time I had visited Rome. It is a small city, in terms of area, but gigantic in terms of architecture and population. Estimates were impossible to confirm, but officially at the time of the visit I now describe, there were around a hundred million people living in the mile-high towers of the City; roughly the same as in the whole of America. Space was at a premium, so there was a vast subterranean metropolis, too. The mob was kept entertained at vast amphitheatres, stadia and the circuses, and fed by balloonists, flying up and down the spires and pits of the tenements and palaces, delivering bread and meat. The citizens lived in those palaces, linked by spiralling viaducts and roadways. But for two thousand years, "Rome" had meant the centre of this titanic city; the Imperial Court and Senate, the Pantheon, the Forum. All roads led here, to the milliarium aureum, and nowhere else on Earth was quite like it.

In ancient days, the Forum contained the Senate House and temples. As Rome expanded, the governmental functions were incorporated into the Imperial Palace on the Palatine Hill. The religious heart of the city gradually moved west to the Janiculum, and now temples, churches and pagodas radiated out from the Global Pantheon there commissioned by Urbanus Octavius to celebrate the world's new unity. This left the Forum to concentrate on commerce. Despite efforts of some Emperors and their Senates to curtail its growth, the Forum sprawled and new building congealed together the various ancient fora, then shot upwards in ever more spectacular attempts to lure investors, shoppers and merchants. Architecturally, all the authorities I read agree on two things about the Roman Forum: (I) the successive layers of building mean that riding the new levarators from base to summit made for a fascinating living archaeology lesson, the nearest thing possible to time travel, and (II) there was and is no uglier building on the face of the Earth or under its oceans.

As for my history of the Forum, it took a year, but it was duly written and published. No doubt, if you are interested, it would be easy enough for you to find a copy. It was a rather dull work, truth be told, but I made all the contacts my brother thought I would and more. It would be a little while, however, before I met the Emperor.

III.

One of the contacts I made was, of all things, a Scotic aristocrat, Tertius Angus Inducula.

His daughter was of marrying age. He and my father made it known that she would be a suitable match. Some time after my History of the Forum was published, it was arranged that I would meet Angela one afternoon on neutral territory; a fine restaurant in sight of the Global Pantheon. We started to talk. She was funny, feisty. She had the palest skin, and red hair, as is the way with Celts. I had been sceptical of the match, but she was a clever girl with a quick tongue. I thought she was the most beautiful creature in the world, a Britannic Venus. I was surprised that she had read every book I'd written, and that she had enough fire to complain about the sheer dullness of the subjects I had chosen.

'The history of a country with fields the size of most provinces and those ugly cows -'

'Uri.'

'The history of a big bridge, where if you read it, you realise nothing interesting whatsoever has happened there since the day it was built.'

Angela was the first to notice this, or at least the first to say as much to my face.

'And your magnum opus, the chronicle of a shopping centre.'

'Commerce is the lifeblood of the empire, the Forum its heart.'

'I suggest that you never become a poet, if that is the most original sentiment in your heart. Can I ask what your next work will be on? The setting of plaster?'

Before long, the betrothal had been arranged. How could I resist such a woman? While my father's agents performed the background checks, spying on the girl and paying members of her family's household for information, the wedding preparations were being made. It would take place at harvest time, naturally.

In the midst of one of the most bounteous autumns on record, my friends gathered in Britannia to witness the sealing of the contract and the paying of the first third of the dowry. The family astrologers were due to give their readings at that point, but the night before I persuaded my father to give them the day off. We added the animals they would have sacrificed to the wedding feast.

Angela and I clasped our right hands together, and these were bound. We signed the contract, I slipped the iron ring on Angela's finger, and in doing so, she became my wife.

The villa close to Londinium my brother and I rented was prepared to receive the bride. The torches were lit so that Angela would not lose her way, and we waited while she made her procession to the villa. We could hear the musicians - and the well-meaning bawdy shouts from the gathered crowds - from a long way off. Money and walnuts were distributed to the local poor. Angela anointed the door posts with oil and wool and her attendants carried her in, past the symbolic marriage bed in the atrium.

The feast began. This was, by Roman tradition, a modest affair. We would normally only have cakes and a little wine. The Scotic people, though, have different traditions; dancing, pipe-playing, drinking... and a little brawling as the night drew on. My father and my brothers looked delighted by this state of affairs.

Early in the evening, the woman appointed as pronuba - I never did know her name, she was a friend of the bride's mother - whispered to me that I wasn't expected to stay the whole night. She laughed that it was rather the opposite: the party was designed to distract the guests from the absence of the bride and groom. She bid me retire to my bedchamber.

There, one last spectacle awaited me, a surprise Angela had contrived. I had expected my bride to be there already, but I was made to wait. When Angela arrived, it was on a giant clamshell, driven with a clockwork engine and guided in by the pronuba and slave girls in flowing blue and green silk gowns. Angela stood there quite naked, like Venus risen from the ocean. This was the first time I had seen her unadorned form, and she held herself in such a way to yet preserve her modesty. I was captivated by the beautiful, pale girl with hair down to her waist and called her "wife" for the first time. Her attendants were giggling, and quickly left us alone. I helped Angela down from her plinth and onto the torus genialis and there, without any of the feigned protestations of Roman tradition, she surrendered her virginity to me.

The next morning we emerged to a day of feasting, surrounded by all my friends and family. I have never felt so elated (nor, I have to say, so drunk) before or since.

The next few months, I wrote nothing. There was a little time to follow up and cultivate the contacts I had made since coming to Rome. That done, I returned with my bride to America, where she discovered the joys of my homeland's natural beauty and became fully part of my family. There was, at this time, a series of terrible earthquakes in various parts of the world; Seres was worst affected, but there was also destruction and great loss of life in the western parts of the American province. I went there with Angela, and we organised some relief for those affected.

As we undertook that, one of my readers - a Roman who worked in the Forum - wrote to me. He told me enjoyed my history, but asked why I had not discussed the ghost who had appeared, in plain sight, just over two decades before. No-one had mentioned the story of the old man while I was writing my book, but the coincidence that the man had made his appearance on the day of my birth was irresistible to me, and once I knew where to look, it was a simple matter to locate the magistrate's report. From there, I traced the mysterious old man to his Alpine sanatorium. Something about this business nagged at me, fascinated me.

I travelled from America to meet the old man. After two decades, he had not learned much Latin, but he could communicate simple requests to his nurses. He could not give his name, he couldn't say where he was from. He had the most terrible difficulty understanding the use of tenses, something the most primitive savage or witless child could master given even a merely adequate tutor. I was the first man for many years to attempt any substantial communication with him. He was still sharp; one look into his eyes made me realise that he had intelligence far greater than my own. He kept himself smart, and behaved with decorum. But there was something ... reduced ... about him. Something that made me imagine he could be a disgraced scholar, or even a deposed monarch.

Talking to him – trying to – was frustrating. He regarded me, I thought, with some amusement. The gap in communication reminded me of the times I'd stared at the caged alpha male gorilla in the family zoo. I'd look at him, and he'd look back. Hanno of Carthaginia, the first man to describe gorillas, thought they were a tribe of hairy women and that has become the basis of many jokes. But while watching the captive, it once had occurred to me that this gorilla was almost the same size as me. Its eyes faced forward. Its brain weighed much the same as my own. Of all the thousands of animals in creation, the gorilla is perhaps the only one to see the world much as a man does. Facing this old man, I had the same feeling. Yet I was the gorilla, not the man. This person staring at me had infinite patience, as though the twenty-two years he had been here, my entire lifetime, was but a blink of an eye.

We could not communicate, at first. But the way he looked at me, it felt like he was saying 'I know. I am a mystery, but you're the one to solve the mystery. Go forth and prove that I am not mistaken'. He clutched his wrist, as if it were in pain, but shooed away the nurse when I summoned assistance.

I left the old man and headed to my family's apartments in Rome, feeling unsettled. In the carriage, I read the original magistrate's report, over and over. When I realised what had nagged at me, I cried out in exasperation at my stupidity. The report said that the old man had been wearing "unusual clothes", yet it had not gone into any details. I had no idea what it meant, there was no way I could picture what he had been wearing. There was also the matter of the "jewellery".

I knew from my book about the Forum that the magistrate who had dealt with the old man had been dead seven years. The clothes the old man had worn may have been strange, but there was nothing to indicate they had been valuable. I suspected, although they would have presented a whole array of clues to an intelligent investigator, that they had been burned a long time ago. "Jewellery", though, was more durable.

I approached the magistrate's widow, who laughed at the suggestion he'd ever given her jewellery. The first time she'd even realised how wealthy he was had been when she'd inherited it all. It was simple enough to discover where the magistrate had lavished his generosity. His will had asked for the manumission of his secretary, a very pretty Persian woman who now ran a perfume shop in the Forum. Despite what his widow had said, it turned out the magistrate was a very generous man indeed. One of the items of jewellery he had given to his exotic mistress was, in her own word, "strange". She kept it in a locked box, she had never worn it because it was so ugly. I offered to buy it, without opening the box, and paid the price she asked without bartering.

When I reached my apartment in Rome and unlocked the box, I discovered a bracelet. It was a solid metal bangle half an uncia thick and about five unciae wide. I don't believe it was any of the seven known metals, but it most looked like copper. It was inscribed with strange symbols, a little like Greek. It was marked with an emblem much like a serpent, twisted into two loops and swallowing its own tail. I didn't think it was ugly, but it wasn't very pretty either.

It was alive. It was a little warm to the touch, and it felt as if it were humming.

I dared not wear it; it unnerved me for some reason. I reasoned I feared its theft, and began to wear a small sword, but that did nothing to help my insecurity. I thought to travel straight back to the Alps. Instead, I summoned the old man to Rome. It took two days for him to arrive. He was attended by a nurse, a big man. They were led to one of my reception rooms, a rather spartan affair, with a plain marble floor, a desk and two chairs. The old man carried himself calmly, and looked at home in a new toga I had provided for him. I sent the nurse and my slaves away. The bangle remained locked in its box.

'Hello,' I said to him.

'Hello,' he replied calmly.

'You knew I would find the bracelet? You knew it would mean we could converse?'

'I knew someone would find it, in the end.'

'It's been over twenty years.'

The old man shrugged. It struck me for the first time that he looked to be only in his sixties. Twenty years ago, he would hardly have been "old".

'How does it work?' I asked.

'How do you think?'

I confessed I had no idea, but I refused to believe it was magic.

'Good for you.'

'Instead of needing this ... item ... to translate for you, why not simply speak Latin?'

'Not everyone knows Latin,' he replied.

I laughed. 'They do. I'm sure it is a very useful tool when trying to decipher the ancient texts of the Aegyptians, or the Jews. But if you want to speak to anyone born in the last five centuries, it is an entirely pointless device.'

'May I see it?'

'No. I want the answer to some questions.'

'You have earned that.'

'What is your name?'

He smiled. 'I don't have one.'

I was beginning to feel angry towards this old fool.

'Where are you from?'

'Nowhere you have heard of.'

'There isn't a desert so barren or ice plain so bitter that a Roman soldier hasn't marched across it. There isn't an island, a jungle or a marine trench so remote that we haven't conquered it.'

The old man looked a little sad. 'Where, then, do people escape to?'

I frowned. 'Why would anyone ever want to escape?'

'Do they need a reason?'

'Of course. Enough riddles: tell me straight why any man would want to flee from food, shelter and security.'

'You have a fine civilisation here,' he said, in the tone of voice a mother uses to praise a child's painting. 'One of the nicest I've seen. As a guest of the state, I have been treated nothing but humanely. I had hoped for more freedom, of course. But without the ring ... '

It was an odd name for such a heavy bangle, but I let the remark pass.

'If I gave you it, what would you do?'

'Are you saying that any court in this land would find it to be your property?'

'If it came to that, I am certain any court in the city would find it to be anything I paid them to find it.'

'Ah … and yet no-one would ever want to leave your utopia.'

The old man was annoying me, now. I took the bangle - the ring - from my pocket. Its owner's eyes were now full of fire.

'What else does it do?' I asked. I had no idea what it was. There were myths of artefacts with magic powers, of course; rings that could change one's appearance, certain foods that gave one strength or amorous powers. But those were the tools and gifts of the gods, not of man. And although everyone in the Empire believed in at least one god, and no-one much minded which, all the immortals seemed to have reached a gentlemen's agreement that they never interfered in the affairs of men.

Was this old man a god? To even ask the question was its denial. Jupiter could disguise himself as a man, as could others of his pantheon, but their divinity always shone through. The Christians believed in a god who was born, lived and died in a way as to be indistinguishable from a man, albeit a man who was also a lamb – something like that, their theology always confuses outsiders – but again he was marked out as different, and performed miracles. Emperors, heroes and prophets could become gods after their deaths … but never during their lives, that would be in appallingly bad taste.

Yet this old man had certainly brought an item of heavenly power to Earth. I wondered if this "ring" had once adorned a giant's finger.

'I ask you again, what would you do with it?'

'*Hand it to me*,' he said.

And I felt myself doing just that. His words – merely his words – were enough to compel me. I had seen magicians do this at parties. I was about to drop it into his waiting hand, then hesitated.

'*Drop it*,' he said.

This time, I was ready, and there was just enough doubt in his voice to allow me to see there was an alternative.

I began to withdraw the bangle, and the old man was on me, grabbing at my hand.

I was dazed, and slow to react. The old man was surprisingly strong, and grasped my thumb, pulling it back. The copper bangle dropped to the desktop, bounced off it to the floor, then rolled away.

We were both after it, but it had fallen in the old man's favour, and he took it. I now had a choice; grab him or draw my sword. Some instinct told me to grab him.

He had slipped on the bangle, his fingertips clasping the design on the top.

The room swirled away, as if it was caught in that whirlpool, and another room swirled up into its place. The old man was clearly prepared for this.

I was not.

I had no sense that I had moved. I felt as if I were in the same place. The same sunlight fell on my face, but through different windows. This room was a hall, with a tiled floor. Two centurions were running towards me. One was shouting something, apparently, into his shoulder-guard.

His shoulder *replied*. Squawking, hissing words, but it spoke to him.

I was almost distracted enough by that to forget the old man. Almost. He was looking around for an exit. A dozen paces behind him, I followed the old man through the door, with the centurions pursuing us both.

After a chase through narrow corridors, I stepped through the main door - still swinging where the old man had passed - and out into the Roman streets. Naturally, I expected to see vast spires and tower blocks. Instead, the tallest buildings were barely a hundred storeys high, and there were many a great deal shorter. This was a busy city, but it was the size of a municipal centre in our Empire. The buildings were of a recognisable style, but even the largest seemed almost plain.

Yet this was Rome. I could see the Palatine Hill, the curve of the Tiber, even the shape of the streets. The city of Rome, but with every building different.

The roofs were dotted with silver masts and poles. I would later speculate that these were religious symbols, but this was far less fascinating than the truth. The air smelled of vinegar and soap. The streets were scrubbed and polished. There was no sign of the old man, and I realised I had been tricked.

I hurried back into the building, listened for his footsteps, heard him scurrying along. I was a young man, and easily caught up with him. When I found the old man, he was on the ground. The floor here had been cleaned, and he had slipped on a section of paving that was not fully dried. I caught up with him as he struggled to his feet.

I drew my short sword, provoking further concern from the pair of centurions who had been following me, representing no threat, all this while.

I had little time. I swung my sword at the old man's forearm, bisecting his ulna. His hand, half his forearm and, crucially, his bangle were sent to the floor. The Roman sword is mainly used to stab at close quarters, but its edge is sharper than is generally credited.

The centurions charged at me now, arms raised to brandish some type of edged metal truncheon. There were variations in their armour that I didn't recognise. They were surprised by my presence in their jurisdiction, but let that be no excuse; I was equally unprepared to be there. I stabbed the first guard in the heart and – with an astonishing lack of discipline – this caused the other to hesitate. Rather than grant him a swift death, I slashed low, cutting the tendons of his legs. His commanding officer would be left with someone to punish. It was my sincere hope that the officer, too, suffered for the ease with which I was granted victory by his men.

I picked up the dead man's shoulder-guard. It was still burbling away to itself. Whatever the secrets of this talisman, it hadn't protected its owner.

Which reminded me.

The old man was lying on the floor in a pool of his own, dark blood.

'Your sword is sharper than it looks,' he stammered.

'This is Roman steel,' I told him. 'With it we conquered a world. Did you really think that an old man, even a magus, could withstand it?'

I retrieved the bangle, and slipped it onto my own wrist.

'You said you didn't believe it was magic.' He sounded disappointed in me.

'Tell me how this works,' I shouted.

Angela was staring at me. There were two house guards in front of her, three of the larger slaves behind her. Behind them was the nurse who had brought the old man here.

Here.

I was back in my own apartments, several rooms away from where I had been.

'What happened?' she asked.

'Where is the old man?' the nurse asked.

I was uncertain. 'He … made me hallucinate,' I told them. He had managed to use his sorcery after all. What more cunning way to trick me than to make me imagine I had succeeded in overcoming him? It had all been a waking dream, induced by the old man.

'But where is he?' Angela asked. The windows of this room were too high and too narrow for him to have climbed through. There was only the one door, and Angela's party had arrived at it before he could have escaped that way. In older days, he could have perhaps have taken a pick and dug his way down to the heating vents, but this was a modern building, and he would have been a wizard indeed if he could have slipped out via the pores of a microhypocaust.

I confessed that I had no idea where the old man had gone.

'What is that you are holding?' one of the guards asked.

'It's covered in blood,' Angela exclaimed.

It was, of course, the piece of armour I had taken from one of the centurions I had felled. Concrete proof, then, that the place I had been was one with a physical substance, not something conjured by my brain, or the old man's.

It was no longer speaking, it was just hissing, like steam falling on hot iron.

I sent the slaves and guards away. Angela arranged for the nurse to return to his Alpine sanatorium, with a small bribe to prevent him from asking questions and to discourage him from discussing the matter with his colleagues. He seemed happy enough to be rid of the old man.

Angela asked me what had happened, and I tried to recount events as honestly as I could. Angela is a clever woman, and managed to draw many details from me that I would have failed to recover alone. The rich red walls of the room in which I found myself. The tiled floor. The painted panels on the walls of the corridors.

We had put the bangle down on the table.

'What happened to me?' I asked.

'You were transported.'

'No. I was in the same exact spot. I know that with all my heart. Entirely the same place, at entirely the same time. Yet entirely different. It was Rome, though. Just not the Rome out of that window.'

'Two Romes,' she said. 'How?'

I told her that question did not matter for the moment, and she might as well ask why there was a Moon, or an ocean. It existed, I had walked there, breathed the air.

'And this old man came from the other Rome.'

'I hadn't thought of that, but you're right, it must be the case.'

Angela was examining the shoulder guard. 'It is not so very different from the armour you wear,' she said.

I examined it properly for the first time. It was heavier than the armour I knew; Angela was not to know that, of course. The metalwork seemed less ... assured, I think is the word. It wasn't as well-crafted, from the quality of the metal to the ingenuity of the fastenings. Its owner's blood had dried, now. I located the source of the hissing. There was a small metal grille on the top of the plate. The hissing came from the grille. On the underside, a small wooden box had been clipped into place. I moved to unclip the box.

'Careful,' Angela warned.

'What for?'

'It could be a ... I don't know. An evil spirit.'

I started to laugh, but checked myself. The bangle was alive, after all. But we would not solve this mystery without taking some risks.

The box came away from the metal very easily. There was a flexible wire extending from it, fitted into the underside of the armour. Inside the box was a collection of what looked like thin metal cords, glass beads and tiny pieces of pottery, all arranged together in a way that seemed almost ritualistic. There was a tiny metal cylinder that was held in place by a spring. It looked as if it could be easily detached. I did that, and the hissing stopped.

'A tiny spira?' Angela asked.

I shook it. 'No. There are no cogs or springs in here. And where would you put the key? I think it's full of liquid.'

I passed it to Angela, who tried shaking it for herself, but she wasn't so sure.

'I could cut it open.'

'Undoubtedly. But could you put it back together again?'

I admitted I couldn't. I replaced the cylinder, and the hissing started up almost immediately.

'Speak,' I said into the grille. But it didn't reply.

'We should get this to an expert,' she suggested. 'A Seric, perhaps, or a Greek.'

'I don't think this is from either of those places.'

'There's a name here,' Angela told me, squinting at the box.

Marconi.

'Certainly a Roman name,' Angela said.

'Have a slave search the directory. Perhaps there is a Marconi listed who can discern what this object is.'

Angela moved to leave. As she did, she asked. 'I wonder what is happening this evening in that other Rome?'

Whether her theory of an other Rome was correct or not, this was a good question I hadn't thought to ask. Had the old man died from his injury? If a skilled surgeon had reached him in time, he could have survived a clean break like that. What arrangements were being made as we sat here talking? Whatever its nature, there was another land, one where I had trespassed and murdered.

I knew what I would do in their circumstances: I would plot my revenge. I would come looking for the man that had shamed them. I would take back my property. These men were Romans, and I felt sure they would do as I would do. I summoned my brother and Angela's father.

I told them, and understood now, that nothing less than the security of Rome was at stake.

I decided to set aside any philosophical or theoretical matters. While I waited for my friends, family and other allies to arrive, I concentrated on the practical. I attempted to piece together what I could of this other Rome. It was a hopeless task. I summoned a scribe, Laton, skilled at drawing, and described the centurion's armour to him. I stood looking over his shoulder, and together we recreated the uniform as best I could recall it, complete with truncheon. There was the shoulder guard, which I sent for analysis at the naval base at the Straits of Hercules, along with a note to Quintus Saxus, urging secrecy. The hissing wooden box would have to wait for the moment. The rest was down to my memory. Again, I had Laton draw sketches based on my description of the rooms and the skyline of the city.

I had the scribe virtually interrogate me on points of detail. We had slaves bring samples of materials and paint. I decided that the floor tiles were a type of Italian terracotta. I could recall the approximate dimensions of the hall, the orientation and size of the windows (long and tall, plainly glazed). I could remember there being paintings hung on the wall, large ones, but I had no recollection of what the subject matter had been. I didn't recognise any of the paintings.

By the time my allies arrived, I had a portfolio of drawings, with a sheaf of explanatory notes. I was happy that every fact at my disposal had been drained from me. I served a fine dinner to my assembled allies, and I explained what had happened, swore an oath that it was as I said (naturally, everyone but Angela, who had been present at my return, was sceptical). I asked what we could infer about this *other Rome* from the facts as we had them, and what we should then do with these facts.

It added up to nothing, as far as we could see. We could make suppositions. It was Rome, therefore the heart of empire. From that, we could suppose that the centurions were not country bumpkins, they would have the latest armour. The metalwork was not good, the truncheons they carried had looked brutal, but were hardly technologically advanced. Looking at the picture of the centurion, my brother and I practically fell over each other to suggest improvements; the ease with which I had found chinks in their armour cheered us all no end. The men weren't well-drilled. They had made the most basic mistakes. They outnumbered me, they were on their home territory, and still they had lost. This enemy was most certainly mortal.

The hall wasn't a home. It was more like an art gallery, or part of some public building. Yet so much was the same. They were Romans, shouting in Latin.

But then there was the hissing box. The centurion had spoken into it, and the box had answered him. That was how it had seemed at the time. Titus wondered if I had been mistaken. Perhaps the armour was alive in some way. The centurion had been giving an order to his armour, telling it to prepare for combat. If that was the plan, I retorted, it hadn't worked. The hissing box remained a complete mystery to our scholarship.

We turned our thoughts to what we would do in their place. How would we seek revenge?

First of all, they would need a method of getting here... and that would seem to mean a bangle like the old man's. We talked through the logical implications of this. I sent Laton away to discover any and every documented example of strange materialization. Anywhere in the world, but limiting his search to the last twenty years. What I didn't tell the poor fellow was that I wasn't expecting him to discover very much. People didn't just appear out of thin air. And so we could deduce that not everyone in this other Rome had a magic bangle that allowed him to travel to our Rome.

But there was a paradox: if the old man was special, wouldn't that make him valuable and powerful? If he had friends, wouldn't they have come looking for him? Wouldn't they keep track of the magic bangles as a matter of course, if only to prevent them falling into the wrong hands? It had taken me less than a day to find the Persian woman who'd been given the old man's. Did he not have a brother or son willing to rescue him?

The logical conclusion, from the facts available, was that the authorities in *other Rome* didn't have the ability to cross to our Rome. Logic dictated that the old man should have known where to find the exit if he had been to the hall in other Rome before... but would I know every room in my Rome, and after twenty years away? No.

I speculated that the old man was from elsewhere. I believed now that he was not a native of that other place. Had he not spoken of the many civilisations he had seen? He hadn't been able to speak Latin.

'What are you suggesting?' my father asked. 'That there is yet another Rome, a third?'

'Indeed.'

'How many Romes, Scriptor?' my brother asked. 'Five? Ten? Fifty? A hundred? Five-hundred? A thousand?'

My mind ... expanded at that moment.

'Of course! Is it any more fantastic to imagine there are a thousand Romes than *merely* two?'

Until that point, my friends had been patient with me. Now they all, in turn, and in their different ways, suggested I get some sleep. It is, if you like the word, something of a paradox that our perspective has changed so much since that evening, isn't it?

IV.

The next morning, the "war council" I had assembled gathered for breakfast. Angela and I were the last to arrive; I was feeling foolish. Wasn't the simplest answer to this problem that I had dreamt the whole thing? That, surely, made more sense than conjuring an infinity of worlds into existence.

My wife and I discovered that the others had come around to my way of thinking. At least, they accepted the possibility of what I had said. They recommended that we contact some thinkers; philosophers, scholars and other men of learning who could consult the authorities and see how this could be. My brother had a more practical suggestion. He thought I should use the bangle to see if I could return to the other Rome.

I had shied away from this idea, and I cannot say why. There was something about the other place that concerned me, scared me a little. I told my friends that I would go, but that it must be done correctly, that things must be prepared. On that first journey, I had held onto the old man, and been transported with him. It stood to reason that - if I could activate the bangle - I could take people with me.

This required careful thought, but it was not as unusual a situation as might be supposed. Even in a togafied world, there were plenty of regional customs. A Roman merchant, soldier or diplomat can't just walk anywhere and treat everyone the same way. These local differences are important, and are frequently a matter of the greatest pride. The Serics, and many other people in their part of the world, eat food with sticks rather than their fingers. The Jews don't eat pigs or work on Saturnsday.

These customs are known, mind you. We knew nothing of this other Rome, and we quickly agreed on a scouting mission there as a first stage. I went with Angela's father, Angus Inducula - who knew Rome well, but could still see it with an outsider's eye - and Laton, who could make sketches of what we saw. We took old Roman coins. These were still legal tender here, but did not bear the face of our Emperor. We also took a few strips of gold and silver, in case the coins proved invalid. We carried daggers, yet carefully concealed. We wore togas, ones in the classic style.

Our family jurisconsultus, Pristrix, was consulted. Under ancient Roman law, the Emperor had to authorise all contact with foreign countries. This hadn't been enforced, for obvious reasons, for many centuries, but was relevant to us. Pristrix suggested that if it came to court, we could simply claim that we had been in Rome, the very opposite of a foreign land.

I finally realised now why the old man had appeared in the Forum. Whatever happened to Rome, surely the Forum would survive in some form. The same could not be said of many other places. The equivalent of my apartments were some type of gallery, or other public space. Would the sorcery of the bangle protect us? Would it prevent us appearing in a wall, say, or a hundred storeys up in thin air? Angus Inducula, Laton and I considered all the options. The Palatine Hill was an obvious choice, as the seat of government, but wouldn't it also be the most heavily patrolled place in the city? We considered spots on the banks of the Tiber, or in some of the parks. We thought perhaps somewhere very remote would be best. In the end, we did what the old man had done, and went to the Forum. Angus Inducula had officinae there, and we went to the ground floor of those.

Clasping hands, I touched the whirlpool design on the bangle, and tried to imagine that other Rome. I'm not sure what I did, to be honest, but it worked. A moment later, the three of us were standing on the floor of a small horreum. Warehouses are functional spaces, and there is little variation in design. It was still the early morning, the air was still as crisp and cold as it had been in our Rome.

Angus Inducula and Latron were clearly disorientated. However much faith they had in me, however much they had believed my story before we set out, it was quite another matter to be walking around in it. Cautiously, we made our way outside. Even before we did so, we noticed all sorts of things. The amphora and cistae were of strange design. The floors were cold, and laid out in bare concrete.

'Space in this Rome is not at such a premium,' Angus Inducula said. 'It would be impossible to afford the rent on a warehouse this big in our Forum.'

'It's also very quiet,' Latron noted. 'I don't think many people live in this Rome.'

'These goods aren't from far away,' I noted. Nothing from America, Seres or any further than Northern Africa.

So it proved.

On my previous visit, I had seen people in togas like ours, so felt confident in walking the streets. The plan of the city was eerily familiar, and the signs almost always bore the same names. It was a little like walking through a model of the real Rome. There were many slaves around in waterproof outfits, sweeping and spraying the streets.

It was then that I saw it.

A glint in the blue, uncluttered sky. A dot of silver, with a white line of cloud trailing after it. The three of us all stared up.

'A metal bird,' Latron said. 'A flying vehicle.'

One of the locals eyed us suspiciously. How provincial we must have seemed to him!

This was our first aeroplane. But very quickly it was followed by others. There were half a dozen in the sky, and we determined that they were taking off and landing from a camp to the southwest. You must understand that this was the first time we had encountered other people who could accomplish things we could not. How was it that these people had the secret of flight, or that they could build talking shoulder-guards, yet their Rome was so ... diminished?

'Perhaps these people have abandoned the ground, and walk in the clouds,' I said.

We soon found a bookstall. The books proved expensive. These were bound paper books, not clockworks. I picked up two guidebooks to the city, both recommended to me by the vendor.

'Tourists?' he asked suspiciously, as he passed one to me.

'From Scotia,' I answered, instantly worried that would ring false here.

'I've never been,' he replied. 'It's meant to be nice. Clean air and water.'

He turned away and started dealing with his next customer.

We sat in an eaterie in the shadow of the Flavian amphitheatre. The Romans here had either always maintained the building as Vespasian had built it, or had recently restored it to its ancient form. Either way, it didn't resemble the modern arena of our Rome. The guidebooks I had bought would need thorough study, I decided. This could wait until we returned home.

The food was overcooked and unadventurous, and cost many times what we would have expected to pay in our Rome. Oddly, there were no pigeons seeking our attention.

A young woman passed us. She was ever so pretty. Small and dark, in a short dress. Pitch-black hair cascaded down her back. The three of us must all have been staring at her, as she looked our way, a little confused by the attention.

'I'm sorry, miss,' Laton called. In our Rome, a slave would have to be careful. Here, we had already recognised that when different classes of men spoke, there was less formality than we were used to.

The woman looked puzzled, then unhooked something from her ear.

'Did you say something?'

Music was coming from the thing she had taken from her ear. There was a black wire leading down to a small wooden box clipped to her sash. The music was so faint as to be impossible to identify.

'Sorry, miss, no.'

She frowned, then walked away.

We all agreed on two things: she was very pretty, but didn't look rich. She was the wife of a craftsman, say. So the Marconi devices - something that all the money in our world could not buy - were so inexpensive they could be bought here by ordinary people.

Our next task was obvious: we had to acquire at least one example of this magical music box for ourselves. Achieving this task was more complicated. We did not know what the things were called. As our poor luck would have it, no-one else walked by. I was sceptical about what we could say if someone did; we could scarcely ask him what the name of such a common item was, or offer to buy it from him in the street. Angus Inducula sighed impatiently, and told me that in such a situation, we would simply ask where the man bought it.

As it happened, we found a shop selling them. The window display had what the sign called "shiners" of all sizes, from the portable devices to ones that were pieces of furniture the size of a large trunk. The three of us going in together might have drawn attention to ourselves, so I volunteered to go in alone.

The shop was brightly-lit, the candles arranged to show off the trader's wares to best advantage. I saw the prices, and realised I had enough gold to pay for a shiner that wasn't the very best, but which was large, with many features. Instead, though, I bought three or four of the smallest - and so, I reasoned, most simple - devices, and a larger one.

'Do these allow you to throw your voice as well as hear music?' I asked, remembering the guard talking into his shoulder. The man, though, looked at me suspiciously, and I did not press the point, claiming he had misheard me.

I decided that between the bookseller, the young woman and now this salesman, that our expedition was in danger of raising suspicion. We returned to the horreum with our shiners, and thence to our Rome.

Angus Inducula sent one of the music devices to his brightest Seric craftsmen, to see if he could get it to work (once again, it did not function in our Rome). I retired to my apartments and devoured the history of this other Rome.

I was fascinated to learn that this was a new, different world history. From what I could glean from the books, all was as I recognised it until the ninth century, when there was political turmoil that – when compared with my history - set the expansion of the Empire back by many years. Indeed, thirteen hundred years later, the boundaries of the Roman territory had been little further developed than in the time of Claudius, with a little more exploration around the African coastline. The Empire had become bogged down in the battle with the German people, and that drained much of their resources. Little was known of the world beyond the Empire. America and Oceania remained undiscovered.

Then a miracle: a Tuscan genius, Leonardo, emerged. Studying in the Great Library at Alexandria and with Arabian scholars, Leonardo invented the "helicopter", a flying vehicle. He also discovered the secrets of light and magnetism, and in particular the "shining wave", an invisible form of light that could be manipulated to transmit sounds, called anisocyclorum.

It took only a few years for these Romans to spread across their world in their helicopters, their armies invincible by virtue of their flying machines ... and as I read of this, I wondered why their Rome was so primitive compared with our own. I quickly found my answer. The world harboured plagues and illnesses in every corner. Sickness spread just as fast as the Romans; faster than any physician could cope with. Indeed, the men of medicine were the first to fall foul of these new plagues. The simple peoples of the world (and the writer made it clear this meant anyone who wasn't a Roman) died at a rate that would make the most efficient army blush. The Empire was literally decimated, but elsewhere in the world, the human race was reduced to tiny, self-sufficient communities.

The other Roman Empire built great walls around itself. Four centuries after Leonardo, this second Rome traded with itself, and ruthlessly wiped out even the slightest sign of plague. Men still flew, but such transport was heavily regulated. Few left their home cities, and all they knew of the world was from the anisocyclorum of the shiners. This was a scared, xenophobic Rome. Not, then, the sort of place that creates bangles that travel to new places. Now, more than ever, I was sure that the old man was from elsewhere.

It was, however, a Rome with many treasures to offer. Between them, Angus Inducula and Quintus Saxus could duplicate the shiner receiving devices using the materials of our Rome ... but neither could infer the vital secret of anisocycla, making their efforts entirely useless. As to the helicopter: only a year before, the greatest men of learning had said that powered heavier-than-air transport was a theoretical absurdity, and we would have to make do with balloons and gliders. We had not seen these helicopters up close, and had no pictures of them, let alone plans that would allow us to build them for ourselves. Such things were as magic. Acquiring knowledge of these vehicles would clearly be our top priority.

We drew up great plans for a raiding party. I undertook a couple of scouting missions with fellow soldiers. We got to the air vehicles' camp and made detailed sketches of the vehicles. We completely failed to locate the "shiner transmitters", because we had no idea what we were looking for.

On the third such mission, it occurred to me that we were approaching this the wrong way. We were treating it as a military matter, but these were Romans, and the diplomatic approach would be far more appropriate. It was going to be far simpler to buy these helicopters than to work out how to build them, how to power them and then how to actually fly them.

I told this to my father and my father-in-law, and told them it was time we involved the Emperor. Both men were unhappy, as they wanted to secure this valuable new resource for themselves without Imperial intervention. But I had already thought of this. We would still have a monopoly on travel between the Romes, as we had the only bangle.

And so it was that, in the space of a week, I met two Roman Emperors. I wrote a letter outlining - to an extent, at any rate - what we knew of the other Rome and how we could get there. This missed out a few details about the acquisition of the bangle. Angela had pointed out that the Persian perfumier, the Forum magistrate's widow, the Forum authorities, the nurse at the sanatorium and any number of people claiming to know the old man would all lodge claims to the bracelet with the courts. I claimed it was an ancient American artefact, discovered during construction works. I asked for an audience, to demonstrate the wonders of this other Rome, and reassured him that the other Rome was no threat to us.

A secretary arrived at my apartment within the hour, and interrogated me until well into the evening. Satisfied with my answers, he then ushered me immediately into the Emperor's presence.

This was Emmanuel Victorius, a man I had only seen before at a distance or on coins. On his death, he was deified, but at the time I met him he was just a man. He had a reputation as an administrator, and he wasn't a scholar. But he remembered my writings, and was fascinated by the story I told him now. Finally, he asked me what I wanted to do. I told him that I wanted to head a diplomatic mission that could reap great benefits to our Rome. My final flourish was to reveal the existence of the helicopters, something I had carefully omitted from my previous testimony.

The Emperor admitted that he wasn't sure whether to believe me. I offered to take his secretary to the other Rome, for just a moment. A piece of theatre, but an effective one. The Emperor was still shaken by our vanishing into thin air a minute or so later, when we returned. As we talked afterwards, he seemed more concerned that no-one else should know of this. I swore the most solemn oath. The Emperor then set out a course of action that was extremely wise, and which I followed. He had a slave fetch a small clockwork statue and gave it to me, a gift for the Emperor of that world from the Emperor of this. He also drafted a letter, from Emperor to Emperor, an official greeting that granted me authority to act on his behalf. The Emperor proposed that he would take twenty percent of the proceeds from our trading arrangements, in return for granting a monopoly on inter-Roman trade. Neither of us, at that stage, appreciated the scale on which we were now operating.

The Emperor was extremely concerned I was not captured, as he didn't want the bangle to fall into anyone else's hands. I had given this some thought, of course, but the Emperor convinced me to give more attention to the matter. It was he who came up with the brilliantly devious solution. He gave me a gold ring, which I placed on the little finger of my left hand. I could touch the bangle on my left wrist while pretending to rub the ring. Thus, anyone watching would think it was the ring, not the bangle, that contained the magic.

I instantly saw the wisdom of this simple deception, and it has saved my life on over a dozen occasions since. As it happened, though, the authorities of this other Rome were open and enthusiastic. After a week in quarantine, I was granted an audience with the Emperor. This was Julius Mundus, a young man who held a handkerchief to his face as he addressed me. He and his advisers had been much troubled by my appearance in their gallery with the old man, and were somewhat relieved that I was a Roman, with no hostile intention. I apologised for killing their guard, but they agreed with me that he should have been better at his job. The old man had died, I learnt, and - in accordance with their customs - his body was quickly incinerated to prevent the risk of spreading infection.

I negotiated a simple trading arrangement with the Emperor's representatives. We would give gold and some medicinal herbs and writings in return for a team of helicopter craftsman and pilots and components to build the first few vehicles. A second treaty gave us plans for shiner transmitters. Within a year, the company I established - financed by my father and father-in-law, with the Emperor as a partner - was producing its own helicopters, ones that operated using clockwork, not the crude chemical energy storage the other Romans used. Within six months, every fashionable Roman home had a shiner set. The social commentators were divided on whether to approve or not. They quickly settled on becoming orators on the shiner, denouncing the new technology while reaching an audience of millions instead of hundreds.

No-one on my Rome had the slightest clue of the true origin of these new developments. The Emperor urged caution; both air transport and the shiner had the potential to destabilise our utopia, and both were strictly regulated. Those that counterfeited the technology were sentenced to execution. We knew it was necessary to control this progress, lest our Rome fell prey to the rapid changes that had devastated the population of the other Rome.

* * *

The Emperor of other Rome visited our world. He was kept from public view, but quickly became agitated. He explained that he had imagined we were somehow equals. He saw now the superiority of our civilisation. Our Emperor would have nothing to do with this view: Julius Mundus was a Roman Emperor. He pledged - and signed the most solemn treaty - that no Roman Emperor would ever have authority over another Emperor on his native world. But even then, it was clear that our Emperor was first among equals in this arrangement.

I, for my part, had a busy few years. I would never let the bangle leave my wrist. It would have been possible to confine my activities to this other Rome. Their world was as large and their history as long as my own. But Pandora's Box had been opened. There were many other worlds, each as large and as old. I led the expeditions *beyond*.

I travelled to yet more Romes and carefully studied their histories. Each was a story of a Rome both like and unlike my own. The dozen or so worlds the bangle had enabled me to reach by this time seemed to have started from the same seed. These Romes were brothers, and like brothers there were many commonalties, many points of resemblance, but having the same background and upbringing did not prevent each from having its own personality. In each of the dozen Romes, the history of mankind was to all discernment exactly the same until the time of Augustus. From there, there was a divergence. Often the most trivial thing. A series of bad harvests, say, or the assassination of a particular person. Battles were lost because the armies weren't expecting rain to fall or ice to thaw, or because the general who won it in our world was killed, imprisoned or assigned elsewhere in theirs. Different Emperors married different women, sired different children or enacted some wide-ranging social reform.

The face of history.

The Gaulish scholar Pascalicus once remarked that if Cleopatra had a less attractive nose, then the whole face of history might change. It was intended as a quip, and concerned the distant past, but it may be among the most profound things a man has ever said. Imagine two identical worlds, with identical Romes. They start off from the same point. But everywhere there are slight variations. A battle won here is lost there. A man destined to be Emperor here died in infancy there, or is born a woman so can't succeed. Cleopatra's nose is longer there, and so Rome remained a republic.

In certain company, this thinking might once have been construed as treason. Our history, so it was thought, was the divine will. Many other Romes had the same beliefs about their histories. I shall write more on that subject when my narrative reaches the appropriate point to do so.

We also learned something of the geography. These Romes were strung out in lines, not unlike a road map. If you want to travel to Londinium from Rome by road, first you must travel through Lugdunum, Duriocortorum and Portus Lemanis and so on. There were, it transpired, a maximum of four "directions" you could travel from each Rome. From my native Rome, which we listed as

Roma I, I could reach Roma II, that Rome ravaged by plague; Roma III, where Yung Lo's Serics had won the toss of their coin ... and promptly decamped to Rome and become utterly togafied; Roma IV, a world where a breakaway Christian faction caused problems for the Mithraic majority; and Roma V, where the Mare Nostra had been drained until it was little more than a river, and used to irrigate the Sahara. These numbers became our new north, south, east and west. So, if we headed out past Roma IV, we were heading "fourwards", the opposite direction was "twowards", and there was also "threewards" and "fivewards".

Within two months I had discovered that from Roma II, you could reach Roma I (fourwards); Roma VI, where the head of the Vestal order lead a world where women, not men, were the sex engaged in politics (threewards); Roma VII, a world ruled from a Roman Emperor based in Constantinople (twowards); and Roma VIII, where the Battle of Actium had fallen a different way, and the culture's main influence had been Aegypt, not Greece (fivewards). The emperors of that world were entombed in ever-larger pyramid tombs, and by now these rivalled the Alps. These were among the most magnificent achievements anywhere in the Known Worlds, but also a massive drain on their treasury.

At this point, the philosophy was a little vague. We consulted wise men, who wondered if perhaps the stars in the night sky were all distant *other Suns*. This seemed farfetched to me, even then. But the men of learning were in agreement: the other Romes were up in the sky, each orbited by its own star. They admitted that they had so far failed to calculate the epicycles of these stars. The men of learning hoped to find some correlation between the constellations and the distribution of the other Romes. They spent their time in elaborate games of join-the-dots. They told me that Roma II was north of us, and that the sun which beat down on it was probably Polaris, but offered little evidence for this assertion.

In practical terms, there were many Romes almost identical to others. Many maintained an Empire the size it was in ancient times; little more than Europe, a little of Armenia and Libya. None of these worlds could conjure up a foe capable of defeating Rome, but in none of these did Rome have true mastery of the world. In every history, though, Rome prevailed.

Always, we maintained the strictest secrecy, revealing ourselves only to the Emperor (or Empress, in a surprising number of worlds), Senate, Supreme Council or whatever other central authority the Roman Empire had. Thus, a vast, invisible trading network was set up. I stress that nothing we did was done to undermine a local Emperor. Our Emperor was very insistent on that. We brought often very simple remedies to boost the fortunes of their Rome. Those who had difficulty feeding their populations were taught simple sowing techniques or matters of animal husbandry such as how to domesticate the hippopotamus. Those with no gold were pointed to the seams they had not discovered. For every problem one Rome felt, another - frequently our own - offered a solution. Every time, we helped a Rome to solve its own problems, we never invaded or imposed.

My Rome, top of this pyramid, was the greatest beneficiary.

It was we who dictated what was traded. It was our world that gained the greatest number of advancements and refinements. Suddenly, there were new types of food and wine, new plays, new scientific knowledge. So much of it that my family ploughed a great amount of our profits into vast academies, recruited the greatest minds of all the worlds to teach and learn. And, to keep this process secret from the masses, this was done in secret locations across America.

These institutions were the finest places. They contained the distilled genius of more than a hundred and fifty Earths. They were vast, self-contained camps. They were the best-defended fortresses in the Known Worlds, but even to visitors they resembled Arcadian gardens and temples. Our job was compilation and assimilation of knowledge. Vast difference engines clacked away all day, every day, cataloguing the libraries of all these worlds. Slaves and scholars worked tirelessly to take the writings of each world, to compare them all, to pluck out the best of everything.

This process was overseen by the Emperor's cabal, but it was controlled by my family, mainly my father, my siblings, my wife and my father-in-law. As I continued to explore (accompanied by a number of my most trusted friends, or the Emperor's diplomats), my family consolidated our position at home.

Then, one Earth, CLII, proved to be very different.

I and Quintus Saxus - who now worked for my family's company - set off from Londinium in June. But I arrived in midwinter. In every other Londinium, it would be summer. Why not here?

That, it transpired, was the least of our problems here. This place was desolate, ruined. A great disaster had befallen it. This was not entirely unusual. We had discovered worlds ravaged by tidal waves, floods, earthquakes, famines, plagues, barbarians, insects ... but this was an entirely different thing. The sky was red cloud, every villa and temple in the town had been brought to ruin. Fires had raged, roofs had collapsed, and then the whole devastated scene had been covered with drifts of snow.

Quintus Saxus, brave young man, found the first evidence that this was a place where the face of history had been altered almost beyond recognition.

He found the skull of a dragon.

It could be nothing else: it was larger even than an rhinoceros', with teeth that would shame a shark.

'Has this world fallen to dragons?' I asked, nervously. On these first expeditions, I never carried anything more than my short sword, as it was not my intention to appear aggressive. On every world, we had found some new technique or improvement that we could add to our library of military arts. However, there were few worlds that had produced weaponry more *useful* than my Roman steel. Yet there was one where the study of magnetism had obsessed the men of learning. The legionaries of that world carried magnetic crossbows that could bring down an elephant. I had practised with such a weapon, and would have felt far more comfortable if I had carried one now.

Everywhere we looked, there was a different type of skull. These reminded me of something, and after an hour or so of trudging through snow, uncovering examples of dragon's bones I remembered what it was.

'Stone skulls like this have been found in our America,' I told Quintus Saxus.

'But those are mere curiosities,' he said. 'We have all seen trees whose bark is contrived to look like a face, or stacks of stone that look, from a distance, a little like a woman. Those stones are just elaborate examples of that.'

This was not my field of expertise. But I had seen bones, and the dragon skulls were bones. Recent ones, too; it was no more than months since they had been picked clean. On some of them, patches of dry skin and scales were yet attached to the skeletons we had discovered.

Then we heard the voice.

'Thank the gods. Thank the gods.' It was such a weak voice, but it was the only sound in this world, as white and dead as the bones we had found there. We hurried to its source, and found a young woman. She was swamped in bear furs, and was almost a skeleton herself.

'My name is Regina,' she said.

'You are a Roman citizen?' I asked. She was nothing more than a savage.

'If there is still a Rome,' she answered. We must have looked shocked, as she quickly added. 'But of course there is. We wondered how much of the world had been affected.'

As we shared our rations with her, she told us what had happened. Six months before - as far as Regina could judge - there had been a great disaster. Fire in the sky, followed by tidal waves. All contact with other cities had been lost in the turmoil, but the people of Londinium thought they had been spared. Then the sky went dark. Stones showered from the sky, killing anyone outside (and a fair number inside). The rains came, and they were burning acid. Yet even this was not the worst of it. In two months without the sun, everything died. The plants and crops could not grow, even the animals and people capable of living nocturnally had nothing to eat. Millions perished of starvation, or fighting over precious resources.

'It must have been what the fall of Atlantis was like,' Regina said. I thought at first that she meant this world had lost the sea city in an earlier disaster, then I remembered that few Earths had built sea cities, and she would be referring to the legendary city mentioned by Plato.

'Was it the dragons?' I asked.

This confused her, so I found and showed her one of the skulls.

'This is the Wembley Arena,' she told me.

I failed to understand.

'The fights?' she asked, as if they were the most famous thing in the world. 'This is where we staged our contests. On feast days, the Tyrants were let loose on the Double Beams. On regular days, we'd have gladiators fighting the Speedy Robbers or the Winged and Toothless. We were always told the fights in Rome were on a much larger scale.'

I understood around one word in five she was saying. She hunted for, then found, some advertising reliefs on a fallen wall. These depicted strange battles; men fighting what looked like vast reptilian creatures the size of elephants.

'These really happened,' she insisted, even though to us they looked like something from some ancient legend.

I knew then that she would have to come back with us, where she could relate her story to our men of learning. It would be a year before they had an answer to what had happened, and before that, I would need to accompany Regina here twice more to remove what we could from the frozen libraries and museums. A disaster in the ocean to the west of Britannia - a vast volcanic eruption, perhaps - had thrown up burning rock and created great tidal waves. All but a handful of living things on this world were killed in the firestorm or the subsequent, unnatural winter. Further expeditions proved that the explosion had been somewhere in the Americas, and that the human population of this world was now numbered in the hundreds. We rescued everyone we found.

Could such a thing happen to our Earth? Astonishingly, some of the scholars claimed that our Earth had experienced such a terrible catastrophe, many thousands upon thousands of years ago. Regina went to her grave many decades later still claiming that this ancient disaster must have killed the Terrible Lizards of our world. But no man of learning took this theory seriously.

I have yet to tell you everything that happened on the day we first met Regina. I bid Quintus Saxus look after the young woman while I slipped back to the Londinium we had come from. There, I quickly had slaves bring warm clothing, provisions and firewood. I returned to the frozen Earth within a few minutes.

I was making my way back to Quintus Saxus and Regina when I found a nine-toed footprint in the snow.

I thought perhaps one of the Terrible Lizards - a smaller one - had survived and was prowling around. I was wary, but also keen to see one of the strange creatures. I followed the tracks. It was about the size of a man, a large man. As I continued to follow the footprints, though, their nature changed. In mid-step, one of the feet became four-toed, then, half a dozen steps later, so did the other. A score of steps later, and the creature I was tracking had two hooves, then it was wearing boots.

A man stood about twenty paces away, at the end of the trail. It wore dark clothes, and was large and pale-skinned. It had one orb set in the centre of its face. This eye shone with a golden fire, like the sun. Like the sun, I couldn't look directly at it, and had to avert my eyes. The man, or cyclops, or whatever it was, stepped towards me, its feet crunching in the snow.

'Thought we wouldn't find you?' it said, in a hissing, snarling voice that seemed to come from all around me.

The man was on me, faster than I would have thought possible. It was grabbing at my hand.

'Give me the ring.'

I tugged my hand away, tried to hide my ring behind my back.

The man pushed me over, onto my back, trapping my arm in the snow underneath me. This hurt, but I ignored the pain, reasoning that a cold, twisted arm was the least of my problems. The man grabbed at my shoulder-guard, and each of its fingers grew fingers in turn, and each of those fingers grew fingers, and they all began plucking away at the segments of the armour there. I could feel the shoulder-guard collapsing under this scrutiny. The fingers were now thorns, scratching the flesh of my shoulder away. Each touch was agony; sharp barbs each with its own unique, burning, itching or paralysing poison

The man had grown wings, little leathery things sprouting from its shoulder blades. Watching it, I felt this wasn't a creature changing form so much as one gradually revealing itself to me.

'Give it up, old man.'

It thought I was the original owner of the bangle, I realised.

'You thought you could escape us?' it rasped.

'I'm not who you're looking for,' I managed to say. 'Look at me, I look nothing like him. I'm half that man's age, if I'm a day.'

The man swung its sun-face at me, stared at me. I managed to stare back.

'You killed the owner of this ring?' it both stated and asked.

'Yes,' I replied, simplifying the story a little.

'A rare pleasure,' it cackled. *'A pleasure you have denied me.'*

It flipped me over, freeing my arm and pushing my face in the snow. I closed my eyes, and saw only the afterimage of the sun.

'The old man was hiding,' it told me quietly. *'He and twelve of his friends decided to remove themselves from the board. We don't know why. But we can guess.'*

It had my arm in its grip. As I lay there, the fingers became teeth, and those teeth began sinking into my wrist. It meant to amputate my hand.

'They're plotting some illegal move against their enemy.'

'Let me guess,' I managed.

'Oh ... not me,' it giggled. *'But you know what they say: your enemy's enemy. The point is, they are plotting something. And they need those rings to do it. Now, we could waste a century or two trying to work out what it is they have in mind. We could try to think like they do, get into their heads, as it were. That was what some of my brothers wanted to do. But I came up with a better idea. Track every last one of them down, kill them and eat them. Sic gorgiamus allos subjectatos nunc. Them and their rings. Your old man was the eighth.'*

I pushed myself upwards, as powerfully and suddenly as I could. The move had the desired effect, and the man - or what was left of it - was thrown away from me.

The thing that faced me was indecipherable. It shuffled forwards on snake legs, unfurling bat-wings ten foot wide, covered with patches of tiny, broken feathers. It had a man's torso and head, but these rippled with scales and fur. It had the arm of a crab or lobster, and another like a lion's paw.

'You can't defeat me. Sigils and incantations from the depths of inner time encase me. I'm protected from anything you can throw at me. Unhappen my timeline, and I'll still

be there. Bind me with ritual and you'll find it's you who's trapped. Seal me into a black hole and with one bound I'll be free. Drop me into a star and I'll suck it up and breathe its fire into your face. Kill my ancestor and I'll sprout two more in his place.'

It had to die. This wasn't just what I thought, it was what I knew, what every part of my body was telling me. This thing didn't belong here. Not in this world, nor in any world. I turned and drew my sword.

'Wait! Not fair! No-one uses swords any more.'

Its glowing eye was the beast's only constant feature, and it was there that I plunged my blade.

The head was the size of my own. The sword slid easily into the eye, and a foot of steel should have emerged from the back of the creature's skull. Instead, the sword kept sliding in, meeting little resistance.

I could have kept up my thrust until my whole arm was in there, instead I withdrew the sword. The blade had all but gone, and what remained had rotted, as if it had been dropped in a cauldron of acid. The hilt was freezing cold to the touch, and I dropped it.

The creature was reeling. It shouted obscenities at me as cracks appeared in its head and torso. Golden light poured from the cracks.

I turned and ran, throwing myself behind a pile of bricks, some wall that had fallen and been covered in earth and snow. The cold snow was a blessed relief for my torn shoulder, numbing the pain.

The creature exploded, the ground shaking with the force of its death-throes.

When I looked back up, it was gone with only a crater in the ice to indicate that it had ever been there. I slumped back, packed my shoulder wounds with snow. I could barely move that arm. I tried to use the other to unclip my shiner and summon help.

Quintus Saxus and Regina had heard the explosion. They came running, now, and stood over me as I started to fade. Quintus couldn't understand why I had sunburn. I ordered them both to search the snow. Within minutes, they had found seven bangles, identical in every respect to the one I wore on my wrist. Regina leant over me, her cracked lips telling me I was going to be all right. Trusting her judgement, I allowed myself oblivion.

V.

There were now eight bangles in our possession, not simply my own. This meant that others were capable of exploring the other Romes, that I did not have to take diplomats and negotiators from our Rome to the other Romes in person. I had spent, by now, half a decade travelling from one Rome to the next. Each new world represented a new challenge, yet each challenge sapped some of my energy. Now, at last, I could rest for a while.

This did nothing, of course, to diminish the importance of keeping secure the travel routes to the other Romes. Just because we had eight bracelets now didn't mean that we handed them around to everyone who asked for them. This included the Emperor. It was always a fundamental part of our strategy to make the Emperor rich, to give him a generous cut of the profits from the new patents and knowledge we were uncovering, but ultimately to keep him at a distance. Finally, my father had exactly what he had always desired for the family: power. Power, if truth be told, greater than that of the Emperor himself. The true Emperor resented this, of course, but we had given him wealth, knowledge and status. Crucially, the secrets of our success and the true source of our new knowledge and technology was kept secret from all but a handful of people.

Members of the Senate speculated openly that my father was somehow in league with malevolent spirits; the only way they could think of accounting for our family's new-found success. As ever, though, they were forced to concede that whatever had happened, it had happened for the good of Rome and the Empire. Their jealousy and confusion didn't stop every noble family from attempting to use the courts to limit our commercial activities... or from ordering a fleet of helicopters from our officinae.

My father was now almost permanently at the Imperial Court with a team of jurisconsulti, and lately, the Emperor's staff had begun to pick at every contract that was signed. I was worried about this. On one of my visits to Rome, I met with my father.

'When this was a fresh deal, the Emperor was happy to take our money,' I reminded him.

'After that, he was more than happy: it was more money even than we had promised,' my father replied ruefully.

'We both benefit from this arrangement, why is he causing trouble now?'

My father looked uncomfortable. 'Do not speak like that of the Emperor.'

I was impatient. 'We've made a lot of enemies,' I told him. 'However, we have initiated a revolution here. The shiner alone would have done it. Or the helicopter. Look at the effect that had on Roma II.'

'Hardly the best example, son.'

'No, but I would say that the effect has been as beneficial here as it was malign there. Everyone can deliver their messages and co-ordinate the arrival of goods more efficiently using the shiner. The Emperor was wise to ensure that the courier companies were the first to invest in the new technologies They could have been driven out of business, instead they reap huge rewards.'

My father shook his head. 'That is not how it is seen in Rome. Many people increase their wealth, yes, but *relatively* we are many times richer than we were only a few years ago. Our success is regarded with suspicion.'

'We caught another spy last week,' I told him. The spy had not sought protection by informing on his master, so we didn't know who had sent him. Still, that meant we could take our time to discover the truth.

'We must proceed slowly,' my father warned.

'The Emperor is plotting something.'

My father wasn't happy. 'I told you not to speak of the Emperor that way.'

'Sir, I have met a lot of Roman Emperors, now. And I can tell you from personal experience what I could already have told you from reading history books. Emperors are men, with men's jealousies and motivations. This Emperor is no different.'

He was angry with me, now. 'The Emperor is above politic.'

An extraordinarily old-fashioned and faintly ridiculous view, but one my father believed in more than he believed in the ancestor spirits. I was not going to change his mind, so I had to change my line of attack.

'That's as may be, but there are flawed men all around him. Men who seek favour and to enrich themselves, and feel that the way to do that is to undermine our family.'

I summoned a slave to bring in a statue of Minerva, sculpted by the Bernini of Roma LXIX.

'What is this?' my father asked.

'A gift for the Emperor.'

'It's disgusting.'

It most certainly wasn't. What it was, though, was erotic. That particular Rome has a ... keen interest in matters of coupling, and indeed tripling, quadrupling and all 'plings beyond. Every religion there, even those familiar to our world, emphasises the celebration of fertility. Not one of the sculptors, painters or tesselators has ever needed to learn how to depict clothing. This was an unpainted marble statuette around two feet high, a woman of extraordinary beauty, an owl resting innocently on her shoulder. This was the goddess of knowledge, and from her expression and posture there was no doubt this included carnal knowledge.

I had kept the statue of Venus by the same sculptor for myself. It reminded me a little of Angela, in her more unguarded moments.

'The Emperor will appreciate this,' I assured him. 'He'll place it in his private office.'

'I daresay,' my father conceded, 'as one would hardly put it on public display.'

'The owl conceals a microphone. We will be able to listen to the advice he receives in private.'

My father went as white as the statuette.

'The anisocyclorum can't be detected,' I assured him, 'and I was sure to use counterfeit components. If it is discovered, it will look like the work of one of the other families. Anyone but us.'

My father was staring at the statue. Finally, he agreed to give the gift. At first, it was of little use, as - despite my father's guess - it was indeed placed on display in a reception room. But soon it was moved, and would prove most useful.

We were, as you can see, worried about security and about our position. We did nothing to reveal the existence of more bangles to anyone except our most trusted people. Thus, an exclusive band was created, ten men and women who possessed all the qualities needed. These were myself, then a group of nine people who took it in turns to travel to the other worlds. My brother; Quintus Saxus; Don Vulpisus of Roma II; Diana of Roma VI; Regina, the young woman we saved from the frozen Londinium of Roma CLII; Terrance Ollacondire of neighbouring Roma CLI, a veteran of the Brianist uprisings in Judea; Angela's father

Angus Inducula; Aeneicus, a remarkable clockwork man from Roma D; and Antonius, from Roma DII, from the caste of British priests skilled at learning languages known as protocol druids.

All of us were well-read, imaginative and skilled fighters. Those we brought in also had little connection to our world; Quintus Saxus had only an elderly mother. They operated away from our Earth, in conditions of such secrecy that less than a handful of people there knew of them.

What of the seventh and eighth bangle? One of these we stored in a tiny, deep vault at the family villa. If all six rings carried by agents of Rome were lost, there would still be a way to travel to the other Romes. The last bangle was sent, in conditions of total secrecy, to a research camp in the middle of America, and the greatest minds of all the Earths were fetched there to divine its secrets.

I was acutely aware now that there was another force *out there* that was hunting down the old man's brethren. That meant there were at least another two factions operating between worlds, and on a scale we could not comprehend. We could operate the bangles, but we had not the slightest ability to create them. We could not communicate between the Romes, except by using the bangles to travel there in person.

But now there were nine other people to share the burden of travelling between Romes, I could spend some time at home. I had seen little of my wife Angela in the last few years, although we had made the most of our rare times together: I had managed to father two boys and a daughter. I spent several blissful months with my wife now, watching my children grow, allowing my injuries to heal. This was a time for consolidation; I had travelled ever onwards, and been unable to take full stock of the Romes I had explored. Simply as an historian, I had much to consider. Traditionally, historians hadn't much bothered with hypothetical situations. They would often write on the potential consequences, with such statements as "had the battle of so-and-so gone the other way, then the result would have been what-have-you", but these were rhetorical flourishes, not serious studies. Now, history was as practical a discipline as engineering or warcraft. Learning from history was no longer an academic exercise.

By now, the first maps of the cosmos were being drawn up.

Cartography was complicated by the fact that the links between Romes were not always as we might expect. Roma III and VI linked up, for example, so it was possible to travel directly from Roma VI to Roma III (it baffled some people that you didn't head threewards to get there, but fourwards). But from Roma VIII, it was only possible to travel to Roma II and no other Rome.

Sailors can circumnavigate the world, and it was thought that perhaps the heavens were also a sphere; that if we travelled far enough, we would return to the point we departed from. We had no idea how many Romes we would have to pass through to get home. Some of us began to suspect that there wasn't an infinity of other Romes. The Romes we encountered often followed similar patterns, and some had followed a different path to converge at almost the same point in modern history. When Roma CI was discovered, we thought it was

Roma LVIII at first, until we discovered that Constantine there had worshipped Mithras, not Christ. Mithras favoured one Constantine in battle exactly as Christ did the other, and sixteen-hundred years later, both Emperors Flavius Venerarius served as absolute rulers of almost identical Empires with an official religion and a distinct lack of tolerance for other faiths. There were other Earths with even more trivial differences, although no two of these Earths were truly *identical*. And everywhere, the laws of nature applied. Only the *possible* variations of history happened. So it followed that there were a finite number of Romes. Finite, though, encompasses some very large numbers indeed, and there was no sign that this well of new Romes would run dry.

With five or six people exploring at once - I did not entirely stop travelling in this time - we quickly discovered over six-hundred worlds. We came no closer to understanding how all these Romes had come into being, or indeed exactly where they were. This was deeply frustrating; I often felt we were like mice let loose on the floor of a vast, beautiful villa, completely incapable of understanding where we were. We scampered over each tile in turn, carefully noting each one's colour, but remained ignorant of the picture stretching out beneath us.

Nihilominus, patterns started to emerge. Threewards of our Rome, around Roma DC, we discovered more and more Romes which were cul-de-sacs. That is, these were worlds that led to no new worlds in one "direction"; heading all the other ways, most Romes still had four links to other Romes. So we had, it seemed, found one edge of creation.

Our finest mathematicians and cartographers worked flat out to divine the structure of this new cosmos, and even looking at their simplified charts could make a man dizzy. Those of us that travelled into these unknown realms had to memorise a vast number of facts and figures. We recognised the dangers of getting lost, and so we established a system of signs. Everywhere we could, we set up an office in the Forum at Rome and in Londinium. These would have a small staff of slaves from the local world, and they would all think they operated a legitimate import and export business. In reality, much of their work simply involved passing messages and invoices between the two offices. Its true purpose was to hold maps and supplies for any of us who passed that way.

What we hadn't found was the world of the old man and his brothers, or the domain of the creature that had been hunting him. I was, I admit, dreading both of these encounters. My dreams were haunted with the image of the beast I had killed in the snows of Rome; all the more distressing to me, as it had no fixed image. If it were not for the scars on my shoulder, and the existence of the other rings, I would have liked to dismiss my slaying of the monster as a dream.

There was a more immediate threat at home.

The Emperor moved the statue of Minerva into his private office, and we started to learn what he told his confidantes. As I had suspected, we were a "problem" to the Emperor and his coterie. While the Emperor never said it himself, his allies were keen to curtail the power of our family. At the moment, this was through a simple matter of bogging us down with spurious lawsuits.

I met with my father again.

'How do we stop them?' he asked.

I had, of course, considered this very carefully. 'We remind the Emperor that he is better off with us than with others.'

Up until this moment, we had only used the bangles to explore and make contact with the other Romes. Now, we used them against our political opponents. Travelled to the adjacent Earths, selecting locations there that corresponded with the secret or most secured places owned by our rivals. From there, we returned to our Earth, bypassing all the walls and guards. We could move almost anywhere, perform impossible feats. The range and variation of our tactics were impressive. Senator Pampinus had been a particularly vocal advocate of curbing my family's new-found wealth. Many had been persuaded by his calls for a windfall tax against our good fortune. We discovered documents at his holiday villa that showed just how much he stood to gain by this… and just how much income his family estates had failed to declare over many decades. When these letters were circulated, the Imperial tax collectors moved in and seized his assets.

In such ways, all our enemies fell. They were caught in personal or financial infidelities. The satirists complain about the standards of those in "public life", but we all have a private side. It is a fact of life that we do wrong when none can see us. We all hold thoughts we dare not voice in public, but might entrust to a friend. We have all done something we shouldn't, however minor or ultimately harmless. It is a peculiar phenomenon, but those with the least to hide go to the greatest lengths to hide it. Take Canterius, a Christian with the ear of the Emperor, one of those who had spoken ill of us within earshot of our statue of Minerva. He had a beautiful young slave. His rooms happened to overlook hers and it was his habit to watch her dress every morning. This is not honourable, but ours is a world where many men happily bedded their slaves, female or male, willing or unwillingly, and few of them felt they were doing anything wrong. This unmarried man made no move to lay a hand on his woman, she was of age, she was unaware of his gaze. Who among us can say we haven't given furtive or lascivious glances at some point? However, when we left a note in his room one morning, telling him we knew what he did, hoping to scare him, he took his own life.

There were, of course, a few men who lived blameless lives. Or, at the least, ones who we could not catch in flagrante delicto. Paragons of virtue, so it seemed. Men who didn't swear or ogle or lie or cheat. Men who could account for every denari they'd ever spent. One of our enemies, Caudex, was a man of such character.

It was easy enough to slip into his room one night and slit his throat.

This move against our opponents took a week.

The Emperor suspected our involvement. He summoned my father, warned him, noted that only our enemies had died, reasoned that such a result could only be achieved by sorcery. There was a delicate balance, the Emperor said. That balance could be lost. Did my family really want the secret of its success to be made public knowledge?

The night before, my father and I had discussed this very question. Now, he gave the answer that we had carefully formulated:

'Do what you will, you remain the Emperor.'

We had calculated that the Emperor would stay silent. The elimination of our most vocal rivals demonstrated our power. He gained from our arrangement, and could only lose if someone found a way to curtail our activities. Not that we could see any way our explorations of other Romes would end, unless we willed it. Even then, though, we accepted that their were limits to our knowledge. There might well have been a way to disable the time bangles. For that matter, they might simply cease to function. We knew nothing of how they worked, and our best defence was that our enemies possessed even less knowledge.

The Emperor grew angry, though, and did not act as we had predicted a rational man would. Nevertheless, we had planned for every contingency. When the Emperor ordered the publication of a proclamation revealing the origin of Rome's new wealth and our family's part in it, it did nothing to damage our interests. In a ten minute shiner address that evening, the Emperor told the populous everything; the existence of magic rings, the other Romes, the new devices and learning found there. He ordered the publication of what maps he had, and the circulation of a digest of what we knew of the other Romes.

So, the secret was out. The Emperor had flung open Pandora's Box.

Had he hoped to destabilise my family? If so, it was in vain. We still had a monopoly on travel to the other Romes, the last week had just given us a new taste for the more direct forms of addressing our enemies.

What happened next was extraordinary, though.

Nothing happened.

Men went about their business. The Emperor was believed, but there was something so *immense* in what he had announced that people could not incorporate it into their everyday lives. They had their helicopters, shiners and new plays and medicines. It didn't matter where all this had come from. Most people, I think, knew how impotent they were to change things. If their lives had changed, it was only to their benefit. I had walked the streets of the other Romes, I had years to get used to the ideas, and yet there was still a part of my mind that failed to believe it. This was not the end of the matter, but if the Emperor hoped that the mob would be so shocked and enraged that my family would topple, he was sorely disappointed.

My family's business continued. Laws were passed that opened up the markets of the other Romes to rival firms. This had little practical effect. By now, we had been operating for five years, and had contacts from here to Roma DCXXI. We controlled access to the other Romes both by finding reasons to confine certain individuals to our own world, and by charging exorbitant fees to those we did allow to travel. A round of lawsuits followed, playing into our hands and further slowing down the efforts of our commercial rivals to catch us up. Years passed.

So, what of the other Romes? Around fifty were isolationists who wanted no trade with us. There were a dozen distinct reasons for this; at the one extreme, some worlds were extremely enlightened and wanted to remain intellectually pure, at the other there was rampant xenophobia or superstition. We chose not to trade with around a further hundred Romes. These were ruled by tyrants or sadists, their worlds ravaged by adherence to the dark arts. Or they were worlds like Regina's, depopulated by some natural disaster. Or they were simply so backwards as to not be worth bothering with.

This left us with a little short of five-hundred Romes. Each Emperor reached their own decision as to what their people would be told. The majority did not tell everyone about the other Romes, but limited the knowledge to a cabal. Others gradually released the information. A few made public announcements. On only a few of the other Romes did the news create great perturbation. Most Romans simply accepted the new order, and wondered how they might profit from it.

Trade continued. Now, the cosmic charts of the Known Worlds were on the walls of every schoolroom of Roma I, the names and main features of each other Rome were learned by rota. The people grew used to the new idea, just as they had become used to the existence of America and Oceania.

This familiarity, though, began to breed ... if not contempt, then some idle questions. A young child or a sceptic can ask awkward questions of a high priest. Why was it that a man who sacrifices to Neptune is exactly as likely to drown on a sea voyage as a man who ignores his religious obligations? Why does a farmer who spreads laetamen made of thrush droppings or digs in crop of lupine by the dark of the Moon see his crops flourish, whether he seeks a blessing from Ceres or not? These are good questions, and those and ones like it mean that the Global Pantheon has sometimes been likened to a Forum of Ideas. Rival religions jostle to explain how the world really works, and how their gods hold the answers.

Now, though, our people began to wonder about the implications of all these Romes. Remember that I was born into a world certain of Rome's destiny. Rome prevailed. But now we knew that slight variations in events would topple towers, or prevent them from ever being raised.

People began to ask one question. Oh yes, there were many ways of phrasing it, and many different motives for asking it, and many different answers reached. Quot capita, tot sententiae. But what they asked was whether our Rome had been particularly blessed. Was it perhaps that we had just been fortunate to be born on the world that we were born on? If all the things that could possibly happen happened, then logically, there would be an optimal version of Rome. We lived, so people began to say, on that "Terra Optimus" not because our rulers had been wise or favoured by the gods, but because there had to be a Terra Optimus somewhere. We had won a lottery, not earned our great fortune.

This was logic. Whether it was sophistry or the premise was false, it didn't matter. It was, as all things had been shown to be, possible. Some Gaulish philosophers tied themselves in knots with the implications; if all things were possible, then were all things true? That was a false premise, as not all things were possible. But we had lost our sense of superiority. Not all roads led to utopia. Our Rome was merely one of many.

There was also, as someone pointed out, the possibility of a still better Rome somewhere out there. This, we never found. But some began to question whether ours was really the best. Some of the other Romes had better sculptors, or more elaborate gardens, or more magnificent temples. Who was to say that Roma XXXI, where the Senate held a veto over every decision of their Emperor, wasn't a better way to govern? What about Roma DCII, where women could have up to three husbands? Or Roma XX, where no gods were worshipped? Or Roma XI, where the law prevented wealth from being inherited, all estates going to the Emperor? So many variations; elected Emperors, universal serfdom, compulsory vegetarianism. There were worlds where anyone not following a holy book would be executed. Many of the Romans were extremely happy with their lot. Who were we to say that ours was the perfect way of doing things?

There were riots in the streets of Roma I for the first time in over a century. Authority and the social order had been challenged.

I was away from Roma I at this time. My thoughts turned to what I called earlier "the edge of creation", the other Romes that didn't lead to any new other Romes.

I had never travelled to one of these. By now, there were thirteen of them known. Our best maps and charts showed them as a straight line, with nothing beyond. Elsewhere, the other Romes sprawled out in every direction. There was no limit to them, seemingly no pattern. Scholars clung to the belief that the other Romes were up there in the night's sky, but had completely failed to associate them with the known constellations. Here was the one place where there was order, however baffling that order was.

Being on Roma DCX felt no different any of the other Romes. I imagined I would have had the sense of standing on the defensive wall at the edge of one of the ancient frontiers, one foot in civilisation, one poised on the precipice. But no, this Rome went about its business, oblivious to its location in the ranks of the others. That is not to say that the history of this world wasn't an interesting one. The Emperor Nero had embraced Christianity, made it the state religion, and within a century all other faiths had gone, either suppressed, absorbed or simply withered away. Rather than settle the matter, though, this simply ushered in almost two millennia of schism. The Empire was split into West and East, one based in Rome, one in Constantinople. The two existed in a permanent state of war, with the two Pope-Emperors both organising crusade and counter-crusade against each other. The whole world was conquered and involved in this local dispute. The cynics were right: hand the world over to religious men concerned with peace and loving thy neighbour, and blood will flow.

This was one of the more martial of the other Romes. There had been two-thousand years of what they called "the arms race"; as one side developed a new weapon, the other was forced to develop a new defence. Continue this process for centuries and, even allowing for the depredations and losses of war, their military techniques and equipment had progressed far beyond most of the other Romes. There were weapons and tactics here undreamed of even by those in my Rome.

A fascinating world, then. Quintus Saxus had been the initial emissary from Roma I, and managed to establish diplomatic contact with both Pope-Emperors. Neither side was more attractive than the other, both had drifted from the ideals of Rome embodied in our own history. But the military learning of this other world was clearly of value. There was a valuable secondary market: many Christian individuals and institutions across the Known Worlds were wealthy, and there was a healthy inter-Roman market for Bibles. Followers of Christ, whichever Rome they are from, all seem fascinated by the slight variations in their faith from place to place.

Quintus Saxus and I sat in the company offices in this other Londinium, staring at navigational charts of the other Romes. No two resembled each other, save that they all showed nothing in one direction beyond this world.

'There must be something there,' I said. 'It is simply that we cannot reach it.'

Quintus Saxus was less certain. We still didn't understand how we travelled between Romes. We willed it, it happened. It was as natural as taking a step forward, or looking up or down. How does a man look upwards? He just does it. When we set out for a new other Rome, we don't have any supernatural sense that it is there, any more than we have a mystic ability to sense the sky above us. It is simply there.

'Perhaps the other Rome in that direction was completely destroyed,' he speculated.

'Like Regina's world?'

'You misunderstand. There, the cities were devastated, but the world survived. Perhaps beyond here nothing remains. The world has been consumed.'

I thought about this. 'Why only here? Why would there be a row of other Romes that ceased to be?' I hesitated. 'Unless they were consumed by the same thing.'

I thought of the shifting demon I had destroyed on Regina's frozen world. Imagined it swelling until it could swallow the whole Earth.

'It is possible,' Quintus Saxus said.

We would have no defence against such an attack, I thought. Less able to prepare or prevent a world being consumed than Caudex had been able to stop his throat being slit. Our only comfort would be that whatever was munching on these worlds had many more to reach before it reached Roma I.

There were, of course, new Romes being discovered almost every day that passed. I could have spent the rest of my life finding them, if only I had faced another direction. But I was fascinated by this gulf. There was something at work here, something important. Something *more*.

This Britannia was an island fortress, a stronghold of the Western Empire since the time of Artorius. Londinium was not the provincial capital, that was

Artorius' old fort to the west. Londinium was a vast diplomatic and religious centre, crennelated temples surrounded by thick walls. Perhaps drawn down there by the lighthouse, I found myself walking to the docks, part naval yard, part commercial centre. My mind was still consumed with the mysterious gap on the maps of the heavens.

I confess I got lost among the endless rows of amphorae and boxes. Many of the vast ships were of the same design. Many of the men and women I passed were in some form of uniform; naval, religious or military. It meant I could walk in circles, thinking I was going in a straight line. Or vice versa.

Eventually, I had to ask for directions. A middle-aged woman smiled at me, and directed me to the *tubulus*. This, I quickly discovered, was a system of underground roadways. They were straight and well-lit; ironically, this subterranean system was far better in those regards than anything on the surface. I learned later it had been built as a shelter from an Eastern attack a century before. The attack had never come, but the subterranean world had developed a life of its own. There were shops, businesses and even some dwellings down here.

The map for this system, which the locals (with a breezy disregard for proper Latin grammar) had coined the *tabulus-tubulus*, was fascinating. Instead of strict geography, it simply listed the places one could exit this subterranean world. It strung them out in lines. Each route was colour-coded, and there were some places where the routes intersected.

The map was appallingly designed. It gave the impression that the exits were evenly-spaced, when some were ten times further apart than others. It gave no sense of the geography of the surface, so it was possible to go down into the system, walk ten miles, return to the surface and discover that you were in sight of where you had entered. I realised now that all maps were just tabulations of routes, like this one, they weren't true records of geography.

I returned - after an unnecessarily lengthy walk - to the company offices. I stared up at the map of this world. The exact projection of the continents and oceans differed immensely from those of my own, with Rome at the centre of this map, which was circular. It was entirely accurate, though. I found myself staring at the Oceanic islands, ones pushed to the margins of this map, creating, so it seemed, a halo around the world.

Islands are not distributed evenly across the face of the Earth. Some are so close together you can swim from one to another. Those of the Contraterranean, the vast ocean to the west of America, have almost the whole sea to themselves.

The other worlds are as islands. I knew this with all my heart. So far, they had been close together, close enough to swim, but now I was faced with a gulf. Beyond this Divide lay more Romes. I simply needed the right route.

I closed my eyes and imagined the stars. Wait until darkness takes hold of the sky tonight, hold your arm up, see how many of those countless points of light you can obscure with one hand's span. What I had done so far was hop from one point of light to the next one. Of course it had been easy.

I knew little astronomy.

But I imagined all the Romes laid out like a road of stars, packed thick, ranked roughly within a confined band. Imagined that the Romes I had visited were all part of the Via Lactea.

Now I imagined a *second* Via Lactea. One equal in size, just as full of stars, running alongside it. Between the two roads, darkness.

The Divide.

Yet Darkness was nothing. Literally nothing. This would not be swimming a sea, this would be swimming *nothing*.

The ground underneath me shifted and shook. There was an unearthly howling.

I opened my eyes, and found myself in another office. It was dark. Small windows blocked with thick, black curtains. The air smelt wet and heavy. There was the smell of cabbage and litter, and things I didn't know, not from any of the Earths I had walked. The howling was all around, coming from at least three different points outside.

I pulled the curtain aside and, once I had blinked the sunlight from my eyes, I saw a city unfamiliar to me. The Thamesis wound the same path. Around it, though, a mish-mash of squat, dark buildings, smudges against a coat of grey fog.

The drone of aircraft filled the leaden air. I could not see them.

'Is there someone up there?' a voice shouted from the street. The language ... it wasn't Latin. I didn't recognise it, but the bangle allowed me to understand it.

I looked down to see a man in a uniform cut from a dark cloth and a simple white helmet with the letters MP painted on it. A man from the thousandth Legion? A man who's first name, like my own, was Marcus? Or something else entirely? I had no way of telling.

I threw open the window.

'Can't you hear the bloody siren?' he shouted up at me. 'If you're going to stay, that's your own business. But if I was you, I'd get out of that dressing gown and into to a shelter.'

'Siren?' I echoed, picturing the harpies of mythology. Was this the domain of the beast I had killed? It had talked of brothers; was this Londinium now under attack from its demonic sisters? Had Quintus Saxus been right, and this world was, even now, being consumed? Their screams filled the air.

'It's the invasion,' he told me. 'It's happened, they're here.'

This "MP" was terrified. He shot me a look that said he'd wasted more than enough time on me, then hurried away down the street. In the Rome I had just left, he would have been heading towards the closest entrance to the tubulus.

I instinctively tried to get back to Roma DCX, but there was nothing. The bangle was dead on my wrist.

I whirled around, feeling trapped, feeling claustrophobic. I searched the room for something that might help me. This was an office, but nothing like the warm, bright and inviting places that my family's company had set up. There were pieces of furniture that were cheap and badly-designed. The desk almost fell apart as I steadied myself against it. Printed matter here took the form of pamphlets and codices, and there was a set of dusty shelves packed unevenly with both.

Resting on top of this was a shiner, marked with strange symbols as well as familiar letters. I turned it on. A man's voice, brave and resolute as any Roman.

'We shall defend our island, whatever the cost may be. We shall fight on the beaches, we shall fight on the landing grounds, we shall fight in the fields and in the streets, we shall fight in the hills; we shall never surrender.'

Yet for all the pride, this was not a triumphal speech. Read it again, examine the words. See that, for all the noble sentiments, this was a man declaring a retreat. This was a man who knew the battle was lost.

Whoever this was, he was on the losing side.

PART TWO: BRENNT LONDON!

VI.

There was an obvious answer, albeit one that was entirely incorrect. My first supposition was that this Britannia had somehow managed to hold out against Roman might. It was more than an uprising or short-lived rebellion, as the architecture of this Londinium that I could see out of the window bore none of the marks of Rome. So it followed that the invaders here were actually delivering security and civilisation to this place.

My instincts, though, prevented me from running out to greet the liberators. Instead, now the black curtain was lifted, I had enough moonlight to search this office.

This was little better than a slum. The carpet was worn and malodorous. The bookshelf, desk and two chairs that made up the only furniture here seemed about to fall apart. Everything was covered in dust. I don't think the room had been used for some weeks. There was a picture on the wall. If I hadn't just been examining the cartographic quirks of Roma DCX, I wouldn't have recognised it for what it was: a map of the world. The projection was impractical and distorted, but it was easy enough to orientate myself. What confused me, though, was that each continent was broken into coloured fragments. I thought at first it was meant to be decorative, then realised that each province had its own section. The people of this world had circumnavigated the globe and discovered longitude. Beyond that, my untrained eye could pluck little of value from the map.

The desk contained a mysterious object, a resin box with a dial on it. The dial was marked with ten strange symbols. A piece could be lifted, and was connected to the main body with a coiled wire. There was a sound from one end, but a strange dead thing, like putting one's ear to a conch shell.

Next to it a large codex marked "London Telephone Directory". While the bangle allowed me to understand speech, I could make very little of the written language here. Bits of it were frustratingly close to Latin. I felt I could decipher it granted a little time. Those three words, if I had but known it then, served as judgement on this world. The first was clearly a diminutive form of Londinium, the middle was a compound Greek word, meaning - if my schooling hadn't entirely deserted me - "far sound", the last was pig-Latin. The language here was a mongrel, it was broken bits of other languages pressed together.

Something had gone very wrong here.

I reasoned that the resin box was the "far sound", and the name suggested it was some primitive form of shiner. I opened the Directory, and was confronted with a list of names in alphabetical order, each followed by a string of the strange symbols that appeared on the device. Instead of broadcasting, then, you could only speak to one person at a time, and you did so by turning the dial in the correct combination.

If I seem to have reached these conclusions without much mental effort, that is because I had by now visited many worlds, seen many different things and ways of behaving. I had become accustomed to quickly inferring how such exotic everyday items worked. I had seen devices like this on a couple of worlds.

Lest I forget, the howling had continued outside all of the few minutes I had been exploring the room. Some time before, I had realised it was merely a way these people raised the alarm, not the battle cry of a mythological creature. It was certainly a sound to set a man on edge, and loud enough to percolate through every room of this city.

Unable to leave this other Earth, I reverted to my military training. When caught behind enemy lines - that was the distinct sense I now had - one should keep moving, evade capture, try to assess the size of the opposing force. Above all, I had to survive. I would need equipment. Roman legionaries are notorious as "Marius' mules", men who spend their time lugging almost their own weight in kit around. On a routine march, a soldier - wearing full armour and helmet, don't forget - would carry two javelins, a sword, a dagger, a pick, a spade, spare clothing, a blanket, spikes, a tool kit, a dish and a pan and a little food.

What the civilian doesn't know is that in times of war or where there is danger of ambush, almost all of that is carried on carts. I was travelling light. I had my sword and a small tool kit. I was wearing a sensible, practical toga, but from the appearance and manner of the man with 'MP' on his helmet, I would hardly blend in. I wore a leather vest that acted to protect my chest, and that could usually be concealed under clothing. Inside my bag was a full suit of light-wearing armour, which was always useful to have around.

The people of this "London" had been directed into their shelters. This would mean that the streets would be emptied. I left the office, walked through three almost identical rooms before finding a staircase. I climbed down to ground level. The door had been locked, but it was easy enough to open it from the inside.

Once outside in the street, I turned to look back at the office building. It was a three-storey structure, made of brick. It was dirty, blackened by soot. It is not possible for any city to have clean air, and a haze hung over them, even on my world. You could smell the tenement pits of my Rome long before you could see them. But this was different, drenched in smoky fog. There was a quality to the air entirely new to me, a man who had breathed the atmospheres of several hundred worlds.

There were also explosions, distant things. I listened out, and heard the projectiles falling. They seemed to be coming from far above me, not from some catapult a few miles away. Now I was listening, I could hear the drone of engines thousands of paces above me.

Aerial bombardment. Such a thing was possible, but I had never before been caught in such an attack. I tried to come to a strategy, but the best I could do was rue not listening to the MP man who had ordered me to the shelters. Around me, in the distance, there was the unmistakable crump and whizz of ballistic launchers unleashing their payload. I couldn't see them, and judged them to be miles from me, perhaps on the higher ground to the north of Londinium. They were firing rounds into the air, presumably in futile effort to hit the air vehicles. I could not see how they hoped to aim their weapons in this fog and darkness. They were trusting in Fortuna to guide them. I have never found her the most reliable of the gods, and she is particularly unhelpful in military affairs.

The bombardment was focussed on another quarter of the city, but the sirens still sounded. I heard further alarms, and realised that vigilis would be patrolling the street, ready to douse the fire.

I hurried away, keeping to the shadows. This office building stood in a side street, but I soon brought myself to a main thoroughfare, with shops. Many were boarded up, and it was almost impossible for me to decipher the signs. What was certain was that none was marked "vestarius", and I couldn't see any with clothing or cloth displayed in the window. Until I addressed this, my manner of dress would mark me out as an alien.

About halfway down this street, I found an open door. This area had been evacuated in a hurry, and someone had been negligent. It looked like tenement buildings occupied the floors above the shops all along this road. I pushed myself inside. There was a small vestibulum, barely wide enough for me. The tiny window would have been inadequate at the height of summer, and had been incapacitated by a thick black curtain of the type I had seen in the office building. There was a small apartment wedged in at the back of the shop on the ground floor. The door to this had been locked, but it was easy to prise it open with my sword.

There were worse slums in my Rome, or so I had heard. This room had been kept clean, and there was something of the Spartan about its lack of furniture or decoration. There was a cracked mirror hanging over a tiled fireplace. There were a couple of ugly padded chairs, a wooden cupboard. The rugs were thick and relatively new, but there was nothing better to be said for them.

The story of this world would be a fascinating one, I had decided. It seemed so much less than all the ones I had visited. So dark and dank, literally benighted. Even Regina's frozen world had once had its Terrible Lizards and its arenas. This world had no grandeur. I thought of the word "London". So much less noble than "Londinium". Was it diminished, dilapidated? Or had its history never soared in the first place? This world was strangely like my own, but somehow it had failed. As I searched the flimsy cupboard for something of use, discovering only cups and plates, I found myself imagining a potter in his workshop. In skilled hands most would be of good quality, but accidents happen. Every pottery had a pit round the back where the broken shards of hopeless pots and bowls were hidden from view. Was that the secret of the Divide? Was I now amongst fragments of worlds that had somehow been discarded by whoever cast whole worlds? The bangle on my wrist remained resolutely inert and unhelpful, but if I understood the language here, then it was clearly not entirely dead.

The kitchen yielded little of use. I took some twine, but there was no food to speak of. I moved to the third and final room, where there was a small bed and a cupboard as tall as I was, full of its owner's clothing.

There were bracae for my legs and lower parts. There were undersubuculas and woollen over-subuculas. There was a sort of tunic to wear over them. All of these were murky colours, somewhere between blue and green. They seemed to be civilian clothes. They weren't of the poorest quality, and were suitable for an artisan of reasonable income and judgement.

I stripped and changed into these garments, putting my own into a canvas bag I found on top of the cupboard. The owner of this flat kept his clothes clean and neatly pressed, but was somewhat taller and narrower than me. He had small feet and so I put my own sandals back on. I then returned to the main room of the apartment to scrutinise myself in the mirror.

I looked uncomfortable. I wondered how the men of this world arranged their hair; such a thing seems trivial, but it is immediately obvious. Were I to get it wrong, it would be like carrying a placard declaring I was from elsewhere. The only man from this world I had seen had been the MP wearing his helmet. I quickly searched the flat for a codex or a magazine that might have a picture to guide me. There was only one to find, lodged under the mattress, but at first it appeared to be of little help. It contained black and white engravings - exquisitely detailed representations, it had to be said - of semi-naked women. Page after page showed light-haired, long-legged women playing on the sand or in the sea.

The women wore their hair long and generally straight, they wore cosmetics and the fewer clothes they wore, the more they contrived to cover themselves with an arm, a well-positioned leg or some convenient item. There was little that could be called erotic, and I wondered if the true appeal for the man who lived here was that the publication depicted a world that seemed so much more sunny and alive than the place he lived, even if everything but its cover was monochrome.

Towards the back there were small advertisements. Here, at last, were pictures of men. They wore their hair swept back and greased. This was easy enough to simulate with a quick visit to the kitchen cupboards and sink. I took the opportunity to drink some water, which surprised me by looking and tasting as clean as I could have hoped for. There was nothing here, though, that I could use to carry water.

I had outstayed my welcome, and hurried out. I lingered in the hallway, before deciding I didn't have anything like the kit I needed. Upstairs was clearly the home of an old couple. I found a small flask that contained some alcoholic drink I didn't recognise, which I poured down the sink and replaced with tap water. In the kitchen and all around the house were items that marked the occupants as Christians. There was a crucifix and some sort of lararium dedicated to the baby Jesus and his mother on the mantle. This gave me an idea. I searched the place and found a small Biblia printed up in the fractured language of this world. There was a personal dedication scratched in the front, one I would have found difficult to read even if I had the language. Conversely, more than I hoped for, three volumes further along the same shelf, I also found a slightly heavier Biblia in Latin. So, the mother tongue was spoken in at least some places here.

It would take some time, but I knew this would be an invaluable way of learning to read the language of this land.

There was a small pile of heavy coins on one shelf. I tipped them into a pouch sewn into my garments. In a drawer, I found a remarkable tool. At first I thought it was a folding knife, but I discovered it opened up with a number of other useful items such as a pick and a file. This world was a conundrum. Air vehicles, advanced printing and now this efficient piece of kit, but in a murky, war-torn version of history.

Once again I felt I had lingered too long. I hurried downstairs and into the night. The howling alarm had stopped. There was the beginning of dawn in the air, manifested by a slight fresh breeze and the merest hint of new light and warmth. I walked the streets, carefully noting the course of the streets. There were tall buildings and ones with spires that allowed me some sense of direction.

Ahead of me, with the rattling of a metal gate, a small crowd spilled out. The sign above them was marked Hobb's End. This was one of the shelters, then. There were perhaps three dozen people, mostly women, mostly very young or very old. There were no men of fighting age, except myself, of course. I tried mingling with the crowd. A few of them looked at me, but no-one said anything to my face or acted on any suspicions.

'We're right to stay,' an old man said. 'The others will be coming back, tail between their legs.'

'More room in the shelters for us,' a middle-aged woman behind him chipped in. A few managed a weary laugh at the remark.

'I could do with a drink,' someone else said.

Everyone wore dark clothing much of which had been patched or allowed to fray and fade. There was every mood imaginable in the crowd. Some were sullen and downbeat, some cheerful. One old couple joked about which buildings they'd hoped had been destroyed by "Jerry". I had many questions but, all too aware that a man who asks questions at time of war is likely to be a spy, I kept my mouth firmly shut.

The people were drifting back home, the crowd was thinning. I turned my thoughts to what I should do next. My immediate physical needs were catered for. I was neither thirsty nor hungry. It was a cold day, but I was well-dressed to face that.

The obvious thing to do was to find out more about where I was. Within ten minutes of wandering, I had found no obvious way of achieving this goal. This was a large city, comparable with many of the larger Londiniums that I had seen. The roads were paved with a hard black substance that made me think they were designed for heavy traffic. There was manufacturing industry here; the bricks and glass of the buildings testified to that.

It was early morning, but even so, I expected to see more people around. In my Rome, say - indeed, in most Romes - there would be legions of people around.

Tradesmen, deliverymen, slaves sweeping the streets. Since the shelter had emptied, I had seen no-one. I had assumed that the city was under siege, but beyond a few unmanned road blocks, there was little evidence of any urgency or military activity.

I stuck to what I understood, and walked along the embankment of the Thamesis. Every world is identical in all respects of geography and geology. Without men, each would be indistinguishable from the other. Whatever the nature of the people living there, whatever local names were given to the places, the Alpes mountains separated Italia from Gaul, the Fretum Gallicum separated Gaul from Brittania. The coastline of this Brittania would be the same, to the exact stone, as mine. Sol lucet omnibus. Many of the towns and cities were in the same place. Either they were truly ancient, dating back to the history common to my Rome and all the other Romes, or they were simply rational places to build, as they were close to rivers and at some strategically useful location.

I had lived and worked in Londinium for many years now, and the curves of this river were familiar to me. Not exactly identical; men had built channels, sluices, embankments and bridges that interfered with and obscured the true path of the river in both this world and mine.

This morning there was the additional problem of a thick fog that restricted my view to a few hundred paces. This was a forbidding place. There were small, dark boats bobbing on the river, some moored to dilapidated wooden piers, some anchored a little way out. The roadway itself was of good quality, though. The race living here was not without skill, although the hints of narrow, winding streets didn't speak well of their ability to plan, or the sophistication of their municipal government.

I had walked a thousand paces or so before I saw an extraordinary site, one that literally disorientated me: an Aegyptian obelisk, just standing on a plinth. Once again, all I could imagine was that this was some broken version of history. I am no expert on Aegyptian matters, and found myself wondering where the rightful home of this obelisk was. Did its counterpart still sit in the African sands of my own world?

I continued on my way, intrigued by a large building at the limits of my visibility. The city here had small parks, strips and triangles of grass and trees. It was green and leafy; as with the Londinium I had left behind, it was summer here, despite the fogs. Behind the trees, great slabs of buildings. Ahead of me, though, was a building that seemed to have grown rather than been designed. A long, flat building with spires and fortifications, including what I took to be a large clock The surface of this structure was broken up with statues, pillars, inscriptions and a mess of other detail. It was, I have to say, one of the most truly ugly buildings I have ever seen, but it was also one of the most fascinating. I stopped across the road to stare at it, to try to understand its nature, leaning against a plinth.

There was a banner flying over the building, I noticed. This was a strange thing; two red crosses on a blue background, slashes of white and red around it. Another sign that this was a land ruled by Christians, another sign that this place was fractured.

It was a full five minutes before I saw whose statue I was resting against. Boadicea. A tribal leader who had resisted the Romans and died. I had only heard of her because of my residence in Britannia and a keen interest in history. Here there was a vast metal statue of the woman, in a fanciful clothes and equipment. Here, had she repelled the Romans, condemned the Britons to millennia of tribalism, albeit with nice roads for their chariots?

That was the obvious conclusion, based on the evidence.

I looked up at the clock tower. Numerals ran around the face, XII at the top, VI at the bottom, and two hands. A vast piece of clockwork, I suspected. It wasn't a sundial, obviously, in this sunless country. Not a water clock, either. It was only my supposition that it was the time being displayed.

The bangle at my wrist was alive again.

I could scarcely believe it.

I took my chance, leaving this benighted world. I felt that sensation of swirling away, then found myself ...

...in exactly the same spot.

Except it wasn't. This was an other London, cast from the same deformed mould as the other. I tried to move again ...

...and yet another London. Was the fog here even more thick?

...and yet another. This time, though, the clock tower had been burned to the ground, and some time ago.

... and another London. This was much as the first few, and the clock tower was intact. It was noticeably more busy than any of the scenes I had so far been privy to.

Rather than travel any further, I attempted to take stock of my situation. This was the middle of a large city, and sooner or later if I continued to travel from other London to other London, someone would see me suddenly appear like a ghost. Just as the people of my world had seen the old man arrive in the Forum, and condemned him to twenty years in confinement.

There was a long queue of people crossing the bridge over the Thames. It was an orderly line, one being overseen by men in blue uniforms and strange conical helmets. There were people weighed down with bags and cases, people with handcarts, horse-drawn vehicles, and also horseless vehicles that were too noisy and smelly to be clockwork. In the background there was a pigeon.

The strange building with the clock tower was another focus of activity. Men who were undoubtedly soldiers by their bearing and uniform were piling up bags and setting up barricades. They were obstructing the way for the people trying to cross the bridge, and vice versa. It barely took moments to see that everyone here was tense, and tempers were frayed.

By now, it was light and the heavy fog was lifting.

I went up to one of the blue guards.

'Excuse me, sir, what is going on?'

He looked at me a little disbelievingly. 'Don't you read the papers?' he asked. I shook my head.

He pointed over the road to me. 'See the woman at the base of Big Ben, there? I'm sure she'll help out,' he told me.

A vendor was setting up across the way, in the shadow of the clock tower. An old woman. She wore the same colourless, worn garments that I had seen on other Londoners. She was selling copies of what was clearly a news sheet. Would I be able to understand it? With effort, and reference to the two Bibles, yes, I'm sure I could. I crossed the road and approached her.

'A copy of Thetimes,' I said, pronouncing it thet-a-mis, as such a Greek name seemed to demand.

'The Times,' she corrected me. I worried briefly that this was merely an almanac or even instructions for understanding the big clock. But I handed over one of my stolen coins and took the sheet away to examine it.

It was four sheets, on a thin paper that wasn't sure whether to soak up the ink or pass it on to my fingers. It had been printed in the Seric manner, using moveable type. It consisted of densely-packed rows and columns of words. I found a bench and tried to interpret it.

THE TIMES

That, at least, had been explained to me. In small type below that:

6 JUNE 1940.

Junius! The same summer month I had left behind. The symbols I did not understand, but they were the same I had seen on the strange farspeaker machine and its directory. These were numbers. It was the VIth of Junius, I knew that. So the "6" glyph should be the number VI. It was the year MMDCXCIII. So those four symbols together might stand for two thousand six hundred and ninety three. Why, though, would these people measure the year, as we do, from the foundation of Rome? In such a fractured place, I could not begin to guess what they commemorated instead.

It was a cool, crisp morning in June, and the clock struck ten.

I could make out one word in three or four printed here. It wasn't enough, and I had no sense of the meaning. I would need to find someone to talk to. I had the letter I always carried, marking me as an envoy of the Emperor of Rome I, but in this Londinium at least, it looked as if this would count for nothing. I could escape this world, slip to the next. But what would be the advantage when every world was the same?

I knew I would have to understand this place before moving on from it. There were mysteries to solve, and more people in this London than any of the others I had seen so far. These might furnish me with answers. There were also a few subtle differences between this and the first London I had seen. Here, more doorways and windows were barricaded or just boarded up. There was a small patrol of soldiers crossing the bridge to my left. Fortunately, they were heading away from me, but I had the growing sense that I would need to keep my head down to avoid suspicion.

I stepped forward to keep out of view of the patrol. I think I remember hearing the vehicle coming now, the screech as its driver tried to swerve to avoid me. It may be that I only remember it because I was told afterwards what had happened. Whatever the case, there was an impact, I was hurled over the front and roof of the vehicle. I remember a feeling of helplessness as I fell to the street below.

After that, I remember a woman's voice.

'He's awake.'

I was lying on a bed, surrounded by smells ranging from the utterly strange to the utterly familiar. I knew at once from some quality of the air that I was in a valetudinarium, surrounded by others who were injured. My senses felt numbed, as if I had been drugged. I was in light cotton garments. A military valetudinarium would usually be staffed by male slaves in my world, but there were establishments run by religious orders where women would tend to patients and invalids. I could expect some overturning of the natural order: this was a world where female barbarians were feted with statues, after all.

I opened my eyes, and found myself squinting in bright daylight.

'You were hit by a car,' the woman said. 'Unlucky of you. It was just about the only thing heading south of the river today. That was an hour or two back. Doctor says there's no serious damage.'

'Where am I?'

'This is the hospital,' she answered. 'On Horseferry Road, not far from where you were hit,' she added, when I looked confused.

'The bangle I wore?' I said. I could not feel it on my wrist. Already I knew it could not be far away; how else would I understand the language here? But if it was lost, so was I, so my concern was genuine.

'In your bedside table,' the woman told me, moving over to open it for me. I shifted my head slightly and saw the bangle and The Times resting on the canvas bag that had been stuffed in there. My leather vest and sandals were also there.

'A heavy bag,' she said. 'All your essentials in there?'

'No,' I said. Was she implying I was a vagabond?

'Sounds like pots and pans in there,' she said. She was referring to my armour, packed in the bag.

'A funny thing,' the woman told me, tapping the leather vest. 'Did you have it made? It probably saved your life. You made those shoes of yours, too? Funny-looking things, but hard-wearing, I bet. Make do and mend.'

'You've looked in the bag?' I asked. My dagger was in there, so was my toga and the letter from the Emperor.

'It's all right Mr. Baretti, no need for that. There was an envelope in your jacket with your name and address on it. I take it you were heading North?'

I didn't correct her, and was careful to mask my expression.

'My family will be missing me,' I said neutrally.

'We've got a 'phone, you can call them.'

By now my eyes had adjusted to the light, I looked at her face for the first time. That, I admit, caused any self-control I had to desert me. She was a young woman of twenty-two, small but with a good figure. She wore an austere grey smock and a headband that looked as if it were made from white card. But in a strange way, this only accentuated the familiar curve of her hips, only made her red hair more vivid.

'Angela?'

My wife seemed puzzled. 'Yes,' she replied, finally.

She must have come here, to my rescue. In which case, then, why the confusion? There was no-one within earshot.

'Do we know each other?' she asked, before suggesting perhaps I had been a patient here before. She apologised, saying she had worked here for three years, and had tended to hundreds of people. She seemed a little embarrassed at this.

'I'm sure I would have remembered you,' she added, blushing.

With a strange feeling in my heart, I realised that this was the first time Angela had laid eyes on me. She was a native of this world. What you must understand is that this wasn't a woman that looked like Angela, a *doppelganger*. It wasn't a resemblance, it wasn't as though I was gazing on Angela's twin. This was so much more than a person with merely the same face or with the same blood flowing through her - this was Angela herself, the same *soul*, the same *individual*.

I had already known, intellectually, that this was possible. Every Earth we had found had its Augustus. Almost all had a Jesus, the founder of the Christian faith. Every Britannia had its Artorius and Concuthasta, every Arabia its Muhammed. There were dozens of examples, hundreds, of great men and women of history. The destinies of these people were rarely the same from Earth to Earth. Many Augusti, for example, never married Livia, or were Republicans, or didn't live as long or achieve so much. The Romes that they built were often recognisable, but markedly different from the history I had grown up with. Many of the greatest men of one history were obscure in another. And so it was that some few great men living had counterparts in other worlds. Usually these were men of learning or artists, generals and even the occasional politician. My Rome and many of the other Romes had, to pick examples, a scientist named Albertus Unuslapis, a writer named Bellator Agricola Putei and an artist called Picasso, although their genius found expressions in different ways, those best suited to their circumstances.

But this was not an historical or public figure, this was my wife. In none of the other Romes had there been another me. I had not dined with an *other* Quintus Saxus. As far as I had been able to determine, neither I nor any member of my family had an equivalent in any of the other Romes.

Fortuna, the goddess I had poured scorn upon only a short while ago, had delivered me to my wife. A woman I knew would help me to make sense of the world I had found myself in.

VII.

I was feeling a little sore, but had nothing a Roman soldier would call an injury. The physicians ran simple tests on me. Luckily, I had thought to check the envelope for "my" name and address, B. Baretti, from Dartmouth Park Hill, Highgate, and so they declared that I hadn't lost my memory. My first initial was a "B". I picked Ben, after the clock. Ben Baretti. A strange name to my ears, but the doctors seemed happy enough with it. If I lingered here, though, I would be caught out. I knew almost nothing of the detail of this land. My age and physical condition, I learned, meant that I would have been conscripted into the armed services. As with the other London that had been subjected to aerial bombardment, this Britannia ... this "United Kingdom" was at war. The enemy were approaching, and the city had been, at least in part, evacuated. Angela already assumed that as I was still in London, and I had been found by the Houses of Parliament, that I must be part of the defensive effort. I gave vague but ominous hints that I worked in military intelligence, and they left well alone.

That morning, feigning weakness, I had Angela read the news sheet, the "paper", to me. She was happy to do so, and I loved to hear her voice again. The Britons and the Gauls were fighting the Germans. In the last week, German forces had wiped out a vast British expeditionary force at a place called Dunkirk. That was on the northern coast of Gaul, perhaps their equivalent of Gesoriacum. The Germans had pressed their attack, and launched an aerial and naval assault on the south coast of Britain. Angela told me that there were rumours German forces had landed in Cantiaci (Kent, in their broken language) and a full scale invasion was underway. They'd heard a lot of "planes" and "cannon" the night before, and most thought that the German "tanks" would soon be rolling down the streets. I had no idea what any of this meant, and found it difficult to picture.

The first of these mysteries was solved quickly. Aircraft could be heard overhead at irregular intervals, flying in both directions. Each time they went past, all eyes in the ward were raised to the ceiling and there was some debate which side the planes belonged to. The man in the bed next to me had been a member of the Royal Air Force, he told me, until a recent eye injury. He talked me through the differences between the "fighters" and the larger (and louder) "bombers", then between the British and German engines. There was a daunting number of types of plane: the Wellington, the Whitley, the Hampden, the Blenheim, the Spitfire and the Hurricane on the British side, the Heinkel, Dornier, Junkers, Messerschmitt, Storch on the other. My guide wasn't always sure which was passing overhead, but was able to give me a good spectator's guide to aerial combat in this theatre of war. I knew better than to ask all the questions I had, lest I appeared to be a German spy.

It was clear that I should not linger in this place for long, and I discharged myself that evening.

* * *

I discovered what time Angela's shift ended, and timed my own departure so that I could be downstairs waiting for her. I had wondered whether to make it seem a coincidence, but gave her more credit. Instead I asked her directly whether she would go for a drink with me. She agreed, smiling, and I left the choice of venue to her. She lived close by, she said, and selected a "pub" called the Blue Post.

The streets had cleared from that morning, but the sense of tension was still in the air. It was early evening, and in the British summer that meant many more hours of daylight.

The Blue Post was another dark, damp place, but a friendly one. The carpet smelled as if it were soaked in beer, and the air was thick with smoke. It was busy, many workers stopping off here on the way home from work. I ordered beer, and - rather to my surprise - Angela did the same. I was distracted by Angela. She was so beautiful, and she was scared of an imminent German attack. I tried to reassure her. Capturing a city was a major undertaking for an invasion force. They would want to establish a bridgehead. They would secure their supply lines and cut off their enemy's before engaging in street-to-street fighting. They would almost certainly want to lay siege rather than launch a swift attack.

'Rationing is bad enough as it is,' she said.

She told me that the aerial attack on London had begun a few nights before, and come as a complete shock. The Britons had been at war with Germany for months, but it had meant little up until that point. They had feared bombardment at first, many had evacuated the city and gone to the country. But nothing had come, and gradually the displaced population had started to drift back. Now, though, the war was real.

'People seem tense,' I told her.

'No-one has slept for the last couple of nights,' she told me.

'You don't seem too afraid.'

Angela blushed. 'It sounds foolish, but ... I feel a little giddy.'

'Euphoria,' I told her. 'You won't be the only one feeling like that. Not everyone despairs or panics at times of war.'

She nodded, but I don't think she understood. To a Roman, one raised in a world safe from the threat of invasion, the prospect of war led to a rushing sensation. I relished the fight to come.

'You don't want to evacuate?' I asked. 'Don't you have family in the North?'

'The accent,' she said. Her voice, like my Angela's, had the distinctive tones of the Scotic people. I had simply guessed that her family came from the same region in both worlds. 'My family are here in London. My father works for the government.'

'And you have chosen to stay behind to tend to the injured?'

'Yes.'

'You're a good person.'

She shrugged. 'With all these people leaving, London's going to be so quiet.'

'There are still plenty of people here,' I said.

'A lot didn't want to leave, especially the old ones. Most think the city will be better protected than the country. Some people just don't believe it, or want to defend their homes.'

'Brave,' I said.

'There has to be order,' she said. 'We have to stand firm.'

She looked at me, and reached out her hand. I took it in mine. It was cold, and I rubbed a little warmth into it.

'I don't really believe it myself,' she said. 'Mr. Churchill seemed sure of things the other night on the wireless. But I bet he isn't in London any more. The King's stayed, that's what they're saying. Refuses to go.'

'You have your own wireless?' I asked. The shiner was still beyond the reach of most families in my Rome.

'Oh yes. A present from my parents.' She hesitated. 'Do you have one?'

I shook my head.

'You could come back to my flat if you wanted to listen to it. I could cook you something.'

I hesitated for a moment. She was watching me carefully.

'I would like that,' I said, thinking I understood the true nature of the offer, but not wishing to make presumptions about the customs of her race.

She lived three streets away. We walked side by side. She was careful not to make eye contact with me. She commented that it was a cold evening, for summer.

Her "flat" was her dwelling, a place much like that of Mr. Baretti, if a little more upmarket. She unlocked the heavy front door and we went up three flights of stairs to a room that, by my standards, was small and damp. She had brightened the place with colourful prints, pressed flowers and other decorations. The room had what Angela called the "blackout", the same heavy curtains over the windows. Before putting on the electric lamp, she checked that there was not so much as a chink of light escaping out into the street.

Alone now, for the first time. Angela made a token effort to show me the wireless, a heavy wooden box. I made a show of admiring it. Neither of us made any move to switch it on.

'My landlady doesn't allow guests to stay the night,' she told me, head flat against my chest, her words humming there. 'But she turns a blind eye.'

I was not the first man she had taken to her bed, then. That had been my suspicion for some time. Who were these men? Who was the first? How many had there been? The thought of being a cuckold should have repulsed me, but I admit the thought of her lovers intrigued me and even excited me.

That first time, a moment's verecund hesitation.
Then we found ourselves kissing, not simply wanting.
Your gentle hand on the nape of my neck.
A friendly embrace eliding to more.

We pressed together, my hand brushing your face.
Your hands around my waist. Kissing.
Our lips barely parted. My palms flat, tracing,
Not touching, the swell of your chest.

Your hands rose to mine. We clasped fingers,
Pulled ourselves close and I felt your heart.
We circle around, like the start of a dance.
I hold my arms out, waiting for you.

Your fingers at your sides, point to the floor.
Now they twitch up, unsure where to touch me.
Or how. You straighten a loose strand of hair.
Clutching your hand there and reining it in.

You took a step back, fingers touching your
Mouth. Dark and intent eyes fixed upon mine.
Your Rubicon crossed, you lead me to bed.
Lay there. I knelt over, naked as you now.

A handful of endless seconds pass as I gaze at my prize.
Flat on your back, feet pointed towards me.
The length of your leg, the bend of your knee, the curve of your hip,
The flat of your belly, round of your breasts.

Flushed skin sharp relief against white sheets.
Limbs languid and yet poised to bear my weight.
Desire in your eyes, pupils
Dilated. Mouth eager, breath loaded.

Ready, you stared at me, but not at my face.
Without a decision, your leg moved aside,
Revealing and offering your most sacred place.
After due ceremony, I came inside.

It is rarely as simple as the poets would have us believe, and there is always something lost in translation.

I struggled to work the various fastenings of Angela's clothing. Each item seemed to have at least one puzzle for me to solve. Her skirt had both a buckled belt and a baffling toothed strip. Her blouse had a whole column of small discs slipped through tiny holes. Her shoes were tied with laces, she wore silk leggings, kept up with clasps tied to the same contracting material. She wore a garment that cupped her breasts, one which was hooked together, for the moment.

Angela put my hesitations and clumsiness down to nervousness, and I was happy to play along with this notion as it put her at ease. I was quietly confident.

Not that I flatter myself that I have any great knowledge of or aptitude in the amatory arts. But - unknown to the woman herself! - I did have knowledge of Angela's curves and secrets. As she lay before me now, divested of all her strange apparel, it was confirmed to me that this was the same body. She hadn't been plucked and pampered in the Roman manner. She was perhaps a few librae lighter thanks to food rationing and a less sedentary routine than the Angela to whom I was married. This Angela, as far as I could tell, had borne no children. Yet, this *was* Angela, it had been far too long since I had feasted on this woman and I fell hungrily onto her. My ardour fed hers.

She wore few cosmetics, and her scents were just as I remembered. But as we lay together, whispering endearments, for the first time, my passions were cooled. Her murmured encouragements would not really be the Latin epigrams I was hearing, I realised, but would be in the fractured language of these Britons. I was a little disconcerted. It struck me that every part of her life history must be different to the Angela I knew. Yet, as I discovered the touch and the taste of her body anew, it transpired I knew it better than she did herself. In time, she progressed to making sounds more universal in their nature, and utterly familiar. Her little cries and yelps enflamed me, prompted me to make further sorties. From the look in her eyes, what inevitably happened as the urgency of the situation overtook us both had never happened to Angela before in this life.

Afterwards, she smoked, the smell of pyrimidine reminding me of America. Both of us were breathless and exuberant, eager to talk, but with little to say to each other. It was impossible to tell whether it was still light outside. I realised there hadn't been a plane overhead since we'd been in the Blue Post, and that I hadn't eaten since breakfast, although I wasn't hungry.

Angela had just taken a red leather book from a drawer. It was full of addresses and now she added my own to it. She was surprised I didn't have a telephone number.

'I feel like I've known you so long,' she said as we laid together.

I smiled, and agreed our meeting was meant to be. I was unsure what else to say to her. I could not speak to her with a husband's intimacy. I had no wish to lie to her, so I would not invent details of my imagined life as Mr. Baretti. I could not, of course, tell her the truth. In the end, I sang the praises of her beautiful body, a topic that required no deception. She, in turn, fussed at my bruises and the acid scars on my shoulder, admired my muscles. I hadn't been shy, she told me, but that hadn't surprised her as she had been told that Italians were good lovers. It was the first time I had ever been called an Italian, but in the terms of this Earth, it was an accurate label. I was careful to stress that I had been born in America, and she blushed and apologised.

'I didn't mean to imply anything,' she said. 'I know you're on our side.'

So, the "Italians" were in league with the German people? This truly was an upside-down version of history. It was cold in the room, but we had thrown the sheets back. As I lay there, stroking Angela's hair and side, letting her kiss my face and chest, I tried to imagine how such a world had come about. There had been a Boadicea, there were Bibles in Latin and numbers as well as necromantic symbols. There had once been a Roman Empire here. Now, though, there were only vestiges. Hints in the architecture and the language.

In every other world, history had taken a different course, but one that could have happened to my own Rome. Assuming that to be the case here, what was the crucial difference that had defaced this world's story?

This world has fallen to the barbarians.

I realised this with such a start that Angela asked what was wrong. That had been Rome's ancient struggle. We had triumphed against the tribalism, intolerance and illiteracy of those around us. Provinces like Britannia had been given cities, roads and a written language. We had lifted them from savagery. What would have been left behind if Rome had ... gone away? Ruins. These Britons had tried to comprehend the grandeur that was Rome, they had done their best. They had innovated in places, but this had led to the creation of dangerous vehicles and ugly buildings. They had embraced the Christian religion which teaches that this world is a broken, sinful place but the next life will be better. They lived through wars and invasion in their dark, damp little dwellings. The men waged total war, leaving the womenfolk to a life of work and promiscuity.

Despite that, Angela was beautiful here. There were the seeds of hope.

I dreamt that night of warm and airy rooms and Angela.

I was relaxed for the first time in a long time. There was something else there, a homesickness. Angela was the only thing here that had anything but an abstract connection to my own world. She had given me a reason to stay on this Earth. She demonstrated that whatever I might have thought, this could have been a worse place.

I left with Angela early the next morning.

She was heading to work, smiling and yawning. There had not been an air raid the previous night; as we'd drifted to sleep, she had worried that we'd be woken by the sirens, and her landlady would find us together. She hoped the lack of activity meant the German invasion had been repelled. I didn't share my suspicion that it meant just the opposite.

I was returning, so I told her, to work. I had let her fill in the details, a matter of picking up on what she said and prompting her. I was an American journalist, it transpired, one trying to provoke my people into joining the war on the side of the British. It was her suggestion that we met back at her flat at lunchtime, which she defined as about a quarter past midday. This gave me the morning to investigate this world further. The fog had lifted, and the landscape of the strange patchwork city that served as the capital of the Britons was revealed to me for the first time.

I was in good spirits.

I found a library, and this was opening up. This did not seem like a city preparing for invasion. I had passed a boarded up "school" (which looked a little like a schola) and realised I hadn't seen any children here. There were few men below fifty who weren't in uniform. There were defences at the Houses of Parliament, as I walked past it. This city was a large area to defend. If I'd been the commander of the garrison, I would have had most of my men on the walls, the rest as a mobile force able to reinforce wherever the enemy attacked. I would also hope that the generals had posted a couple of legions in defensive positions between here and the enemy.

I climbed the steps to the library, which was being run by a pair of stern old men. I found the section containing the histories. Written matter here was bound in codices, with the titles printed on the spines, often in gold lettering. Most of these titles were, to me, strings of meaningless letters. I found a large Latin / English dictionary in another part of the library, but to trudge through the history books would have been slow work even if they had already been translated for me. Instead, I gained an impression of what had happened from the titles, running along the history shelves in chronological order: *Greatness and Decline of Rome; The Monuments of Ancient Rome; The Pagan Background of Early Christianity; Gothic Art; The Dark Ages; The Black Death and the Peasant's Revolt; Heresies of the Later Middle Ages; Religious Poverty and the Profit Economy*. I found an encyclopaedia and picked my way through its short entries, starting with "Roma", finding an entry on the Roman Empire. Rome had fallen nearly fifteen-hundred years before, as far as I could tell. And in its place? I read of Vikings, Christian tyrants waging war on one another and the unbelievers, bubonic plague and warring empires. The extermination of the American people was glorified here, seen somehow as emblematic of freedom. The American continent was a place of Depression, where rich men threw themselves from the tall buildings of New York. The world had been subjected to famine and plague, piracy and democracy, revolution and slave uprisings, civil war and religious persecution, genocidal conflict and great fires, racial segregation and the burning of witches, gas warfare and class struggle.

And what did the great British historian Edward Gibbon, 1737-1794 AD, have to say about the human record so far? He said, "history is indeed little more than the register of the crimes, follies and misfortunes of mankind". The only surprise was that the human race here hadn't wiped itself out long ago. I'm sure these books contained every secret of the fall of Rome. Epic battles and treachery, tyrant Emperors and malevolent barbarians. The particulars seemed unimportant, now. I found myself almost crying to imagine my beloved Angela adrift in such a world.

An old man was sitting at the table across from me, reading today's *The Times*. He told me:

'The world's gone to hell. The War to End Wars, that's what I fought. Here we are again. I blame the whole bloody lot of them. You think this newspaper is the truth? They're coming, you know. I was on Wimbledon Common last night. Heard the artillery. They got through our lines, or they weren't in the right place.'

I asked him what he thought the Germans would do next, trying to get the measure of the man. He looked at me suspiciously, wise enough to keep his mouth shut when he had to.

So, the German army was on British soil, and making its advance.

I left the library, heading back to Angela's street. As far as I could judge it, I had a little time before noon, but I didn't want to risk missing her. The city streets were quieter than the day before. There weren't any planes. This unnerved me. If the Germans were establishing themselves on British soil, then every Royal Air Force plane would be vital. The German invasion force would need to disembark, and they would be vulnerable as they did so; it was ever the same in warfare. If the British weren't defending themselves, then it could only be because they had nothing to defend themselves with.

Angela joined me after about ten minutes and we sneaked into her flat. With the walk to work and back, with only a half hour break, and with the constant threat of her landlady interrupting, there was a sense of urgency to our lovemaking. We were already longing for each other, though, the four hours since we parted had been too many. Had we all day, we could not have contained ourselves longer than we did, or reached a more satisfactory conclusion.

'I'd stay, but we're busy.' Angela told me as she shrugged herself back into her uniform. 'They've told us to clear patients out.'

Her skin was flushed, her red hair still wild.

'They think the invasion is coming?'

'You don't know? The Germans have a beachhead from Hythe to Dover. A dozen miles long, and they're establishing themselves up to a mile inland.'

I cursed myself.

'I'm not naive, you know,' she told me. 'When the Nazis arrive, I know what they'll do to the women.'

I wish I could tell you that the soldiers of my world would have behaved with more honour. All I can do is tell you that I found such practices disgusting. What I said to Angela was that the city was not in immediate danger. This, I felt, must be the case, or there would be more evidence of urgent preparations.

On the way out, while Angela wasn't looking, I pocketed a small folding map of London I'd seen on her bookshelf that morning.

As we got outside, she lit a cigarette. 'I'm scared, okay? I admit it. Tonight, can we stay at your place? It's further north. I don't feel safe so close to Whitehall. It's the first place the Germans will head.'

I said nothing.

'My place is so miserable,' she said. 'My landlady isn't a nice person. She's probably heard us, you know.'

I insisted we meet here, at her house.

She lent in, meekly. 'I didn't mean to upset you. I ... okay. Be here at five-thirty. But I can't stay at my place tonight.'

Angela kissed me on the cheek and hurried away.

I couldn't yet read the language of the Britons, but I could memorise the names on the map of London.

The map was beautifully detailed, an example to the cartographers of any world. If Angela could buy this, then I was sure the German army had a copy. Little wonder if they had made the progress the old man thought they had, with such clear routes laid out for them.

Angela had been gone for only a few minutes when I heard the first planes. It was a drone, coming from all around. A harsh, heavy sound. Those weren't the swift, small fighters I'd heard before, those were bombers. The air raid sirens started up, all but drowning out the din in the sky. Around me, people picked up their pace, and the city grew even more tense.

I could hear artillery on the ground firing.

'Stand firm,' an old man shouted at me, running past.

The ground had started to shake. I could hear dull thuds and panes of glass breaking.

Angela's front door opened.

A stout middle-aged lady stepped out.

'Here!' she shouted. I thought she was offering me shelter, but as I stepped towards her, she looked horrified.

'I only wanted to tell you that you're not welcome here. I'll be having words with young Miss - '

I was vaguely aware of the black blob falling behind the building, and I was vaguely aware what it meant. If you looked out of Angela's window - you'd have to dislodge the blackout a little - there was a patch of grass, a rather derelict looking "back yard", as she called it. The bomb had missed all the buildings, but landed neatly in the yard.

The building was obliterated, nevertheless. It burst open, full of light, then the roof avalanched down, completely consuming the poor woman on her doorstep. Only as I was thrown from my feet did I hear the projectile in the air above the building.

Like all soldiers who narrowly escape death, I wondered if I were being deliberately targeted. Then a building a hundred paces further down the street exploded. Angela's tenement building, all three storeys of it, was rubble, now, with patches of fire. Windows all down the street had either cracked or entirely shattered.

Blood roaring in my ears and eyes, I got back to my feet and tried to locate the landlady in the pile of bricks and roof slates, but it became immediately obvious this was a fool's errand, and the woman could not have survived. I offered a quick prayer, to a god no-one in this country had worshipped for fifteen-hundred years. This wasn't to intercede on behalf of the dead woman's spirit so much as to give thanks for sparing me from her fate.

VIII.

The air raid continued, and I was helpless.

I had my sword and my armour in my bag, but what use were they against an aerial bombardment? I hurried to the nearest Underground station, where I was ushered in by a couple of men in the MP hats I had seen on my arrival in the first other London.

This Underground was an subterranean trackway network, tunnelled deep under the whole city. It made for an impressive shelter. There was light and heat and ventilation. There were several hundred people here. The siren had only sounded a few minutes before, but already this place reeked of bad breath and urine.

'You've got a cut on your head,' one of the Military Policemen pointed out. I dabbed at my temple. A chip of flying glass or brick must have done it. The MP had no intention of helping, he'd done his bit by telling me. It was a small cut, but I had to keep my hand to it for a little while to prevent any blood from getting in my eyes.

There was little else to do down here. Everyone else was clearly a veteran of this type of conflict, as they had brought a book or a newspaper, or a pillow so they could catch up with lost sleep. The children occupied themselves by drawing pictures, or chasing each other around. I had imagined that it would be possible to feel the ground shake and to hear muffled sounds, but there was nothing. It was as though I had slipped into another world.

The temptation, of course, was to do just that: to gather up Angela, use the bangle and take us to an other Earth. There were two important reasons that I would not do this. Whatever else it was, this was Angela's home. I could not ask her to abandon it any more than I would have abandoned my Rome. I shared her instincts to stay, to fight and to die. Dulce et decorum est pro patria mori. I wanted to man the barricades. When all else fails, a man can do nothing better than to kill his enemy. As my tutor said, they can only take one of your lives, you can take many of theirs.

More preferable still, though, was the possibility that I would discover a way to help Angela and her people win the fight to restore their homes and whatever liberties they enjoyed. With my guidance, I believed, a new and better society could be forged here. There is no better crucible for social change and improvement than a time of war.

All that said, if I could have taken Angela to my Rome, I would have done so quick as boiled asparagus. My home was a place that was brighter, richer and somehow more real than this *Vandalised* history that she had been forced to endure. Perhaps it was at this moment that I first imagined the forces of Rome arriving on this Earth, led by my brother Titus Americanius, legions in glinting armour, swinging their swords and sweeping aside the barbarians and ending the dark age that had engulfed the world for fifteen centuries. A seductive image.

The second reason for not taking her was that, from what I had seen of the adjacent Earths, they offered little in the way of respite. No two of the other Romes were as interchangeable as the cities I had seen flitting from other London to other London. The air raid sirens had sounded in one, I'd seen the clock tower of the Houses of Parliament toppled in another. It was not a case of out of the boiling pot and into the fire, more a case of jumping straight into another boiling pot.

I had a greater duty. I had discovered a whole new cluster of other Earths, and I had to report this to Rome. For the moment, I didn't feel I knew enough. The reports I had were hearsay, not solid fact. Rumours fly around a battlefield, as man is separated from man. Then, I had only a tenuous grasp of the history and geography of this other Earth. I could not draw up a full report for my Emperor without far more information. So, that was my plan: reconnaissance of this world, and the German invasion of Britannia in particular; return to my Rome with news of this group of other worlds, with a suggestion that Rome intervene to restore their true history. Finally, the removal of Angela from this world to the safety and wonder of my own Earth, once her own was set on a fair course..

There was no keeping track of time down in the shelter.

Eventually, the all-clear was sounded. As we shuffled out, blinking, into the daylight, I asked if anyone knew the time. One woman checked a device at her wrist, and told me it was nearly six. I hurried back to Angela's house, or rather the crater where it had stood.

Angela wasn't there.

I felt, as all lovers feel, that she couldn't be dead, because I would know. We shared a bond, one that had brought us together though we had started from points a hundred worlds apart. If a bomb had fallen on her hospital, I would have seen her die in my mind.

This, of course, is not the case. Now I had the urge to find her again, to claw through the rubble, if I had to. I had concluded that it had been her fate to die today, whether she stayed in bed or went to work, by the time Angela turned the corner. She naturally expected to find her home where she had left it, and spent a whole minute looking around, as though she had misplaced it.

I put my hand on her shoulder. 'I saw it happen,' I said.

'If we'd taken a few minutes longer this afternoon...' Her voice was dulled.

'Your landlady is dead,' I told her.

Angela nodded.

'Well, that settles it,' she said coldly. 'Your place tonight.'

I had spent over five hours in the shelter with nothing to do but think, and this complication had not occurred to me. It took a moment's hesitation on my part for Angela to see that something was wrong, and to jump to a conclusion.

I tried to hide any reaction.

'You're married, aren't you?' she said quietly.

I was, of course, married.

'No,' I said.

She believed me, and now couldn't understand my reluctance. 'So what's your story?'

I had stolen the identity (and clothes) of a man from an other London, not Angela's own. I should have seen that discovery of the charade was inevitable. My deception was so basic that it couldn't withstand a wisp of an examination.

If anyone else on all the Earths had found me out, I would have reached my hand over to my wrist, slipped away to an other London. Yet I had wanted to find out all I could of Angela. She would have wanted the same.

Angela asked me whether I was a deserter, and got her answer from the expression of anger on my face.

'Like I said. I'm an American. I'm from New York.' The truth, or the nearest I could get to it without summoning an infinity of Romes.

'You don't have the accent,' she told me. 'I didn't mention that before, but - '

'America is a big place. We don't all sound the same.'

She was watching me. She wanted to believe me. I, for my part, did not wish to lie to her. Eventually, she simply told me she would spend the night with her parents. I had warm memories of Angus Inducula and his wife.

'That seems appropriate,' I replied.

She looked at me, trying to understand me.

'What do you mean?'

'London is in trouble,' I said, 'but I don't believe the Germans will attack London straight away. They'll try to encircle the city, cut it off. It's possible that the British generals have decided to withdraw their soldiers, rather than let them be trapped here.'

'They'd let London fall?'

'You've walked the streets here. You can see it's not ready to repel an invasion. Either it's genuinely undefended, or the alternative is that London is being set up as a lure. The Germans could think it was an easy win, march in and the trap will be sprung; the bridges will be destroyed, the invading army trapped here and attacked by city defence units who know all the streets and the secret ways of moving around.'

'But London is doomed either way?'

'Either way there will be a bloodbath, and civilians will be caught in the crossfire.'

'If you're here, does that mean the Americans are coming? They're sending troops?'

'Not that I know of, no.'

'We're trapped.'

I told her that we weren't yet, but that I believed she had to leave London soon to avoid this fate. She told me that she couldn't leave her job, that she had stayed up until now, and she would stay until death.

I took her hand. 'You're a brave woman. But I know the Germans, and they won't admire your courage or reward you for it.'

'Where would I go?' she said. 'No: I'm going home. My parents will know what to do. They have their own shelter.'

With that, she set off. I started to follow, but she turned on me, told me I wasn't to come with her. I was speechless, and she was firm in her belief. I could think of no way to settle her mind without revealing the truth.

'We will meet again?' I asked, already feeling sick at heart.

Angela looked at me carefully. 'The battle for London is about to begin. There are more important things at stake than what happens to us.'

An honourable sentiment, but one that every part of me wanted to fight. Instead, I agreed to let her leave.

'Where will you go?' she asked, her concern genuine.

An excellent question, of course, and a difficult one to answer. My instinct was to leave London, discover all I could from a distance. Most descriptions of a war are written by victorious generals or distant academics. I had more of an ant's-eye view of proceedings. I wish I could tell you that I somehow divined the deployment of both sides, the course of the battle, the outcomes of each combat. I did not. All I saw was the occasional aircraft and then the aftermath, all I heard was the distant crump of a ballistic weapon, the design of which I could only guess. The British would launch a counterattack, they would have strongholds. However powerful an army, it is almost impossible to subjugate an entire nation. It would profit me more to meet up with this counterinsurgent force than to stay in London. As it was, though, I was almost entirely ignorant of the positions of German forces and which were the British fortress towns. I did not even know any of the place names. As this world's history encompassed Roman settlement, I could presume that this Britain had once had a Verulamium, a Lindum and an Eburacum, but had no idea if they still stood or were now called that. Was it a safe just to break the last syllable or two from the name and hand what was left to Angela, to tell her I would seek haven in "Eburac"?

'I'm leaving London,' I said. 'Going North. Using back-roads where I can.'

'You have a car?' Angela asked.

I didn't even understand the question. 'No,' I answered truthfully.

'Well ... good luck. Please tell your countrymen what's happening here. They have to help us, or we're lost.'

I swore an oath that I would, and then my unmarried wife kissed me passionately and hurried away, into the evening.

I thought I could steal a stallion.

During my wanderings around the city, I had seen horses tied up in a number of yards and semi-public places. Most were large, common animals, the sort used to pull carts. But I had seen one courtyard near the Houses of Parliament where smaller, more agile, beasts were tethered. Truth to tell, I was not a skilled rider. I could ride, obviously, but would not be able to charge an enemy, and I prayed that I would not be pursued at any speed. Having a horse, though, would only maximise my chances of survival.

I returned to the courtyard with the horses. The mounts were the property of the police force, which I took to be some sort of city defence along the lines of the prefecture. There was activity inside their large building, but no sentries. It crossed my mind that taking a horse might weaken the British war effort. For want of a horse, the city might be lost. Then I remembered the aerial bombardment, the artillery pieces and the mysterious "tanks" and gas attacks that the people here feared so much. If I were altering the course of events here, it was only to spare the life of a horse.

I grew angry at how poorly-defended this Britannia was. Even the mighty Julius Caesar couldn't conquer this island. A single Roman legion, I felt, could have held off a German landing, but once they established a bridgehead, repelling them would be all the more difficult. In summer, with long days and smooth seas, crossing from Gaul would be easy. I imagined every beach on the south and east coasts full of landing craft disgorging German soldiers and materiel. Millions of Britons would be murdered, injured, tortured and raped.

These were perfectly good animals. Not pampered racing animals, not old carthorses. They were easily led, and looked as if they could gallop if they had to. They were elaborately saddled, and had iron shoes nailed to their hoofs, not the leather slippers I was used to.

What, then, was my plan? I checked the map I had taken from the library. There was a London street called Highgate, the nominal home of Mr. Baretti. This was the start of a wide road that the locals in my world called Ermine Street, the main artery through Britannia leading all the way north to Hadrianopolis, the so-called City Wall. The road in this world seemed to broadly follow the same course as the Roman one, with the rather more prosaic title "the A1". This was not, of course, the back-road route that I had told Angela about. But it would serve me as I left London, it would ensure I was heading in the right direction.

I loitered in front of this police building for a full ten minutes. London was succumbing to darkness and silence. I thought I could hear aircraft in the skies above me, but these were faint buzzes and hums, not the sounds of an aerial attack.

I had no plan. If I were really to draw up a report for my Emperor, I couldn't confine myself to the affairs of one world. The reality was that nothing bound me to this London except Angela, but that was enough to keep me here. I loved my wife. I would not leave her here to the mercy of an invading army.

I took one last look at the horses. I could be well away from London by morning, moving swift enough to evade any invaders. But that would make me a coward. I hurried back to the ruins of Angela's home. I didn't know where her parents lived, but there was, if Fortuna blessed me one more time, a way to find it. It was dark, but we Roman soldiers have no quarrel with the night. Rooting through the rubble, I found Angela's distinctive address book in the splinters of her bedside cabinet, and from that it was easy enough to deduce which of the addresses was that of her parents. It was in a place called Belgravia, a few miles' walk.

The air raid sirens started when I was about halfway there. The streets were already empty, there was no sign even of military patrols. Few of the other Romes had extensive histories of aerial combat, but many Romes - my own included - had adopted Seric rocket technology for military use. It was always a scattershot affair, in my experience. You can't kill more than a fraction of a population, merely drive the survivors away or into deep shelters... and priority for spaces in those shelters will always be the very fighting men and prominent citizens you are trying to eliminate.

The absence of people now suggested that the Britons expected a ferocious assault in preparation for an invasion. Angela had spoken of a complacent population, one that felt secure in their vast city. None of those millions of people were evident now.

The battle for London had begun.

As I reached Belgrave Square, the bombing was underway. There was a row of smoke all along the horizon to the east, lit with red fire. There were squeals and roars from the sky, clattering fire of projectile weapons, the whistling of falling bombs. In reply, distant thunder: ground batteries firing streams of dots higher than the clouds, following pure white lines of light thrown out by powerful beacons.

I made the decision to change into my full armour. I had been considering this for some time. There were two reasons to do so. The first was that it was practical. If nothing else, the Britons were firing bolts of metal into the sky. These all had to land somewhere, and pieces of hot metal were now fizzing down like shooting stars. My helmet would protect my head, the metal strips of my armour would, I was sure, deflect any light weaponry the Germans had to offer. The second reason was symbolic: I would find Angela, I would stand before her, a Roman warrior, pledged to protect her, radiant in gleaming steel. It would prove my true nature to her, it would give her and her family great hope.

A faint black shape passed overhead as I donned my helmet. I thought nothing of it, then.

I did not understand the sequence of necromantic numbers this world used, but I knew I was looking for a "6", the symbol that stood for VI. I felt confident I would find it. In the event, it announced its presence to me.

There was a sharp rattling sound, then smashing glass. I ran to the scene, and found a black-clad figure, carrying some sort of projectile weapon that he was using to spray metal pellets at the front of a house; one marked with the "6". In front of the house, behind a barricade of fallen bricks and sandbags, a Briton had a smaller version of the projectile weapon, one that could fire only single shots. Behind him was Angela, reloading a similar weapon.

The man defending his home was unmistakably Angus Inducula. He was a little fatter, with a small moustache, not the proud bristling beard, but his fighting spirit was the same on this other world. However, he was clearly not a warrior, and was going to lose the fight, and in short order.

I intervened.

Much has been said about the character of the Roman soldier, and perhaps as much has been said about the German people. Hard to imagine, now, but this was the first time that fighting men from each world had faced one another.

Let me describe the combatants, so that you might picture the scene and compare those involved.

The paratrooper was still in his grey jump-smock and padded, rimless helmet. He wore his SS uniform underneath the smock, black tunic and trousers, black leather hobnailed boots and belt. He was wearing the medals he'd been awarded. He was lightly-armed, carrying just an MP40 light machine-gun and P-38 pistol. He carried a knife, but did not seriously expect ever to use it in combat.

He was nineteen or twenty.

I could scarcely have looked more different. I wore segmented metal armour, the lorica segmentata, overlapping curved plates of steel that covered my shoulders and torso, reinforced and augmented with small plates and discs in places, held together with leather straps. This was flexible, but heavy. My legs were almost bare, protected by a short leather skirt and cingulum, an apron of studded leather strips that protected the groin. I wore my sandals, caligae, which were strong, light and comfortable. My helmet was tight-fitting and practical. I would normally carry a range of weapons: the pugio, a dagger; the gladius, a short sword; a pilum, a light javelin; and a heavy full-length shield. Today, I had just the gladius.

Both of us served in armies that placed a great deal of emphasis on a gruelling basic training, we'd both done four months of marching, swimming and exercise that made us physically fit. Both armies maintained that standard once training was over and kept their soldiers working. Both, despite their reputations, produced soldiers that weren't mindless drones, but skilled individual fighting men. The Germans, like the Romans, knew the importance of keeping formation, and went through seemingly endless drills and combat exercises ... but in the heat of battle, each man could take initiative, and knew that it would be his individual strength and sense of purpose that would win the day.

In this situation, though, at close quarters, there could only be one result. I was stronger, more used to hand-to-hand combat, and I had the element of surprise. I removed the German paratrooper's weapon from his hands and stabbed him in the heart. He died quickly.

Angus and Angela continued to hide behind their barricade, staring at me. My armour must have reflected the fiery sky. I walked over, carefully lowering my sword so that they did not, in their confusion, think I was a threat. I understood that I must be making quite an impression upon them. This would have been their first sighting of the glory of Rome.

The two of them stood, slowly, taking me in.

'Ben?' Angela asked, astonished.

'I have lied to you,' I confessed. 'My name is Marcus Americanius Scriptor. I am the ambassador for the Emperor of the greatest of Romes in all the Known Worlds, and I bring with me full Imperial authority.'

I stood before Angus, my father-in-law, and saluted him, in the Roman style.

'What the fucking hell?' he said, in his familiar Scotic accent.

Angela also seemed lost for words. 'He's a patient of mine,' she said, after a moment.

'A head injury?' Angus asked, enigmatically.

His daughter nodded.

'How the ... why did he follow you here?'

'Sir,' I intervened, 'I can speak for myself. There are many worlds where the river of history flowed along a different and better course, and the Roman Empire never fell. I am from such a Rome, indeed one with the optimal version of history. There, I am married to your daughter. You, sir, are one of my family's most trusted friends and business partners. There are as many Romes as there are stars in the sky. Indeed our philosophers believe that each star represents an other world.'

Angus and Angela were now oblivious to the air raid around them.

The city was under attack. German troopers were being dropped from large transport planes. There were two waves; the first squad, the larger, was dropped in Hyde Park. This was a diversion, and many British soldiers fell for the ruse, moving swiftly to form defensive lines. This sucked men away from the true target of this assault, the nearby grounds of Buckingham Palace. Would I have fallen for such a simple tactic? From the lofty heights of time and space I am now afforded, it is easy for me to say that I would have not. On the London streets that night, matters were more obscured, event followed event most swiftly. Even so, my instinct was that the apparent German attack would be suicidal, were it the only aim of the invading forces.

I attempted to warn the city authorities, but Angus was unsure how we could relay such an anxiety. I suggested the farspeaker, but the device used a system of "lines" and "exchanges" that had been disrupted by the German bombing.

By now, Angela was pointing into the sky, where a German was descending in a harness attached to some sort of air sail, like the fallwarders I had seen in some of the more advanced other Romes. I swung my gun up, killed him while he was still thirty feet above the ground. But there were more black shapes in the sky. An eerie, silent sight like clouds from a sycamore.

These men wore the black uniform of the SS. The customs of the German people require some explanation. They spend all their time in warlike pursuits, and thus are run by their military. Their Fuhrer, Adolf Hitler, was the supreme leader of every soldier, but they divide their forces between the land, the sea and the air, and so between the Wehrmacht, Kriegsmarine and Luftwaffe. The Schutzstaffel - literally "defence echelon" - were something different still. They were the personal guard of the Fuhrer, and numbered almost a quarter of a million men. They brutally suppressed political opposition in Germany itself, they made sure factories and their workers were devoted to the war efforts and ran vast prison camps. The administrators of the occupied territories came from their ranks, and no victorious Roman general in our history ever punished a defeated people so severely. They revelled in names like "Death's Head".

These men were fanatics, but they were also an elite fighting force, and their devotion to their cause did nothing to dull their prowess.

Many years later, talking to the servants at the Buckingham Palace of this world, I discovered what happened that night.

Scores of German paratroopers alighted in the large ornamental gardens of the Palace. More than one German came to grief in the waters of the lakes, there. There were iron and wooden spikes in the ground; like the stakes in my own pack, but designed to impale anyone coming from the air, rather than those charging a rampart. Many more Germans died that way. Those inside who peered over the shielded windows saw muzzle-flashes and explosions across the park.

Within minutes, the wall of the Palace had been breached. Soldiers from both sides had rushed to this place, shrouded in darkness and confusion. The Germans were knelt all around, behind trees, statues and other cover. Their weapons were propped on their knees. The British soldiers defending the Palace were easy pickings, as they were framed in the light of the windows.

The Germans fired some sort of propelled bomb. It arced into a window on the first floor, blowing out glass and blackout material. There was a huge explosion from deep inside the Palace.

Thoughts now turned to the King and his family, and getting them to safety.

The decorations - the finest paintings, furniture, ceramics and sculptures of this world, some not without merit - had long been removed. It made the Palace seem empty to the servants. There was now machine gun fire all around them. This, in confined quarters, was deafening. The echoes added to the melee, made it very difficult to judge the distance and bearing of the attackers.

The strongholds of my family villa are ceremonial, and have indeed never been used. I got the sense that this had, heretofore, been the truth for this "palace", too. But the King knew it was a time of war, he had made his preparations. There were many barricades to man, and these had been cleverly designed to offer the enemy little comfort. But the German forces pressed on.

Their leader was a man holding the rank of hauptsturmfuehrer, called Otto Begus.

In subsequent years, I met him on a number of worlds. He spoke good English. He had a craggy face, which was sunburned. This was a career soldier, solidly-built. His uniform was the same black one worn by most of the other paratroopers, with an SS regimental design on his sleeve. The boots were almost knee-length and glossy black. Even the pistol he carried was black.

Before the Palace had been secured, he ordered the swastika raised. He had found the flagpole, but not yet the royal family. Knowing there would be tunnels and hiding places, he ordered the servants rounded up. He began shooting them, one by one. Yet still, none of these loyal slaves - many ex-military men - would betray the location of their King.

Begus had been in command of operations to capture the royal families of Denmark, Holland and Norway. The plan was not to harm the British royals. They were to become agents of the Reich. The young princesses would be publicly threatened, and the British commanded to surrender.

What would have happened? On many worlds, the same operation was mounted and the British proved to be susceptible to such threats. On most, they continued fighting. On some, the Germans committed crimes against the princesses, murdering them. This merely strengthened the arms of the British soldiers in resistance. The Romans long ago learned that smashing an icon merely increases its power.

In any event, the Germans had been tricked. The royal family had left two days before, and had been flown to Canada. The men that had died, on both sides, had sacrificed themselves for an empty room.

I was otherwise occupied.

Angela and I were surrounded by SS men who had landed in the gardens of this opulent area and regrouped in the street. There were six of them, all with projectile guns, surrounding us.

Their Untersturmfuhrer was laughing.

Angela stood resolute, unwilling to show her enemy weakness. The Britons had a saying; that in times of trouble, they should show a stiffened upper lip. A great virtue, a sign that they had the potential to be civilised.

Unlike the Germans. This was the first time I had talked to one, not merely killed it on sight. The officer had been handed the sword they had taken from me. He looked me up and down, a barbaric sneer on his face.

'I thought the Romans killed themselves rather than falling into enemy hands.'

I was hardly listening. I was calculating. Five German soldiers and an officer almost in reach. Grab the sword, run him through, slash left, then dart right ... no, they'd be able to cut me down. And if any of them thought to use Angela as a shield, they'd be able to pick me off with their guns.

The officer was looking at me. 'You look ridiculous,' he told me. 'What are you supposed to be? Did we interrupt a costume ball?'

He weighed my sword in his hand.

'I'll fight you,' I said. 'Me with that sword, you with your pistol.'

'A Luger versus a Roman short sword?' He laughed.

'Yes. I'd have your heart in two before you fired one shot.'

The German smiled, thinking it over. 'An intriguing offer. But no.'

He hefted my sword one last time before ramming it into my belly, between two bands of my armour.

I had never felt such pain. I had heard that this was the case, and never quite believed it. My vision and hearing were blurred by the agonies I felt.

'The girl next,' the Untersturmfuhrer ordered.

Angela was knelt over me. She was unable to reach the wound to treat it, because of the armour.

'Hold me,' I said. She mistook this to be me asking for last comfort.

As she hugged me, I touched the bangle at my wrist, willed myself and Angela to an other London. Here, the same street was a smouldering crater. Before I had even caught a wisp of smoke, I moved us again, again, again and - with an extra push of willpower - once more.

My calculations were right. I had crossed the Divide and returned to a world ruled by Rome. I recognised at once that this was the garden of the vast Temple of the Western Christ on Roma DCX. The smell of the oil lamps, denied to me in Angela's world, was sweet perfume to me. It was a dark, still night, just as it had been in London. Christian Priests hurried to attend to us. Now, though, and not for the first time in this narrative, I allowed myself unconsciousness.

IX.

I woke several days later, with Quintus Saxus standing over me.

'Angela?' I asked.

'She is being tended to by clerics,' he replied. 'She is perfectly safe. They have been asking her about the history of her world.'

'Not just her world,' I said. 'Beyond the Divide, all the other worlds have a common past.'

'They're identical?'

'No. There are differences, but only slight ones.'

'All the Romes share common history,' Quintus Saxus said. 'The history of the world on all of them is identical until Augustus's birth.'

'I believe the common history of the worlds beyond the Divide is identical until much more recently,' I said. 'Within living memory, in fact.'

A slave had brought water, and I sipped from this. My stomach wound had been treated, but as I sat up, it was clear that I would not see action for some time. Quintus Saxus told me that Angela had saved my life, stemming the flow of blood in the crucial minutes until the surgeons arrived.

'I lost my sword,' I told him, feeling ashamed.

'The last time you did that, you did it slaying the sort of beast even a Greek poet couldn't have imagined. Word has been sent to your family that you have been found alive,' Quintus Saxus assured me.

'What was in the dispatch?'

'Simply that.'

I thanked Quintus Saxus, and asked him to send for Angela.

She appeared after a few minutes, in a fine dress of Seric cotton and a wool cloak. She was a little unsure of the garment, clearly worried it would either unravel or she would trip over its hem.

'Hello,' she said. Angela still looked startled. I remembered the profound - and deserved - sense of disorientation I had felt when I had first breathed the air of Roma II, and gave her a moment to recover herself.

She kissed my forehead.

'You saved my life once again,' I said.

'You have ... changed ... mine,' she said, with the endearing understatement that often characterises the speech of the Britons. 'So, this is where you are from?'

I shook my head. 'This is just one of the worlds my people have discovered. We call this place Roma DCX. I am from - '

'Rome One?' she guessed.

I nodded.

'And it's even more beautiful than here?'

'Oh yes. This is a relatively backward other Rome, although I'd never say that to the locals.'

'I don't know anything of its history. The scholars that Quintus sent are more interested in asking questions than answering them. I'm not sure I was much help. I'm no historian.'

She declined the offer of wine from a serving girl.

'Quintus told me you are married, and to ... me?'

I did what little I could to explain.

'You love her?'

'You're the same woman, Angela,' I told her. 'Were you to stand next to her, it would be even more than standing next to her twin. So I love you.'

She gave a weak smile. 'That's what Quintus said. He thought I was ... her ... when he first saw me. I've had a few days to think about it. I think I'm OK with it. You must be the first man in history to have cheated on his wife with his own wife. You Romans have a reputation for decadence, you know.'

I told her that I didn't consider it cheating, that I would never cheat on her.

At Angela's bidding, I described our wedding night.

She was interested in the most trivial details. I had to explain three times things that any Roman would have found obvious. It baffled her most that on the night before her wedding, she had offered her bulla - which I had already thought to explain was a lucky amulet worn by children - at the household shrine, and burnt her toys.

Angela's outfit for the wedding had been easier to explain. She'd worn a white woollen dress that she'd woven, tied up with a sash. Her hair had been elaborately woven [repetation] into six crines, although I confessed I never understood quite why, as the flame-coloured veil covered it entirely. She'd worn jewellery bought for her by her parents, and striking orange shoes.

She seemed amused, that I, for my part, only had to turn up tidily-dressed. I explained that I needn't have turned up at all; my brother actually missed his own wedding day because he was heavily involved in a covert action against Gaulish separatists on Roma XXXI, and sent a letter instead. For my role as groom, I'd worn my second-best toga.

When I had finished my description - with, as I'm sure you will remember, Angela's appearance on a clockwork clamshell - Angela told me it sounded like a fairytale, not something possible in real life.

My Earth, I told her, often seemed that way to me, now.

'How long have we been married?' she asked.

I answered that it would be ten years, this autumn.

'And I'm the same age there?'

'You're exactly the same woman.'

'But ... I'm twenty-two,' she said.

I nodded, absently.

Angela said nothing more, but there was something cold about her manner for the rest of the day, and she refused to say why when I asked her. To this day, I do not have an explanation for this. I think she was starting to see that the history of my Earth wasn't merely different from her own. It must have been sobering indeed to think that her world was not the one that was *right*.

It was a month before I was strong enough to return to Roma I, a pleasant month of recuperation with Angela, aided by sunshine, wine and lovemaking. The scholars spent a further week or so questioning her, then drew up a report on her world. Despite Angela's protestations, the information she provided made for a thorough document, one that was very honest about its shortcomings and voids.

I learned much from reading it, and Angela was happy to clarify. I had a slave read her a popular history of Roma I. She, like I, could understand the spoken word, but not the written one. This was some magic property of the bangle.

She was becoming comfortable with the trappings of Rome. The little things still bewildered her; she would thank the slaves, and found it difficult to eat with her fingers, for example. We were staying at a small villa, guests of the Western Pope Emperor (he, of course, was entirely unaware of the Divide, and stayed in Rome, planning his strategies against the East). We ventured out once, taking a balloon ride to the Rhine-Danube Wall, the symbol of this world's own dividing line. It was made from great plates of metal, bolted together and resembling a line of shields, thirty paces high. The wall - actually a double wall, one on each bank, patrolled by legionaries from both sides - had stood for a thousand years, and was one of the seven-hundred wonders of the Known Worlds.

Angela thought it was incredible. Truth to tell, the first time I had seen the structure, rather than just hearing about this Iron Curtain, I wasn't very impressed. Along its length there were patches of rust. At one point some time ago, an insurgent had daubed *Romani ite domum* in letters ten paces high and it had never been cleaned off. But the countryside was beautiful, the gods had granted us good weather, and the bird's eye view of the world was most pleasant.

That night, as we lay together in the observation dome of the balloon, heading back to the villa in Londinium, Angela had another question.

'You live in a palace?'

'In your terms ... well, yes, I do.'

'What's it like?'

I thought about that for a moment. 'The Vatican,' I said finally. There was nothing else on her Earth that really compared. Her eyes lit up at the news. By now the reality of the Roman Empire was evident to her, she was embracing these better places.

We travelled to Roma I, shifting from world to world without much pause, passing from company officina to company officina. The whole journey took a few hours, and left me tired.

A messenger from the Imperial Palace was waiting for us in the office in the Londinium of Roma I. I was to have an audience with the Emperor as soon as I arrived. The helicopter was waiting. I kissed Angela goodbye, and told her I would return at the earliest opportunity. She was taken to the family villa by sedan.

Having recently taken a flight over one Europa, it was strange to see another.

The lands of Roma I were more prosperous, more developed, more fertile and so more beautiful than any other. Unruly natural forests had been tamed, ornamental lakes added. Above all else, every settlement was large, from the farm buildings sitting in their tended fields to the vast and beautiful metropolises. I tried to imagine the "Europe" of Angela's world. London, I knew. A stark contrast between it and the ordered lines, flowing traffic and clean marble of Londinium. Paris stood where Lutetia Parisiorum should be, freshly-occupied by the Nazis. Columns of German troops and military vehicles were sweeping across Gaul, burning and levelling wherever they met resistance. Crops stood untended in fields, men and women lay dead in ditches. And Roma was Rome, a city of ruins led by a man called Mussolini, who puffed himself up and had declared himself one of the Caesars. Some took him seriously, most thought him a rather comical figure sitting among ancient ruins, dreaming grandiose dreams.

As my helicopter landed on the appulsus of the Imperial Palace, I gathered my thoughts. The Emperor would ask my advice. What I planned to propose was ambitious, and not without some risks. Romans would die. I wanted an army to be drawn up, a vast force that could destroy the Nazis, and their paltry dreams of a Thousand Year Reich. A thousand years! There were books in my family's library that old which no-one had yet got around to reading.

We would have a huge advantage: our armies knew of the other worlds, the Germans did not. We could topple the Nazi regime, hone our skills against a foe, annihilate him, then flit to another world and start the campaign again, learning from any mistakes. How long would this war last? I had no idea, but Rome would spread its benevolent influence to these savage worlds, make them safe for the good, decent people there whose only misfortune was to have been born in darkness.

I was summoned into the Imperial presence. All but his chief advisors were sent away before the Emperor bid me make my report. I was surprised how old and frail he now appeared.

I explained only the basics. That there were many other worlds out there, ones shrouded in war, want and despair. That on each of these worlds there was a scourge, a German warlord, named Adolf Hitler, an ugly little man who dreamt of imposing his barbarism on the entire population. He would leave worlds of smoke, shrieking dive bombers, death and oppression. I explained that the people on these worlds lived in tiny "nations" that fought amongst themselves, each with their own languages and beliefs.

I spoke for an hour and, I believe, passionately and accurately presented the situation. I would let the Emperor digest the information, read the report, then I would suggest my solution.

The Emperor listened carefully. 'There is no Rome?' he asked.

'The largest Christian church is there, and wields great power in the spiritual sphere. It has influence, but no army beyond the ceremonial. Italy is just another nation among many, run by a pale shadow of Hitler.'

'You have not met this man?'

'No.'

'Knowledge of other Romes has caused unrest here.'

'It has upset the status quo,' I admitted.

'A status quo that has served this Rome well.'

'I have seen a hundred lesser Romes, and none as great or greater.' I agreed.

'What do you think would happen if news of this ... "Divide" and the worlds beyond it became common knowledge?'

'I think most people would thank the gods that they were born on this side of it,' I said, perhaps a little too swiftly.

'"Rome fell",' the Emperor said. 'A phrase that does not occur in any of the histories of any of the Romes of the Empire of Empires.'

'No,' I said, trying to work to the moment where I might reveal my plan. This phrase "The Empire of Empires" was still a new one. I had perhaps heard it three times before.

'A dangerous phrase,' the Emperor said. 'Do you know what they argue about, now? Men of learning stand outside the temple of Jupiter and squabble over whether the Jupiter worshipped here is the same Jupiter worshipped in Roma II, Roma III and so on.'

A theological question I hadn't considered, but one for which I had an instant answer: My Angela was my Angela, whatever world she was on. I kept my own counsel, though.

'Cults springing up everywhere. People don't trust the gods. Worshipping the ancestors... why, it used to be a healthy thing. But now some men have raised temples to them. Wear skull-masks, you know that? Picked up some cultish belief from some other world, like a sailor picks up the clap.'

'I was not aware of that,' I replied. Most Romans, I imagined, would continue to honour the gods in our Roman way. That is to say, we didn't bother them too much if they didn't bother us too much.

'These cultists are obsessed with death and change,' he went on. 'And that's the very opposite of what Rome should stand for, isn't it? No,' he said, changing course again. 'It has brought us wealth, when we already had in abundance. It has brought us inventions. Toys. But I begin to wonder if discovering that magic ring of yours was a great curse, not a blessing.'

'It gives us further responsibilities, sir, but I believe - '

'I forbid all travel across the Divide of any kind whatsoever. It is best left alone. Draco dormiens nunquam titillandus. All references to it are to be suppressed. No study of it is to be conducted, the scholars who compiled this are to have their tongues and fingers removed. All evidence of the world is to be destroyed. There is to be no discussion of this decision. If I hear a single rumour, I will hold you fully responsible. The penalty for this will be death.'

He tipped the report into a lamp, where it caught fire, twisted and curled its way to ashes.

I imagined Angela dragged to a funeral pyre. I had not mentioned her in the report, few knew of her.

'As you wish,' I told him.

His two advisors, silent the whole time, looked on admiringly. I wondered about them. I did not recognise either, and they both had a quality I didn't understand. There was a secret there. Once home, I would have them investigated.

The Emperor was an ass, and I had no intention of following the orders of a ass.

He had his spies, though. I quickly arranged with Laton that the scholars who wrote the report were to be declared dead, that all the necessary paperwork would be completed. Roma DCX was very distant, it would be all but impossible to check up, and that was all the action required to make the Emperor think I had complied with his repugnant order. I had a copy of the report. The only other people who knew about the Divide were Angela and Quintus Saxus.

I was not there to witness, or soften, the meeting of the two Angelas.

I had written to my wife explaining about her counterpart. There had not been time for a reply. It did strike me that the Angela I married may have been offended, threatened or scared by the thought there was an other her. Later, she would confide that she had felt sickened by the thought I loved another. But from the moment they met, the women (or woman… I never reached a satisfactory vocabulary) adored each other. I've attempted to explain this before, both in this narrative and to my friends, and it is difficult to believe that there was no jealousy or rivalry. These were not like sisters, these were the same woman, as much at ease as you are with your own self. Angus Inducula, their father, embraced his new daughter, as did our children. It was as though they were one. Like so much in Roma I, it just seemed somehow *right*.

One of the more interesting consequences of one Angela meeting the other has no doubt occurred to the more salacious-minded of you. Such people may not believe that it had never crossed my mind. Both Angelas suggested it to me, though, independently on the same morning three days after meeting, adding that they weren't sure what their counterpart would think it proper and they weren't sure how to raise the subject with her. Both, though, used the exact same form of words. I quickly brokered an arrangement which, that night, proved extremely pleasant, successful and indeed educational for all three of us.

The next morning, I found Angela from beyond the Divide exploring my chambers. She was preoccupied with one statue in particular, one of a woman as naked, yet not as beautiful, as her.

'I recognise this,' she said.

I held her, pressing myself against her back, nuzzling her neck. 'You do? It's a tatty old thing. It needs repainting.'

'I remember being told at school that the Romans painted their statues. It's odd to see it, though. It's lifelike. Like a waxwork. I'm trying to imagine it without the paint.'

'I'll have a slave strip it down to the marble, if you think it will help.'

'You don't have to do that … where was it found?'

'Found? In some sculptor's yard, I imagine.'

'I mean where's it from?'

'I'm not sure. I can find out. It's been in the family for years. I think this is a Greek one.'

'It's a statue of Venus. From Melos?' Angela said.

'The Greeks call her Aphrodite, but yes, I believe you're right,' I replied, amazed by the deduction. She had given no indication of being an art historian.

'It's still got the arms here,' she said. Once again, a most bewildering utterance.

'This is over two-thousand years old,' I told her. 'We can make much better now. Would you like that?'

She seemed confused by the question for a moment, then: 'You want to make a statue of me?'

I nodded.

She laughed. 'This is an extraordinary world,' she told me. 'It's utopia. It's amazing. I feel so at ease here.'

I called for a slave. As he arrived, Angela ducked behind the statue. I laughed at the sight of a soft nude body behind an almost identical one of painted marble. She only emerged when the slave had been sent away with instructions for my chosen sculptor.

'You were saying?' I laughed. 'There's no need to be shy, they're trained not to see anything they shouldn't.'

She was reticent, now. 'It will take me a while to get used to your servants.'

'Slaves,' I corrected her. She flinched at the word.

'Another of the necessary things your world has lost,' I told her. 'As you say, this is utopia. And soon, your own world will be, too.'

I prepared my course of action. I kissed both my wives goodbye, and slipped off to Roma DCX.

Not one of the loyal company men I had summoned here so much as commented when told they were to oppose the Emperor's express orders. Regina pointed out that he was not many of their Emperors. Ollacondire began a familiar discourse of his about the dubious origins of regal authority.

It was clear to me that the worlds beyond the Divide were of great interest, and we knew almost nothing of them. At the very least, we needed some idea of the extent of these other worlds. Drawing up a map, compiling brief reports on each other world, perhaps discovering the specifics of the military capabilities of the worlds' forces.

Regina had reviewed the report I had had drawn up. 'I agree that we should not ignore this,' she began, 'but these other Germans pose no threat to us. We have no indication that any of them are aware that there are other worlds.'

Quintus Saxus had anticipated this objection. 'They pose no threat now, that is true. However, who is to say that one of these worlds won't develop the ability to reach us?'

I had also thought on this, and I had another answer. 'That is not the issue, in any case. People are suffering there,' I said. 'We Romans have much to teach them. In millennia past, Rome would find a land of wood huts and transform it into one of marble cities. Men who were mere painted savages would become scholars, architects and other great men. Thus, the whole of the human populace was improved. In days gone by, when we discovered lands, even whole new continents, we didn't ignore them and hope they would somehow fall back into the sea. As Quintus says, we ignored the existence of such places at our peril, and when we embraced them, Rome only reaped the rewards.'

The others all agreed with this reasoning. Now we turned to practical business. We had to decide the extent of our actions. I had seen five other Earths beyond the Divide, and had an instinctive sense that there were more in every direction. To me, the obvious thing to do was to have one group of us flitting from world to world simply to establish how many other Earths there might be. Another group could examine specific worlds of interest in more depth, living among the people there, collecting reference books and other materials.

Don Vulpisus had stayed silent through most of this discussion, a contrast to his usual witty self. Finally, he asked:

'Your world, Roma I, is one where every decision made was the right one. Statistically, as we know, such a world had to exist. It is the optimal version of our common history. It follows, does it not, that there is such a version of these Nazi worlds? One where every turn of fate went their way? Germania I, if you like.'

We all agreed this had to be the case.

'We should locate this world,' he said.

I told him that I would join him searching for this world. It would tell us a great deal about the extent of Nazi capability and ambitions. Regina would travel out into the cluster, as far as she could, just to gain some knowledge of the extent of the Nazi-dominated realms. Quintus Saxus would - in conditions of utmost secrecy - recruit a small team of explorers and scholars from across the Known Worlds and ferry them to particular other Germanias, where they would learn what they could.

I was acutely aware of the Emperor's prohibition of travel across the Divide. What excuse could I have offered, if challenged? He had told me to my face, summoned me to his Rome to tell me. If this had been a minor matter, buying a horse that my Emperor had requested I shouldn't buy, then it would have been held against me for years. I've seen allies of the Emperor push for legal charges on matters like that, and it can be the straw that breaks the back of a man's good reputation. This was of a different order of magnitude. This was mutiny, treason, the breaking of an oath ... and probably a dozen other high crimes as well.

But weighed against the suffering of billions of people, the Emperor's orders had the moral authority that an ant's would have. I began to wonder then if this was the great purpose that the gods had created our near-infinity of Romes for. Fashioned for millennia, brought together by fate, we were to bring light and hope to the dark worlds beyond our shores. Had I reflected on my actions that day for a mere moment, I am sure I could have detected a dangerous arrogance in my thinking. But I did not, and that is something I regret to this day.

X.

The eighteenth time we destroyed the German oil refinery at Hythe on the Kent coast, we encountered a problem.

Like trained soldiers, Don Vulpisus and I had honed our techniques. On worlds that were practically identical, the same plan worked every time. Now, with months of practice, we knew exactly who to contact on the British side, what to say to them to convince them. We could pass on the clockwork calculating machine that could swiftly crack the Aenigma codes used by the German military, then a set of maps that detailed German supply lines. British officers on any number of worlds had learned the code phrase that marked us out as saviours: grillus gravis jaceo.

We had to move swiftly. This was one of many worlds, and while each was at a slightly different stage of the war, the variations were slight. In every world, the lamps were going out across Europe. This was a fixed target, and an important one. The German tactic was "blitzkrieg", or as it would more properly be called bellum fulgur. They threw every plane, war machine, ship and man at a target in a vast co-ordinated attack, overwhelming the defences of their victims. Such tactics can be effective, of course, and the armies of Rome have done the same (one need only think of Sulla marching six legions into Rome itself), but it is a brutal method. We Romans prefer to plan, to rely on the discipline of the men at our disposal. Above all else, a lightning war comes with one great risk: there is no time to establish or consolidate supply lines, and the armies can charge ahead so far and so fast that they find themselves cut off and surrounded, deep in hostile territory.

The Germans relied on their aircraft to scout the area, to discover the build-up of enemy forces and either disperse them or lead armies to break them up. By now I had seen "tanks" for myself. A tank was a currus loricatus that could move twice as fast as even a running soldier, with turret-mounted ballistic launchers. They could overrun even an entrenched line of soldiers, smash down the walls of buildings or defensive structures. They had their limitations - principal amongst them, they became death-traps for their crews when their ability to manoeuvre was restricted - but on open ground, they were a formidable weapon. The German Kriegsmarine, their navy, was also formidable by the standards of this world. Do not misunderstand me, they would not have lasted five minutes in close quarters against a Roman fleet, but the German ships had enormous launchers capable of firing a projectile over the horizon.

These war machines had one thing in common; all were fed by oil. Simple vastatio tactics against pipelines would inconvenience the Germans. The British resistance forces could manage such attacks with little difficulty. But that was to cut off one head of the hydra, not to kill it. Destroying the Hythe refinery would leave the German tanks with just the fuel they were carrying. Forewarned of this, the British forces could goad the Germans deep into the countryside and surround them. Commando attacks on German radio masts and strategic bridges would leave the Nazi forces unable to move far or co-ordinate with other units. The technology of the Nazi worlds was dependent on oil-powered engines. The raw liquid had to be vaporised in special stills, removing various components until it became "diesel", and this was achieved in refineries; networks of storage vessels each the size of the cathedrals of these worlds, linked with vast metal aqueducts and pipes. Oil burns easily, of course, and these refinery complexes were heavily-defended. The greatest defence is secrecy. The British were not always aware of where these refineries were.

On the first three other worlds we had succeeded in destroying the refinery, and the Germans had been swiftly routed. Conquering islands the size of Britannia is never an easy task. Without fuel, the German planes were grounded, the tanks became statues, the supply boats couldn't make it across the water. The soldiers soon ran out of bullets. The conflict was bloody, but the Britons knew the battlefields, and were fighting for their motherland.

On each of seventeen previous worlds, I had been with the British commandos as they made their amphibious assault on the refinery. We left the river Humber in a submarine, which surfaced only a few hundred paces from the beach closest to our objective. Naturally, the Germans imagined the real resistance threat would come from the land. We arrived in small rowing boats. Half our number dragged the boats up the beach, the other half obliterated the trail they made. We concealed the boats in the grass, then evaded patrols and got through the fence. It was then a simple matter to set the explosives, and a swift retreat to watch from a safe distance as the refineries became infernos. Only the faces of the guards changed; on every other world, with only slight alteration, even their patrol routes were identical.

This time, on the world we designated Germania LXI, we failed.

We had arrived on the beach, dragged our canoes up out of sight. We were dressed in black, and we carried the bare minimum of equipment. The Britons believed that I was the Italian engineer who had helped design the refinery, explaining away my detailed knowledge of the area. There was, as always, a degree of mistrust between myself and the commander of the Special Air Squadron, a man called Pilgrim. As with Angela, this was the same man I had fought alongside a dozen times. It was unusual, to say the very least, to have to make his acquaintance each time. It was easy to assume a familiarity that I had not earned. Every time, his handpicked squad of ten men contained a few new faces, but these were mostly men I knew.

Repeating this operation time and again gave Don Vulpisus and I a luxury unique in warfare. We had fought this battle before, learned from our mistakes, and had a chance to try once more. It was very difficult, I admit, to treat the operation with the due seriousness. It felt more like a training exercise fought with wooden swords than a true battle. However, the Nazi patrolmen here were entirely ignorant and unconcerned with how many other Earths I had walked upon, and would happily put a bullet through my heart, regardless of the feelings running through it. The men and women dying in the wars here were as real as the ones from Roma I. By now, I was almost a blinkered horse. Defeating the barbarians was the most important matter.

Around the perimeter was a barrier like a metal net, through which lightning had been made to course. A lethal wall, but one that the Britons knew how to neutralise. We clipped a hole in it, passed into the refinery complex.

The man beside me, Beal, I had seen die three times. Our victory would be measured by the destruction of the Nazi oil reservoir. We had always achieved this goal, but often at some cost. Beal was a young man, a brave and intelligent one, but he was perhaps a little too thoughtful to be a soldier. I hope that if nothing else, this narrative of mine demonstrates that a man can be a thinker and a fighter. But a warrior needs passion, something to give himself impetus. The Britons had a word, "guilt", that stayed their hands. They said that killing another man was never easy. I have killed many men, and every one of them deserved it, each in their different way. This Beal was like the one of Germania XIII who had confessed to feeling guilty after killing his enemy. I will have none of that. There is a more noble act than dying for your country: making your enemies die for their country. If I had the chance to kill a barbarian, nothing would stay my hand. Indeed, along with the "sten gun" and "pistol" of the Britons, I carried my sword. As I often say, there is something special about the blade. To feel your enemy's flesh part, to get a splash of his blood on your wrist. The Britons carried knives, they attached sharp spikes, "bayonets", to the ends of their guns. There were some who understood that particular pleasure.

Beal was a brave man, though. He was also a good climber, and could move around silent as an owl. He used that skill now, hurrying on ahead of me, off into the darkness, up and over a fuel line thick enough for a man to swim down.

I set an explosive charge at a crucial place in the pipeline. Not only would the line be destroyed, it would shower a large area with burning shrapnel. In other worlds, we had set the charges off and started a chain reaction, one that had swept around the whole refinery, turned an area of a hundred jugeri into a hill of flame.

The thought warmed me. Soon I would be observing this firestorm from a nearby hillside. It would make for a better spectacle, I am sure, if I could relay tales of burning men and vehicles fleeing the fire. The reality, though, was that the heat would turn the hardest metals to splashes of liquid. The skin and fat and bone of everyone down there would boil away into the air. You are perhaps imagining a smell like meat drifting up to our place of safety. But no, the diesel oil had a sharp smell all of its own, and burned in black clouds that choked all other scents.

Perhaps I had grown complacent. I found myself remembering the future. I was anticipating that the next day, the column of black smoke would be visible over the horizon, and the smell would drift across the whole of Britannia.

In hoc signo vinces.

I had seen this happen, so I allowed myself to imagine that my task here was completed.

I was disabused of this when Beal's body fell to the ground from high above me. His throat had been cut with such force that the head was now barely attached. The blood was spraying from his neck.

And now the Germans ambushed us, doing to us what we would have done on a larger scale; lulling us into the midst of the territory, letting us get ahead of ourselves, then ruthlessly springing the trap, wiping us out. I could hear shouts all around me in German. I was unable to call a warning to any of my comrades without giving away their presence and my exact position.

Nazi soldiers in black uniforms and silver buttons, the SS uniform I had first seen in Angela's London. Three of these self-proclaimed "Death's Head" men moved on me, now, guns in their hands. I swiftly dispatched the nearest, surprising him with a thrust of my sword into the stomach. One of the others fired at me, missed and hit the pipeline.

Fuel spewed out like water from a fountain, and the sound echoed off the metal pipes, drums and other structures. The shot fired had put an end to any stealthy aspect of this adventure.

I tried a desperate ploy. I have seen this done by legionaries on guard duty in colder climes, although it is deeply discouraged by their officers. Strike the edge of a sword in just the right way with another blade, and it acts as though it were a flint. Sparks fly. It's used by the men of Hadrianopolis to light fires on cold nights on guard duty, or simply to pass the time.

I let loose a spark by striking my sword against the pipeline. The fleck of metal fell. I was already diving for cover behind a concrete barrier. The designers of refineries are well aware of the dangers, and provide many walls and places of shelter. Like any shield, though, these only work if one is ready to use them.

There was a wave of fire, a fierce deluge that overwhelmed my attackers and quickly snuffed out their screams. But this conflagration was contained by the lay of the place, and quickly burned itself out.

I was aware of our plan, and ran to where Hawkins was meant to be planting a second set of explosives. I found his corpse, a knife in his back. Over it were four Nazis, including an officer.

'He is not the one,' the officer said in German.

He was taller than the others, closer to the Aryan ideal. There was a quality to this man that I found familiar. It was as if I recognised him.

He turned to face me. He grinned, baring pointed teeth.

I stumbled back. There was never a battle won by a man who believed he would lose. I felt now, with all my spirit, that I would lose a fight with this person.

There was an alternative to fighting.

I shifted across to an other world, back to Germania XVIII, the world immediately onwards of Germania LXI. Don Vulpisus and I had long agreed this arrangement, only to be used in extreme emergencies. This was the first time either of us had implemented it. Now, I found myself facing Don Vulpisus, who wore an expression of the utmost terror that I knew must mirror my own.

We agreed to move another world onwards, for safety. We found a quiet spot, deep in the woods. Neither of us was pleased with the thought that we had fled a battlefield. Nor, though, would we waste any time mourning this lack of honour. Don Vulpisus suggested that the Germans had been waiting for us. I agreed, but was more concerned with the bigger picture. I told him I believed that the deeper we travelled into their worlds, the further the Nazis had tightened their grip on power.

'That has been troubling me,' Don Vulpisus replied. 'Why would such an order exist? If you look at the Roman other worlds, there are no such patterns. Roma I is the most advanced, but there's no progression from world to world. They do not become less advanced the further you travel from Roma I. Roma CCII is probably the second most blessed world we know.'

' ... but Roma CCIV is one of the least,' I agreed.

Much time and effort had been put into trying to find an order for the other worlds, but there was none. The only common factor was summed up by that new phrase, "Rome never fell". Just because no civilisation ever surpassed Rome didn't always mean that Rome grew; if it did, it never grew in quite the same direction, and there was no telling whether a newly-discovered other Rome would prove to be a place of social and technological innovation or one where Rome ruled a desolate, impoverished world. Roma D has clockwork soldiers that talk and fight like men, and their shiners can send pictures, not just words. The Senate of Roma DI is made of wood and collapses or burns down faster than elections can be arranged to refill it.

As best we could establish, the histories of all the Nazi other worlds was identical in every single respect until some time in the autumn of 1918, at the conclusion of what was called the Great War. It meant that everyone born before 1918 had an exact counterpart in every world of this cluster, which is how we pulled off that same trick with the Resistance over and over again. Most people conceived before the point of divergence had been born, but there were other Earths where the mother or child met with accidents before that had been possible. Angela, incidentally, was born in the winter of 1918 on both Roma I and Germania V, and there was no evidence there were other Angelas in any of the other Earths. The exact moment of divergence - and, as ever, the exact mechanism of how this whole cosmos operated - eluded us. I had begun to think that each of these worlds had grown from a common seed. I had no idea who had sown them, or what they intended to reap. But there was clearly some form of design at work, at a level so high that I hesitate to even credit the gods with it. There was a degree of order; the Romes and Germanias didn't jostle among each other, there was the Divide between them.

'It may be because the histories of the German worlds are so close,' I said. 'The point at which they diverged is recent. So they somehow affect each other.'

'A natural phenomenon?' Don Vulpisus asked.

'What else could it be?'

'Intervention,' he said.

That single word sent a chill down my spine.

'You think that someone here is travelling between worlds, yet working for the Nazis?'

'Yes. How else could our foe have known about the attack on the refinery? They had seen it before, they can compensate. Exactly as we have, they can develop tactics, learn from them, apply them on many Earths. It makes them unbeatable.'

'We can't be sure.' But already I wondered about the man with the pointed teeth.

'No, not without collecting proof. Scriptor, there's an obvious danger here to Rome.'

All other thoughts were washed from my mind. 'They could cross the Divide.'

'If we can, all we can do is assume that they could.'

'They could drive their tanks and fly their planes into Londinium DCX. That world is relatively well-defended, but even so... the Nazis would certainly have the element of surprise. Would the people of that world even understand what was happening? They would think it an attack from the Eastern Empire.'

'Almost the entire military of both Empires is lined up facing each other along the Iron Curtain. Remember the history of my world, Scriptor? The Goths and Vandals likened the Roman defences to an egg; a hard shell, but a thin one with nothing beyond it. Once they got through, it was two-hundred years before we repelled them and restored order.'

'The descendants of the Goths and Vandals from these worlds could do the same to so many Romes.'

Don Vulpisus nodded, casually sipping from his flask. He was ever one to remain cool in a crisis. 'Are you going to tell the Emperor?' he asked sweetly.

I would, of course, be executed if I so much as mentioned it. Indeed, my head might be travelling towards the floor, independently of my body, before it had finished the sentence.

'There are a handful of us,' I complained. 'We are not going to be able to fight a multitude of armies. How will we ever find the Nazi travellers?'

I realised I could answer my own question.

'Wait! We know that the German armies alter their tactics. All we have to do is discover at what point in the command chain this happens, infiltrate it and confront the traveller.'

Don Vulpisus put down his flask.

'"All we have to do?"' he echoed, incredulous. 'We go to Berlin and sneak into German High Command, then see if we can spot anyone there from an other Earth?'

He laughed.

'The plan may need some refinement,' I admitted. 'But that has to be the gist of it.'

'We don't know for certain that there *are* such travellers. It is a theory.'

'We can test for evidence. Establishing that must be our very first priority.'

'And we must also renew our quest to discover the optimal Nazi history. Indeed, we must redouble our efforts. That must be the most likely candidate for the world with the ability to travel between worlds.'

That logic was inescapable; the old man had arrived in my Rome, Roma I, the best of all possible worlds, not some backwater. And he had done so almost by definition: for any world that received such a boon (and was equipped to exploit it) would gain the huge benefits that would make it the first among Romes.

We were careful to leave word for the other Romans travelling to the Nazi other worlds, and moved on, making separate ways after arranging to return here within an allotted time.

Next, I went to the world Germania LD. In Kent, I found the defences between Dover and Folkestone abandoned. I walked around it. The weeds had begun to reclaim the concrete walkways. Sand from the nearby beach had drifted against some walls. A quick check of the few oil drums here proved that they were almost empty. I found a poster honouring Rear-Admiral Conolly, "leader of Free Britain"... although the gist of the writing beneath suggested he lived in Nova Scotia.

The war had moved on from this place. If the Nazis had no further need to be here, the front was elsewhere. Everything I knew about the deployment of forces led me to conclude that the war was now being fought to the north, up in the Midlands of England. The tide of events here had already overwhelmed the Britons. A full analysis of the situation of all the other worlds would need more scouts and tacticians than I could summon, but it was clear that Don Vulpisus was right: the deeper into the barbarian other worlds we travelled, the better the Nazis were doing.

I was becoming adept at travelling across territory occupied by the Nazis. Within half an hour I flagged down a Nazi motorcyclist, dispatched him and took his uniform and vehicle. Few would dare to challenge me, now, as I moved through the road network. Locally, though, I could face problems, as the rider I had killed would be missed. I would have to leave the area quickly. There was still enough fuel at the refinery to top up the motorcycle's supply, and to furnish me with a couple of containers' worth to spare. I decided to head into Berlin itself, to go to the heart of the barbarian lands.

The roads were deserted here. The war had been and gone; I could see evidence such as tyre-tracks and the occasional abandoned vehicle that spoke of a vast military convoy heading west, to the coast. But the tarmac had grown sandy, the air was clean and quiet. It was quite a relief, after half an hour or so on the road, when a dozen black bombers passed low overhead, the rumbling of their engines shaking the ground.

It was now late autumn, the days were short, but the nights were still warm. I planned to find a convenient barn or shed each night. I drove on, and discovered a convoy of military vehicles that had been reduced to burned-out husks. These weren't German vehicles. This must have been a British unit sent out to resist invasion. Almost all stood in a line on the road, a sign that they could not have had a moment to react to the attack. It must have come from the air. I dismounted and searched the wreckage, already knowing that there was no chance anyone had survived this long. The metal was cool to the touch. This attack had been weeks ago. There were, I estimated, two-hundred charred bodies. Some of these men had fled from their vehicles and died in the ditches. A couple had struggled into the neighbouring fields. They had been left here by the barbarians to be picked at by crows and wolves.

I rode on.

I could smell Ashford before I saw it, a gentle evening wind hinting of soot and flesh. The column of smoke on the horizon was the next sign. Within minutes, the town was in my view.

Ashford had been razed to the ground. No building stood unharmed. As an intact church steeple appeared on the horizon, I was filled with hope that part of the town had been spared, but the steeple was the only thing that had survived of the building. The rest was ribs of stone and charred wood. Few roofs survived in the town, most buildings were now rubble.

Again, my instincts were to go into the heart of the settlement, and search for survivors, find out what had happened, look for signs that the Nazi dominance wasn't total. Unlike the convoy, I thought it likely that at least a few men or women there were still living. I would also liked to have examined the battlefield, tried to discover what methods the Germans had used. There had clearly been air support, but even before I reached the town itself, there were bullet-casings littering the road. Bullet-casings and bones. There had been a land battle here, albeit a brief and one-sided one. There were civilians, including small children, and soldiers in two types of uniform, including Germans. There were tracks of heavy vehicles and many boot-prints.

A massive, swift assault. Air attack to soften up the enemy and take out key defences, followed swiftly by ground forces sweeping in and destroying everything in their path, moving on to the next settlement without pausing even to bury their own dead. I admit to feeling at least some admiration. It had taken the Roman Empire many centuries to conquer all the European lands. The Nazis had achieved it in months. They would, I assume, return here, once all opposition had been crushed. For the moment, this whole sector had been depopulated.

The packs of dogs could remain overnight in this town of the dead, but I could not. I found a farmhouse a way off the main road. This was no villa, but it was a far larger dwelling than it might have been. The barn had been levelled, there were bullet-marks in the walls. Inside the kitchen, I found an old man and woman and possibly their young grandchildren, neat bullet-holes in their heads. I moved them outside to the back of the place, covering the bodies in some sacking material I found in a small tool shed. I could not cremate them without drawing attention to the house, so I dug a grave and tipped them in.

After that, I was ready to eat and sleep. There was enough food here to satisfy me; the people of the barbarian worlds place many foods in sealed tins that preserve them almost indefinitely. I had with me a small shiner, a relic of Germania XXXII adapted for clockwork, which worked on all the other worlds. I spent several hours listening to various frequencies until the coil unwound, then turning the key and listening again. The strong, nearby signals were all military, and all in German. More distant, voices in the languages of the Gauls and Britons, endlessly repeating the same proclamation about the "Ordinances of the

Military Authorities". This covered everything from espionage and requisitions to hunting and fishing rights. On other frequencies, an extremely aristocratic Briton was bragging about German supremacy. Birmingham, Wolverhampton and Coventry had all fallen. The people of York, Manchester, Leeds and Liverpool would do best, this man was suggesting, to just lay down their arms.

Paradoxically, this gave me hope. One is permitted a certain amount of boasting in a conflict, one should never be slow to point out an enemy's weakness. But this was so often bluster and bravado. If the Nazis truly reigned over the British islands, then they wouldn't need to brag, and not so crudely. My guess was that the people of the Midlands were putting up more of a fight than the Germans had anticipated.

I decided it would profit me to stay here and monitor these shiner anisocyclorum. I knew a little, now, of how these things worked. I could fashion a yard of metal that would allow my radio to pick up more signals. As night fell, I would be able to hear things from greater distances than during the daylight.

As darkness came, so did the stray signals from farther afield. I heard American news broadcasts, in the British language. Their "President" was on the verge of signing a non-aggression pact with the German government. The announcer said that almost every member of their Senate had agreed, some with heavy hearts. Another broadcast told of a "superman" who was single-handedly saving the American city of Metropolis from a volcano. Yet more tried to sell any variety of products to me.

I turned my attention East. From both German signals and ones in a new language, that of the Russians, I learned of fierce fighting. There was confusion, but clearly vast movements of men and military equipment. It hadn't, until that moment, occurred to me that there might be another front in this war. Wasn't the conquest of the lands west of Berlin enough for them? There is nothing new under any sun. I say this, because what I felt now was not an original sentiment: these barbarian armies reminded me of nothing so much as a plague, spreading through the slums and tenements of a great city. Nothing could stop it. How could they muster such military power? More importantly, how could they be stopped?

I worked through the night, slept through the next day. From time to time, say once every hour or so, aircraft would pass overhead. These were usually the heavy winged "planes", but late one afternoon a vast dirigible threw its shadow over the farmhouse. It was escorted by two small groups of tiny fighter aircraft. Every air vehicle was heading north. Other than that, the only sounds were those of nature; birdsong, the braying of a horse, the sound of a stream or the wind through the forest.

I had written many notes, carefully recording frequencies and codes. When the shiner fell silent, or I had already heard the information it was relaying, I went to my papers and reviewed them. I knew enough now to infer a great deal about what was being said and - just as importantly - those things left unspoken.

On the second night, I sensed a change in the tenor of some of the German broadcasts from Britain. I found some Aenigma messages that remained cryptic even when decoded. Senior officials from Berlin were visiting the country. Some parts of Britain, then, were completely subdued here by this time.

I had hoped to move on today. My plan was to go to Berlin. From there, I could flit from other world to other world, until I found the version of history that had proved optimal for the Nazis. Now, though, I felt I should remain at my vantage-point a little longer.

In the mid-afternoon, I looked up. I had heard something, I was sure of it. Something akin to thunder or an earthquake. But there was nothing after that, and I returned to my work.

News came just before dusk. The British city of Hull had been destroyed by a new weapon. All the German shiner frequencies came alive to report this. I listened for several hours. The weapon was a pyrobolus atomicus, although what that meant and how it related to the theories of Leucippus were unclear to me. This time, though, I sensed that the German boasting was justified.

I could receive the American shiner signals at nightfall. I eagerly tuned into them. If anything, the American reports were more lurid and seemingly exaggerated than the German ones. The "Reich ambassador to Washington", whatever that was, had released a statement. The weapon they had used could parsed the atomus, unleashing unprecedented power. I had heard of nothing like this in any of the other Romes. If such a thing were possible according to our science, then I am sure I would have known. The ambassador said that they had many such bombs, and would destroy a city a day until the Britons surrendered. Coventry would be next.

An hour later, word came that the Britons had offered their unconditional surrender. Herr Hitler was in Britain, and would witness the signing of the formal agreement himself.

I felt numb. The dirigible that had passed overhead that afternoon must have contained the German leader. Perhaps the bombers each contained pyroboli atomicuum. I had the sensation that I had been near enough to touch them, and that, had I know, some intervention on my part may have been able to stop this.

A whole city destroyed. The fantasy of Emperors that their enemies simply vanish in an instant, as if it were as easy as smudging out a name on a map. This Germania, at least those of this world, could now do it. The histories of these Nazi worlds were not so very different, and there was now some evidence of contact between them. If they hadn't already, then soon every one of the Nazi other worlds would have the capability. The cities here were smaller than the largest of my world. How many of these bombs, though, would it take to destroy the Imperial Palace? What defence was possible against this? I felt a sense of helplessness. That night, the whole of Western Europe was under Nazi control. They would sweep East, crush the Russians, or simply annihilate them. Then where? The answer was simple: wherever they wanted.

This was important enough for me to head back across the Divide and make a report. With a heavy heart, I willed it ... and nothing happened.

I tried again, and this time, *agony*. It was as if I had been struck by lightning. I had to tug the bracelet from my wrist and throw it across the room. It crackled and hissed to itself in the corner for a full ten minutes.

Afterwards, I gingerly stepped over to it, poked at it. It was safe to pick up. I wore it again, but thought better of trying to use it.

I assumed I was trapped here, at least for the moment. But the next morning, after fitful sleep, I used the bangle and it worked. It didn't let me go back to the last world I had visited, however. It only let me travel onewards. The bangle had suffered glitches and malfunctions before, and while I hoped things would return to normal soon, I thought little of it.

XI.

A month or so later, I found a strange variation in the familiar pattern of the German other worlds.

As I have said, most of these worlds followed a strict conformity. You have seen how the first five Londons I saw were almost identical; in one, a stray bomb (or perhaps merely a lax fire brigade) had led to the decision of the Houses of Parliament. This was a war, and war is both unpredictable and capable of forging great changes in the face of history. In some worlds, British defences were more elaborate, their air force better able to repel the Luftwaffe, or else someone in the German chain of command suffered some failure of nerve. So, the level of success the Germans enjoyed varied from world to world. The fact remained, though, that in every one of the other Germanias I had found, the Germans were winning. As I travelled, I was becoming more convinced that Don Vulpisus was right, and that a common plan was being executed on every world. What I could not say with any certainty was that this was due to external influence. Another, more comforting, theory was that the Germans were all simply using an old, and perfectly sensible, plan. A little over twenty years ago, there had been another war with France, Britain and Russia, so any nation worth its salt would have learned lessons and made preparations.

Dresden LXVIII was very different.

For my last few journeys, I had avoided the battlefields of Kent or London, and gone to Berlin itself, a journey with a fair few legs which involved smuggling myself in a freight train, or stealing some form of motor transport. I had avoided Berlin, fearing that the heart of the Nazi empire ought to be avoided until I had a better idea of the disposition of the German forces.

I had also done much research on the so-called Eastern Front, where the Germans fought the Russians. There was much variation between the other worlds. In some, the Germans and Russians had yet to engage; in most, it was a vast and bloody conflict, one where tens of millions were deployed on both sides of a battle-front a thousand miles wide and fifty to a hundred miles deep. Always, though, the area I was in now was so full of military equipment, either mobilised or ready to mobilise, that it resembled a vast military camp.

This Dresden, however, was an ordinary city, the first for a long time which didn't bristle with anti-aircraft guns and road blocks. There were many posters, displaying the image of Hitler alongside the swastika. There were the usual exhortations to honour the fatherland, to beware of outsiders and to pull together.

There was also violence.

Within minutes, I saw three young men beating an older man. I hurried to the victim's aid, quickly driving the ruffians away. Such are the violent instincts of youths, unless they are harnessed by the army.

The man I had saved was not the decrepit old man I had imagined. He was in his early fifties, of medium height and build. Thoroughly unremarkable. I passed him a flask of strong drink. He sniffed it, said he was omomnio, then decided to take a swig anyway.

'They didn't recognise me,' he said.

I asked if he was all right. He was bruised, but had no serious injuries. Now he was in my debt, I wondered if he might tell me everything I needed to know.

'You don't recognise me, either?' he asked. His eyes were wild, his face clean-shaven. I didn't know the man, and put the question down to the edge of paranoia that was readily-detectable in his voice.

When it was clear that I didn't, he relaxed.

'Italian?' he asked me. I nodded, not wanting to be drawn into a discussion on my origins.

'No,' he told me, 'You are a worker. There is an old saying: a bayonet is a weapon with a worker at each end.'

I found myself agreeing. Me; agreeing that I was a proletarius! A completely absurd and insulting notion, but one that had me nodding. It was as if he had an influence on me. I had felt like this before, when the old man had tried to compel me to hand over his magic bangle, all those years ago in Rome. This wasn't a magic power, though, simply a manifest strength of personality. I had met a number of men like him in my time.

It was only when I passed yet another poster of the Fuhrer that I recognised the man I had rescued. This was Adolf Hitler himself, somehow transposed into the gutters of one of his provincial cities. He could see the dawning of recognition in my eyes.

'I wanted to build a utopia,' he told me. 'An ideal society where the workers owned the factories they worked in. Not the old families, not the banks, not the Jews. You see, if you were a German, you'd have been made to read Mein Kapital at school, you'd understand what I am saying. I see your scepticism, but you have to admit it was working, yes? Everyone with a job, with a sense the nation was right. I was expecting the other countries to fight, even if it meant they'd take on Russia, too. We were like Spartacus, yes?'

I raised an eyebrow. Indeed, it certainly sounded as if he were a traitor and a criminal. What deviant society, though, could model itself on such a man?

'That's what we called ourselves, back in '19. Spartacists. We took control of every city. The people... the people have always wanted this. Rosa and I rallied them. Beautiful Rosa ... '

He was on the verge of crying.

If what Hitler was saying was true, he'd been in power for almost a quarter of a century. Not a bad run for a Emperor, or a Fuhrer, or whatever the dictators called themselves here.

A thought struck me. 'How?'

'I know what you are thinking,' he said, misjudging me, I feel sure. 'Hitler still rules in Berlin. But that man isn't me. It's a man who looks like me. They came one night. I don't understand it. They didn't storm the palace, they didn't get past the guards. They were just there. Like phantoms. They... Rosa... '

He took another swig of his drink.

'They beat her in front of me, stripped her. Humiliated me by humiliating her. Showed how powerless I was.'

I imagined this happening to Angela, and I felt angry for this man.

'Then... I escaped. Ran away. They thought I wouldn't abandon her, but I did. It meant I was wandering the streets. Hitler was still the leader of Germany, but not the same Hitler. I couldn't call on any favours, I didn't know which direction to turn. No money, no clothes, nothing. Now ... now I am *this*.'

'When did this happen?' I asked.

He laughed at that. 'Is it really so difficult to tell? What a judgement to make on all that I've done for Germany, that you can't tell the difference between the values of International Socialism and that ... thug.'

I suggested that he humoured me. He told me of the burning of the Volkstag two months before, the Enabling Law passed by terrified politicians that gave the (in his version of events, that I had no reason to doubt) false Hitler any range of new powers. The purging of the civil service began, the education system was handed over to new institutions. Any resistance, however minor, was instantly crushed.

'It was so easy,' Hitler said. 'Their tactics so transparent. They declared free speech; anyone could say anything they liked from now on. Big cheers from the crowd. But Party officials made careful note of everything that was said. Then a month later, they reversed the law, they rounded up everyone who'd said anything they disagreed with. I saw Rosa on the television last night,' he finished sadly, 'I could tell she'd been drugged. I don't know what else. Believe me, I know what they can do to a person. That first week, they crucified most of my followers, on crosses in the shape of swastikas. Tens of thousands, lining the autobahn from Berlin to Dresden. Men and women. Then the bomb he dropped on Stalingrad. Those were our allies. And even if they weren't ... they were civilians. Workers. Not our enemy.'

I considered all this carefully. An other Hitler. There were many explanations, of course. Most generals have doubles and decoys for their own protection. There were many millions of people in the world, and it wasn't hard to find someone the same height and build, with the same hairline. But the tactics were so effective, I immediately concluded that there had been external influence. The detail of the bomb; Hitler never said as much, but it was clearly an pyrobolus atomicus. Knowing what I did, it was clear that the Hitler now ruling Berlin was a Hitler from an other Germania, bringing his own technology and agenda to a new world.

The next thing Hitler told me confirmed my suspicions.

'There was a man ... more than a man. A blond, with strange teeth.'

'Pointed teeth?' I said.

The fallen leader looked at me. 'Yes. Herr Abschrift.'

The ramifications were enormous. It meant that one Germania was operating across the other worlds, that these operations were conducted at the highest level of the Nazi Party, and that the Germans were unafraid to intervene to divert the course of history in the other worlds they knew of. There was, in other words, a Germania willing to declare and execute a war against another Germania.

The Emperor of my world had always held that he was primus inter pares, with the emphasis heavily on the notion of equality. A Roman Emperor was a Roman Emperor, and every Emperor respected his counterparts' rights to rule as master of their own world.

There had always been some of us who had idly speculated about more direct action against the more dangerous or deviant Emperors. Ultimately, without the ability to travel between other worlds, or indeed to even legislate against any restrictions on such travel, none of the other Emperors represented a threat. We could have toppled any Emperor we wanted, and while we never so much as voiced that sentiment, it was obvious to any Emperor who thought about it for a moment. The deterrent was there, and it was a stronger defensive barrier than any threat we could have made.

No such gentlemen's agreement operated between the Hitlers, that was clear.

The Hitler of Angela's world, and by extension the ones from most of the other worlds, called his political philosophy "fascism". There were many appealing aspects to it; it was a dictatorship, an emphasis was placed on the fatherland, there was a powerful military and ruthless suppression of the weak. To many of the rich and powerful in other countries, though, there was a specific attraction to the creed. Every nation, to one extent or another, was in the throes of a workers' uprising. A "class war", as it was known. You are nodding your heads now, remembering the reference to Spartacus. Yes, indeed. As you have recalled, that escaped gladiator led a slave revolt, managing to rally 90,000 slaves and other disaffected working men to his cause. In almost all of the Germanias, Hitler's National Socialist Party had a pathological hatred of these militant workers, the "communists". This world, then, was one turned upside-down, one where Hitler ruled the communists. Here, Hitler modelled himself on Spartacus, perhaps unaware of the fate of the man and his followers.

The Hitlers of all the other worlds I had encountered hated communists. Hitler of Germania LXVIII was a communist, so they hated him.

I have already said that I considered - no, it is more than that, I knew it to be the indisputable truth - that the Angela I married and the Angela I liberated were the same woman. For one Hitler to usurp another, to degrade his wife ... I could not. It would to be to harm oneself, to literally strike one's own cheek. Hitler was an evil man.

And vice versa.

This Hitler was, logically and inevitably, exactly of the same character as the one that had usurped him. Communist or fascist, there was no difference. There was no need to ask what he would have done to his counterpart, had their positions been reversed: that was not a hypothetical situation.

There was also a new word, one this mysterious Herr Abschrift had said: "Mirraflex". He was somehow associated with this word. Neither of us knew, or cared to guess, what it might have meant. I spent an hour or so asking Hitler questions. After that, I killed him, making sure it looked like the work of the young men I had saved him from. Then I abandoned this world, cursed with a second Hitler.

The next world, I initially designated as Germania LXIX, one that conformed far more closely to the normal pattern. Hitler was a fascist, and he was triumphant. The newspapers had many pictures from the Hull and Coventry craters, which were only now fit for the photographers of the Reich to visit. The cities had been destroyed four months ago. This would mean the bombs here had fallen before the first I had heard of

In the absence of any better plan, I set off for Berlin. Starting off from Dresden, it was easy enough to find a railway service that would take me directly to the capital. The carriages were full of jubilant German soldiers, all surprisingly young. A simple mix of eavesdropping and asking questions led me to the discovery that they had been reservists, ready to go to Britain. They hadn't been needed, and had been given a week's leave. The mood was triumphal. These weren't the battle-hardened; they reminded me more of the population of a city who, hearing that an army has earned a great victory, start talking about the way "we" won. War becomes a circus or gladiatorial conflict. Such civic pride and loyalty to the Empire is, of course, a great virtue, but it is often mistaken by the citizen as a substitute for military service, not a gift granted by those who serve.

There were transport systems like this on many Romes, but this was - as I had come to expect - dirty, slow and cramped compared with the magneticus of my world, or the vacuum tubes of Roma D. It ran using some sort of aeolipile, like that proposed by Hero around the time of Augustus. This meant that the drive unit trailed steam and dust behind it ... into the passenger carriages. The decor suggested that it was civilian transport, commandeered for military use. It was not best suited for it.

We had passed into Germania, leaving behind the exclusion zones and battlefields. The land here was not untouched. A great army had passed through here, and there were plenty of almost-abandoned airfields, vehicle lots and barracks. Even these, though, eventually gave way to green countryside, forests and the occasional town and city.

The train was an express, but while it didn't stop at any stations, it frequently slowed down or shuddered to a complete halt. This did a little to transpose the soldiers' elation with frustration, but it also gave me more time to learn about their hopes and fears. I was able to tell the men about the pictures of the destruction of the British city. Most were pleased to think Germania had such a thing in their arsenal. A few reflected that such power would change everything. There was one young man who wondered whether anyone, even the Fuhrer, should have such a weapon.

I had felt this sensation before, for the one sleepless night when I had worried that the people of Roma II had the ability to cross to the other worlds. Before then, I had always known that Rome was supreme. Since then, my thoughts had often returned to the old man's people, the builders of the magic rings, and to the demonic creature that had hunted them down. But that felt, to me, like someone else's war. A war among gods, like a lightning storm at sea. I could not fight a war with the ocean, or stop the motions of the earth. But other men ... I was a citizen of Rome, a citizen of the best of Romes. It was my place in the scheme of things to be above all other human races and civilisations.

It is ironic, then, that my nerves were steadied when I entered Berlin, and the heart of the Nazi empire.

A city is a statement, a capital city only moreso.

Words are cheap, paintings can be created for very little money. Even spectacles, festivals and theatrical productions can be mounted on a relatively modest budget. Cities are different. They take so much time, effort, money and above all else *power* to alter. My Emperor was the most powerful, most wealthy man who ever lived. It had long been the done thing for an Emperor to try to make his mark on Rome. To commission a new building or complex or roadway. A few new bridges here and there, tearing down a vast building to put one even more vast in its place. But even the Emperor could do very little to alter the skyline or road plan.

Hitler had ordered the centre of Berlin rebuilt, and so the crude power fantasies of the Nazis were being imposed on that ancient city. At this time, work was fully underway. The collapse of the Germans' enemies in the West meant that there was a new impetus and sense of pride. More than that, of course, there was a new influx of slave labour and other resources.

My train drew into a vast, incomplete new railway station. It was an ugly, imposing building of granite and concrete, and it set the tone for the capital city of the Nazis. Leaving with the crowd through the main concourse, I stepped out onto the far end of the new three-mile avenue. At the far end, to the north, the Grosse Hall. When completed, it would feature a colossal dome possibly a thousand paces in diameter. There were more impressive structures in my Rome, but few to match it elsewhere in the other worlds, and it would be petulant of me to pretend it wasn't an impressive sight among the diminutive buildings of the old city, even half-completed, as it was here. At this end of the avenue, a frame for the domed hall, was a triumphal arch five-hundred paces high. Again, there were arches larger than that in my Rome, but this was truly gargantuan. Remember that to these people, Roman civilisation had ended fifteen-hundred years before. This arch could comfortably fit the Arches of Titus or Constantine under its opening, possibly even if they stood on top of each other.

But ... there was no inspiration here. Domes and arches? They had simply taken what they had seen elsewhere and ordered a larger one. And there was another thing. The dome would be so high when finished that clouds would form *under* it. Perhaps a quarter of a million men could stand on the concrete floor beneath it. But all that did was diminish any Emperor who would wish to stand there. He couldn't make a speech. Even the most brilliant mechanical contrivance couldn't help; the words would just bounce from or soak into the walls. No matter how artfully arranged, even the most imposing figure standing in that hall would become a dwarf. No thought had been given to this. They had simply ordered the largest hall their structural engineers could manage, then draped it with banners displaying their broken cross. This was the work of megalomaniacs, not a thinking race. Building a palace a mile wide simply meant you were out of breath before you were out of the front door.

You may be thinking that such sentiments are rich fare when served by a Roman. And you are right, of course. The Circus Maximus has grown and grown over the years until its track could have encircled this Berlin, with enough seats for its entire population. Everything about Rome has swollen over the centuries, as successive emperors have used ever more skilled architects and new construction methods to outdo the past. Rome has been built over and rebuilt and remodelled, and no Emperor has ever decided to tear something down and replace it with something smaller.

But that is our prerogative. We were the first race to build a triumphal arch, the first people to cast domes from concrete, to build stadia and amphitheatres. All the Germans were doing now was trying to ape us ... no, not even us: our ancient forebears. They were trying to recreate the grandeur of Rome, whereas I was from a world where such grandeur had been continuously torn down and replaced with something ever more impressive, ingenious and wondrous.

These were not men fit to be the masters of a world, they were errant children. Just as children played with oil lamps, these Nazis played with parsing atomi, but scratch the surface and they were mere barbarians, one step away from fur loincloths and rusty axes.

So, I had reached my goal. Berlin. I had no doubt, now, that this would be recognised as Germania I, the other Earth with the optimal version of history, at least as the Nazis would see it. Everything here had gone the way they had wanted. This wasn't just the capital city of the German Empire of this world, it was the capital of the whole Nazi cluster. I firmly believed I could discover that the attacks on other worlds were being co-ordinated from here.

Every second person was a man in uniform. As I understood it, there was no immediate military threat to this Berlin... or, as far as I could see, any distant prospect of the Germans' enemies mounting an assault that had any chance of reaching here. Yet this wasn't a jolly, confident place. The grey buildings merged with low winter's cloud and the grey of the army uniforms to create a sense of imprisonment. There were splashes of colour; blood-red banners marked with the swastika, gold trim, and enormous posters extolling the many and varied virtues of Germania, Berlin, the National Socialist Party or confining their adulation to Hitler himself. On many of the other Germanias I had seen, the starved, hollow-eyed populace looked nothing like the strong, confident men and women on the posters. Here, though, there did seem to be some truth in the images. The men seemed taller, the women more comely. As with Roma I, there was little discrepancy between the ideals of Germania I and the actuality.

My stolen uniform allowed me to merge with the crowd, indeed to attract the attention of some of the female population. However, it did not compensate for the lack of any real plan on my part. To reach my goal, the heart of Nazi power, I would need at least three legions, not simply a German army uniform which had apparently been designed by a man who felt that wool and cotton garments could stop a bullet. It was obvious that the secrets of the atomus would not be conveniently displayed for me, that I would not be presented with an opportunity to meet Hitler in person, or to chair a meeting about the other worlds where all my questions would be answered. I did have my letter of authority from the Emperor, and it did cross my mind that a straightforward diplomatic approach might be a good idea.

I was not to be the master of my own destiny, however.

Within ten minutes, I was surrounded by Nazi storm-troopers.

It was as if the city's population had melted away. There were dozens of German soldiers, all with their machine-guns.

'Check him,' one of the junior officers called out.

I was compelled by two of the soldiers to press my fingers into an inky pad, then onto a piece of paper. I asked him what he was doing. I wondered if it was some form of poison. But it looked like ink, it made marks on a piece of card like ink. The junior officer scrutinised the marks I had made, compared them with another image on a piece of green card.

'Your prints,' he then told me, 'match those discovered on a knife found in the back of a German officer.'

The bangle, as I have said, no longer let me return to the worlds I had already visited. I felt I had to try it, anyway. It was dead on my wrist. A familiar Nazi soldier stepped forwards, looking as he had on our last encounter. The man with the pointed teeth. He raised his arm, to reveal a bangle of his own on his wrist.

'You're not going anywhere,' he told me. 'You left a trail of fingerprints across a dozen Earths.'

I asked for clarification. I knew that each man had ridges and grooves on his fingers. It was not until then that I knew these were unique. The Nazis, arch-controllers of their population, had records of these fingerprints, including - now - my own.

I was surrounded, under arrest, with no prospect of escape.

I was a prisoner of the Nazis, at the heart of their Empire.

'So you are the Roman ... ' the Nazi officer said.

'Herr Abschrift,' I replied graciously.

He looked surprised, then smiled, revealing his fangs. Then he stared down at my wrist.

My bangle caught light, melted from my arm, burning through the cloth of my stolen uniform, searing my flesh.

Red hot drops of metal hissed and plinked to the pavement.

I knew true terror at this moment.

'That was stolen property,' Abschrift told me. 'Where is the man who was wearing it?'

I told him proudly that I had killed him. He reached out for me and, impossibly quickly, he lashed out with surprising speed and force, hitting me hard in the solar plexus. I doubled up with pain.

'You have intervened,' he told me, 'in a war that should not have involved you. You have helped spread imbalance. You have entered a sphere of affairs that is not for the mortal. You have forced a response.'

I looked at him again. Like the old man, he was somehow more ... it is hard to explain. It is the difference between a painted portrait and its subject. The painting inevitably is less than the man. This was not a man, this was something greatly older and more powerful.

'I have killed your kind before,' I told him, 'and I have easily slain a beast that's killed many of your kind. You may rule this broken, ugly world, but I am a Roman. Kill me, and see how a Roman dies. But be warned: you will also see how a Roman kills. My comrades will hunt you down, kill you where you stand and then toss your body to a pack of Molossian hounds.'

'I don't rule here,' he told me, unimpressed by my rhetoric. 'This ... this is a war game, not the War I'm fighting. But let me show you the extent of my game.'

I was marched to the Great Hall.

We entered the great arena at the heart of the domed building. This was a building designed to be dramatic; I was led under tall arches into monumental entrance chambers, up many flights of wide stairs to one of many viewing galleries. Ours, though, was the only one occupied today.

'A closed session,' Abschrift explained. 'This is quite an honour for you.'

There were dozens, hundreds of - no, perhaps a thousand - men sitting in an immense semi circle. This was the Nazi Senate, then, and it was in full session, under the unfinished dome. My first efforts were spent taking in the room, a vast public space that looked like an amphitheatre nestled in a yet greater space, partly enveloped by a cracked eggshell which was barely lower than the vaults of the sky.

Then I turned to mortal affairs. Wasn't this a dictatorship? Why encumber a dictator with such a large parliament?

At the centre of the Hall, on a raised platform, stood Hitler himself, in shining ceremonial armour. He ought not to have cut such a striking figure. He was of average height and build, his face was prematurely old, his tiny moustache faintly ridiculous. Yet his voice boomed, and he was clearly a leader to be reckoned with.

He bid one of the Senators make a report.

'My forces have engaged those of an other world, beta alpha one five. The Hitler of that world was killed by Ernst Rohm, who declared himself Fuhrer seven years ago.'

Almost all the other members of the Council began hissing and deriding the name. It was a strange sound, like a male choir, each member in harmony with his neighbour.

It was then I realised. Each man in the hall was the same height, the same build. All had the same presence, the same voice.

Each man there was Adolf Hitler. This was a congregation of Hitlers from a thousand or more other Germanias. I understood at last why this chamber had to be so large. I had failed to understand how Hitler had planned to fill it.

'The Council of Hitlers,' Abschrift whispered. 'I have enabled them to meet like this, to pool their resources.'

'We struck against him,' the Hitler was continuing, 'wiping out every one of his deviant followers. We executed Rohm.'

'The Hitler of alpha alpha nine was discovered murdered,' another Hitler rose to announce. 'This man, as you remember, was a deviant. A communist, a traitor to the German race.'

'Found murdered?' a couple were asking.

'Yes. A gang of youths saved us a job,' Hitler joked.

There was a deep laugh from many of the Council. From my vantage point, I could not see one among them who seemed disturbed that, in a sense, they had just received news of their own funeral.

'Eight dozen worlds,' the Hitler in the centre of the chamber screamed, thrusting out his arms. 'The tide has turned on eight dozen rogue worlds. Gleichschatung has been established. The rightful ruler raised or restored to power. Sieg Heil!'

Every one of the hundreds of Hitlers stood and thrust his hand out, the salute of the Nazis. In unison, they repeated the chant: *Sieg Heil. Sieg Heil. Sieg Heil.* Their voices merged, rose beyond the very apex of the incomplete dome above us, then echoed from the stone and concrete walls, growing in volume and intensity.

Sieg Heil. Sieg Heil. Sieg Heil.

'Nearly a thousand worlds, united in purpose, confident of victory,' Abschrift whispered to me. 'Do you really think you have any way to stop them conquering everything?'

Sieg Heil. Sieg Heil. Sieg Heil. Sieg Heil.

PART THREE: ROME WASN'T BUILT IN A DAY

XII.

To conquer the Earth.

The Nazis had not done this before. They dominated many hundreds of worlds, true enough, but this was not the same. For a start, by the standards of their opposition, Germany was a large, developed land, rich in resources and in a strategically advantageous position. The infrastructure was in place, as were the armies. Many of the lands around them had large sections of population who were of German descent, and others who were sympathetic to their policies and philosophies.

Even then, even in Germania I, the Nazis did not subjugate every nation. When I talk of German victory, of their world domination, I mean that they were placed in a position where no other nation - or any group of nations - could realistically challenge them. On a tenth of the worlds, they signed and honoured treaties that meant no fight with Russia. A third of worlds had the Britons either surrender or draw up a pact with Germany that avoided conflict. Over half the German Earths saw the United States of America stay out of what they saw as a "European conflict", for a whole range of reasons from ideological sympathy to military unpreparedness. Most expressed sentiments like those of President Richard A. Russell of Germania XII:

'The United States will survive as a happy and fertile oasis of liberty, surrounded by a cruel desert of dictatorship.'

There was no need for the Nazis to invade such countries. They were neutralised, incapable of stopping the Luftwaffe and Panzer squadrons sweeping down from Europe to seize the Arabian oil fields, and then to take control of any African or Indian territory they chose. With every acquisition, the Nazi empire was more irresistible, their allies stronger, the resistance against them more hopeless. They didn't occupy every jugeri of land, but the Greater German Reich became the dominate power of each of their worlds.

There were four phases to the war in most of the arenas where it was fought. On every such Earth, whether it came from Stalin, Churchill, Chamberlain, Coty, Daladier, Russell, Roosevelt or any of the countless others, the rhetoric started the same way: the Nazis were evil, but not our problem. Gradually, this line shifted. Soon, nations were speaking of working with the Nazis, perhaps using what influence they had to get them to abandon some of their more blatant brutalities and atrocities. Then, things shifted again. Leaders told their nations they shouldn't envy the Germans' success, but should try to match it. Within ten years, it became the case that most of the nations of most of the Nazi Earths were openly trying to emulate the German model. Each Britain, each America, each Russia had its own fascist dictator, its own idea of what had gone wrong with their nation, and its own variant on which groups among their population were to blame.

We are back to Cleopatra's nose and the face of history. In every war, there is the possibility of defeat, of bad fortune. There are points in any campaign where victories can occur. It took a number of years for these to be played out across the barbarian worlds. Nazi thinking was controlled by a document, the Hossbach Niederschrift, drawn up in 1937, that varied in no important respect from other world to other world. One of the key elements was that Germany must start its expansion within five years, before its weapons grew obsolete and while its recruits were still young. Many other Earths fell in 1940 or 1941, with spectacular invasions of the British Isles, or of Russia. America was successfully isolated in others, its military and industrial might being denied to the Nazis' opponents. European resistance to the Nazis tended to collapse in 1943 or 1944 in those other Earths. Some other Earths saw massive alliances set up against Hitler. The might of Britain, its Empire and America combined to create a great invasion force, one that swept into France, or Belgium. Fighting was fierce, but in every one of these other Earths, the landings were repelled, or the armies were massacred as they made their way inland. Broken, the enemies of the Nazis surrendered or otherwise came to terms. Some other worlds avoided war completely, or saw only limited skirmishes. Here, weak or compliant political opposition gave Hitler everything he wanted. On every one of the barbarian worlds, aided no doubt by Abschrift and his overlords, Nazi strategists skilfully identified the schwerpunkt, the one crucial pivot on which history swung. In one world, it would be the result of the civil war in Spain, in another the weakness of the Russian Red Air Force. In some worlds America could be persuaded to join Hitler in a campaign against the British Empire, in others fascist uprisings were promulgated in Scotland and the North of England. There were a dozen ways to neutralise the Russian threat, a hundred ways of buying off the French. Each series of events had to be engineered with the most delicacy, and not every attempt succeeded, but gradually the Nazis came to dominate every world, by force of the gun or by diplomacy. The risks they took all paid off, given time.

Germania I, of course, was the ultimate expression of this philosophy. Here, all the nations surrendered to Hitler, either capitulating immediately, or after short, one-sided wars. On this other Earth, every mad dream of the Nazis was given form. The Russian people instigated a revolution which saw Stalin sent in chains to Hitler on a special train. They welcomed German liberators with open arms... and were confined to the cities, rife with disease, when the Wehrmacht arrived. Moscow was bulldozed and flooded to become a great lake, all without the city's population being evacuated. The British - once enough blood had run down the palace walls - were welcomed by Hitler into his great enterprise. The price was the colossal British empire, which was handed over. Overnight, Canada, Australia, India and much of Africa - along with countless islands - became part of the Reich, and the sun never set on Nazi Germany. The Crimean was German.

A puppet US Senate set up hearings in which public figures, even actors, were denounced as communists. SS-US officers rounded up Negroes from Manhattan jazz clubs and sent them to Nebraskan gas chambers. Switzerland, the Channel Islands and those in the Mediterranean were turned over to Strength Through Joy. Electricity was generated in Sweden, and by 1950 every Jew had "gone East"; so far East, not one was ever seen again. For the first time, the whole of this Earth was under one rule, and Hitler was the garish master of a garish world.

The capital city of Berlin was completed to the letter of Albert Speer's designs, the plunder of the world stored in the vast Reichmuseum. Around the world, architects jostled to ape this vast, brutal city of grey concrete. Cities flattened by war were remodelled in this new style and linked by wide, winding autobahns. The motivation wasn't pride, but fear: every administrator now wanted only to find favour with Hitler and his circle. The cult of their leader became ever more elaborate and all-encompassing. When, on the 30th of April 1945, the Hitler of Germania I and his wife Eva announced the birth of a son, August, the celebrations lasted for months, and the child was endowed by the official statements with supernatural ability. At the age of three months he could speak in full sentences, before the year was out he had uncovered a Jewish plot against his father. Or so it was claimed.

Across hundreds of worlds, the path to this victory was the same, the only variation was in the detail. The Council of Hitlers, using technology supplied to them by Herr Abschrift, were able to fight the same war on a hundred fronts. More importantly, they could ship men from one world to another to act as reinforcements.

Did they even know, I wondered? One of these Nazi worlds looked much as all the others, especially in Europe and North Africa. If the foot-soldiers encountered something unexpected, some city putting up resistance that they knew had fallen, well, they were more likely to think that their newspapers or radio broadcasts had lied to them. Reality, in the Nazi state, was whatever the authorities told you. In many ways, the people of these worlds had been well-trained for life travelling between different worlds. The young schutzes and oberschutzes would do what they were told, they'd know not to ask any awkward questions. At what level were their commanders made aware of the true nature of the war they were now fighting?

Little matter. By the year 1951, the Nazis had triumphed in all but a dozen or so of the other Earths beyond the Divide. The remainder would soon fall.

The ambition of Hitler did not end there. Now, the leader of Germania I commissioned Von Braun, engineer of the missiles that had levelled whole sections of cities even before the Nazis had parsed the atomus, to build rockets that could carry men beyond the Earth into the celestial void. The plans, enthusiastically trumpeted from every newspaper and newsreel, were to build cities that circled the Earth, and vast rockets that used atomic power to take men - Aryan men - to the Moon. This, I admit, led me to some admiration for the Nazis. We Romans had known since the time of Hipparchus and Ptolemy how large the Moon was, and how far away. Not one of us had - up to that point - ever seriously speculated about bridging that gap. A German sternmatrose planted the swastika in the Mare Tranquilium on the seventh day of Octobris, 1957.

The assault on Roma DCX was a different matter. The Germans had prepared for wars against the French, the Russians, the British, for campaigns in Africa and the Atlantic. Somewhere, no doubt, there was a plan to invade everywhere on Earth from Abyssinia to Zululand. They had no contingency plans against, by their way of thinking, the ancient Romans.

The military planners of Germania I fell eagerly into drawing up invasion strategies. Most must have thought it a whimsical exercise, perhaps a few entertained treasonous thoughts that being asked to do this was evidence of Hitler's insanity. In those days, there were still men who resisted Hitler, even in the highest echelons. In July 1944, across a number of worlds, Hitler was assassinated by a conspiracy of his officers. The exact method varied; most commonly, it was a bomb in a briefcase. On many of these worlds, Hitler's body was found in the rubble. On a couple it was even filmed or photographed. But the next day, Hitler appeared in public, miraculously unscathed, to announce a new wave of purges. Across all the Nazi-controlled worlds, the conspirators and every counterpart of the conspirators were rounded up. Many of these men would have been entirely innocent. As every possible variation of events was played out, many could be assumed to be loyal followers, even fanatical devotees, of Hitler. All were taken to their Bendlerstrasse and shot, the ultimate form of guilt by association.

In such a climate, all the wishes and instructions of the Fuhrer were taken seriously. So it was that classical scholars found themselves dragged from their universities and seconded to espionage units. Logistical charts and maps were drawn up. Officers were given refresher courses in speaking and reading Latin.

Scouts were sent across the Divide. Roma DCX, as you will recall, was in the throes of a bellare frigidus, East and West constantly on the alert for enemy spies. This suspicion and vigilance made it difficult for Nazi agents to operate. In their position, I would have tried to divide and conquer. Offer assistance to one side, wipe the other out, then strike against my former allies if they proved too independent-minded. But Hitler had a different mentality, a victor's arrogance that saw all Romans as the enemy. Indeed, the Council of Hitlers had kept all knowledge of the Roman worlds beyond the Divide from his Italian ally (on most of the other Earths), the fascist dictator Mussolini. A limited man, Mussolini dreamt of restoring the glory that was Rome. In practice, this merely meant plans for large statues of himself, draining a marsh or two and scoring straight roads across the face of Rome to link one landmark to another. Mussolini was ever in thrall to the Nazis, any attempt to think for himself was almost cruelly mocked and thwarted by the Germans. His loyalty to Hitler remained intact, but Hitler was wise enough to realise that the Roman worlds beyond the Divide were Mussolini's dreams given form, and so were to be denied to him.

The Hitlers' first objective had to be to blockade Roma DCX, to prevent any word of the attack reaching another Rome. Herr Abschrift - as we have seen -

was able to exercise some control over the rings that allowed travel between worlds. If it had been a simple matter to shut them all down, if he could engineer the same malfunction at a distance as he had with my own ring, the Nazi conquest of the Empire of Empires would have been relatively simple. However, if you are receiving correspondence from a friend and it stops abruptly, then you will be suspicious. So it would have been if all contact with Roma DCX had been lost, let alone if all those travelling between worlds lost their ability. Moreover, Abschrift's powers were subject to limitations. Quite what they were, I was never made privy to, but I understood that he was only able to control the rings with considerable effort, and over limited distances. Even then, his hold was not infallible. His most useful ability was to know if a ring were present on an Earth. From there, he could track it down.

Or, as he did here, he could simply wait until there were no rings on Roma DCX, then give the signal for the invasion. The only way we had of passing messages from one world to another was via a courier, one of our hand-picked band. So, when the Nazis came, they could do so without the slightest risk of tipping off another Earth. The only risk was that a Roman explorer would subsequently arrive at Roma DCX, and get away to report what was happening. As we have seen, Abschrift had some sort of device that could stop a ring from functioning. He could trap anyone who ventured to this world.

In the event, the Nazis had more than three weeks without such an interruption.

Their methods of transporting themselves between worlds were far more advanced than mere bangles. I had walked past the most important structure in the German capital without noticing its significance. The vast triumphal arch at the heart of Berlin functioned as a doorway from one Earth to another. And there was no need to hop from one, then to another, then to a third. It could create a gateway to any point on any Earth where the same structure had been built.

This led to an absurdity, a story that would be a salutary message to all Romans, were the moral not already that of one of the oldest pieces of literature. A group of Nazi agents on Roma DCX posed as rich merchants, and flattered the Western Emperor that a great arch should be erected in the centre of Rome to sing of his triumphs. Anyone could have told the old fool that he had no triumphs. The recent history of his world had been centuries of deadlock. Skilfully managed stalemate, I might add, but hardly something to compose epics about.

Not only did the Western Emperor explicitly endorse the building of an arch, he helped to pay for it. He matched, denari for denari, the money the Germans had raised. The arch took several months to build, and the entire Nazi Supreme Command must have spent it mocking Rome and our vanity.

The priests and Emperor gathered at one end of the Via Dei Fori Imperiali. Games and races had been organised in all the stadia and circuses. The statues had been garlanded. The streets filled with men, women and slaves. Offerings were made to the gods. And the very moment the arch was completed, the air in the centre boiled like water in a cauldron. Then the Nazi invasion force arrived - almost all of them men and machines from Germania I - Junkers 98D dive bombers screeching out of the archway and over the Forum and the Imperial Palace. In pinpoint raids, all but two of the smallest bridges in the city were demolished. The First and Second Panzer divisions now powered out into the bright morning, securing the bridgehead, then moving out to level buildings and foster panic. PzKpfw IX medium tanks inflicted massive casualties on a city that had elaborate methods of detecting an attack from the East, and which had complacently depended on the fact that any attack would have at least a four momenti warning. The city of Rome was heavily fortified, but all the defences - naturally, and understandably - were pointing outwards. It took almost an hour for the ducis on the ground to redeploy their forces, and by then the Nazi infantry had marched out of the archway, captured the Emperor and killed or rounded up the imperial family and virtually all in the political class.

The first suspicion of the people of Rome was that this was a sneak attack from the East. The Easterners had an embassy and informers in Rome, and they quickly sent word to Constantinople of what they had seen. As yet, of course, they had no idea of the exact nature of the invasion, even the identity of the invaders. The Eastern Emperor convened his military advisors, but they remained baffled.

The Western army, massed - ironically - in the Germania of this world, was unsure whether to abandon their posts to defend Rome. The commanders were split: the balance of forces along the iron curtain was precise. Removing one cohort might be enough to make the East think it was time to chance an attack. For centuries, there had been a peculiar logic at work on this other Earth. No sane Emperor, from either side, would commit his forces to a frontal attack, as both the East and the West maintained almost perfect defences against such an operation. So, paradoxically, maintaining these defences became a matter of the greatest importance. Meanwhile, generals on both sides planned more subtle, gradual or indirect attacks.

The practical effect of this was that when the Nazis attacked Rome, the two Roman armies facing each other on the Rhine both thought that it was a trick dreamt up by the other side, the precursor of an attack. Both thought the urgent shiner broadcasts from Rome were faked, both thought the other side was creating confusion. When, four days later, the same reports started coming in from Constantinople, many of the wiser heads nodded and said they expected such a bluff from the enemy, and this just proved this was a phoney war.

Two vast armies, each ten times the size of the German invasion force, sat where they had for hundreds of years. Some of the legionaries were the great-great-grandchildren of the men originally posted to Germania. None had fought, all had spent their whole lives waking up in the morning expecting this to be the day the last battle of their world was fought. When it came, they were facing the wrong way. Generalleutnant Falkenhorst, the veteran Nazi commander, now in control of both Rome and Constantinople, summoned the top Eastern and Western Roman commanders back to their capital cities, and had them imprisoned. The legions on the Rhine were now leaderless.

Only now did some of the junior officers understand that things had gone very wrong. We should not blame the Western Romans for assuming that the Easterners were to blame, nor vice versa. Few among them would have even have heard the theory of the other Earths, let alone expect to face the hordes of one in battle. Those small number of the political elite who knew the secret of the other Earths would have been told that each other Earth had a Roman Empire, that travel and communication between the worlds was limited and benign.

But the fact remains that, at the time when the whole concept of the Roman way of life was at threat, Roman decided to fight Roman, rather than face the real threat. Most accounts have the Western army moving first. Some say it was one impetuous legatus who called his men to charge, and in so doing committed both armies to war. Ten thousand men died in the first hour, and the Nazi commanders, monitoring the situation from the commandeered war rooms under the Imperial Palace in Rome, could scarcely contain their laughter. It is a common tactic to divide and conquer. Rarely is an invading army granted the gift of their opponents primed and ready to divide themselves without any external intervention.

Within ten days, the Nazis had complete control of this world, and none of the other Romes had even the slightest suspicion of this fact.

By the German reckoning, this was the year 1957, by my way of thinking it was the year MMDCCX.

At this point, I had been the prisoner of the Nazis for sixteen years. An account of these times would be dull, at best. Life in gaol is one of routine. It is always a problem for a storyteller. How to convey the length and emptiness of each day, how to depict a life almost devoid of incident? I had a small cell in Spandau Prison, in the west of what had once been Berlin. This was a red brick building, built as a military prison about a hundred years before. There were four watchtowers, and I was kept in one of these.

At first, I was tortured. They used wrenches to pull a number of my teeth, and sawed off my left index finger. I was tied to a chair that was far too small for me, the injuries were left untreated, and led to blood loss and infections. I was deprived of all sleep, and in a matter of days I became delirious.

This was to be to the Roman Empires' advantage. I had seen so many other Romes that now, in my weakened state, the details blurred. In the forum of the Roma CLI of Terrance Ollacondire, there is a gigantic marble foot, contrived to appear as if it is hovering, like the sword of Damocles. An impressive spectacle. In my mind, it became a stone sword, and I ascribed some random number to this other Earth. My captors recorded every word I said on a magnetophonium. It gives me no satisfaction at all to tell you that so much of what I said was nothing but nugae. I felt I was telling the truth, I confessed all I knew. The only thing I kept from them was the existence of Angela. She was my strength, my guardian spirit, coming to me in my sleepless dreams. Her face was indistinct, she said and wore nothing. As I sat on my chair, she simply stood over me, her pale skin shining in the darkened room, broken only, at my eye level, by a notch of flame-red hair. She was something the Nazis knew nothing of, the only secret I kept from them.

After some months, torture had told the Germans all it could. I was given a bigger cell, assigned a nurse, Freiden, a pretty blonde girl of sixteen who visited me every other day. She was not my only company. At first, scarcely a day went by without some senior Nazi official arriving. Few spoke to me, some merely watched me, as if I were some rare animal in a private zoo. It was around a week before Herr Hitler's first visit. He said nothing, just stared at me, giving no hint of his thoughts. He would return half a dozen times, still saying nothing, staying around an hour. Soon, though, I lost my novelty value. From this point, my only regular visitor besides Freiden was Herr Abschrift. I thought at first he was indulging in what the German language calls Schraudenfreude, but everyone else would call feasting one's eyes, or merely "gloating". But I soon realised he prized me. I was something special to him, and I got the distinct sense he preferred my company to that of any Nazi.

Within a few months, we were ... not friends, but certainly possessing that which was akin to friendship. He brought a latrunculi set, made me teach him the rules of the game, and then played me, over and over. This was an act of some kindness. I knew from Angela - the Angela, that is, from the Nazi side of the Divide - that there was a game like this on these worlds, but the pieces and their moves were different. Abschrift joked that he had bought this set in the ancient past of Germania I, before Rome had fallen here. This was a newly-carved set, though, not one more than fifteen centuries old which had faded with age or become worn from use. As with my thoughts of Angela, this was a link with home. My Roman clothes and equipment had been taken from me, and without the bangle, I had been forced - literally - to learn the German language. The game pieces became tangible symbols of home for me, a source of great hope.

Freiden also proved a source of comfort, both spiritual and physical. She wore the uniform of the German army, and, over the years, held the rank of Oberschutze, then Gefreiter and Unteroffizier. Yet she was no monster. She was genuinely kind to me, not simply brisk and efficient. Freiden was happy to tell me of her life beyond the walls. Although I never told her as much, she reminded me of Angela... who, of course, on one Earth had also been a nurse and who had once tended to me as the German girl did now. The story of her life provided me with a human narrative, something that grew over the years. A shy young woman when we met, one with a domineering father, she matured before my eyes. Within two years, she had a secret lover, a soldier a year younger than her. This man I never met, nor saw a picture of, but - like so many of her friends and family - he became vividly real to me, an ersatz companion. They were soon engaged and married. Her husband, though, was cruel to her - I surmised as much from a bruise on her arm, and she admitted it - and wanted Freiden to do nothing but breed children with him. This led to several months of absence, when she fell pregnant, but she lost the baby and in such a way that ruined her chances of having another. Her husband had an affair, which she meekly accepted, then divorced her. Her father blamed her, and she had lost her religious faith and many of her friends. I became the man she confessed to. This, in turn, led to some small physical intimacies over the years. Never very often and never very far. A kiss, a caress, a touch. For our own different reasons, these were guilty pleasures, and rationed in such a way that the brush of her mouth or my finger was always an unexpected treat, a charged moment, however slight. We never talked of it.

From Freiden and Abschrift, I learned a great deal about the course of events from the German point of view. Of course, neither intended to tell me anything. My nurse must have been under strict orders not to do so, Abschrift's natural instinct would be to keep me in the dark, although he was an honest man and not prone to lying. But each gave me micae of information, and added together I could assemble a picture of what was happening. I was still interrogated from time to time, and the questions I was asked let me know exactly what my enemies did and did not know about the Roman Empire and my activities. In the years leading up to the attack on Roma DCX, they and I were almost entirely ignorant of any developments in the Roman worlds.

By this time, the Emperor of Roma I was an old man, having hit his century ten years before, and was not expected to live more than another few years. Advances in medicine and public health meant that the life expectancy of the young of Roma I was now around a century and a quarter - assuming, of course, the absence of warfare or political intrigue - but earlier generations remained lucky to see their ninety-fifth year. The long age of his rule was coming to an end, and for someone there would be the literally once-in-a-lifetime chance to take the reins of the greatest of Empires, one that was now even more prosperous than it had been, thanks to the contact with the other worlds.

It meant that the political class of Roma I was fully occupied when the attack on Roma DCX came. There was an heir to the Emperor named, his adopted son Eugenius. But, as was always the way, there had been other heirs named over the years, and there were also legitimate claims of succession to be made from other members of the Imperial household. And although the guidance given in the Emperor's will on who should succeed him was by tradition compelling, while the Emperor lived his will could always be altered. After his death, the army and Senate could always fail to ratify the will or dig up another version of the document - old or faked, it rarely mattered - with a name more acceptable to them on it. One must never underestimate the influence of the Roman people in these affairs, either. History is full of the mob taking to the streets and forcing change, but they rarely have to do that; the fear of the mob is enough to curtail the activities of some of the more ambitious men. The Emperor must always be acceptable to the people, even if those people don't have any direct say in his appointment.

The life of the career politician is dedicated to these practical considerations. Such men exist in a sea of events, rumours, scandals and financial realities. They spend their lives there, trading gossip, making deals. It becomes all-consuming, but it is an oddly effective system. All of them, it seems, translate their power into money and sex. There are plenty of bribes and mistresses, examples of insider trading and buggery. But the system allows the political class to identify the particularly heinous, the dishonest, the bankrupt. Such are the whims of the gods of politics that a small lie, repeated, will topple an otherwise competent man, while his incompetent, but honest, colleagues thrive. To survive a game with such unclear rules, men must have a certain cunning. But above all else, they must keep up. They must immerse themselves in the news, play their parts, bide their time. There is little else to such a life.

Rome has prospered under the rule of such people, but my view is the common one: these are odious, petty men. My distaste, I am sure, stems from a childhood where my father pushed me to become one of this political class... and from the knowledge that what I chose to do instead was far more important and productive.

The eyes of every Roman politician was on the succession, then. Once again, Rome proved to be its own worst enemy. Within a month, it was clear that Roma DCX was the scene of some terrible calamity. This information was never made public, but was common knowledge among the politicians and senior soldiers. Complicating matters was the Emperor's injunction on discussing the Divide or what lay beyond it. Those that knew of the Nazi Worlds also knew not to speak of it in public.

It meant that the Nazis had a whole year on Roma DCX without anything but the most cursory contact with other worlds. In the event, Herr Abschrift had neglected something. While he had set up some method of detecting the arrival of a traveller from an other Rome, he hadn't counted on a traveller arriving from beyond the Divide. There were, it was known now, five other Romes along the Divide. Diana was the first to realise that she could travel from one of these, into one of the Nazi worlds, then back to Roma DCX without being detected. The main gates of the Nazi fortress were impregnable, but they had left the back door open.

What Diana reported was not all bad news. After a year of occupation, the whole of the Earth had not been subjugated. The remnants of the Western and Eastern armies had joined up to resist the occupation. While there was a puppet government, led by collaborators and traitors who spoke of "reunification" and of a "greater Rome", it was not popular. The certainties of the last few centuries had been replaced by a new order, and this always scares the population. The persecution of the Jews was welcomed in some quarters, but most Romans are tolerant of other religions and races, and found the new rules that required the public identification of Jews and often the confiscation of their property to be unfair and baffling. The Nazis were behaving true to their barbarian roots. Himmler was systematically raiding Constantinople, removing the statues, prising off the mosaics. Rome was the scene of all the depravities a conquering army could imagine. Fuelled by a lurid imagining of Roman life, bacchanalian orgies were held and prisoners were forced to fight to the death in the Flavian amphitheatre or into work gangs ordered to tear down symbols of Roman rule.

Fifteen-hundred years before, in this fractured history, the German leader Odovacar had seized control of Rome. Now, his descendants did exactly as he did; organised races in the Circus Maximus and parades through the Forum. In creating such a caricature of Roman life, they both mocked and honoured us.

The Nazis and the Resistance each had their strongholds, each had to contend with vast movements of refugees and the associated problems of unrest and shortages. It was clear the Nazis had not allocated quite enough men or material to this war, but that they had done plenty to destroy the weapons factories and training camps of the native Romans. This was not the sterile deadlock that this other Rome had become used to: battles were fought, great routs took place, cities were burned to the ground and leaders on both sides assassinated. But neither side had quite the strength to overcome the other. The Romans built great military camps in secret places all around the world. The Nazis, who had expected to subjugate the world quickly, then use its own resources to fund the occupation, waited for reinforcements to come from beyond the Divide. I knew from my conversations with Abschrift that the Council of Hitlers was unhappy, and believed that enough military might had been committed to do the job. There are few generals who ever believe they have a surplus of men and arms to fight a war. The luxury of knowing that there were many hundreds of Nazi worlds, all with armies and tanks and ships and planes, had led the Nazis to complacency. It had led them to believe that such resources were ready to be moved to this front. Even on the worlds completely dominated by the Nazis, though, the armies were needed.

You must also understand that the military planners of Roma I had never, in their entire history, put a foot wrong. They had made mistakes, or been the victims of circumstance, but each and every time, they had learned their lesson... or been replaced by someone who had. They were not infallible, and they were certainly not smug, but they knew their craft. They were agreed that Roma DCX must be retaken, but unsure how this was possible.

Travel from other world to other world was achieved by the bangles. There were now only seven of these in the possession of my family's business. Using them, we could transport equipment and men from world to world. In practice, a man wearing a bangle could link arms with two colleagues. Up to another four - we had found - could grip or hug him. So we could transport seven people at a time. Each man could be wearing a pack, carrying a bag and have items attached to him... but only about as much as they could lift. We had conducted experiments, but everything to be transported had to be in direct contact with the man wearing the bangle. The rules were not obvious to us, and there were many loopholes and anomalies. The conclusion, though, was that Rome could not mount a full scale counterattack. We simply did not have the ability to send armies and war machines from one other Earth to another.

One thing the strategists in Rome realised was that all the other Known Worlds could now harbour Nazi spies, saboteurs and agent provocateurs. Such people operate best when the authorities do not suspect their existence. With the armies of every one of the several thousand Romes that had been identified looking out for German agents, it was easy enough to spread the net. Around a dozen were quickly rounded up. They yielded some useful information, but their greatest value was their equipment. They had devices that operated like shiners, except from Earth to Earth. These proved relatively easy to duplicate. At first, they were used simply to listen in to the German anisocyclorum. These were in code, but the Nazi's primitive encryption methods could be cracked with even the simplest clockwork abacus. It meant that both the network of spies, and their masters, based in the Nazi-occupied Rome could be monitored. Listening posts on all the adjacent Earths were set up, as was an army of slaves whose job it was to collate the intelligence that now poured in. British engineers from Roma DII were able to learn the German language very quickly. My father, taking an idea given to him by the Angela from beyond the Divide, commissioned a detection system that was able to monitor any movements between worlds.

That account makes it sounds as though all the Romes were now geared to war with the Nazis. This was not the case. Simple communication between Earths had invaluable commercial benefit. Once again, my family found good fortune. The aged Emperor of Roma I insisted on the usual caveats curtailing the new technology.

My father and Angela, I might add, never gave up hope for me. Don Vulpisus knew of my intention to head to the optimum Nazi world. I was missing, but presumed alive, deep within enemy territory.

The monitoring of the activity in the void between the other Earths led to some interesting discoveries. From the earliest days it was in use, the operators would hear anomalous noises or see momentary flashes of light on their scrini. At first, these were put down to either human or machine error, but patterns began to emerge. As well as a form of weather between the worlds, one with storms and periods of calm, there were travellers unknown to us. Not many of them. Barely one a week was detected, anywhere in - or rather between - the Known Worlds. But they were there, like shooting stars in the night's sky, leaving a wake in the medium between the worlds quite unlike those using either the rings or the Nazis' more brutal techniques. Regina and Terrance Ollacondire were sent to follow one of these signals.

I was already dimly aware of who they would find. Over our games of latrunculi, I would ask Herr Abschrift about his own origins. I lay it out here as though it was one, free conversation. In fact, each piece of information was prized from him. A sesterce of information here and another one there, and so on, until I had saved up a miser's hoard. He was not from one of the Nazi worlds, I already knew that. He clearly wasn't a Roman. I speculated, to his face, that he was from beyond another Divide, another great branch of history which split into innumerable boughs and twigs.

He laughed at that, and told me that he was from the True history. He was from Earth, then? Here he was less than candid, telling me that such was a matter for philosophers. Pressing him, he told me that it was fair to consider that he had *originally* been from Earth. I had already come to realise that people from his place of origin would never answer a direct question with a direct answer.

Why, I asked him, was he so sure that his was the one True Earth?

It was, he told me.

I asked him again.

'You spoke of the branches of history,' he said. 'Let us use that analogy. Your world, and every world you know of, is grown from a seed that has fallen from a great tree. They follow the patterns of that tree, adapting them for the soil into which it has dropped. But they remain mere saplings.'

Didn't all the mightiest trees start that way, I asked? His Earth may be the first, but why would that mean it was the greatest? Must the son always be inferior to the father?

'Your Earth is a parody of the True Earth, a mere dream of history.'

His world, then, was even more perfect?

'You do not understand.'

That is why I ask questions.

'Your world is ... limited. Condemned to repeat, to echo. Never to innovate. It falls into patterns, things you would dismiss as coincidence or destiny, but which just demonstrate a lack of imagination.'

E fructu arbor cognoscitur.

I thought at once of meeting Angela as a nurse in London. There was, I believe, only one Angela on this side of the Divide. Yet of all the hundreds of worlds, each with billions of people, I was carried to her. There had been other examples which I had ascribed to Fortuna's guiding hand.

I found it very difficult to imagine Abschrift's other Earth. My instinct was to imagine a place of larger, more magnificent cities, stronger men, more beautiful women, brighter colours, taller buildings, cleaner seas. I remembered the condescending look from the old man all those years ago, when he had looked at me as if I were a child.

Thoughts of the old man led me to another realisation: over the years, Abschrift was ageing. He had started out as a youthful man, probably in his mid-twenties. Sixteen years later, he could pass for thirty. Slowly ageing, then, but a contrast with the old man who, if you remember, in the time it took me from being a new-born baby to being a young married man with a career, didn't appear to age a single day. I raised the issue with Abschrift. He was a servant of such people, was he not? Or perhaps they were gods and Abschrift a demigod.

This made him smile. Those who had forged the rings looked like men, he told me, but each one of them had the power to bring any of the human gods to their knees. Immortality was the least of their abilities.

These, I asked him, would be the "Mirraflex" I had heard of.

That was just one of the political factions, Abschrift told me.

So his masters fought amongst themselves? How mundane. It was always something that disappointed me about the Gods, at least the Greek interpretation of them. They acted like human beings... no, they acted like the very worst characters in the theatres: flouncing off, adopting pointless disguises, impregnating every woman they so much as touched, getting angry over the slightest things, or setting out on the most ridiculous quests. The Roman way with religion had always been to avoid the more saporoperean aspects of the pantheon. Our Gods were more static and stoic, more self-contained. You could worship Mars and Venus without imagining them squabbling with each other, or fornicating the first chance they got.

'They don't just fight amongst themselves,' Abschrift said quietly, 'at least not in the way you mean.'

If such a race of beings could defeat an army of gods, then who could fight a war with them, I asked?

'Who indeed,' Abschrift replied quickly.

The lords who commanded Abschrift were divided into houses, chapters and factions. Abschrift was the servant of one House, Mirraflex. They had a reputation for brutality, but a distaste for it. Abschrift was their agent; a soldier, an aggressor. He had been sent here on a mission, and I concluded that - like the formless beast I had slain, so many years ago - his orders were to track down the original bearers of the rings. The Nazis had issued leaflets to their soldiers on the Russian front declaring that Russians weren't people, they were untermenschen. Subhumanus. And if that were true, if Russians were not true humans, then that justified any sanction against them. Abschrift thought like this, yet thought that my whole world was a submundus. Romans have always erred in the other direction; admiring our foes, singing of their virtues, sternly warning ourselves that our enemies have much to teach us. Not that we were ever any less ruthless in orchestrating the destruction of those who opposed us. But his was the Nazi philosophy. My history was not real history. It was a dream, that is what Abschrift had said. If I wasn't real, if none of the Hitlers or Romes were real, then what did it matter? These weren't true people dying. And he trod heavily, as he trod on my dreams, his boot in my face, forever.

Nothing mattered to Abschrift, except his mission.

He asked me about the old man several times, but I knew little and told him nothing. Interrogation reveals much to the interrogated, as much as it does to the interrogator. The questions Abschrift asked told me much of what he knew and didn't know. One question troubled him: had the old man explained his own mission here among the Romes and Germanias? Travel in obliquum or seitwarts, between the worlds, was not without great risk. Abschrift gestured to the latrunculi set; the old man and twelve of his colleagues had removed themselves from the board, placed themselves on other ones. It was utterly wrong to do such a thing. An illegal move. More than that, a dangerous one. What had this baker's dozen of conspirators been planning? Had they tried to raise an army? Had the old man talked of weapons, either ones he had concealed, or ones he hoped to uncover? He was clearly operating in secret, against the interests of the Great Houses. He had associates. What did he want?

And although I never told Abschrift, I thought I knew.

All those years ago, the old man had looked sad when I talked of my world as a utopia. He had asked me where people escape to. All wars lead to a displacement of people. The old man, and those who had left with him, had escaped Abschrift's "True history" and all its factions, in-fighting, paranoia and plotting. He had fled this War among the Gods, looking for a safe haven. And when a War rages across infinity and eternity, then where is there to flee to?

At a time close to the end of my captivity, as yet unknown to me, the Emperor of Roma I finally succumbed to old age. His youngest son, Eugenius, emerged safely as the successor. The customary purges and reshuffles affected the senior military, and once again plans to recapture Roma DCX were delayed. All the time, the Nazis' grip on their conquered territory grew stronger, and all the time they were preparing to launch further attacks. Roma I did a fine job of containment, and had good intelligence: it was far more easy for our spies to report on the state of Roma DCX than it was for Nazi agents to assess the extent of the Known Worlds. As another year passed, the situation was akin to watching the house next door burning down. The German incursion was clearly going to spread, if not extinguished.

However, Emperor Eugenius finally allowed discussion of the Divide, he increased the circle of military planners to include those from Roma I's strongest and most technically advanced counterparts. Finally, Rome had begun to accept the challenge.

Shortly after this, Terrance Ollacondire and Regina arrived on Roma XIII, following the detection of another traveller there. This was a world I had never visited, although you can see from the number ascribed to it that it was not far from Roma I. Our scouts had reported little of interest. Many centuries ago, the Emperor Hieronymous had successfully unified the various state-sanctioned religions. This, though, was a creed obsessed with death and the afterlife. To my tastes, at least, it took devotion too far.

Don't get me wrong. Even those of us who don't put our trust in the protective spirits recognise the value of honouring our ancestors. Whatever we have, we owe to them; whatever we are, we come from them. We should honour the lars. Even in my cell, many worlds from my own, I contrived a way to offer a libation to them, dedicating a small shelf as a lararium.

The people of this Rome, though, inhabited a necropolis. Bodies were inhumed in elaborate tombs, cemeteries forming long avenues and twisted alleyways. Underneath the city was a vast catacomb. In my Rome, such developments were curtailed on the edge of the city. Here they encroached into the centre, like weeds. Soon, the people lived and worked among the tombs. There was no distinction between the homes of the living, and the homes of the dead. Those ambassadors we had sent were seen as mere phantoms, and had soon left declaring this to be an other Earth of superstition, with nothing of value to teach us.

The fashion among the women of this world was to use cosmetics to bring a pallor to the skin, to darken their eyes, to dust their hair until it was grey. In my Rome and in others, rich men pay for professional mourners. This was a world of them; eyes red, lips trembling. Instead of music, the sounds of wailing wound through the streets. Regina and Terrance Ollacondire had considered disguising themselves to blend in, but there was no need. The locals simply accepted them as spirits. Regina saw this as a sign of their faith, but Ollacondire suggested it was simply symbolic of their struggle against reality. He and Regina walked the narrow streets of this Rome without being challenged.

They made their way to the Senate building, then to the debating chamber. In a room identical to a hundred others on other Earths, a fat middle-aged man in a dusty toga sat on his throne, patiently listening to one of the empty benches. This was the Emperor of this world, Crolix LI, and he shared a palace on the Palatine with the ghosts of all his predecessors. His Senate was one of spirits, and - like all the men of that world - the Emperor spoke to the dead as though they were the living. Where Regina and Ollacondire heard nothing, Crolix could perceive the most eloquent debate. He would intercede from time to time, then nod sagely. Regina and Ollacondire watched, astonished, as he told an empty room to come to order.

The symbols of Rome - the wolf, the eagle and so many others - had been replaced here with necromantic signs. Oil lamps had been replaced with fatty candles. Behind the throne was an extraordinary effigy. It was tall, with stick-thin limbs. This scarecrow wore thick black robes. Its face was a bird's skull, like the desiccated remains of an Aegyptian sun god.

The Emperor listened to the debate for what seemed like another hour, then called for a vote. Unhappy with the result, he stormed from the room, making sure before he left to genuflect towards the effigy. Crolix walked straight past Regina and Ollacondire, without acknowledging their presence, and called for a cohort of non-existent Praetorian Guards to fall in behind him.

Regina and Ollacondire stepped down onto the Senate floor. He moved over to the throne, looked over at the ranks of empty benches. She spoke to herself, breaking the silence to say that she sensed no presences. The ghosts of the Emperors were not in this place.

'Perhaps they're in recess,' the effigy suggested, stepping down.

Both my colleagues doubted their sanity. Both wondered if the dead truly trod the paths of this other Earth. Then reason prevailed, and Regina grabbed the man, tugging off the skull, a mask of bone that concealed an ordinary man's face.

'I nearly soiled my armour, because of you,' Ollacondire squawked, drawing his sword and digging it into their captive's ribs.

'Miserable bloody Romans, no sense of humour,' the man replied.

XIII.

The man behind the mask was Consobrinus Patruelis, a representative of an organisation known as Partes Paradoxum. This was, of course, the very traveller between worlds they had been dispatched to locate, and he was here on his own. Patruelis quickly settled his differences with Regina and Ollacondire, and admitted he was bored with Roma XIII, and eager to move on. The world was superficially attractive, he claimed as the three of them left the Senate, walking past yet another funeral procession. The religion - or "methodology", as he termed it - fascinated him. The three of them could agree this was a world of extremes.

When Regina accused him of being a Nazi spy, his sheer lack of comprehension was its own denial. Regina asked how he travelled from other Earth to other Earth. He laughed when he saw the bangles they were wearing, and revealed that he was from the same place they had been forged. He had come to this world for inspiration, he said. Where he came from, the idea that history was flexible was taboo. 'Wars have been fought over it,' he added. 'Or rather, wars have been fought to ensure that no wars are fought over it.' Here, he said, there were many thousands upon thousands of worlds, each with their own histories, each a functioning civilisation. The group to which he belonged, he said, revelled in difference, in pointing out the absurdities of the rules, and the hypocrisy of those who would enforce them. He saw our possession of the bangles as proof that 'they couldn't keep their Great House in order'.

It was immediately clear to him that the Nazis had not independently developed the ability to travel between the other Earths, and that Rome faced attack from more than one other Earth.

'It means that the War is spreading,' he said.

The three of them moved up to the Palatine, found a grove in which to sit and confer. Regina got straight to the point, as was her way: would Consobrinus Patruelis and his faction ally themselves with Rome?

He was cagey. 'I am not a soldier,' he told them. 'I cannot fight a war for you.'

'You are not wearing a ring,' Regina pointed out. 'How did you get here?'

'There are certain procedures ... ' he said, his voice trailing off.

'Answer the question,' Regina suggested, drawing her sword.

'Spatiumtempus can be made to fold,' Patruelis told them.

'How?'

'You wouldn't understand. All right, all right: the processes and equations of time are, or form, a *loa*. A traditional tempusnavis is not so much a mere vehicle as a multifaceted *event*. It's the calculations that are important, not the actual object. We in Partes Paradoxum exploit this "fact", and via ritual and complex invocation access the power of the loa to introduce non-linear pathways to causality, building alternative time-structures from the framework of raw history that - '

'You pray to the gods,' Regina translated.

'Er ... essentially.'

'Essentially?'

'Well ... '

'Is that all there is to it?' she pressed.

'Confess!' her companion added.

'Well ... er ... yes.'

'The first blow has been struck, Reg.' Ollacondire concluded.

The very next day, back on Roma I, the Emperor listened to this report and ordered the conversion of one of the larger palaces into an immense temple to Clepsydra Metiri, goddess of time. It was to take the form of a huge sundial, and inside great pumps and pipelines formed the largest water clock in the Empire of Empires. The walls were lined with clockwork mechanisms, all telling the time perfectly.

This took many months. Patruelis advised on the design. He was given the title consultor physicus, and a large budget. When completed, those that stepped into the Temple felt that they had stepped out of time itself, that they existed nowhere. From here, then, they could construct vessels like ships of the sea which could travel wherever they wished, providing the right offerings were made. The men of science were forced to concede that they didn't understand how the Temple worked, but a series of tests proved that it did. A fleet of ships that could travel between the other Earths was quickly commissioned.

The obvious strategy was to launch a counterassault on Roma DCX. Such a thing was now possible, at least in theory. When complete, the fleet would be able to ferry many thousands of soldiers to Roma DCX from an adjacent other Earth. The novice might think that a war is won by men thrusting swords or throwing javelins. Such men play their part, of course, but they need to be fed and transported. They need weapons and medical care. The Roman army has always been unrivalled in such logistical feats. Roma DCX was known territory, and some of its leaders and tacticians had been spirited away to an other Earth, or remained in contact with other Romes. Great plans were drawn up for such a landing as the Known Worlds had never seen before.

The Emperor, though, grew restless. He understood that the Nazis not only had to be driven back, but had to be utterly destroyed. At the very least, their ability to travel between worlds had to be ended. It would not be enough to recapture Roma DCX, which in any event was heavily-defended.

The Emperor's solution would be bold, and brilliant. He would take the fight to the enemy; striking at the other Earth across the Divide that bordered Roma DCX. It would cut off Roma DCX, which could then be liberated at the Empire's leisure. At a stroke, we would have a foothold - a gradus - in enemy territory, and the enemy would lose their foothold in ours. As the Temple was completed, so plans to capture a Nazi Earth were nearing completion.

Countless other Earths away, I had finally left Spandau.

I had been told the night before that I was to be moved, but not where. Smart clothes were brought for me. I had the anxiety all prisoners must have in such a situation, that my utility to my captors had been exhausted, and I was to be executed. Some part of me speculated that there had been negotiations with Rome, and a treaty signed, a condition of which was my safe release.

A few weeks before Herr Abschrift and I had been talking about the nature of existence. He had seen me reading books on astronomie and questioned me about what I felt the nature of the universe to be.

I should have said already that my captors gave me any books or journals for which I asked; they delighted in finding old manuscripts in Latin, which I learned had been the language of scholarship on this side of the Divide until very recently. Romans are practical people, interested only in daily life, not abstractions. While all the celestial bodies have been charted and catalogued, this was because most of the citizens held the belief that the stars somehow controlled human destiny. Hipparchus' theories did enough to satisfy us, and we had no real equivalent branch of science to the Germans' astronomie. Most of what I read in German science books seemed fanciful, much was clear nonsense, designed to glorify Hitler and his beliefs, not give any true explanation for the natural phenomena. But much seemed sensible. The people of this world, lacking the stability, peace and guarantee of a labour supply that had been granted to my Rome, had proved ingenious at investigating and exploiting the natural world to balance the deficit. There were hints, in some of the older books from before the Nazi triumph, of theories that dwelt on the nature of the atomus. This was now felt to be "Jewish science", and all studies in this area had officially stopped. I wondered just how much of the pyrobolus atomicus was the product of the race that Hitler so thoroughly and irrationally despised. As in every world, the phyleticus osor here wouldn't find any hypocrisy in enjoying the fruits of the labours of those they condemned.

As, I suppose, was my position now. I read the German science textbooks and learned, while hating the Nazis who fetched them for me. There had been great developments in the field of astronomie. The universe was far larger than had been thought even a generation ago. There were more stars in the sky than could be seen with human eyes. In 1924, an American astronomer called Edwin Powell Hubble had demonstrated that Earth existed on just one continent of stars, which he called a galaxy, and it was thought now that there were many such galaxies, making up the universe.

I told Abschrift that each of these galaxies must represent a group of worlds. The Romans in one, the Nazis in another. The distance from one star to another was immense; too immense to put into numbers. But the distance from one galaxy to another was many times greater than that. Abschrift listened to my theories patiently, occasionally asking me to back my speculation with some piece of evidence. This was one of the longest conversations we ever had.

In the end, he simply told me I was "sinnreich", or ingeniosus.

'You speak Latin,' he said. 'What is a universe?'

'Universus means the whole.'

'Yes. A universe is a whole cosmos.'

'*The* whole cosmos,' I suggested.

'No. There are many universes. Each is a whole. Each has only one Earth. It is impossible for one universe to contact another, by definition.'

This sounded like Greek sophistry, to me. I reminded Abschrift that neither he nor I now sat on the world of our birth. I went further, pointing out that he had facilitated the Nazis' contact with other Earths.

'What happens here is of no concern,' he told me.

Because we were not the True Earth?

'In der Tat.'

But if men - not to mention gods and monsters - from this so-called True Earth can come here, then surely men from here could travel to the True Earth and influence affairs there? I thought about this a moment longer, and continued that even this was not necessary. Merely by being here, those thirteen men from the True Earth were affecting events back home. Their absence had been noted, and was clearly felt to be important enough to warrant Abschrift's masters sending him to track them down. I never talked about the beast I killed in the snows of Regina's world to Abschrift, but it had been given a similar task. What I had learned led me to doubt that the monster and Abschrift fought on the same side.

I had no intention, I ought to say, of allying myself with either Abschrift or the beast. There is an old saying, that my enemy's enemy is my friend. Let us not forget an older saying: a plague on both their houses.

Abschrift nodded. 'You understand,' he told me. 'Whatever reason the old man and his colleagues had for leaving, they should not have done. Pandora's Box has been opened, and we must shut it, whatever the consequences.'

I masked a smile. His use of the old myth was presumably intended to create a connection between us. It merely emphasised his lack of learning. Pandora's Box had been closed, and swiftly, but it had been too late, and the consequences could not be contained or reversed. Abschrift may have worked for his gods, they may have granted him some of their gifts, but he was a mortal, and a fallible one.

Several days later, I was escorted from my cell and down onto the small lawn, where a staff car was waiting for me.

For seventeen years, now, the prison had been the extent of my world, and "outside" had meant this tiny garden. I had been allowed to exercise outside, for up to an hour a day. I knew every brick by now. At first, I had imagined scaling or smashing every wall of this paltry German keep, killing every man here before making my departure. If Abschrift or Freiden had been here, then they, too, would have died. Abschrift was a soldier, and he would go down fighting. I often fantasised about delivering the final blow myself, or insisting I performed the execution. Freiden was kind to me, and I to her, as I have recounted. But she was no friend, or an innocent victim of the Nazis. I would not wish her death to be a cruel one, but I wished her dead.

Latterly, as captivity had dulled the edge of my fighting prowess, I had conceded that I would need assistance, and imagined being liberated by a Roman legion. They would ram down the gates, swarm over the battlements and drag every German guard to his death.

It was strange, then, to see the gates crack open with a terrible squeal, and to be driven through them, out into the heart of Berlin.

The staff car was a Mercedes Benz, black and shiny on the outside, like a beetle's carapace. Inside was upholstered leather, polished wood and chrome. There was a driver, and an SS officer I had not seen before had joined me on the back seat. He introduced himself as Sturmbannfuhrer Ranzigg. My hands had been bound, but not tightly. I was no expert, but recognised there was hope that I could work myself loose of the restraints.

Much of the journey was on the new autobahns, and driven at tremendous speed. The window of my cell had faced inward, the small garden had been surrounded by the high walls of the prison. This, then, was the first time I had seen the city in almost two decades.

We slowed as we reached the edge of the Tiergarten, became entangled in traffic. This gave me my first close glance of the outside world, so much brighter than the photographs in the journals I had been reading. Swastikas flapped from positions on every corner. SS men patrolled the lazy streets. Much seemed normal, for the barbarian worlds, at any rate. A couple of pretty shop girls passed our car. They peered in as they walked past, smiled at us. I could see the driver in his rear-view mirror, grinning back.

The most obvious recent incursion onto this place was the vast televisifica screen now set up in front of the Brandenburg Gate, filled with the face of Hitler. He was announcing some further consolidation of his victory, his angry voice making it sound like an affront. This shocked me. Not the device. I had not been granted such a thing in my cell, but I knew of their existence. And what else would such screens show here, but the exalted leader? No, what surprised me was how aged Hitler was, now. A swift calculation, and I knew he was approaching seventy.

I barely had time to register this. The car was now on the Wilhelmstrasse, and would soon be on the new Reichstrasse heading towards the triumphal arch. Four motorrad outriders had joined us, and all five vehicles were ushered onto a special lane that led under the arch.

The reliefs on the side of the travertine masonry were glinting, like sunlight caught on gold. I think, instead, this was arcane energy, what in former times would have been called magic. A moment later, we were under the arch, and it was as if we were in a tunnel, one made of polished blue and silver metal, bright light twisting the patterns. There was still noise from the tyres, though, just as if we were on concrete. The outriders alongside us continued in a straight line, unperturbed. A minute later, and we emerged from under another, identical, arch, into the centre of London.

Ranzigg informed me - in his own terms - that this was the other Earth that faced Roma DCX across the Divide. I had been to this Germania before, as you will recall; indeed it was the first of the barbarian worlds that I had visited. I had arrived in a dusty London office, been assailed by the wailing sound of what I now knew had been a Luftschutzsirene. Seventeen years before, that London had been a dark, fractured place. Nothing, though, prepared me for how it had changed.

This had been Trafalgar Square. The column in the centre was gone, replaced by the archway from which we had emerged. The buildings all around had been dismantled, so that the area was a large piazza, a flat expanse of concrete, half a dozen wide roadways radiating off like the spokes of a wheel. Apart from those impositions, the surviving great wedge-shaped blocks of buildings looked untouched.

One half of the piazza was full. Neat rows and rows of grey and green tanks, armoured cars, trucks, artillery pieces, fighters and bombers. There was little sign of activity at this stage, they simply seemed to be parked, with a minimum of guards on duty, but it was still early in the morning.

Our car accelerated out of the piazza and down one of the new roadways for several minutes, then turned off onto a more ordinary street. I was no expert in the geography of this London, but by my estimate, we were heading west. Every so often, at the side of the road, there were slave gangs. They looked like native Britons, for the most part, but there were also some Africans among them. They were all male, and ranged from the youthful to the extremely elderly. Some of the gangs were marching to their allotted place of work, others were toiling to pave the roads, or clear up piles of rubble. It had been many centuries since a whole race of men from my Earth had been subjugated in this way. This was the just fate of the hardened criminal, not that of a general population. A few of the more daring among the slaves looked up to see the staff car and its escort, but there was little defiance in their eyes.

The steady drone of aircraft engines filled the sky. It was an overcast day, but there were many squadrons in the air, all heading the way we had come. It occurred to me that the vast Piazza Trafalgar, or whatever the Nazis had renamed it, would serve as a landing strip for the aeronavis. Reinforcements for the war in Roma DCX? I suspected that it was more than that; that this London had been prepared as a staging post for the next phase of the operation, a blitzkrieg against further other Earths beyond the Divide.

The car had left London now, and was out in open countryside. We were travelling at great speed along a smooth, well-paved road. The fields were being tilled by women in grey overalls, their hair tucked under red head-cloths. There was little traffic, mostly farm vehicles that moved aside quickly if they saw us coming.

Our destination became obvious three-quarters of an hour after leaving central London. It was a vast stone keep. Had I not seen the castle itself, I would have seen the airship masts. Three Zeppelins were casting their alien shadows over a building that looked much as it must have done for many centuries. We entered the town that surrounded it, and now we were just one of many staff cars, each trying to assert our authority and to reach the castle. A sign said this was Windsor.

'Go round,' Ranzigg told the driver. 'You know the back-streets.'

'We were told to only use the main routes.' But the SS officer didn't need to say anything, the driver knew better than to offer up more than a token protest.

Instead, he nosed out the traffic - losing one of our outriders in the process - and headed down a side-street. Soon we were driving along a narrow country road. Heavily-wooded, and with a high brick wall on one side. If I had not lost my bearings entirely, this would be the perimeter of the castle grounds.

Sturmbannfuhrer Ranzigg visibly relaxed now we were moving again.

A moment later, one of the outriders was smashed from his mount when a large stone slammed into him. A second skidded in the road, tumbling away from his vehicle, and our car ground to a halt.

'Keep moving!' Ranzigg yelled. But the car had a large metal pole transfixing the engine. A mere moment later, the driver was impaled by a second.

I had worked my hands free. Rather than deal with the terrified Ranzigg, I made escaping the vehicle my priority. I pushed open the door, threw myself out onto the road.

The two surviving outriders were standing guard, scanning the trees at the side of the road, from where the attack had been launched. They held MG-42 light machine-guns, a weapon I knew. It was reliable, but the rate of fire was so tremendous that it needed frequent reloading. They had yet to shoot a single round, of course.

They weren't looking in my direction, but Ranzigg would soon raise the alarm. I was considering my course of action when my prayers were answered.

Six Roman legionaries charged from the woods, three to the right, three to the left of where the German soldiers had been watching. They wore a lightweight version of the standard armour, helmets of a familiar design, but stripped of any showy crest or other decoration. The swords they carried were utterly familiar, though, and a welcome sight. Two legionaries attended to each outrider, a swift stab to the heart and a slash to the throat seeing them off.

The other two men ran towards me.

'Civis Romanus sum,' I told them. 'I am Marcus Americanius Scriptor.'

They hesitated, but believed me. Just as well, or I would swiftly have joined the ranks of the dead.

'There is a German officer in the car,' I shouted.

The six men, between them, dragged Ranzigg from his back seat, threw him to the ground.

'I am Quintus Glabellus,' the leader of this party told me, as we headed for cover. A name derived from his bald head, shaved closer even than most other Roman men. Behind us, one of the legionaries pulled Ranzigg with him. The other four were clearing away, as best they could, evidence of the ambush. They had found a ditch in which to conceal the car, and the motorbikes and bodies soon followed.

'In what legion do you serve, centurion?'

'The glorious Sixtieth Legion, known as the Draco. From Roma I, sir, just as you are.'

'How did you know where to find me?'

'We didn't, citizen. We're on a scouting mission.'

Glabellus quickly told me of events in Rome; the new Emperor, and his plan to recapture Roma DCX.

'Rome hopes to go on to conquer every Nazi Earth?' I asked. There were, I was sure, at least as many other worlds on this side of the Divide as on my own.

'I don't know the long term plan, sir, but I know my history. All we need is a buffer area. Keep the barbarians away from the Empire.'

'I've learned much of these worlds during my captivity,' I said.

'We'll have need of that, sir.'

I did not ask of Angela. How would this soldier know what fate had allotted to my family in my seventeen years away? Instead, I concentrated on the matter in hand. I learned that the Roman attack was imminent, and that this party was one of the final scouting missions.

'Something is happening here,' I told Glabellus, explaining how I had been taken from my prison and brought here, and that many senior Nazis seemed to be converging on this point.

Glabellus and his men were here to investigate the same meeting.

I interrogated Ranzigg, but the SS man said nothing. We left his body in a ditch. It was Glabellus who proposed the next course of action.

'As you are clearly invited to this meeting, why not go there?'

This gathering, for all I knew, was my public execution, but it was a lot of trouble to go to for that. Why drag me halfway across the galaxy?

So it was that I returned to the site of the staff car. I was found by a Nazi patrol, a couple of SS men who must have been in their cradles when I had first arrived on this Earth. They gave no indication that they were anything other than natives of this world. They spoke German, but the accent was heavy. These were British youths.

'Our car was attacked,' I told them. 'They looked like British Resistance fighters. I played dead, as these German men died defending themselves.'

They sneered at my cowardice, but the two men were certainly keen to move away from this place. They escorted me right through the palace gates, without once noticing that I now carried, concealed, a portable shiner.

Glabellus had given me quick instruction in this ingenious device. It was the size and weight of a large coin. Previously, the smallest such device I had seen had been a dozen times larger and heavier. There had been much technological advance while I had been away. It emitted its signals on channels that the Nazis were not known to use, but Glabellus urged me only to use it sparingly, lest they detect it.

This castle had once been the property of the royal family of the Britons, and from the style and appearance of the building it was old. At least for this world, where such things are measured in terms of decades and centuries. Now the swastika flew from most of the flagpoles; there were a few other banners here, the significance of which I was unaware of. The upper ward was full of black staff cars, autocinetum from a number of worlds, judging by slight variation in styles. They were being guarded by SS men, all in their best dress uniform. I was reminded of the Praetorian Guard; these soldiers gave off that same air of mixing ceremony with fighting prowess. It was tempting to imagine that they were here for show, but I had no doubt that these were handpicked, well-drilled men.

The Zeppelins moored over us eclipsed the whole castle, making this late morning seem like evening. Glancing up, I saw Hitler... disembarking, surrounded by a retinue of bodyguards, advisers, senior officers and civilians.

I was passed from one set if guards to another, to another. They seemed more concerned that my clothes looked smart than what they might conceal. Then I was marched into a reception room, the Waterloo Chamber, one full of a mix of people. Apart from the guards and the occasional waiter, most of the men here were in their forties or fifties. These were all veterans of the war, and the war had been a long time ago, now. There was one exception, a youth who had not reached his fifteenth year. He had cropped blond hair, but brown eyes. Vain old men colour their hair, dabbing out the grey, but this was the first time I had seen a young man with hair treated to make it lighter. The most remarkable thing about him, however, was that this unbearded youth wore an army uniform and held the rank of general. Was he from a world where the war had gone badly? The histories tell of many conflicts of attrition, ones only resolved when one side had wiped out every fighting man of the other. In such places, the women and children manned the barricades. I would find out soon enough who this young warrior was.

There was a seating plan by the door, which my escort now consulted. The high table was marked simply "A. Hitler" on the list, but there was more than one of them. Three of them I saw at once, sat at the high table, attended by servants in smart, fussy uniforms, two bodyguards apiece even here in this stronghold; especially here, surrounded by the ambitious, the impatient and the seething. The Hitler I had seen outside had not yet had time to get down here. The Hitlers were as old and drawn as the man I had seen on the teleficium of Germania I. More so. That man had been the ruler of the Nazi utopia. These were lesser men, their worlds not as securely under their control.

It has long been the Roman way to remind the Emperor that - during his lifetime at least - he is a man. At parades and coronations, a functionary is employed to whisper m*emento mori* into his ears. Remember that you are mortal. All around the room, there were nervous glances towards the Fuhrers. Was this septuagenarian really the master of the world? How long would that remain the case? He looked so much more frail than the man on the posters.

It was the undercurrent running through this gathering. No-one, of course, would dare voice the sentiment, or hint at it. But whatever control the Nazis exercised over public proclamations, whichever books or authors they burned, however strong their military, however they dictated what was taught in school, they could not control a single man's private thoughts. Each man had an 'interminable, restless monologue that had been running inside his head for years'. And it was, I had come to realise, the things unsaid that defined us. I had grown up as the proud member of a civilisation where values and identity were things known, not things to be defined and analysed. We simply were what we were. There were lawyers' ways of determining if a man was a Roman, but it was the feeling in the stomach that mattered, not the words in the mouth.

I came from a world with an absolute ruler. I well recalled the dread I had felt as a young man, when I had sent my Emperor an impetuous letter. I could read those German thoughts, then, as I was walked through the group to my table. There were few women, mostly wives bored to be here, but being loyally convivial. Here was an ambitious army officer, a little too old for his rank of hauptmann, hoping to do better under Hitler's successor. There was a merchant, fretting at the prospect of uncertainty, after so many years of Germany having it her own way. Most nervous of all, though, were the Hitlers' own retinues. The history of Rome has a number of common themes, but among the most consistent is that when the Emperor dies, his entire court is swept away with him. Surely the same would hold true here.

The Nazis boasted that what they had built would endure a thousand years. Now, though, some were fearful that the whole Nazi edifice would collapse with the death of Hitler, no more than a decade away. While I had been imprisoned, I had turned my mind to this subject. There were many thousands of permutations of history in the barbarian worlds. No doubt, on some of these other Earths, left to their own devices, the Nazis would build a lasting, stable civilisation, one that started to rival the longevity of the great empires of their history: the Aegyptian, the Roman and the Papal. But none of the other Earths were left to their own devices, not now. Just as Herr Abschrift had said, mere contact between worlds would change their destiny. Their course would be deflected. The Nazi worlds were already more homogenous than those of the Romans. Decades of co-operation between the worlds, an interchange of men and material, had served to eradicate difference, not celebrate it, as the Romans had. The German people, the Volksmasse, were one unified group, whichever other Earth they hailed from.

If a farmer grows just one crop, then he becomes vulnerable to the whims of fate. One form of blight, or too much rain, will destroy his entire yield. The prices at market might fall, ruining him. All farmers cultivate diversity. I had seen little of Nazi agriculture, but I imagined huge regular fields, tended by slaves or vast grey machines. No one method is perfect, or is suitable for every changed circumstance. This vast, uniform Greater German Reich could never endure a thousand years.

One of the Hitlers - I assume the man native to this other Earth - stood, and the chatter around the room died down without further prompting. Hitler began to speak. I cannot convey how compelling this was. The stare of the eyes, his posture, every gesture. It was an extraordinary effect, and while he spoke, all thought of a world without him was suppressed.

'By now, the armed forces of this and many other worlds have departed for their next great venture. The tausendweltreich prospers, but there is an enemy at our borders. A race enemy. Fifteen-hundred years ago, the German people faced the greatest empire the world had yet seen. We signed treaties with Rome that they ignored. As they absorbed lands that were ours since the dawn of history, they destroyed our towns, butchered our people, sold our women into slavery. It has taken centuries for us to regain our rightful place in world affairs. Still, the so-called "educated" classes around the world call us "barbarians", because we stood against Rome. They forget that the barbarians crushed the decadent, complacent Roman Empire in the end. Our chariots raced through their streets, their temples burned. Now we have a foothold in the Roman Empire. Rome wasn't built in a day, they say, but it didn't take the Reich much longer than one day to make the Eternal City topple. In a version of history where Rome never fell, Rome has fallen. Rome will fall again. The way has been prepared, through the sacrifice and toil of the people of this world. Two days from now, the armies of the Greater German Reich shall gather in London, and then the greatest invasion ever seen shall pass through the archway and sweep across the Roman worlds. A blitzkrieg that will be the largest in any history.'

All doubts swept away, the crowd were standing, almost screaming 'Heil Hitler!'. The chorus continued for several minutes. I remained seated. The Hitlers did so, too. The only other person not on his feet was the youthful general. He had his back to me, and was simply nodding.

This had been to my advantage. As all eyes had turned to the high table, I had reached into my jacket, and opened the shiner channel. Normally, I would be worried that the device was unable to hear a man so far away, but Hitler's oratorical skills were, for one moment, to his great disadvantage. I knew that every word would be heard by Glabellus and his men, concealed in the woods within a mile of here. I knew that every word would be relayed to Rome. Forewarned is forearmed, they say. Rome was poised to attack. Now they could choose their moment, and strike with a force that would make any German lightning-strike look like a tiny spark.

As the crowd's acclaim began to die down, the young general turned round and looked me straight in the eye.

Then he smiled.

XIV.

There would soon be larger invasions and greater slaughter, but until that day there had been nothing like it, in any of the Known Worlds.

The Emperor of Roma I had already been planning an assault on this other Earth. The physics (or magic, if you prefer) of Consobrinus Patruelis, and the toil of many thousands of craftsmen, had given us an armada of vessels with the ability to cross the Divide in great numbers.

These vessels, navispars, resembled large iron triremes, the oars replaced by rows of hieroglyphs that encased them in the subtle incantations of space. At the prow, a great ram. A tall mast to capture the anisocyclorum of shiners rather than the winds. Each vehicle could carry three centuries, around two-hundred and forty men, their weapons and vehicles. They sailed not on the sea, but - thanks to manipulation of the magnetic field of the Earth - hovered a couple of paces above the ground. This magnetic field, and the thick armour, meant the outer alvei could withstand even direct hits from heavy artillery.

The Emperor committed twenty legions - over one-hundred-thousand men - to the assault on this other Earth. They had already mobilised, and were poised on five worlds close to the Divide. Many of the battlefields of the Roman and Nazi worlds had seen larger forces assembled in their long histories, but none so well-trained and co-ordinated, none so clear of purpose. The finest officers and men any of the Romes had at their disposal, led by my brother, Titus Americanius.

Just before dawn on that most auspicious of days, there was a rush of wind and the sky over London went dark, as it suddenly accommodated many hundreds of navispars. A dozen or so headed for Windsor, powering there in a matter of minutes. The remainder arrived at the piazza containing the arch. One legion was all it took to secure the square, and the few dozen guards in the area were put to the sword. A cohort surrounded the arch itself, made the incantations that shut it down, preventing reinforcements from arriving from an other Earth. Bombardiers then took apart the unmanned German vehicles parked there from the safety of the air. Fuel dumps, useless to the Roman army, were simply set ablaze.

The first wave of navispars lowered themselves to ground level, and the men began hitting the ground and falling into formation. First out was the aquilifer of the Third Legion, who planted his standard in front of the arch. Soon, eighteen more standards had joined it.

Within ten minutes, every sign of German occupation had been scoured from this sector of the city, and it resembled more a vast Roman parade ground. Five minutes more, and the Londoners emerged. A handful at first, waving white handkerchiefs (a sign, apparently, they meant no harm). The Roman legions welcomed these poor people, dominated by the Nazis for nearly twenty years. Dressed in grey rags, white eyeballs peering from grimy faces, these emaciated creatures had been treated worse than any slave, even a convict, in the Roman Empire. The legionaries would have been shocked by what they saw. They would have offered the people rations and medicines. And, as word spread, many more Londoners would have emerged from derelict buildings and subterranean bolt-holes. Rome was the great liberator, civilisation would rule here.

Not so many miles away, in das Windsorschloss, I was summoned from my cell in the Round Tower and rushed to a control room deep underground. I had no time to retrieve my shiner.

Hitler - the one who had spoken the previous night - was hunched over a large table, covered in a large map of Southern England. There were many dozens of purple blocks on London, and a mere handful of blocks bearing the swastika scattered around the whole area. There were half a dozen very senior military men here. I recognised a few of them, including a couple of Rommels (one with an eyepatch), a nervous-looking Heinrich Mueller and a more confident Freidrich Paulus.

'The war has begun,' a man who looked a lot like General Udet told me, as two young soldiers tied me down to a wooden chair.

'It will soon be over,' I suggested.

Hitler's mouth twitched. Was it his attempt at a smile, or an indication of his trepidation? The others maintained an exclusion zone around him, staying two feet away, as though there was an invisible wall dividing him from the rest of the room.

The only exception was the young man, who seemed almost oblivious to the presence of the Fuhrer.

Hitler saw that I had noticed this, and smiled. 'This is my son, August. Not my son, exactly. That of my counterpart on alpha alpha alpha.'

The young man sneered at me. 'We thought you might like to see Romans dying. We're all hungry to see that.'

That simply provoked a smile from me.

Hitler had moved over to a couple of serious-looking junior officers manning telephones.

'Wind direction?' he asked.

'Southerly, mein Fuhrer.'

'Unleash Fenris,' Hitler commanded.

In the Norse myths, Fenris was the offspring of the trickster god, a huge wolf who would consume the world when released from his chains. I knew in an instant the only possible meaning of the order.

'It's not just an archway, Herr Scriptor,' August Hitler told me, 'and we knew about your radio.'

No-one alive now witnessed the atomic explosion that destroyed central London, but our scientists and poets have imagined what they would have seen.

A flash of light bright enough that a man ten miles distant, facing the other way with his eyes closed, would have been dazzled. A perfect circle of light, a sun on the face of the Earth, fifteen paces across. A single second later this energetic force had whipped up earth and rubble into a surging nimbus boletus that would grow to eight-thousand storeys' height. The winds created by such an explosive pressure were strong enough to blow down all but the strongest structures. The buildings of stone and concrete lost their roofs, windows and doors. All of the men within a mile of the explosion would have died in that first moment, destroyed by fire, crushed under falling buildings.

Then a moving wall of heat, that burned away the skin and eyes of all those within four miles of the arch. Wood, paper and the like evaporated in the firestorm, of course, but so did tile and glass. The wind moved faster than Aquilo could have ever marshalled; so many thousands of miles an hour it was impossible to measure. Then, the sound. One that made the air ripple like disturbed water, forceful enough to pull down weakened walls and shatter bones.

A quarter of an hour later, and clouds were just beginning to clear. The centre of London was a crater over a mile wide and two-hundred paces deep. Buckingham Palace, the Houses of Parliament, St. James' Park, Covent Garden, Charing Cross Station and the roads and buildings surrounding them were now burning gravel, raining down on the whole city. The Thames discharged into the crater, hissing and steaming. The rim was so hot it burned the air. For another half a mile beyond, there was little recognisable; exposed sewers and Tube lines, foundations if they had been dug deep enough. Miles away, around Knightsbridge and Bloomsbury, the largest and strongest buildings still stood. The blast, though, had killed all but two in a hundred of the population, and most of the houses were bare frames. Fires were spreading, uncontrollably. Five miles from the arch, the living barely outnumbered the dead, but almost all of them had serious injuries. Further out, in Brixton, Highgate and Putney, the buildings were merely heavily damaged. The top floors of the tallest had been sheared off, their contents and inhabitants scattered to the winds. Here almost everyone survived, but most were injured in some way, usually by flying debris, and all had ringing ears and burning skin. For those ten miles away, there was a strong wind and a shaking of the ground like an earthquake. Everywhere, a black rain of dirty water and debris.

Every one of the Roman expeditionary force in London was dead, of course. Few would have even survived long enough to be swept away with the fire and rubble, to realise they were dying. More than nineteen legions, their equipment, their weapons, their standards, had melted away in around the time it had taken Hitler to order their destruction.

I stumbled backwards, as if I had been struck, while the Nazi officers calmly reported the successful detonation of their bomb.

'My son's idea,' Hitler was saying. 'It didn't occur to me. Any of me. We've beaten the Russians, the British. Perhaps it takes my son to beat the Romans. Tomorrow belongs to us, Herr Scriptor.'

'Since the time before Augustus,' I started quietly, 'a man who kills a Roman citizen might as well slit his own throat. Rome will avenge this. The spirits of those men will follow you and watch justice done.'

August Hitler just smiled. 'No,' he said simply.

I swore an oath at that moment that he would die at my hand.

One vexillation had not been in London. A dozen navispars, containing half a legion, had been dispatched to Windsor.

As they made their way over the vast, scarred city, then the lush green fields, they would have been sending dispatches to the main force, and vice versa. They arrived around the time the bomb was detonated in London. Could they have imagined the fate of their colleagues, when those signals abruptly ended?

No matter. Now they arrived at the Windsorschloss. Before the Nazi sentries had time to respond, the attack was launched, magnetic bolts swiftly puncturing the three Zeppelins moored overhead. Had the planners expected what happened next? The airships burst open, section after section became flame, and the burning wreckage showered over the castle, setting the roof ablaze, blocking the main gate, devastating the courtyards. Scorpions were employed to pick off the guards from the walls. The navispars circled the castle, cutting off the escape routes.

Then the legion deployed, dropping out of the ships on lines, taking up positions, forming into units. Ramming teams set up at the main entrances, swiftly breaching defences that had long elided from the formidable to the ceremonial.

The SS men guarding the castle were not expecting an attack on this scale, and were outnumbered five to one. As they reached for their Walthers, Lugers, Mausers, Sauers and Dreyses, then fumbled to load them up with ammunition, the legionaries tore into them with their swords. German cloth was no match for Roman steel. Those Germans who tried to put up a fight were beaten down, their heads cracked open. Roman legionaries, segmented armour glinting silver, swords held out in front of them, kevlarian shields deflecting the few bullets that were fired, surged through the castle like water through a burst bank.

The sounds of hastily bolted doors splintering open and German screaming percolated down to the war room. Hitler looked scared, and his officers reported that all "radio" signals were being jammed. The senior officers scrambled to get to defensive positions, hurrying from the room.

I took my chance. I lurched down on my chair, breaking it. Now I was free. I smashed the skull of the nearest leutnent with the edge of one of the broken chair's legs, then twisted my weapon around, faced the sharp end away from me, bound over the table, and plunged the point into Hitler's eye. This was an old man, and whatever inner strengths he had, they were not physical. I twisted the stake, screwed it down through the matter of his cerebrum until I felt it reach the back of his skull. He was still screaming, but could not live much longer.

I had not forgotten August Hitler. He had drawn his pistol, and now levelled it at me.

But I had calculated my moment correctly. The door of the war room burst open.

'Gladius!' I shouted, and the centurion who was first through he doorway had the wit to obey my request without question. I caught the sword effortlessly, despite the many years since I had held one. The weight was natural to me, an extension of my arm, as my instructor had told me it should be. Now I swung the sword round, a slashing blow to the Little Hitler's throat, a silver streak in the dark.

It found only air.

'He vanished,' the centurion said.

'Gone to an other Earth,' I told him.

'Let him go. Wasn't it the ancient custom to let one man survive a battle, so that he could return home and tell his people the circumstances of their defeat?'

I told him how the "defeated" Hitler had just obliterated London, and he paled.

'My brothers, sir, served in the Sixteenth ... ' he said.

'And I too have lost a brother today,' I told him.

The centurion disagreed.

'Titus Americanius was the leader of this assault, was he not?' I asked.

'Yes, sir. But Titus Americanius led the attack on this castle.'

When I saw my brother, I did not understand at first. This was my younger brother, yet he was a man more than a decade older than me. Many years, of course, had passed since we had last seen one another. He was still lean, but there was the first hint of grey in his hair. Mine was sal et piper, and much of my muscle was now fat.

Still, we clasped hands and embraced.

'We knew you were not lost,' my brother told me. 'Your wives have waited for you, like ... which one was it? The hero whose wife waited for him.'

'Odysseus?' I suggested, noting with a laugh that my brother had clearly not devoted much of the intervening time studying literature. The image of Angela as Penelope warmed me, though.

'She ... they are safe, your children have grown into fine young people.'

'London ... ' I replied.

Titus nodded. 'They used some unknown weapon. Everyone is dead. The eagles are lost. I cannot return to Rome.'

I kicked Hitler's body. 'The day is not without its little victories. The barbarians have lost at least one of their warlords. Search this castle, and you will find scientists who know the secrets of the atomus. And I have learned a lot.'

So it was that I returned across the Divide. Before I left, my brother tried to inform me of everything that had passed. The new Emperor. The death of Don Vulpisus five years before, on one of the Nazi worlds. The new ally, Consobrinus Patruelis, and the techniques he had granted us. Many new Roman other worlds had been discovered, and the Nazi threat had led to formal arrangements that banded a number of the most significant of the Roman worlds together, under the aegis of Roma I. My family's fortunes and influence had only increased.

For most, though, the war with the Nazis was something distant, even abstract, just as the outcome of battles along the Rhine had made little difference to the everyday lives of those in Rome at the time of Augustus and Tiberius. The Emperor, while allocating great resources to the war, and making speeches about the struggle against the barbarians, had been careful to keep any tangible sign of the fighting from Roma I. When I returned to the Earth on which I was born, it was on board a merchant ship from Roma D. The ship's clockwork captain was fascinated by my adventures and, despite his nature, was able to give me a sense of how the ordinary man was feeling.

The merchant ship arrived in the Atlantic of Roma I, where it set down to become a conventional ocean-going vessel. We were half a day away from my family villa on the East Coast of America. I sat on the deck, free and alone for the first time in many years. It would be reassuring to report that the sun shone more brightly on this Earth, that the breeze was more sweet, the sea darker. But had I been on Germania I, in the same spot, I am sure I would have seen exactly the same sights.

There was no other shipping, at least not for the first few hours. As we approached the family villa, though, we saw the first Balaenae. The design of these vast freighters had hardly changed in two-hundred years, so the last twenty were nothing. As the great Jupiter Libertatis became visible on the horizon, I admit that I wept, knowing I was home.

* * *

That night, I couldn't sleep. I lay, the reassuring weight of my wife pulling down the culcita on either side of me. If I reached out an arm, it found a bare leg, buttock or back. The warmth of Angelas' skin, the rhythm of her breathing was nothing compared with the love radiated. I had thought a great deal about Angela during my captivity, fantasised and idealised. Nothing in my mind was as heady as her actual scents and tastes. As I touched her, and she touched me, the reality was solid, irresistible.

After almost as many years on this Earth as her native other Earth, the Angela I had liberated was now identical to the one I had married. They had both gained a little weight and a few lines to the face. It had only made them more beautiful. The two women who were one woman had endured their own captivity while I had been gone. They had kept each other strong, sat together and talked of the day I would return.

Not that they had spent the years idly waiting for me to walk through their door. The Angela native to this world had become a powerful businesswoman, someone with the ear of the new Emperor. She co-ordinated the family business now that Angus Inducula was growing old. The Angela from the Nazi worlds had become a physician, and had married the medical knowledge of her own world to the technological superiority of Rome. She had discovered - or rediscovered, such distinctions being hard to make these days - many vaccines, and simple but effective surgical and hygiene techniques. The Angelas' nature was not generally known outside my family, and most people assumed she was just one exceptionally talented and hard-working young woman.

Everywhere in the villa, there were little differences. Buildings had been extended, towers had been added, new gardens had been laid out. New slaves, of course, new statues and other decorations. But everything fell so easily onto my eyes. Every change had been an improvement. This world was right. I thought, for the first time since I had left Germania I, of Herr Abschrift, and his insistence that his was the true history. It had never been a claim I had accepted, and now it seemed absurd. Whatever plan Abschrift and his masters had for my world, for all the Known Worlds, I was confident we could prevail.

So far had things changed on Roma I that the new Emperor came to visit me at my family villa, I did not have to go to the Imperial Palace. The Emperor and his entourage flew in two days after I arrived, and were put up in our guest quarters. Think back to the day of my birth, and my father's hopes for our family. My father had become an old man in my absence, shockingly so, if I was truthful, but his dream had been fulfilled.

Titus had taken it upon himself to be ashamed at the loss of so many men in London. It had been his operation, planned for so long. He had been unaware of the pyrobolus atomicus, and now many legions were gone forever. Great dishonour fell on a legion that lost a battle, but the survivors could rally round the eagle standard and rebuild. There were no survivors of London, and no eagles.

No Roman general had ever lost so many men, let alone so quickly and so utterly. Now my brother joined us at the villa, inconsolable. He offered his life to the Emperor during our first audience. The Emperor tearfully replied that he, too, should take his own life. He was the ultimate commander of the armies, the man entrusted by the Senate to protect Rome, and so it was his loss. The two men hugged each other, bawling and offering manly protestations to the gods.

I quickly grew impatient with this self-indulgent nonsense and bid them to fall silent. Neither man could have known or predicted the existence of the Nazi pyrobolus atomicus. It was a secret weapon, rarely used even at the height of the Hitlerian Wars in the barbarian worlds. The loss of life - Roman and native - had been appalling, the methods disgusting. But we now had an example of their secret weapon, and could develop our own.

The Emperor insisted that there was one course of action; we must learn to split the atom, and destroy every Nazi world. The Roman people, now word of the defeat was spreading, were demanding Hun blood. There were already reports of German shopkeepers being molested, German temples being desecrated. We must strike at the Nazis on their own territory. Demonstrate our strength, at the point when they assumed we would be licking our wounds.

Two things prevented immediate retribution. Firstly, building a pyrobolus atomicus was no simple matter, time-consuming and needing special minerals that could only be found in a few places.

I argued most strongly that the Emperor study the history of the barbarian worlds. The face of it was that there were hundreds of Nazi worlds, but by my reckoning there was not one, not truly. The hearts of almost every person on our world was Roman. Even those, I dared to say, who did not like or approve of the Emperor did so because they championed a different version of Rome. All were proud to be part of the Empire, and every citizen would fight to defend their rank and home. The Nazis, on the other hand, were a recent plague, on other Earths with many dozens of nationalities. The maps might say that Britain, France, Poland, Russia and all the other lands were now part of the German Reich, but their peoples were proud, and could be mobilised against the Nazis. Our way was better, we could demonstrate this to the races of the Nazi Earths, and they would rise up. They knew of Rome, their culture celebrated us, albeit in fractured form.

But we must strike back. The counterattack would not be easy, but it was necessary.

The Emperor promised to stay his hand.

On the second day of his visit, he was met by scouts who had been sent to the battlefield of London to search for any sign of survivors or the eagles. They were, it appeared, physically weakened by what they had seen. Millions dead, buildings shattered hulks. They reported on the black rain, and how the survivors had already begun growing sick, as though the atomic explosion had released plagues into the air. Our scholars theorised that this was due to the exposure of corpses, and to the release of poisons. It was well known that when a building burned to the ground, many harmful substances were released into the area.

With a whole city ablaze, every toxin and germ would have been freed.

A week later, the scouts' malaise became more pronounced. They had headaches and no appetite. They began to vomit and defecate uncontrollably. We had already placed them in isolation. They became fevered. Angela ministered to them, diagnosing that they had weakened blood and that their bodies had fallen to the wolf, or "cancers" as she called it. They started bleeding, and lost their hair. They died soon afterwards.

This sickness was known to the Romans of my world. In my absence, seven years ago, the priests of the temple of Jupiter had arranged a voyage to the heavens. They hoped to send men to the celestial wanderer - planet, in the German tongue - that bore the name of their god. But as they prepared for this expedition with test flights to Luna, the men they sent, healthy soldiers, died in much the same fashion as the scouts to that other Earth, and in a matter of weeks. The scientist Albertus Unuslapis had concluded that properties in the fabric and atmosphere of the Earth, every Earth, protected us from the toxic forces that flooded the heavens. The Nazi weapon opened the gates to them.

We would learn, much later, that the poisons in the air, the radiatio atomica, as we came to call it, would remain present for years in London, bringing silent death. Walking in the centre of that London was suicidal. It would be ten years before it was considered safe. Ninety miles downwind, many people died within two days to a fortnight. Twice that far, and still people grew sick.

This was not simply the effect of some large bomb, this was an appalling weapon, an evil. One of the scouts the Emperor had sent was his most trusted friend, his brother-in-law. The Emperor cradled the man's head as he died.

The Emperor returned to the audience chamber, summoned us and commanded that all the wolves and eagles of Rome be mobilised. My plan was the one that would be followed. The Romans would be a beacon of hope, and would liberate the whole of creation. The scourge of the Nazis would be wiped from the Known Worlds.

Germania delenda est

XV.

Each Roman legion - and this is true on virtually every known Rome - is a fighting force unto itself, with a long and proud history, its own traditions and way of doing things. A legion has trained together, exercised together, drilled together, lived together. Each soldier trusts his comrades, to the point where each legion is almost a world. Each legionary was a citizen, and they'd volunteered for tours of twenty to twenty-five years. The legion's fort was their life, containing everything they needed. Each legion was made up of around five-thousand men, with about as many support staff and hangers-on in and around every camp. Each legionary was ready to take on any task his Emperor ordered, and would be willing to march to the end of the Earth to achieve it.

The Emperor now commanded them to march a great deal further than that. Summoning five of his fellow Emperors to Roma I, my Emperor called on them to send their best legions to fight the Nazis. The latest reports from the London wasteland were handed around. The regent of Roma D committed the fearsome "Ferrum Legion" to the struggle before the others had finished reading. The Emperor of Roma CLI committed his "Curcurbita" and "Calceus" legions, his crack suicide squads, his inquisition and his most famous knights. Diana, now Empress of Roma VI, summoned a dozen legions of the ferocious female warriors of her world. In all, the six Emperors between them were able to muster over a hundred legions, more soldiers than it had even been possible to raise before.

Practically every navispar had been lost in London. Those that survived, and those that had been built since in dockyards across the Known Worlds, would be valuable. They were to be used just as ferries, not in the combat role that had originally been intended. Roman armies would arrive in the heart of hostile territory, and then would be left to their own devices.

The campaign I had planned was simple, direct and began swiftly. Four simultaneous landings were made, on four barbarian Earths a little way beyond the Divide that had been scouted and found to have active resistance to the Nazis, but to be otherwise unremarkable. Careful scouting had revealed gaps in defences, or ill-conceived concentrations of troops. The forces of the Reich were becoming complacent on a number of worlds now. It was a lethal combination, often seen in the histories of the Romes: a vast army had stabilised a situation, but not to the extent that it was possible or desirable to demobilise them. It meant a lot of soldiers with nothing to do; never a happy situation, and these men had to be kept disciplined with unpopular drills, or diverted by costly entertainments. The Nazis had cleverly combined the two, so that the idle soldiers were given victory marches and parades, and great festivals celebrating "deutschtum", or Germanness, were arranged. It rewarded the soldiers and kept them busy.

We had other ways of occupying their time. Germania V was the scene of the first great land battle of the campaign. The Fourth and Eighteenth legions of Roma I marched on the German parade grounds at Nuremburg, in classic first formation, crashing their swords against their shields. This caused panic and confusion in the German ranks. As the Roman soldiers appeared, the ballistic attack began, smashing the obvious escape routes for the natives - and the roads any reinforcements would have to take - and spreading mayhem.

The Nazi soldiers were involved in ceremony, not a real military drill. There were tanks and rifles here, but none of them had ammunition. The men had only the bullets in their pistols, if that. They resorted to hand-to-hand combat, but with improvised weapons. Many were young men, unused to their enemy putting up much in the way of resistance. For more than a decade, here, opposing the Germans had been done with stealth, with the concealed explosive and acts of devastation. The men of the Roman legions were generally older, veterans of proper battles and ruthless training. They had known hardship and labour. These men marched through the German ranks as if they were not there, and soon they were not.

No effort was made to hide our attack. On the contrary, we had stationed our own cinematographici artifex and shiner masts around, and now began sending the message to this whole world. Those watching the big screens in the centres of towns would - until the German engineers thought to cut the power - see scenes of crack Nazi troops being put to the sword, and the officers degraded.

Within the hour, riots had started on English and French city streets. The Nazi authorities faced difficult choices, torn between a desire to attack the Roman invaders and a fear they would lose control of areas they already held. Where to reinforce, where to abandon? They couldn't win, but made the fatal mistake of trying to do both, diverting forces for a counterattack on the Roman legions marching through the fatherland, while trying to suppress the insurrection that, by nightfall, was all across their Greater German Reich.

Our first act had been a covert attack on the archway in this Berlin, preventing any reinforcement from an other Earth. We knew, though, that word of the attack would be making its way to Germania I. Three other worlds saw the same sort of landing, brilliantly executed. A dozen other Germanias saw feints and diversionary attacks, usually on the arches that led to other worlds, or surprise assaults on command centres or targets of opportunity. Five Hitlers died that day, three assassinated, two in battle. Our strategists had worked through a number of possible German responses, and had correctly guessed that they would hesitate to use the pyrobolus atomicus. The London they had destroyed was a carefully set-up trap deep in the territory of a conquered enemy. They wouldn't condemn their own people to the same fate, at least not lightly. Germania V and the other worlds we attacked were unremarkable provinces, but contained loyal Germans.

Within two days, we had established a bridgehead, and set up camp. I was on Germania V, in a fort that the Eighteenth legion had thrown up on the outskirts of Berlin. We had invited the tribal leaders of the British, French, Americans and Russians here, and such was our dominance that we were able to offer them safe passage. Defeating the Nazis wasn't easy, but a process that would lead to an inevitable conclusion had begun here. Our aeroplani insectatorii, new Eagle fighters with magnetic engines, had swept across the skies that day, dissecting the Luftwaffe and strewing their remains over Germany. There were a few German squadrons active, though, and our negotiations with the chieftains were punctuated by anti-aircraft fire.

The American chieftain was a man called MacArthur, and he was mainly concerned with the Atlantic Ocean. He assured me that his people could expel the Nazis from the whole of the American continent, and what he called "the Pacific theatre", if only the German U-boat patrols in the Atlantic could be neutralised. I sent word back to Roma I requesting that a few of our precious navispars be used for this duty. Romans from my world had been practising the art of cryptography for millennia, and as I have said, we had long ago deciphered the Nazi codes. We would send signals that appeared to be from the highest authority in Berlin ordering the U-boats at sea to surface, and pick them off. Our bombers could take care of those in port. MacArthur was also concerned with the

Japanese, here as in many other Earths allies of the Reich. That was a problem for another day, I suggested. If Nazi Germany fell, its allies would start rethinking their plans.

The British and French had a harder task; the Nazis had been in control of their territory for a long time, and were entrenched. For the strategic purposes of Rome, this mattered very little. We didn't even need to sack Berlin, only prove it was possible to do so. The Germans of this world had so many problems of their own, now, that they could not spare anything for the greater war effort. Every man and machine was needed here.

The four leaders all wanted Hitler for themselves. An impulse I understood, and I shared their disappointment that he had been killed by an anonymous bomb during an early air raid.

I told the chieftains that I knew the history of their world; I was very open about the fact I came from an other Earth, and while it seemed incredible to them, what better explanation was there? I told them that they all had their own differences, but that they faced a common enemy. Rome, I said, would remain here to provide an international framework. We had much to teach this world, and would rebuild their lands for them. Civilisation would return, better than this other Earth had ever seen. I had set up a large moving mosaic scrinium at one end of our meeting chamber, and now set it in motion. It was merely a set of images from my world. The simple beauty of the American housesteads, the rightly-famed gardens at the heart of Lutetia Parisiorum, a chariot race in Piccadilly Circus, the peerless towers of Nerograd. Images of strong, wise, happy Roman citizens that weren't merely on a poster, but lives that men lived, and our simple message was that this was how it could be here.

This case was made on three worlds. The fourth we had attacked, Germania XIII, was proving a little more problematic, and it would take almost a month before Hitler's cella loricata was stormed and he was dragged out to face Roman military justice. Fighting there proved vicious and costly. In that time, though, we had swept back over a dozen further Nazi worlds, and recaptured Roma DCX. The world where London had been destroyed we avoided almost superstitiously, but we had effectively cut it off from the tausendweltreich. In all, then, we had restored one other Earth to the Roman Empire, and seventeen barbarian worlds were now under our control. Without an archway on any of these worlds, the Nazis were unable to counterattack. None of these Earths had pyroboli atomicuum, and were spared the firestorm and black rain. On some worlds, we found ruined cities that had suffered that fate in the past. For hundreds of miles around, the people were sick, their babies deformed or mentally retarded.

Germania V had become, for no obvious military reason, the regional headquarters of the campaign. If you are keeping track, you will note that this other Earth was the one on which Angela had been born. It was sentimentality, no doubt, that led me to set up fort in the Buckingham Palace of that London. It was, by now, nineteen years since I had liberated Angela. This London had survived Nazi occupation relatively unscathed. The museums, palaces and galleries had been looted, but the invasion had come swiftly, not after the sustained bombings seen on other worlds. The bullet-holes were still visible in some of the buildings that had held out, white dots against the soot that covered most walls here. The Nazis had set up their administration in Whitehall, and fighting had been elsewhere in the country. The Midlands were fields of rubble, cities like Birmingham, Rugby, Wolverhampton and Coventry had been razed to the ground in years of street-to-street combat.

I had much work to do, and stayed in London. I had the men at my command fortify the palace grounds, surround it with ramparts and ditches. I commissioned Gropius, one of the finest architects of my world, to build a new palace in the modern Roman style. This would operate as a command centre, co-ordinating the campaign that now raged over scores of worlds, but it would also give people of London something monumental to look up to, to inspire them. So as not to alienate the natives, the existing Buckingham Palace would be incorporated in the grounds, and I was careful also to order the construction of a temple to the Christian gods - the largest that world had ever seen - by clearing the derelict area of Highgate. I chose not to send for Angela until this work was complete, and had slaves begin a search for her family and friends here. None were ever found.

Elsewhere in the world, the young Queen of England, Margaret, reigned over a British Empire that included almost everything it ever had but the British Isles themselves. She ruled from a sandstone palace in the aptly named Queen's Park, in the Canadian city of Toronto. Oddly, she made no claim on London now, merely dispatched ambassadors to welcome me. America was strictly neutral, Italy and Japan had extended their spheres of influence in Africa and Asia respectively. The German Reich covered Europe, and had been a place of consolidating prosperity, with banditry rife at the edge of its territory. The same challenge, then, facing Rome nearly two-thousand years before. We had stopped the heart of this Nazi empire, razing Berlin and smashing the military infrastructure. The factories and naval bases were gone, as had all central communications and control. The Reich here was shrivelling up into small areas ruled by rival generals, who were little better than local chieftains, and who could be picked off by native resistance groups, let alone the three Roman legions at my disposal.

At my instigation, the Roman Empire made its first diplomatic contact with fascist Italy. I could not spare the time to go to the Rome of this other Earth, but the Italian ambassador thoughtfully prepared a photoephemeris showing scenes of his capital city. The sight of ancient ruins - few of which had survived at all in my Rome, except in name, some of which had never been built - among barbarian buildings and roads was a strange one. The ambassador was a Roman, at least in the sense that it was his home city, and was able to answer many of my questions. He had many of his own for me. It shocked me to think that the old Roman buildings and statues had been raided by successive generations of barbarians for their own structures. Then again, it had ever been thus. Even in my

Rome, some of the marble used in new buildings had originally been quarried in the time of Augustus. Still, there was something disconcerting in seeing the column of Marcus Aurelius surmounted with an image of some saint, or in knowing that the stone of the Circus Maximus had been systematically looted to build a vast fortress for the Pope.

The campaign against the Nazi worlds was co-ordinated from my new palace, long before construction was even completed. In practice, my brother Titus Americanius was in command of military assaults, I took charge of consolidating victory and organising the new order for these barbarian worlds. We worked together, with the level of trust and co-operation only possible among family members. There was a great gallery in the depths of the palace, a long room where every known world in this galaxy - well over a thousand, now - was represented by a large glass map. It demonstrated the scale of the problems facing us, but also the vast reach of the Roman army, now.

I freely admit that one of my decisions was to cause problems for years to come. These liberated other Earths were now Roman worlds, part of the Empire of Empires. There was a constitutional problem, though: these worlds had no emperor, so who ruled here? Since the discovery of Roma II, as I have recounted, the Emperor of my world had insisted that he was but one among many emperors. He was, as he put it, primus inter pares. There had always been the element of polite fiction about this injunction. Roma I was the supreme Rome, power and influence inevitably gravitated to it, and its Emperor was always the supreme Emperor. I could have devised some polite fiction of my own, decreed that the liberated Earths were somehow held in trust by the Empire of Empires, or devised some power-sharing arrangement or complex legal formula. But I was exposing these other Earths to a great deal which was new, and naturally frightening to them, already. I didn't think it would be wise to introduce to them the whole mass of Roman law, a system that would have daunted Theseus had he all the string in the Known Worlds. A man can have only one master, and every subject in the Roman Empire needs an emperor. The simplest solution was to grant dominion over the liberated other worlds to the Emperor of Roma I. On the Roman side of the Divide, every world but one was happy with this arrangement, which they rightly saw as pragmatic and nominal. It was on Roma I, ironically enough, where dissent was heard. Senators stood up to denounce the Emperor multiplying his own powers. Many citizens of this Rome were unnerved to think that they now lived in no more than just one province of their Emperor's territory.

I had anticipated the next problem, which was easy enough to predict from a simple study of Roman history. The peoples of the liberated Frances, Englands, Americas, Russias, Indias and Chinas had been freed from an oppressive regime. Rome, with its firm ideology, authority and military supremacy could superficially be thought of as just another such force. Indeed, in our political parlance, words such as "dictator" held none of the negative connotations they had recently acquired on the barbarian worlds. Our diplomats would often be less than sensitive to these and other local concerns, such as our system of slavery. The nations of the barbarian world were going through an anti-slavery fad, the sort of anomaly or mania that occasionally rises in every civilisation which might see one generation abandoning the eating of meat, or the depiction of the phallus in art, until sanity is restored by their children or grandchildren. Slavery had been, as in almost all the Roman worlds, the natural order of things since prehistory, even supported numerous times in the Christian Bible, for example Ephesians 6:5-6:

'Servi oboedite dominis carnalibus cum timore et tremore in simplicitate cordis vestri sicut Christo non ad oculum servientes quasi hominibus placentes sed ut servi Christi facientes voluntatem Dei ex animo.'

However, slavery had been abolished in the supposedly Christian British Empire, and other nations had followed. Two generations after Europe, even the United States of America abandoned it. Though it continued in many places in the world, it mostly did so illegally. They had polluted their system of slavery with the pandemic discriminatio phyletica that was characteristic of their worlds. I am not exaggerating when I say that you could beat up a Jew here and people would turn a blind eye, but that if you raised the same stick to a dog, then you'd be sent to prison. It was perfectly acceptable, it seemed, to deny a Negro a job or even to state that he wasn't a human being, but utterly abhorrent to house and feed such a man and set him working. The people here had mistreated their slaves, then manumitted them all in one day, without making any attempt to set them up in life. Another mania, that for mob rule, or "democracy", as they called it, hijacking a Greek term, meant that the natives were quite incapable of running their own affairs. The imposition of democracy on Germany had enabled the rise of Hitler and his National Socialists in the first place, and you'd have thought that this alone would have been enough to warn the people of these other Earths. Our diplomats would voice such perfectly self-evident sentiments, denounce the absurdities of these worlds, and the barbarian natives would recoil. I think, in retrospect, I agree with what Angela would tell me: that we were so busy laughing at the multitude of ways the natives had failed that we didn't spend enough time explaining the benefits of the Roman system of government.

So, the worlds we had liberated across the Divide proved reluctant and surly subjects of their new Emperor. All had active Resistance movements set up to irritate the Nazis, and many of these organisations simply switched to resisting Roman advances. The majority of the peoples of the worlds embraced Rome, and I think it's important for me to say that. The average African or Indian, even the average labourer in France or Germany was far better off under Roman rule. Unlike the "capitalists" and "democrats" of the West, we wanted to feed and house everyone, and unlike the "communists" of the East, we had a chance of achieving that. Lots of the natives talked about "equality", but seemed determined to exist in systems designed to exploit or discriminate against the vast majority.

But there will always be troublemakers and malcontents, there will always be those for whom preserving the old way of doing things is preferable to improving it. And we were lucky in one respect; the Nazis tried to encroach on the worlds we had liberated, but they were universally hated. In Germany particularly, Hitler and his cronies were not welcome back (the native Hitlers had all fled or died in the fighting for these worlds), and considered the architects of great misfortune. They could not exploit our problems. It was not just men and armies we were defeating, it was an idea, a thing that couldn't just be run through with a sword. It became obvious that the complete extermination of this idea was the only course of action.

Rome, conversely, was quite capable of continuing to strike and spread deep into Nazi territory. Every month, a handful of Nazi other Earths would fall to the might of our legions. This is to diminish the achievement of capturing whole worlds by military force, of course. Many thousands of Romans were dying and being injured, and it was hard for me not to feel responsible for each death. Even at this rate, it would be nearly a century before we had control of this side of the Divide, and while a century is nothing to Rome, it meant condemning three or four future generations to grow up in time of war. As the conflict progressed, the fighting became more difficult for us. Resources were stretched, German co-ordination between worlds improved, and their strategists developed better defences against us. I sensed the hand of Herr Abschrift in this.

Titus sent me back reports of worlds where, unchecked, the Nazis had total dominance. On one other Earth he discovered, America was divided between the Japanese and the Nazis. The Americans were grateful, thinking the Axis had saved the world from communism. The Nazis had bases on the Moon, and were sending a mission to colonise Mars. Their rocket-planes could fly from Scandinavia to the West Coast of America in forty-five minutes. The Mediterranean had been drained for farmland, and Africa had been razed by giant machines, a billion Africans broken down into chemicals for the utilisation of German industry.

Not every world was as lurid as this. Another battleground was an other Earth with two superpowers. Here, Nazi Germany and the United States of America had long been locked in a bellare frigidus much like that which had afflicted Roma DCX. Two superpowers, each with formidable military might, they had kept each other in check. Now, though, President Kennedy, "JPK", as the Americans fondly knew him, had made overtures to Hitler and his regime. Some years before, this man had stated:

'Strong anti-Semitic tendencies existed in the United States and a large portion of the population had an understanding of the German attitude to the Jews.'

And, now he ruled his country, a period of detente had been initiated between the two nations. Roman generals decided to skirt around both worlds, to pick off Earths where German power hadn't consolidated quite so much.

My palace almost completed, Angela joined me on Germania V. She was forty-five years old by now. Some Roman women are old matrons at that age, but many are youthful, and Angela was one of the latter. She had always been slim, and exercised. This Angela was the native of this world, and the shortages and rationing of her formative years had never left her. The Angela of Roma I followed her lead, and I have to admit that when I met one of them on her own, I wasn't always immediately aware which it was. To be honest, after so many years - and so many apart - I did not distinguish. They were one person, in two beautiful bodies. Rather than agonise over the philosophy of the matter, I simply thanked the gods and enjoyed her company.

One night, I was lying with Angela in the bedroom of my apartment in the Roman Palace. This must have been mid MMDCCXVII, as the structure of the palace had been completed, but the mosaic floor of the Great Hall had barely been started. That had been ready just in time for the Christian festival which marked the winter solstice, the most significant annual celebration of the Britons on this side of the Divide; we celebrated that with a fight that went down in legend, between Cassius Marcellus Argilla, the renowned gladiator from Roma I, and his counterpart from this Earth. Twenty rounds of bare-fisted fighting, and no two opponents had ever been so well-matched.

Volitat par papilio et icet par apis.

I digress.

'This palace feels more like home now than the streets,' Angela told me. 'It's strange being driven past St. Pancras station or through Westminster. The old buildings look so small and dirty.'

'I hope, given time, everyone will feel as you do,' I told her. We were only really safe in the Palace. The Resistance was not large, as far as we knew, but it was ruthless. Roman patrols were shot at, small bombs were placed under our vehicles or by the roadside. A month before Angela had arrived, a man posing as a contractor had got as far as the palace gates and detonated a larger device, killing himself and a dozen other people, demolishing a small section of the curtain wall. All too often, these attacks murdered more Britons than Romans. We were the target - I was the target - but there were several sets of thick walls and an entire Roman legion between the would-be assassins and myself. I slept easily.

'Not everyone lives like we do,' Angela said. 'People are envious.'

'Everyone benefits,' I replied.

'Even the slaves?'

'There's no slavery here,' I reminded her.

'That's what people are worried you'll do; round them up, put them in slave gangs or throw them to the lions.'

'I won't. I remember the words to "Rule Britannia". People forget what it was like in the... the Eastern Quarter?'

'The East End.'

'Slum housing, no sanitation, malnutrition, brutality. At the heart of the capital city of the British Empire. Where was their Royal Family then? We're giving them a better life.'

As I said it, I realised it must have been exactly what the Nazis had said as they occupied this London twenty-four years before. I was at the age now where I was beginning to wonder what I would leave to posterity. Clearly, my actions had been significant. I was happy that I had raised the fortunes of my family and of Rome. But, returning to that hoary analogy again, I had opened Pandora's Box. My children were grown now, and most of them were married. I was a grandfather, although as I was embroiled in the struggle across the Divide, I had not seen my grandson. Thoughts of him, though, made me think of the future. Would he still be fighting his grandfather's war when I was long in my tomb? Beyond further Divides, would we find aggressive Americans, Britons or Norsemen? What of Abschrift's masters; had I condemned two-thousand Earths to be pawns in their war with the formless beasts?

This talk of mortality makes me realise that this part of my narrative has skated quickly through a number of years. It was now, by the barbarian way of reckoning, 1964. On every one of the Nazi worlds - and who is to say, perhaps on most of the Roman ones - Adolf Hitler was born on the 20th of April, 1889. In 1964, it follows, all the Hitlers who had survived were seventy-five years old.

The Romans and their allies had done their best to prevent the Hitlers from reaching this milestone. Scores had been killed, by now. The Council of Hitlers presumably still convened in that vast domed hall in the Berlin of Germania I, but every time they did so, there would be a few more empty seats. That would have been unsettling enough, I feel sure. But in this war of attrition, we were not the only factor. Hitler, as I have no need to tell you, was a fanatical man and one of his concerns was health. He didn't smoke tobacco or use any of the other narcotics, he drank alcohol only in moderation. As an historian, I should record at this point that he most certainly did like to eat meat, though his physicians occasionally advised him to abstain from it in order to avoid a complaining stomach. Nevertheless, he was active and ate healthily, and needless to say had the finest physicians of his world ministering to him. But his was a job with stresses and strains. Regardless of the assassinations and attacks, regardless of the fact that there was a war on, some of the Hitlers were beginning to die of natural causes. His heart couldn't always take the strain, even small falls and ailments could have serious consequences. Old wounds could flare up, the poisons some of the Hitlers placed in their atmospheres and water supplies caused cancers to grow. There are a thousand ways for an old man to die, and each permutation was being worked through on the Earths of the tausendweltreich.

No-one, not even the most fanatical volunteer to the Schutzstaffel, had ever thought that Hitler would oversee the whole of the Nazi millennium. Men are mortal. We all know this, particularly as we grow older, but we understand it at an intellectual level. Hitler saw it with his own eyes. Men, exactly as him, dying of old age. The logical implication was clear, even to a man prone to fits of irrationality and self-delusion. Perhaps he looked to Herr Abschrift for advice. This was a man, after all, who had apparently only aged one year for every three or four that passed. Had Abschrift an Elixir of Youth, or was he simply the result of the sort of good breeding that Hitler advocated, but had not benefited from? Whatever the case, the Fuhrer's erstwhile ally clearly did not share with him the secrets of immortality. The ones we captured or killed looked ever older. War and fear do that to a man.

Hitler had always had an unstable personality. At its best, this gave him a clarity of purpose and the willpower that tore his wishes from his dreams and into our reality. At worst, he was a psychotic, frothing lunatic who couldn't understand that his failure to compromise often endangered Germany. Fearing death, his natural - and deserved - paranoia came to the fore. All the Hitlers had only one son between them, August, born on Germania I, architect of the massacre of the Roman legions in atomic fire.

The Council of Hitlers agreed that August Hitler should be their successor, framed a will in which - on the death of the last of the Adolf Hitlers - he would inherit the mantle of Fuhrer. This strong, blond young man would truly embody the old slogan "Ein Volk! Ein Reich! Ein Fuhrer!". It would ensure stability; he was not yet twenty years old, and would rule the Greater German Reich for many decades. He started appearing on the propaganda posters of every German world, his father's hand on his shoulder. The people were prepared for his eventual succession, and such was the Nazi control of information that the population of each world soon believed that they had learned of his existence many years before, and that he was the natural son of their Hitler.

To ensure the coronation, of course, it was necessary to eliminate any pretenders to the throne. So it was that veteran Nazi generals who won the War, then had gone on to conquer dozens of entire worlds, quietly disappeared. Many politicians who had given Hitler sound advice or helped with the practicalities of implementing his plans were rounded up and shot. A decade of our men infiltrating, blackmailing and assassinating couldn't have been as effective against the Nazis as the Hitlers' own purges. As the surviving Hitlers - and there were still more than four-hundred of them - gathered in Berlin to vote through August's succession, they must have felt that they had achieved some sort of immortality. A dynasty had been formed, the bloodline would carry on. They stood in their chamber, their chants of 'Sieg Heil' echoing around them. When they called 'Heil Hitler', for the first time it didn't mean them.

Hydrogen cyanide gas smells a little like almonds, I am told. I have no idea how this is known, and have no wish to; to breathe even a small quantity of it is to die. I had long ago stood in that council chamber, one surmounted by the largest dome in the Known Worlds. To fill that space must have required a lot of poison gas. But filled it was, and every Hitler died, choking. Those that came to their aid were overcome before they could get a single man of them clear. Every possible permutation of Hitler was there, so, I comforted myself, between them they experienced every possible reaction, from denial to panic. I pictured a hundred Hitler faces, purple, eyes bulging, trying to spit out some last piece of hatred. Then falling to the marble floor, whatever animated them driven from all their bodies.

Every Adolf Hitler was now dead.

The new Fuhrer, his son, blamed the attack on Roman agents. I can only say that killing every Hitler at one stroke had been my dream for two decades, and if I could have done it, I would have done it and boasted long afterwards. I do not believe it was the Romans. Cui bono? The Little Hitler immediately granted himself emergency powers that even his father had not asked for. His rule over the barbarian worlds was assured, he had total control of hundreds of other Earths and a people baying for Roman blood. But now, as word of this mass murder reached me through our network of spies, I smiled. My greatest wish had been granted. Utinam populus unam cervicem haberet. The Greater German Reich now had one neck.

I made the most solemn oath before all the gods that I would be the man to wring it.

XVI.

The Roman Army was in a strong position.

Technologically, we had advantages and disadvantages. As in all wars that last long enough, a certain symmetry developed between the two sides, as we both adapted our weapons and defences to match the threat from our enemy. But we had a large, mobile military and the Germans were on the defensive in their own territory. The Germans had to invest vast resources to fortify every Earth, whereas we could send our forces practically wherever we wished. Our tactics were akin to the "blitzkrieg" the Nazis had once used; concentrate on an overwhelming surprise attack in one place, moving so fast and hitting so hard that no defence could withstand it. The Nazis could not put a guard on every uncia of every world, we had the luxury of being able to strike where they were weakest.

Our great fear was that August Hitler would authorise the use of the pyrobolus atomicus. There were generals who urged the Emperor to build such weapons for ourselves. What was normally done was to take those men to the London wasteland, and then to the field hospitals we had set up on the outskirts of that city. They soon understood the need to contain and protect ourselves. There were two distinct threats. We had seen the devastating use of the weapon against an army on the battlefield; such a tactic could only be a last resort, but it did stay our hand, and prevent us from massing too many legions in one place. There was also the minalarva, that of a smuggled weapon destroying a Roman city. The bombs were small enough to be carried by one person, concealed in an amphora or packing case. With the help of Consobrinus Patruelis - who I had finally met - we developed a way of blocking off the Divide, the creation of a wall with only one gatehouse. In former times, walls like this marked the boundary between the frontier of the Empire and the unmapped, tribal lands beyond.

The gatehouse itself was a variation on the temple to Clepsydra Metiri, and as such it was difficult to say where, exactly, it existed. I was aware that my own image of it, a wall around the Roman galaxy, with a single stone watchtower, was inadequate and inaccurate, but I found it difficult to understand it in any other way. In practical terms, there was now only one route across the Divide; through one enormous set of bronze doors in a new building in the centre of the Londinium of Roma DCX, to a secure area in the grounds of the Roman Palace in the London of Germania V, my command centre. This became known as the Tramontane Gate. Yet none of us ever felt entirely safe, however much the access between galaxies was regulated and restricted.

A new and vicious phase of the wars had begun.

Each Roman victory saw the Germans driven back, and millions of people liberated. We were becoming more skilled in pacifying those we freed from the Nazis. Many in the political classes would now rush almost comically to become togafied. As with fighting the war on each of the Nazi worlds, in peace we didn't face a thousand different challenges so much as the same challenge many times over. While the barbarian worlds were not identical, there was sufficient similarity that we could use the same tactics again and again. A light touch was needed; a token military and diplomatic presence, the promise of financial aid to rebuild. To win the hearts and minds of a population, it is always better to build them new schools rather than demolish the existing ones. The Roman way was preferable to the old discredited systems. On a hundred worlds, new and better civilisations were forged. Travel from other Earth to other Earth - even the knowledge that such a thing was possible - was strictly limited, just as it had been in the Roman galaxy at first. Essentially, these worlds were allowed to heal themselves as they recuperated from the fascist plague.

We won many quick victories at first. But as the Nazis retreated, they consolidated their position. August Hitler ordered men and weapons evacuated from other Earths when it was clear all was lost there, and these would be added to the defences of the worlds closer to Germania I. I sensed Herr Abschrift's hand a number of times, when travel between the other Earths still controlled by the Nazis seemed problematic. Like Neptune, he could ease the crossing of those he favoured, make it all but impossible for those he opposed.

Fighting was fierce. There were so many battles, on so many fields, that it is difficult even for the professional military historian to keep track. Local commanders, of course, furnished me with full reports, which were duly dispatched to the Emperor on Roma I and collated. On the ground, co-ordinating the attacks, deciding where to send legions, and in what strength, my brother and I were more concerned with which tactics worked. After our initial victories came a period when honours were more evenly-shared.

We were well-matched in terms of artillery. Rome had long understood the value of field artillery, and while our magnetic catapults and ballistae lacked some of the range and force of the larger German carriage guns and howitzers, they were far more accurate. We had begun to develop anti-aircraft weapons, although the Germans had, by now, advanced jet fighters and bombers that could fly high and fast enough to evade us, given even a little luck. Our infantry guns were far superior. As for broad strategies, Roman armies had four basic methods of attack: the long range, the medium range, the short range and close quarters. The German army depended on only the long range and the short range. Their basic tactic was to bombard our positions - often for many days - then move in and machine-gun those who survived that initial attack. They had no real equivalent, or at first any defence against, our sagittarians, individuals skilled in the use of hand-held medium-range weapons. The Cretan archers and Numidian slingsmen in particular were able to take up positions too close for artillery, too far for machine-guns, and simply pick off the German officers and other strategic targets. That would weaken the German ranks and allow the legionaries to pour in. While they typically carried knives, the German soldiers had abandoned blades for ranged weapons. In doing so, they had become lazy and vulnerable. They relied on the ability to shoot an opponent from many paces away. When a Roman legionary arrived in front of them, sword down and shield raised, there was rarely anything but a swift defeat for the German soldier. As the war continued, as more and more factories that manufactured bullets were captured by Roman forces, and shortages ensued, this imbalance only become more acute.

Lest you think this was all one way, the German Panzer divisions caused problems for us. The Wehrmacht's tanks were fast and well-armoured. Their guns could blow holes in our shields - by such a dry phrase I mean they could kill and maim many men - and then power through our ranks. Early on, our legions would get into their formations, maintain perfect discipline, find the ideal battlefield, march towards the enemy ... and find themselves attacked full-on, encircled, or both. Special anti-tank auxiliaries were formed and trained, but this new form of combat took a number of years to come into effect. The trick was simple enough; tanks were only fully effective when given the freedom to move. When we had methods of miring and trapping the Panzers, we could turn the tide of the battles.

There were some great victories at this time. The "Ferrum Legion" of Rome D liberated a whole world, even when their supply lines were cut, marching from France to the gates of Berlin itself and laying siege without rest. Germania LI saw what is thought to be the largest sea battle known to history. Legend has it that you could walk from Spain to the Azores, so numerous were the vessels on the sea. Exaggeration, but it is said by men of good standing that the shores of America were lapped by violent waves, as so many ships had sunk and swirled up the Atlantic. Many slaves were taken during these wars, but it was felt best to relocate them - as far as was possible - on their own Earths. Exceptions were made for officers, and for the members of the SS, who were fanatici, and trained to instil such belief in others. It was far too dangerous to let them fraternise with other Germans. Most were executed.

Then, almost exactly ten years to the day after the campaigns began, tragedy struck.

My brother was felled, and not at the hands of the enemy. His vehicle overturned. It was a commandeered Rolls Royce, not even a Roman clockwork. It happened in the Netherlands of Germania CXI. His leg was crushed, and there was so great a loss of blood before the medics arrived that all hope was lost.

I rushed across the galaxy to be at his side. He died in a townhouse that had been converted into a hospital. His last breath was to tell me to take command of the armies, reminded me of my oath to kill August Hitler.

He was conveyed back to Roma I. I did not go with him; my task was here. He was interred in the family tomb, just outside the villa complex. Americanus, my ancestor, has pride of place in that mausoleum, lying in a great bronze coffin in the centre. It's a vast circular space, on three levels, a dome above it. The walls are decorated with reliefs of the family history. There are statues and smaller burial places and urns. My brother was laid to rest on the lowest and most sacred level. Angela wrote a most moving letter to me describing the inhumation ceremony. No-one needed to pay for any tears, all of Rome was united in genuine grief.

I felt nothing.

I was consumed, now, by the war. It had been my only thought for many years. I could not afford to let sentiment or ceremony deflect my sword. The Roman army needed a leader, not a mourner.

The direction of the conflict was soon as inevitable as these matters ever are. We had momentum, we had superior logistics, we had the better weapons. More than that ... it is easy to laugh at such sentiments ... but we had moral superiority. Our men were stronger, our cause more noble. For all their talk of country and leadership, the Nazis stood for death, suppression, uniformity. They would lie and keep secrets from their people. They built death-camps where we built great libraries.

By the year 1970, we had beaten the Nazis back to their heartlands. Now, mere handfuls of other Earths remained completely under their control. But these were the worlds where the Nazis' grip had come soonest and firmest. There was a whole generation here who had known no different to the rule of the Fuhrers. The Romans, they had been told all their life, were cruel and intent on raping their women and watching the men torn apart for sport. Our tactics of isolating the German command structure and working with local resistance movements simply ceased to work. There were no local rebel chieftains with whom deals could be made. Here, the allies of the Germans had prospered, and their opponents had all "gone East". Refugees from the defeated worlds were here, bolstering the German forces. With less to defend, the Nazis found it easier and easier to maintain their borders and marshal their resources. And without Titus, the Roman army found it harder to press an attack.

The Nazi High Command, we learnt from their communiqués, were living in worlds of fantasy. At first, we assumed that the messages, full of talk of counterstrikes and waiting for the right moment, were put out for the benefit of morale. No army ever won with the spectre of inevitable defeat in their hearts. But the more we listened in, the more we realised that the Nazi generalobersts and feldmarschalls believed all this nonsense. They spent their days ordering non-existent units to defend places that had long fallen to us. This meant it became impossible to sue for peace, or to demand surrender. They genuinely thought, despite losing grip on nearly a thousand worlds, that they were in the dominant position.

We had no qualms in conquest the hard way. We assembled great invasion forces, overwhelmed their defences, crushed them. Even here, once the high command had gone, once every member of the SS had been put to death, once the Party had been disbanded, Nazism didn't survive. The populations of these worlds emerged, as if they had been locked in a cellar for the last few decades. Confused, rambling, often very scared, but with no lasting loyalty to August Hitler. The ferocity of the fighting often left little for these people. No factories, no railways, few roads, devastated cities. Disease was pandemic, starvation was the norm. There was no heat or light, no reliable water supply. The survivors fought and died over possession of a single potato or piece of bread.

We could have aided them more than we did, but these were a defeated enemy and many Romans had died destroying their armies. We organised the able-bodied into slave gangs, co-ordinated them in rebuilding the agriculture, clearing the cities of the dead. There had been significant depopulation, even before our legions had attacked. Our philosophers speculated that these worlds would, in a generation or so, settle into a tribal pattern. Within one-hundred years, the population would stabilise at a fraction of its previous levels. The great forests would reclaim Europe, local chieftains would emerge, ruling from fortresses to organise hunting and foraging. In many ways, I expect the Nazi imagination would willingly embrace such a destiny.

Then, finally, our goal: Germania I, the ultimate expression and capital of the Greater German Reich, one-time seat of government of the Council of Hitlers.

There was still fighting on other worlds, but all other theatres of war were squarely in the last act. We had left this other Earth alone. There was a paradox that troubled our scholars; Germania I was a world where everything that transpired did so for the best of Nazi Germany. All that happened on Roma I, as I have said, did so for the benefit of Rome. What, then, would happen when the forces of these two worlds clashed? There is the old puzzle, the one about immovable objects and irresistible forces. That's easily resolved, of course, but now we faced an enemy as successful as us, with the same luck. Not divinely-inspired victories, as we long thought, but simply a statistical inevitability. "How could we win such a battle?", the thinking men of Rome asked.

I came up with a simple solution: we would win the battle with well-trained, well-disciplined men, attacking in force with the most effective weapons.

The Roman Palace in the London of Germania V dominated the skyline of that city. Deep beneath it, only one of the great glass maps now garnered any attention from the strategists. Germania I may have resembled the other worlds of this galaxy, but it was clear, now, that it would be well-defended, both by conventional weapons and by the more mysterious techniques of Herr Abschrift. Here, all opposition had been eradicated, every heart was German. Those that still lived there lived in their personal utopia and had everything to lose.

August Hitler was still enthroned here. It made me smile to think of him, alone in the vast council chamber designed for a thousand of his "fathers". The people of his other Earth seemed all but oblivious to what was happening around them.

We had not conquered every barbarian world, but we had done enough, and I and the strategists grew confident. Rome should make a decisive move, not just nibble at the edges. We must defeat Hitler and his followers.

I took personal command of the legions, and travelled to Germania I. I had spent many years of captivity on this world, all of them vowing to escape. Now, though, my mind soared at the thought of being back. Every available navispar was commandeered, packed with men and equipment. Four great fronts were opened up. We would attack the French and Belgian coasts, giving us control of the Atlantic when we blocked in the German ports. We would attack Berlin from the south, through Dalmatia; from the west via transalpine Gaul; and would move to blockade the oil supplies of Arabia and Russia. The Nazis now only had access to one world's worth of fossil fuels. Our main problem was an array of unforeseen and unpredictable restrictions on travelling between other worlds. Clearly Herr Abschrift had activated some new defences. It didn't matter; we had deployed very quickly and had all the legions here we needed.

There was one decisive battle in particular, which has come to be known as The Battle of Rhine I. The Nazis could have won there, and changed the course of the war.

This was the front I had chosen to join. My initial command post for this world was established in the Nordeifel, and that's where I planted the eagle of my new legion, the One-Thousandth, or "the conficers". I had handpicked these men from every other Earth in the Known Worlds. This was an army that spoke of the colour and scope of the Roman Empire. The tribunes of this fighting force were the survivors of the band of explorers, those of us who had first travelled between the other Earths. We met for a banquet, the night before we embarked for this world. This was the first time I had seen many of my old comrades for years. The Empress Diana - who would not be joining the fight, but had assigned her daughter the task - scarcely looked older, Regina was now a handsome and distinguished woman. Terence Ollacondire ... well, he had always looked older than his years. Quintus Saxus was now an old man with a long white beard.

How long it had been since we were young men and women. How much we had seen. And how many of us had fallen since those days.

We were all keen to finish the Nazis once and for all.

The defences of Germania I, both physical and more arcane, meant that we could not materialise our army in Berlin itself. The forest we selected for our landing site was an important area; there was the Rhine nearby, of course, but also an oil pipeline, and a couple of airstrips. Around here, there was the Voglesang training ground. Despite all the military bases, this was a common route for escaped prisoners. The old border with the Netherlands ran through the forest, so fugitives and defectors who managed to get over the river would camp out here, using the dense woodland as cover. Many would get lost, wandering the hundreds of square miles for days. Our patrols found these people, who gladly shared their knowledge. One thing we didn't know, but which was fairly common knowledge locally, was that one of those "airstrips" was really a missile silo. This we seized quickly, using just cavalry.

The Rhine was Germany's moat. A natural barrier that could only be crossed at a few points, the vast bridges. These were easily-defended, as they usually sat in mountainous areas, and German guns were posted on the high ground on both banks.

This was our only route to Berlin. To take the city, first we had to capture at least one of the large bridges. At the end of the first day, I ordered the legions to form up and begin the march to the Rhine, double quick.

Our army had never been better equipped, the men had been honed by combat. Their morale, now we were on the verge of lopping off the head of the Nazi Empire, had never been higher. Decades of contact and co-operation between Romes, and of concentration on military innovation, had given us superb new weapons.

I was onboard one such device, the cancrus.

It was an armoured vehicle. A new kind of tank, but with a segmented body the size of a house, wider than it was long. The bodywork - carapace - was steel. Around the edges, the surface was enamelled, with gold detailing. There were dozens of hatches, of various sizes and shapes. Great tubes ran underneath. It was ornate, rather than purely functional; a statement of power as much as a practical weapon. On one side, an identifying mark: SPQR. It was supported on eight curved, jointed legs that lifted it fifteen feet in the air. It moved slowly, deliberately, one spiked foot forward, then another. There was a jerkiness to the motion, but a new type of clockwork motor meant it moved almost silently. Sat in the vehicle, enthroned in almost guilty comfort with my eight-man crew, I had a commanding view of the battlefield and the disposition of the forces of both sides. There were another two vehicles alongside.

The Nazi defenders of the bridge on the Rhine had been warned that we were coming. It was impossible to prevent them spotting such a movement of men, but the swiftness of our march caught them out, and we arrived before all the defences were in place. The Germans on the west bank - military and civilian - had started to pull back across the river to the safety of the other side. There was a railway tunnel within fifty yards of the far bank. With a whole mountain on top of it, it served as the perfect shelter, for both the ordinary men and women of the town, and for the officers looking for a secure command post.

The Roman foot-soldiers, all in glinting metal armour, dug in furiously as they reached the river, setting up spiked barricades, finding cover, maintaining their line wherever they could. One cohort marched relentlessly towards the command post on the west bank. Each end of the bridge had two large stone towers. There was a good field of fire from those gun emplacements.

Our artillery took up position on the hillside overlooking the river, and started firing at the German ranks.

We had all but taken this west bank. There were fires in the streets of the small town on this side, and our men worked their way systematically through the buildings, rooting out civilians and soldiers alike. Despite there being Germans here, the Wehrmacht major on the other side of the river ordered shelling to begin. The major had a Panzer division under his command, and deployed half of them along the bank, the other half directly at the eastern end of the bridge, gun barrels aimed squarely down the line.

There were nearly sixteen-hundred German troops here, mostly infantry. Most were sent to find strategic positions. There were already machine-gun emplacements all around. The heavy artillery and anti-aircraft guns were up on the hillside.

The two sides, then, had quickly formed up the way their officers would have liked. Two ranks of troops facing each other, holding territory on opposite side of the river. It was almost a mirror image; infantry lined up on the roads that ran along the banks, heavy artillery up on the hillsides, and a built up area in between, with buildings that served as good cover for snipers and as excellent observation posts.

In between: the river and the bridge. A box girder bridge, painted steel struts making a squarish frame, which was supported on thick brick-and-concrete pillars. Not a beautiful structure, but a strong one. It was about three-hundred yards long, and wide enough for a couple of road lanes, a footpath and a single railway track.

My view from the cancrus was panoramic, encompassing the infantry - I could identify the exact centuries from the standards and eagles poking up from the ranks of men - the river, the opposing force and, of course, the bridge. The legates had set up their own command posts in vineae, small mobile shelters, among their men.

I gave the signal, and a flare was launched.

The burning arrow seemed to hang in the air over the Rhine for a moment.

Then the Romans attacked.

The ballistic assault first. Catapults and ballistae, pounding the artillery positions on the opposite hillside. While the German guns were entrenched, and had the higher ground, the catapults were devastating. Boulders and vast blocks of metal were hurled half a mile, crashing down with practised accuracy. Where the Romans missed, there was still damage to be done; the rocks rolled down the hillside and into the town, demolishing buildings.

Within moments, the firestorm began. Some of the projectiles were rigged with a substance that was flammable in air. The hillside was ablaze, fire took hold in the streets of the town. Others spat out clumps of black smoke. Not a gas attack, simply smoke to add to the confusion, but the Germans didn't know that.

Archers and slingsmen began picking off individual German troops. It wasn't always obvious who the officers were, but where possible, these were the men targeted. A few of the men in the javelin auxiliaries chanced their arm at throwing spears across the river, and a handful hit, but not enough to make it worthwhile, and the order was given to stop.

German gunners responded. Machine-guns strafed the enemy across the river, thousands of rounds turning the air hot and deafening. Snipers aimed for the crested helmets, the officers. The Romans huddled behind their shields, which protected them. German heavy artillery pounded the hillside. I saw that the shields my men carried would withstand the light machine-gun bullets, but not anything heavier. And while the shields were tough, they obeyed the laws of physics; the legions would be pinned down.

I ordered the cancri to attack. The walking machine to my right moved to the head of the bridge. It now became the focus of the machine-gunners in the stone towers. Bullets bounced from the hard shell, flicking off in every direction.

Relief, though, for the legionaries nearest the towers, who now pressed forwards, taking up positions at their bases, out of the line of fire. Classic shield-work was used; one set of men levelling their shields vertically, defending against shots from the opposite bank, another set keeping their shields horizontal, covering themselves against shots from above.

The cancrus reached the first tower, and deployed the vomitorignii. Twin metal tubes extended from the body of the machine, poked right into the highest window of the tower, smashing through the glass, and filled the whole building with liquid fire.

The war machine withdrew, and made its slow way to the second tower. German soldiers there abandoned their positions and either tried to surrender or get across the bridge.

They were all picked off by archers and marksmen.

There was now heavy crossfire on the bridge. No Roman had set foot there, but they had dug into position facing down it. German infantry, with light submachine-guns, were in place on the opposite side, supported by tanks, and others were pressing forwards. Each of the first half-dozen girders now had a couple of German troops ducked behind it, nervously ready to repel anyone who made it onto the bridge. Additionally, the Germans were now aiming their heavy guns down at the bank. The larger guns hadn't been designed for such a short range attack. The targets were the cancri, but these proved hard to hit. Instead, there was carnage as the shells ripped through the Roman shield wall. I ordered my ballistic units to concentrate fire on the German artillery.

This, in turn, freed up the German infantry on their bank a little. The reserve Panzers were brought down from their positions in the town, under cover of the smoke we had sent over. Their guns were also more than a match for Roman shields. The blasts cut away at the walls and road opposite, undermining many of our soldiers. Weighed down, legionaries tumbled down the shallow mud banks and into the water. If they showed any sign of struggling, they were shot down by machine-gunners.

Five minutes into the battle, and the German fighters arrived.

Flying wings. Their latest jet fighter / bombers. Fast and manoeuvrable. They first flew a sighting run over the enemy ranks, then returned for a bombing run. A third wave used machine-guns. One of the cancri was blown off its legs, and crashed into a line of men.

The Roman artillery tried to respond, but it was well-known that this was a particular weakness of ours. The Luftwaffe jets were just too fast and too small for the catapults to hit.

'Shields!' I ordered. Before I'd even finished the word, the horns had been sounded.

The only anti-aircraft defence we had was crude and dangerous.

The spargus threw metal fragments up to two-thousand feet in the air. It made a wall of shrapnel, a cloud of it. The idea was to hit the planes, but all that metal had to land somewhere. It rained off the shields of the men. But it was never possible for every Roman soldier to raise his shield, or to raise it in time. A hundred men died or were injured as the metal showered down over them.

But the attack was well-timed. The jet planes roared right through the cloud of fragments. The immense speed of the aircraft now became far more of a problem for them than an advantage. Each and every plane was torn apart by many thousands of projectiles far faster than bullets.

The flying wings crashed into the hillsides and the river.

By now, the Roman artillery had pummelled the German guns opposite into scrap.

It was time for the infantry assault.

It is a paradox of war. Each man is well-drilled, plans are carefully drawn up, preparations are made. But combat is unpredictable, inherently chaotic. The outcome of a battle turns on a sequence of almost random events and strokes of fortune. There is little order on the battlefield.

A Roman legionary had an instinctive understanding of that. These men were all veterans, indeed most came from army families so that their military experience could be said to have started before their birth.

What drove them? Something deep down, something they would not even have to think about as they formed their ranks of shields or raised their swords. The soldiers now formed a testudo, a "tortoise" formation where they created a wall and roof of shields, then moved as one, pressing forward like a human tank. Behind them, another group was doing the same. Dozens, then hundreds of men started marching across the bridge, under sustained enemy gunfire.

Inside the testudo, it would have been hot, sweaty. It would have been impossible to see the way ahead. Anyone who looked down might see the river below them, through the slats of the wooden footpath. But no-one could see the end of the bridge, or what was waiting for them on the other side. The only considerations were to press forward and to keep shields locked together. All around, the sounds of war would be deafening.

Behind them, the two surviving cancri were stepping down into the river. The water came up to the second joint in the legs. We were now strafing the German Panzers with streams of fire. It didn't do much; the tanks were designed for that. But the cancri crews soon realised that a sustained attack did the trick. Like boiling a pot, my driver joked.

While the Roman legions were at arms' length, the Germans had a chance. The machine-guns might keep us back, might be enough to bring down whole ranks of those neat lines of legionaries. But once we were closer than arms' length, the Wehrmacht troops knew it was over. They didn't have the weapons for close range combat. They might get a few shots off, a few of those shots might find a weak point in the armour; a leg, say, or a face. But there would be another Roman behind that one, thrusting with his sword or dagger, hurling a javelin. The ground was already slick with German blood, now. Behind them, the railway tunnel in which the officers and townsfolk had been sheltering was filled with fire and screaming.

I watched my men pour across the bridge, saw the German defences respond. I could see from my lofty position that we would overwhelm the German lines like seawater over sandcastles. German reinforcements were on the way, and the bridge was now a bottleneck for my men, an easy target for our enemies, but our job now was to hold the bridge, not take it.

The Rubicon had been crossed, the Romans were at the gates.

I watched the German ranks carefully as they began to pull back. And there, for the merest instant, I knew I saw him. August Hitler, come to see his men destroy the Roman legions, instead staring at the fall of his empire. In the history of this world, almost exactly fifteen-hundred and fifty years before, the positions had been reversed. The barbarians had attacked Italy, swept down to Rome. At what point had the Romans realised all was lost, I wondered? When had Honorius accepted that the Empire had fallen? Never, I suspect, if he was truly Roman.

Now, though, the history of this world had been repaired. Rome had risen. We marched to Berlin, and victory.

XVII.

The first stage was to take control of the air. While the Luftwaffe had many aircraft and pilots at their disposal, mostly refugees from other Earths, they were severely limited by the number of landing strips and refineries. On paper, the Roman air legions were outnumbered several times over. Our ground troops launched assaults on the airfields, which were poorly-defended against such types of attack. Each airbase we secured was quickly fortified, becoming a useful home for our aircraft and legions. The German pilots were not easily overcome, however. The best we could manage at first was to secure areas of sky. Our legions could deploy and march under such places, but would not have long - a matter of hours - before the enemy planes returned, meaning the legion had to dig in and set up shelters. These were simple variants on the standard vineae, used in sieges. The road network here was modern and efficient, and this was to our advantage. A Roman legion, on foot, could march six miles in an hour, and ten times that where vehicles were available.

The German generals were skilled, and quickly formed up their defences. They knew that our objective was to cut off the capital city, they knew we would move against the oil refineries. The more realistic of them must have realised months or years ago that they would soon be facing Roman legions marching on their beloved fatherland. German reinforcements were sent to every major bridge, local defence units were mobilised in every town. This was German territory. We had maps of this world, but not all of them were completely accurate; it became clear that they had been using double agents and sending misinformation to us.

The men under my command moved from our position at the Rhine, five legions marching to, and swiftly taking, Magdeburg, to the west of Berlin. Fighting was ferocious, casualties on both sides were high, but the battle was not a long one. Berlin was now in our sights, though victory was not yet assured.

On the 30th of April, 1970, we decided to give the Fuhrer a birthday present. Heavy bombers from the Third Air Legion dropped immense quantities of high explosives on the dome of the Great Hall in the centre of Berlin. It was an extraordinarily strong structure, made from concrete reinforced with steel. The Luftwaffe's fighters and the Wehrmacht's Flak 72s destroyed one in three of the bombers we sent over the city that night, killing many hundreds of pilots. But when the morning came, and the smoke had cleared, the vast dome had a crack three feet wide and running from one side to the other. All we had to do then was wait and watch. Over the course of that day, the crack grew, and before nightfall it had collapsed in on itself. We had a vantage point many miles away. I eagerly explained to my generals how large the dome was, how many hundreds of thousands of librae of concrete had gone into its construction. I tried to imagine the noise that must be echoing around Berlin, the dust in the air, choking its citizens.

Our armies had been training for months in the arts of urban warfare. The Nazis' capital city was a maze of streets with tall buildings, millions of Germans fighting for their own homes, not just the more abstract notions of Party and Country. We were well aware of the threat from snipers, and that it would be all too easy to get encircled. Neither could we afford to take our time; as the threat to the capital had become apparent, the order would have gone out for every spare army division and aircraft in the world to return to Germany to fight off the invader. There were large forests to the north and east of the city of Berlin, and a number of our strategists were worried that we had little way of seeing what was going on amongst the trees. The area was large enough to conceal a number of divisions, and certainly large enough to conceal missile bases and heavy artillery.

We struck out, heading down the road from Magdeburg to Potsdam, legions marching fast with full air support. The road had been blockaded, and was well-defended, but our scouts had accurately located every single pill-box and machine-gun post. We took the defences apart almost forensically, using the marching legions to distract attention from the advance guards who had got round the defences and attacked from the rear. We made a feint with a couple of legions, making it look as though we planned to attack Potsdam directly. Under the cover of night, however, the main force swept northwest. By daybreak, we had secured the airport and captured - with remarkable ease - Spandau Prison. There were no prisoners here, in my former residence. I put sentimentality - and I admit fear and superstition - aside, and we made camp here. This was now our forward command post. Early that morning, intensive bombing from the air legions provided cover as our ground troops dug in. We pulled one legion back to defend our rear.

I have made this sound easy, but our force had been decimated. One in ten of our legionaries were dead, about the same again had been seriously injured. I was a man in his sixties by now, and as my slaves prepared my quarters at Spandau - not my old cell, I assure you - I was so sore and tired I could barely remain standing. My armour was heavier than I remembered, and dug in uncomfortably in my shoulders and sides. I was careful not to show weakness in front of my men, but slumped and wheezed when I was alone. Decimation was the ultimate punishment for a failed legion, and losing ten percent of your number was, so the scholars told us, exactly the point where morale collapsed. We had come so far, but it was beginning to seem as if we were dashing ourselves against rocks.

Regina and Quintus Saxus, among my oldest friends, were both among the casualties, I learned. So few of the select band who had pioneered travel from Earth to other Earth still lived. My father and brother were dead. Angela's father was now feeble of body, if not of mind. Diana ruled her Earth, Antonius was long retired.

That night, Terence Ollacondire and I drank to their memory.

Retiring to my bed many hours later, I read reports from our spies in the city which heartened me a little. The SS were hanging people in the streets, from lamp-posts it was said, fixing signs to the bodies to the effect that the executed men weren't brave enough to fight, so had to die. A clear sign the Germans were worried. Some women and even older boys had been killed this way. The Roman army's methods of motivating its men and for punishing failure were often brutal, but had never displayed quite this level of desperation. We had rattled them.

At a meeting with my generals, though, it became clear that our tacticians weren't so confident. We had not laid siege, and didn't have time to. We had cut oil supplies, but the Nazis would have stockpiles of diesel, and it was a warm spring, so little would have been used for heating. They had water, we could presume they had stocked up with food. It was a large city, with millions of mouths to feed, and given a little time the people could be starved out. But we had word that almost the entire army in the East had been ordered back home. Russia had been pacified long ago, but it was a large country and needed a large military. Elsewhere, all the young men and women on their Strength Through Joy holidays had been urgently recalled from the Mediterranean, and rocket planes had been commandeered to ferry them back. Much of the German navy was converging on the Baltic, missile units were taking up positions.

We could find ourselves surrounded. Herr Abschrift's techniques weren't perfect, but there was clearly something interfering with travel between the Earths. We could not rely on reinforcements or resupply, and - if it came to it - we could not retreat.

We were, though, camped so close to the centre of the city that we were confident now that August Hitler would not order an atomic attack. To do so would be suicide. The possibility existed, of course, that if all was lost, the Nazis would destroy themselves to destroy us. But such a strategy would mean a Roman victory; other Romans would survive, while Nazism would not. It was not my desire to die in that way, but if it happened, my last thought would be one of triumph.

'Waiting only helps the Germans,' I concluded, after assessing the situation. 'We can afford to recuperate for a day, maybe two. After that, we attack.'

On the 3rd of May, the battle-cries of five legions echoed through the streets of Berlin, swirling together with the sound of gunfire, breaking glass and the clash of Roman steel.

I led one such charge, reinvigorated. Our ballistae fired their projectiles right over us. I knew these weapons were accurate, but it was still unnerving to look up and see great masses of metal arcing overhead. Every time one fell to earth, the ground shook, and there was a thunderous crashing as another concrete building fell down somewhere a few miles directly in front of us.

Ahead of our military charge, cohorts had been sent in to disrupt the running of the city. This is easily achieved, and no doubt you can think of a few of the ways. They severed electricity lines, demolished shiner masts, devastated water pumping stations. But there were more subtle forms of attack. They raided the banks; not to steal the money or valuables, but to leave them wide open. The local people would realise the vaults were open and unguarded, and would charge in, trying to loot the jewellery, safe deposit boxes and bank-notes. It is, sad to say, human nature. Few stopped to think just how worthless bank-notes bearing the face of August Hitler on one side and a swastika on the other would shortly be... or perhaps they were confident of victory. In any case, the German police and SS were forced to move in to stop the looting of the banks and other shops and buildings. Divide and conquer; two Germans fighting each other meant two Germans not fighting us.

I was considered liberal by many in my army, but even my instinct was to sack this city and kill everyone in it. This was the heart of the Greater German Reich, these were the men and women at the seat of power. Most, in this totalitarian state, would work directly or indirectly for the government, or would be the wives and children of those who did. All were Party members, and willingly. Every child was a member of the Hitler Youth, inculcated since birth in the hateful philosophies of the Nazi Party.

We had agreed a more merciful plan, though. Not through any desire to compromise or reconcile, but out of sheer practicality. The Berliners had to be given some hope that surrender was a desirable option. Had we slaughtered everyone, then the population of the city would have had precisely two options; get out onto the streets to take us on, or huddle in their homes, prepared to fight to the death to defend them. We circulated leaflets and made appeals over the shiner, suggesting escape routes into the northern forest - we hoped such a movement would block any German force there. We told them, quite correctly, that it was the SS shooting German children, not us. We told them that, as civilians, there was little they could do, and they should get out of the city so that the soldiers could settle their differences.

One thing we didn't have was a clear idea of the location of the Nazi High Command. They would be in bunkers by now, we assumed. It was our most profound hope that they were still in the city. We knew that no-one had escaped to an other Earth, as we could monitor that, but if a significant number of them had got away - gods, if just one of them had, and it was the right man - then we could be in trouble. After almost forty years of Nazi rule, these men would never consider surrender. They had won great victories, planned great invasions, and at one point had ruled a thousand worlds. They would almost certainly find it impossible to believe they could be defeated.

The lower ranks of the German forces, though, were more pragmatic. We soon found that a large number of the "civilians" fleeing along the routes we had opened were wearing army boots. At first we feared a breakout, that these men had been instructed to leave the city, regroup and attack our rear. However, these were just scared young men who'd come up with a way out. We let them go.

Fighting continued for a week. There were snipers or blockades on every corner. Our artillery had quickly reduced the military positions of the enemy. The big German carriage guns were heavy-hitters, but they weren't as mobile as was claimed. The skies were now ours, as were all three of the city's airports. The railway lines were cut, and the advance of the reinforcements from the East had been halted by the destruction of key railway bridges and stations. It was heavy going, and I don't believe even one of our men managed to escape some form of injury. A lot of scars, bruises and broken bones. But we were in close quarters, and so in our element. The Cretan archers almost came to see the German snipers as a sport; a game where concealment had to be balanced with strategic positioning. They ran from rooftop to rooftop, taking out the German riflemen. The ordinary legionaries swept systematically through the city, clearing out buildings, demolishing those that were causing trouble.

Our vast clockwork cancri units couldn't operate in the narrow streets, but could stride through the wide boulevards, parks and display grounds. The huge metal crustaceans did the job they'd been designed for, blasting, crushing and smashing the Panzers. Our horseless chariots swept through the cleared streets, bringing in fresh troops, evacuating the ones who needed medical attention.

The tide of the battle was obvious, now. We could go into almost any ward of the city. We had started to locate the subterranean command centres. In no mood for mercy, we drilled holes down, and filled them with water channelled from the river. By now, the city seemed almost empty of Germans. There was fierce fighting in a number of places. The new concrete buildings were, by accident or design, extremely tough nuts to crack. The Nazi forces had taken up positions in the main railway station and in a large factory. We surrounded them, decided to starve them out. We now held most of the government buildings, apart from the new Reichstag. That we bombed out of existence.

The commander of the German troops was a General Wilding, the son of the previous man to hold that position, so he claimed. He surrendered on the 10th of May. We broadcast the news on all channels, and sent cancri marching around the streets, hailing it. The shooting and bombing stopped within the hour, superseded by silence. We had control of - give or take - the entire four-hundred square miles of Berlin, capital city of the Nazi Empire.

Not that there was much of this city remaining. City blocks were now toppled facades. The ground was all caves and craters, as deep as the buildings had been tall. Grey dust covered everything, making the world here monochrome. Water pipes and gas lines poked up like bones. The dead lay everywhere, dead men, women and animals. The smell quickly grew unbearable on such a warm spring day. Everywhere, among this rubble, were human beings. Their fine clothes were coated with mica dust, they were bruised and tired. All their spirit had gone, though. The Nazi spell had been broken, and now their utopian city of grand buildings and bombastic intent was mere dust.

Pulvis et umbra sumus.

I bid a legion search the city for the body of August Hitler. I prepared a lengthy dispatch for our Emperor, informing him of our victory. Slaves were rounded up and transported off this other Earth; for now, the barriers that Abschrift had raised up had fallen away.

The rest of this world ... well, it would take years to completely remove the taint of the Nazis from this place. Like a disease that takes hold, you can cure the symptoms, but never quite remove the touch of it from the body. But this was a dictatorship, one that had been ruled by the whims of one man, then his son, for forty years. We had lopped off the head of this world.

August Hitler's cella loricata was located close to the Brandenburg Gate. We were led there by informers, who had been promised their freedom in return for the information. The terrified staff of the "bunker" were sure that Herr Hitler and Herr Abschrift were behind a certain door.

They were not. There was a small, sealed room with no ventilation, let alone doors or an escape route. The two men had fled this world.

I left this other Earth and led efforts to track down Hitler. The Prime Emperor and the other leaders of Rome debated long and hard about what constituted victory. There were over a thousand Nazi worlds, countless numbers of which were barely aware of the war that had raged for decades. Maintaining control of this territory would be extremely difficult.

A month later, Herr Abschrift was apprehended at the Tramontane Gate between the Roman and the Nazi ... pardon me, the former Nazi, worlds. I had been looking forwards to returning to this London, its Roman Palace that had been my home for many years, and - naturally - Angela. My wife, though, was on a visit to Roma I. I had to settle for seeing Abschrift in his cell. Thirty or so years after I had first glimpsed this man, he looked perhaps five years older. He wore a smart grey business suit and was barefoot, a look he had apparently copied, of all the things in all the worlds, from Paulinus on the cover of *Via Abbatia*.

Terence Ollacondire was with me.

'The war is over,' I told my former captor. 'Our scholars think that over a billion people have died. Count yourself lucky you are not one of them. '

Abschrift appeared moved by this. Years before, hadn't he dismissed all these worlds, all those lives, as somehow not real? He was concerned about something. He paced around his cell, restless, looking around.

'In a hurry?' I asked him.

'I have sent for my masters. They are coming,' he said. Abschrift wasn't scared, not exactly. But neither was he entirely happy. 'I did not realise what they would do.'

'So you've fled?'

'They'll destroy it all, Scriptor. They annihilate anything that threatens them. They're fighting a war, they're desperate and they won't want to take any risk that an Empire made up of two-thousand versions of Earth will fall into enemy hands. Take me to the gateway. I can seal it off. Not even they can get through the barrier. Seal the gates and you'll be safe. Fail to do it, and they'll destroy everything you've ever known. You think there's been death up until now? Nothing compared with what's to come.'

I had Abschrift released, and we went to the gateway. The great bronze doors were open, leading through to a large hall in Roma DCX; the next room, but in another galaxy. It never failed to amaze me.

I told Ollacondire to return to Roma, to tell them what had happened and to get the gateway sealed. I would remain here. The doors were never to be opened again.

I knew then that I had seen Angela for the last time.

Ollacondire grabbed my arm, looked me in the eye.

'Sir ... if we ... if we don't meet again ... sir, I'd just like to say it's been a real privilege fighting alongside you, sir.'

I nodded. He saluted me as he passed through the gateway. I ordered the bronze gates closed. The sunlight behind them was still visible.

Abschrift was glaring at me.

'A metal door isn't going to stop them,' Abschrift said. 'And we're on the wrong side of it, in any event. Wait ... no, it's too late. They're here ... '

I knew it, felt it in the deepest part of me. The divine was about to intersect with the mundane. I was about to meet the gods themselves.

It was as if there was a great rushing of wind. He stepped out - of what, I only asked that question later - and time itself seemed to lap around those feet. I remember a giant, yet one shorter than me. I remember a radiant face, but it was an old man's. I remember a great, echoing voice, but it was a whisper. There is an ancient school of philosophy that says we are mere shadows on a cave wall. This man was of the breed that cast those shadows.

Deus ex machina.

- You were meant to contain the situation.

'I have done precisely that, my Lord,' Abschrift answered firmly. 'With the exception of this one opening, the barrier prevents all transduction.'

A word with which I was unfamiliar. Referring to a glossiarium afterwards, I learned that it meant the transfer of the cells of one creature to another. Were these gods really so worried about something as small as a cell?

Abschrift continued that Rome was contained behind this wall, this was the only way in or out. The Romans were trapped in, just as he was trapped out.

- You constructed this?

'No. It's stolen technology.'

The god stepped forward, looking around.

- Prepare to erase the timelines within. We'll do that, then withdraw and erase this cluster.

He handed Abschrift a metal disc. Abschrift nodded, and moved towards the control panel, disc in hand.

'I'm sorry, Scriptor. It has to be this way.'

His back was to me. I took my chance, leapt forwards, leapfrogged over him, took my sword and punctured Abschrift's shoulder, then dragged it down with me through his chest. I landed neatly on my feet, my back to the gateway, facing Abschrift, looking him in the eye. I guided his body to the ground, took the disc from his numb hand.

- Who are you?

It was as if He had only now noticed me.

I released my grip on Abschrift.

'I am Marcus Americanius Scriptor.'

- Are you now?

'I have killed your kind before,' I warned Him.

- You wish to kill me?

'No, sir. '

- You seem the violent sort, if you don't mind me saying.

'I am defending my home and family, sir. The people of Rome have no quarrel with you, and no wish to ally with those that do.'

- No matter. You have violated the universal boundaries, disrupted a cosmic balance that you cannot begin to understand.

'I understand that you are fighting a war, and I understand war. I know my history, sir. I know what it is to be deadlocked, I know what it is to fear that an entire way of life might be lost.'

I remembered the old man, all those years ago.

'I know what it is, sir, to live in utopia, and to fight to preserve that. I know what it is when that fight becomes of the most paramount importance, when sight is lost of what you are fighting for, and on whose behalf.'

- War is like fire, Marcus Americanius Scriptor. Unchecked, it spreads. There are things that must be fought.

'I agree, sir. But the first rule of warfare is a simple one: to defeat an enemy, one has to understand what motivates him, what he desires, what he fears most. Know your enemy.'

- If only it were that simple. What if the knowledge of the enemy is so profound that even by understanding it, you find yourself defeated?

'Rome is not your enemy.'

- We are threatened by Rome's actions.

'No, sir. Herr Abschrift here - '

- Who? Oh, I see. "Abschrift"? Very good.

'- Herr Abschrift provoked our response, sir. His attempts to contain the situation simply made it worse. By the end, even he saw that, I think.'

- Well, never let it be said that history doesn't repeat itself. Best it was all over with.

'You mean to destroy all the Roman Earths.' I had no doubt He had the ability.

- And these others, the Nazi Earths. Erase the errant timelines, stop the infection.

'The infection is of your making. I want nothing more than for you, your kind and your enemies to return to your own universe, sir. Pandora's Box, though, cannot be closed once it has been opened.'

- Such sentiments once had meaning. No more.

'You sound as if you have what the Greeks call the "pain of return".'

- An occupational hazard for my kind. I would like things to be as they were *before*, but it cannot be. The very word no longer has meaning ... wait! Wait! You ... you would stall for time?

'Time, as I understand it, is your domain.'

- Give me that.

The device I had taken from Abschrift was about the size of discus, surprisingly heavy, and hummed as if it were alive. It reminded me of the old man's bangle, and had clearly been forged in the same fire.

'Make me,' I suggested, heading to block His way to the gateway.

The old man sighed, and closed His eyes.

Then, where every drop of Abschrift's blood had fallen, a new version of

Abschrift grew like vines; muscle and capillaries spiralling up, filling out into the shape of a man, bone stretching out to provide a framework, skin fading up until it covered him, hair sprouting.

Two dozen Abschriften, naked.

- Take it from his corpse.

All of them leapt at me. I had the disc in one hand, my sword in the other. I swung out with both of them, slashing at skin, crashing the heavy disc into skulls. They were all around me, blocking my retreat, preventing my advance. They were unarmed but, as I believe I have established, Abschrift was a tall, strong man, a natural warrior. As I brought the pommel of my sword down to break a nose here, or kicked with all my strength there, the constant risk remained that one of four-dozen grasping hands would snatch the disc from my grip.

Behind me, the gateway across the Divide remained open behind those metal doors, a chink of Roman sunlight filling me with panic.

I stabbed one of the Abschriften neatly between the ribs, and he died. In the narratives, you will often hear of heroes swinging such dead men around as improvised shields. I am no hero, and Abschrift weighed half as much again as me. Instead, I swiftly withdrew the sword, slashed the eyes of another. These brute creatures, or men, whatever manner of thing they were, were heedless of caution. They had no tactics, but didn't need them. They had me outnumbered, and could rely on strength. They did not fight me one at a time, all of them piled onto me and pressed their attack simultaneously.

The sword was yanked from my hand. With so many of them pushed at me, it had become impossible to use in any event. I punched the nearest pointed-toothed mouth. Now, though, I was being assailed by kicks and punches. I felt a rib break, my grip on the floor was lost. I tripped, steadying myself by grabbing a handful of blond hair. My other hand had curled around the disc, and it was now flat against my stomach. I fell on top of it.

I endured a beating. A foot flat against my back, many other bare feet kicking my sides. Hands grabbed at me, trying to pick away the disc. One arm was round my neck, trying to pull it up, uncaring if my head were torn off in the process.

I could hear nothing now, the blood was roaring in my ears. I could see nothing by a mass of limbs. I tasted blood on my tongue, my nostrils were full of that blood and the smell of sweat. Still the blows came, relentless.

Through all my life, I had been in jeopardy many times. This, though, was the first time I had felt the hand of the ferryman on my shoulder. How, then, did I survive to write this narrative? Some of it was that I was a Roman, fighting to defend Rome. It gave me the strength to continue, though all seemed lost.

The other reason was that, just as I thought I had inhaled my last breath, above all that clamour:

- Stop.

The Abschriften stood back. I lay on the floor for the moment.

- The gateway is sealed.

I managed to turn my head. The bronze doors had swung open, but there was nothing but dead wall on the other side. My friends had done their work, and I had done mine.

'You cannot get through?' I said, weakly.

- No.

The Abschriften were fading away, as if they had been dreams. Soon, only the body of the original remained.

'What is to be done?'

- It has been done already, Roman. You have won.

He helped me to my unsteady feet, handed me my sword, which I could barely lift. Unthinking, I handed Him back His disc.

'Sir. What of the barbarian worlds?'

- You have won a reprieve for over a thousand universes today, Scriptor. You are pushing your luck.

'There are many Romans still here. And the natives of these worlds? They have as much right to life as you and I, sir.'

- Would you build another wall around them? Seal off another thousand universes?

'The Nazis rounded up and exterminated whole races and groups, sir. I will not be party to the same process on a galactic scale.'

The old man hesitated.

- Such a place will have to be policed. All travel between the other Earths must be completely forbidden from this day. All who break this law, everything that they touch, must be utterly destroyed. You will be charged with that duty.

'Rome?'

- No. Rome is safely behind its wall. You, Marcus Americanius Scriptor. It will be your job to locate those who transgress the law, and to punish them. You will be the only traveller between worlds.

'I become the agent of the gods?'

- In your terms ... why, yes.

'What of August Hitler?' I asked.

- Certain assurances were given.

'If I find him, can I kill him?'

- Yes. But you won't find him, he is beyond your reach.

'He has been given sanctuary on your Earth? The "True Earth"?'

- He has been allowed to escape there, that is all. He will get no special privileges. We made a deal with him, Marcus Americanius Scriptor, and will honour it, just as we will honour this treaty. You are not to seek passage to our universe. We shall not allow passage to the barbarian worlds, or seek methods of reaching or attacking Rome.

With a magician's flourish, He produced a scroll which when unfurled revealed a legal contract. He pressed his ring into the parchment, marking it with His seal, a swirling occult symbol. The same symbol which had marked each of the bangles, a serpent coiled into two loops, though on this occasion the loops were interrupted by another form; sharp-edged and aggressive, a shape unlike anything in the Known Worlds but unmistakably military in its nature. The sigil of the divine Houses, during time of war? Perhaps. Perhaps, since the bangles were forged, their republic had become an empire.

The god passed me a pen, and I signed the treaty without hesitation.

I would never again see Angela's face, or touch her skin. But those I loved would endure. Rome would not fall, or be dragged into this War in Heaven.

I had fought the gods, and I had won.

Epilogus

That was nineteen years ago. It is now the year MMDCCLII, by a calendar I have not used for a long time. I realised some while back that I no longer think in Latin, not unless I will myself to. I have lived and fought alone for most of that time, and have had no further contact with the gods. Each of the barbarian worlds has the touch of Rome upon it. The Romans here have settled. Many have married locals, all have brought with them the values and nobility of Rome. Slowly, independently, the barbarian worlds are healing.

I have travelled. I discovered four edges to this galaxy, one of which at least I know has another Divide, beyond which lies another galaxy of other Earths. The nature of those people, the dominant conditions on those thousand worlds, I can only speculate upon. On the worlds of the Nazi galaxy there were remnants of Hitler's regime, often with access to fragments of arcane power. There were renegades and independent operators from elsewhere. I was kept busy. My job has required ruthlessness. I have made pre-emptive strikes, I have killed children. I have changed.

What of Rome? I do not know. Perhaps there is a large statue of me there, now. Or a column, sides filled with an account of my life and victories. Angela will be an old matron now. I imagine her as head of my family, perhaps even Empress.

The masters of the "True Earth" have, to the best of my knowledge, kept to their pledge and within the boundaries of their own world.

I have not.

I did not act with any authority but my own, but the line of Hitlers had to be ended. August Hitler, son of Adolf, second Fuhrer of the Greater German Reich, had fled to the "True Earth". There was much to do in the barbarian worlds, but it was all done within a decade. I was compelled then to destroy the Little Hitler, to hunt him down to the ends of the Earths. He had found a haven, galaxies away from those who knew him, and had received assurances from his powerful allies that he was safe. It was my oath that this should not be the case.

Fiat iustitia, ruat coelum.

I found my way here. I cannot tell you how without compromising those who aided me and so I will not say. I will leave it as a question mark. Finally, three years ago, I trod the ground of the "True Earth". Fearing detection, I had left my bangle behind. It was easy enough to live on this other Earth. I have spent those years tracking August Hitler down, paying my way and buying free passage by operating as a mercenary in Africa, Yugoslavia and South America. This was as fractured and dirty a world as I had seen. There were wonders, as every Earth finds room for those, but there were ruins. This was a history where both Augustus and Adolf Hitler reigned, yet only briefly and neither so brightly as in the other Earths I have seen. The people here weren't any more happy, or even any more clear on their purpose in life. Herr Abschrift had complained that my world was one of patterns and coincidences... but there was some structure to life. Poetic justice, at the very least, prevailed.

A week ago I arrived here, the Amazon jungle. This was my latest lead, one that had meant a flight into Brasilia, then a river journey on a motorboat, then two days and nights trekking through the rainforest with a native guide. Hot, glutinous raindrops clung where they fell on me. The chorus of insects and rustling leaves was inside my skull, like a madness. The scents of this place were likewise dizzying. In all truth, I had no expectation of finding him, not after so many false trails.

The guard I killed was blond, a textbook Aryan in fact, and that raised my hopes. We found him on the outskirts of a small clearing. There was a compound; just a garage, storage shed, a large satellite dish and a small villa. There was a trackway, and my guide told me it would probably lead down to the river. There were two Land Rovers, both muddy and clearly much-used, parked by the garage. The main defence this place had was its isolation. There were three guards on duty - two now - and the compound's mesh fence seemed designed to keep animals from wandering in, not as fortification.

The guard had carried an Israeli submachine-gun. The irony was probably lost on him.

Five minutes later, I had my quarry sighted.

August Hitler was in the front room of the villa, one with a wide window overlooking the garage. He was talking on a cellphone, and as he did so his limbs and head twitched and thrust quite as his father's had done when he'd been making a speech. I already recognised the man, despite the years, but those gestures were the proof.

I bid my guide return home, and paid him slightly more than we had agreed. The Little Hitler was still making his 'phone call while I killed his guards, driver, cook and the two women, one of whom looked like a cleaner, the other a whore.

My sword had been busy. I gave it one more task, and severed the cables leading from the satellite dish and into the house.

August Hitler was on the doorstep in moments.

'What is going on? Why can't I get a signal?'

He saw his dead colleagues, then, and understood. He had a pistol in his hand, which I removed. At the wrist.

What should I have done? A slow death. Interred him deep underground, still alive, perhaps. Walled him into a room and sat outside as his cries grew ever weaker. Inflicted a stomach wound and watched his life seep away from him. A violent death. Challenge him to a duel. Hack away at his limbs. Make him bleed then pursue him into the jungle, where beasts would fall upon him. Burn him alive. Crush him under stones. Stake him out in the sun. Poison him, drown him. Perhaps I could have removed his hands, taken his life and baked him into a pie. I am a historian, I am aware of a thousand gory ways I could have done it.

Yet I am old, and just wanted it over with. I took the Little Hitler's throat in my hands and crushed it. I had no need to keep hold of him after that, he could no longer breathe or call for help. He staggered back into the house, first clutching his neck, then using his hands to try to steady himself. He stared at me the whole time, a look that I interpreted as incomprehension. His skin was already paling, his eyes bulging. He lurched around trying to suck air into his lungs, but the way was blocked. I followed him inside.

He looked at me one last time, then stumbled over, hitting the carpeted floor and unable to raise a hand to cushion his fall. Anima est, spes est. The life had left him. My own beliefs don't allow for an afterlife. As I understood it, Hitler's own gods would ensure for him an eternity of torment and hopeless despair. An eye for an eye, then.

Sic semper tyrannis.

I searched the villa, top to bottom. Checked every photograph, every address book, every computer file and email. No evidence of contact with, or even oblique references to him having contact with, anyone or anything beyond this Earth. No contact with the higher powers that, unbeknownst to all but a handful of the people of this "True Earth", control infinity and eternity. Nothing about any children. Plenty of information about networks of the neo-Nazi groups, drug-pushers and other agitators with whom he was in contact. I have since restored the satellite link, and forwarded the data to the authorities. Volumes and volumes of hand-written notebooks set out his policies and beliefs. No evidence that anyone but August Hitler had ever read them.

I broke up some of the furniture. I ripped out the pages of all his diaries and writings. Then I took it all outside, built it up, placed the last of the Hitlers on the funeral pyre and lit it. I watched intently as the dark, distinct shapes of the wood and the body became pliant. The flames had a life of their own, sparking and hissing, sending points and squiggles of light up into the air. The light and smell of the fire was an intrusion here. As I watched, I rejected the idea of demolishing this compound. The jungle would reclaim it soon enough, leaving no ruin. The bonfire heap collapsed in on itself after an hour or so, and I went back inside. Overnight rain doused the ashes. I picked through them before breakfast the next morning, collected the jawbone, the teeth and the other recognisable fragments, then ground them up to dust and scattered them to the winds.

One more death, after so many, brought me no satisfaction. I had sworn an oath. Now I swore another; let this be the last man I would kill.

There were a couple of empty notebooks. Beautiful things, with heavy leather covers and marbled paper. Difficult to bring to the jungle, difficult to keep pristine. I took one of them and wrote this account of my life and history. It has taken me five days - not half as long as I thought it might - and has been cathartic.

* * *

I cannot return home. I would not wish to. It seems to me, now, that I have completed my task. I should return to the barbarian worlds. Settle on one where the values of Rome have taken root. Germania V, I imagine, birthplace of Angela, location of my vast, pointless fortress. I do not know the fate of my Rome, of any of the Romes. I still dream of the translucent towers of the Palatine, of my family villa casually decorated with statues fifteen-hundred years more exquisite than any other world has seen. Those splendours have seemed to me, as I have written this account, like a man recounting a dream, or even a delusion. I am a man who has slipped between worlds, seen so many versions of the "real" that the word should be as meaningless as dreams and fiction. Was there really ever a Hercules Bridge? Are there clockwork men? Was there once a sun-eyed beast stalking the snowbound ruins of Londinium? Yes. We know that. Everything that can possibly happen happens somewhere. All that which we think of as stories, it is real to someone. That is scientific fact. So I find myself wondering *did it happen to me?*

Then I remember the taste of quails and honeyed dormouse, the sickly tang of Northern wine. I remember singers and dancers interpreting the latest works of Homoinis and Atriensis. Above all else, I remember the touch of Angela's skin. A woman born both among Romans and barbarians. A human being who I liberated and was liberated by in turn.

Let Rome be my epitaph. Whatever has happened, is happening, whatever will happen, I know that Rome will endure, whether as concrete and marble reality or as gilded, marvellous dream. Even here, on the "True Earth", its name echoes through eternity.

Rome will ever be remembered, and is still felt, by the nations of all the Earths.

introducing the all-new novel...

Faction Paradox
WARRING STATES

Warring States
Mags L. Halliday

* Not actual cover art

The air in the Stacks races through the tunnels, pushed by the ghost trains rattling over the dead tracks. Posters for films that never were, and adverts for beauty products that give new meaning to "age-defying", flutter blindly. Occasionally, the icy air slams into abandoned platforms, where insubstantial suicides stand, clothes swirling around them as they stare into the abyss of the permanent way.

Deep in the Stacks, Cousin Octavia welcomes the intermittent blasts of air. She likes it down here, safe not only from surface-level War offensives but also from the tedious internal politicking of the Eleven-Day Empire itself. Down here in the Faction's huge repository of knowledge, beneath a bloodlit London, she could lose herself in research. And if people got lost in the Lobokestvian geography of abandoned underground tunnels whilst looking for her, even better.

Unfortunately, Prester John is good at remembering the way.

'You could visit me in Westminster,' he remarks as he arrives, swirling flyers for *The Defective Detective* in his wake. Octavia shrugs.

'I've found it,' she tells him.

In the city square the crowd gathered, jostling not only to get a good view, but for their eagerness to be seen by the officials. Four men and a woman knelt, hands tied and heads bowed. A mandarin of the sapphire button stepped forward, peacock silks as stiffly formal as the condemnation he was making.

'- are hereby executed, for the most heinous crime of attempting to disrupt the Most Exalted One's Heavenly Kingdom, for the circulation of pernicious and corrupt ideas promulgated by the heathen foreign devils, for -'

As he continued, guards hacked off the queues of the men, holding the plaited hair high. The woman's hair had already be shorn, and not gently. A five waited silently as the official finished his denouncement.

In the crowd, Liu Hui Ying felt the hand of her father tighten about her upper arm. He was scared, she had realised this morning. Terrified that his laxity, his trade with the foreigners, his schooling of her, would lead to his own beheading. These five had been brought down from the north for this, but Chin Liang-Yu had been a school friend of Liu's. So now her father made her watch her friends kneel in the dirt for their ideas.

Five swords fell, the edges shearing through the second and third vertebrae, through the thick muscles and flimsy vessels of the throat. Chin's head rolled, tainting the dust with blood, until its force was spent and it came to rest staring upwards at Liu with something like hatred.

Walking back to the dockside factory, where her family's fortune had been made selling antiquities, Liu felt her jaw tingle with the promise of vomiting, her mouth filling again and again with the taste of it. She swallowed it down, urgently wishing she'd managed to close her eyes. Her father's new-found distrust of her education didn't yet outweigh her cheapness as a translator, and there was a new shipment of vases going to Britain. She set to work.

'Please, convey to your father my gratitude for continuing his business with us at this time,' Atkinson said. He took a sip of pai mu tan. Liu's father nodded with satisfaction as she translated.

'We are always honoured by your visits,' he said, then excused himself to supervise packing the crates. Atkinson took another sip of tea. Liu liked these moments, her chance to practise her language without being watched.

'How was the voyage from India?'

'Easy enough. We had an interesting party on board. Your father might want to contact them.'

'Really, how so?'

'It was an archaeological expedition, from Oxford, who hope to find the Great White Pyramid of China. I told them that it was just a myth, but Professor Grieves seems quite sure.'

'What is it this time? The stars aligned to bring down heavenly fire? Prehistoric germ warfare? Godfather Morlock's birthday?' Prester John is sidling through the room, letting his long coat brush against the precarious mounds of research material. Just reminding her that he can bring it all crashing down, make her go back to the fighting. 'Actually, that last one would be of some use. He'd be really pissed off if I threw him a party -'

'The Holy Grail.'

'Again? We've got a storeroom full of the things.'

'The metaphorical Holy Grail: live forever.'

'Given that we've already given history the slip, why would we want that?'

'Think about it. We give history the slip but it always catches up. Always. Remember the Noose?'

Prester John winces. 'Yes, that was embarrassing. So, what's the plan?'

'I'll need to mount an expedition into linear time to retrieve it. And I can only trace it to China. During the Boxer Rebellion.'

Prester John nods agreement. The distant rumble of a train swirls Cousin Octavia's clothes about her, and her shadow dances.

Release Date: First quarter 2005. **Retail Price:** $17.95.

mad norwegian press

1309 Carrollton Ave #237
Metairie, LA 70005
info@madnorwegian.com

www.madnorwegian.com

the book that started it all...

Faction Paradox
The Book of the WAR

A novel in alphabetical order. Before the *Faction Paradox* book series, there was the War: the terminal face-off between two rival powers and two rival kinds of history, with only the renegades, ritualists and subterfugers of Faction Paradox to stand between them and pick the wreckage clean.

Marking the first five decades of the conflict, *The Book of the War* is an A to Z of a self contained continuum and a complete guide to the Spiral Politic, from the beginning of recordable time to the fall of humanity. Part story, part history and part puzzle-box, this is a chronicle of protocol and paranoia in a War where the historians win as many battles as the soldiers and the greatest victory of all is to hold on to your own past.

Assembled by Lawrence Miles (*Dead Romance*), with illustrations by Jim Calafiore (*Exiles, Aquaman*), *The Book of the War* is a stand-alone work which dissects, defines and pre-wraps the *Faction Paradox* universe, and explains just how things ended up starting this way...

Available now.
Format: Trade PB, 256 pgs.
MSRP: $17.95
Also available as a hardback edition, signed by Miles and Calafiore and strictly limited to 300 copies, from our website. **MSRP:** $34.95

www.faction-paradox.com

1309 Carrollton Ave #237
Metairie, LA 70005
info@madnorwegian.com

mad norwegian press

mad norwegian press

info@madnorwegian.com
1309 Carrollton Ave #237
Metairie, LA 70005

I, Who 3: The Unauthorized Guide to *Doctor Who* Novels and Audios... $21.95

Dusted: The Ultimate Unauthorized Guide to Buffy the Vampire Slayer, by Lawrence Miles, Lars Pearson & Christa Dickson...$19.95

Redeemed: The Unauthorized Guide to *Angel*... $19.95 (upcoming)

Prime Targets: The Unauthorized Guide to *Transformers, Beast Wars & Beast Machines*... $19.95

About Time vol. 3: The Unauthorized Guide to *Doctor Who* Seasons 7 to 11... $14.95

ALSO AVAILABLE NOW...

- *Faction Paradox:* **This Town Will Never Let Us Go,** by Lawrence Miles...$14.95 [softcover], $34.95 [signed, limited hardcover]
- **I, Who vols. 1 to 3: The Unauthorized Guide to Doctor Who Novels and Audios** by Lars Pearson...$19.95 [vols. 1-2], $21.95 [vol. 3]

COMING SOON...

- **About Time vols. 1 to 6: The Unauthorized Guide to Doctor Who** by Lawrence Miles and Tat Wood, $19.95 [vol. 4 only], $14.95 [all other vols.]
- **A History of the Universe [Revised]:** The Unauthorized Guide to the Doctor Who Universe by Lance Parkin, $24.95
- *Faction Paradox:* **Warring States** by Mags L Halliday, $17.95

www.madnorwegian.com

ABOUT TIME

ABOUT TIME 4: THE UNAUTHORIZED GUIDE TO DOCTOR WHO
1975-1979 — SEASONS 12 TO 17
LAWRENCE MILES & TAT WOOD

Six-volume reference guide series to the "Doctor Who" TV show...

In *About Time*, Lawrence Miles ("Faction Paradox") and long-time sci-fi commentator Tat Wood not only dissect the continuity of "Doctor Who" (its characters, alien races and the like), but crucially examine the show as a work of social commentary, looking at how issues of the day influenced the show's production.

Join Lawrence and Tat as they illuminate on the Buddhist-flavoured Pertwee era, the show's "gothic" phase under producer Philip Hinchcliffe and more. Essays in this series include: "When are the UNIT Stories Set?", "Why Couldn't the BBC Just Have Spent More Money?", "Just How Chauvinistic is *Doctor Who*? and "When Was Regeneration Invented?" (And it's not the answer you think.)

Out Now: *About Time 3* (Seasons 7-11)
Out in 2004: *About Time 4* (Seasons 12-17) and *About Time 5* (Seasons 18-21)

Also Coming Soon...
- *About Time 6* (Seasons 22-26 and the TV Movie)
- *About Time 1* (Seasons 1-3)
- *About Time 2* (Seasons 4-6)

MSRP: $19.95 (*About Time 4*); $14.95 (all other volumes)

www.madnorwegian.com

1309 Carrollton Ave #237
Metairie, LA 70005
info@madnorwegian.com

mad norwegian press

dead ROMANCE
Laurence Miles

'All right, let's start with the basics. The world ended on the twelfth of October, nineteen seventy...'

Originally published by Virgin in 1999, *Dead Romance*, considered by many as Lawrence Miles' greatest work, now comes back into print through Mad Norwegian Press. Serving as the diaries of Christine Summerfield, a 23-year-old cocaine user in London, *Dead Romance* chronicles Christine's relationship with the time traveler known as Christopher Cwej... which leads to the fate of the world coming down to a game of rock-scissors-paper against a Horror that defies definition.

This re-release includes:

• Introduction by Lawrence Miles (entitled "Disinterred Romance").

• The text of *Dead Romance* (obviously).

• "Toy Story" (Miles' short story from the out-of-print *Perfect Timing 2*).

• An original essay by Miles on the mechanics of the *Faction Paradox* universe.

• Miles' award-winning short story "Grass".

All told, this book greatly compliments the *Faction Paradox* universe as created by Lawrence Miles.

OUT NOW.   **MSRP: $14.95.**

www.madnorwegian.com

mad norwegian press

1309 Carrollton Ave #237
Metairie, LA 70005
info@madnorwegian.com

dead parrot discs

1-866-DW-AMERICA
(Toll Free!)

doctorwho@deadparrotdiscs.com

All the finest imported and domestic Doctor Who collectibles...
Fans serving fans since 1989!

Doctor Who...

- BBC
- BBV
- Big Finish
- Cornerstone
- Dapol
- Panini
- Product Enterprise
- Stamp Centre
- Virgin
- Telos
- ...and more!

...and MUCH more!

- British Telly & Cult TV
- Sci-fi, Fantasy & Horror
- Anime
- Music & Movies
- AS SEEN ON TV

www.deadparrotdiscs.com

FREE GIFT WITH EVERY ORDER!

▲ *(Dare we say... it's about time*

Our Products Include:

Large Selection of Books
BBC, Target & Virgin Lineups

Audio CDs
Big Finish & BBC
Subscription service available

Video & DVD
Region 1 DVDs & NTSC Videos

Magazines & Comics
Large selection available

Trading Cards
Strictly Ink & Cornerstone

Independent Productions
Soldiers of Love
Reeltime Pictures
Myth Makers
BBV Audios & Videos

Collectibles
Resin Statues
Stamp Covers
Gift Items

Toys & Figures
Talking Daleks & Cybermen
Rolykins
Roll-a-matics
Dapol

DOCTOR WHO STORE.COM

The LARGEST selection of **DOCTOR WHO** on the internet!

EXCLUSIVE!
AE-1 Promo Card
Free with any trading card order.

Mail us at
P.O. Box 2660
Glen Ellyn, IL
60138
USA

Telephone
(630) 790-0905

Toll Free in the US and Canada
1-888-734-7386

EXCLUSIVE TALKING DALEK!
EMPEROR'S GUARD DALEK LEADER
from "Evil of the Daleks"
Limited to 1500

Look for these and other products at
WWW.DOCTORWHOSTORE.COM

Doctorwhostore.com is an Alien Entertainment Company.
We ship worldwide from the United States.

The Comic Guru Presents!

www.thecomicguru.co.uk

One of the UK's leading Doctor Who retailers!

Faction Paradox!
Short Trips!
Merchandise!
Audio Adventures!
Models & Collectibles!
Novels & Novellas!
Comics!

We ship worldwide, too!

Tel/Fax: +44 (0)29 20 229119

OPEN THE DOOR TO A NEW DIMENSION

www.galaxy4.co.uk

ABOUT THE AUTHOR

LANCE PARKIN has written a fair few novels, non-fiction books and edited the diary of Amanda Dingle, a former workmate. He was a storyline writer on UK soap *Emmerdale* for a couple of years, he wrote a biography of Alan Moore and writes *Miranda*, a creator-owned science fiction comic. Current projects include a guide to the writer Phillip Pullman, a comic that's a hush-hush revamp of a character you've all heard of and the last of the BBC Books' regular Eighth Doctor adventures, *The Gallifrey Chronicles*, which features an evil talking mule. Mad Norwegian will publish the forthcoming updated edition of his Doctor Who chronology, *A History of the Universe*, next year.

EDITORIAL STAFF

Series Creator / Editor
Lawrence Miles

Publisher
Lars Pearson

Cover Art
Steve Johnson

Interior Design
Christa Dickson
for Metaphorce Designs

Mad Norwegian Press
1309 Carrollton Ave #237
Metairie, LA 70005
info@madnorwegian.com

VISIT US ON THE WEB

www.faction-paradox.com
www.madnorwegian.com